The Sugar
Pavilion

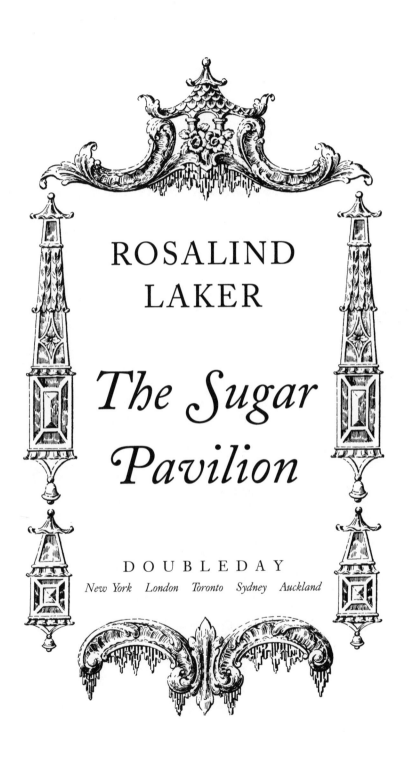

ROSALIND LAKER

The Sugar Pavilion

DOUBLEDAY

New York   London   Toronto   Sydney   Auckland

PUBLISHED BY DOUBLEDAY
a division of Bantam Doubleday Dell Publishing Group, Inc.
1540 Broadway, New York, New York 10036

DOUBLEDAY and the portrayal of an anchor with a dolphin
are trademarks of Doubleday,
a division of Bantam Doubleday Dell Publishing Group, Inc.

Book design by Paul Randall Mize

Library of Congress Cataloging-in-Publication Data

Laker, Rosalind.
The sugar pavilion / Rosalind Laker.—1st ed.
p. cm.
1. France—History—Revolution, 1789–1799—Refugees—Fiction.
2. Man-woman relationships—England—Brighton—Fiction.
3. Brighton (England)—History—Fiction. I. Title.
PR6065.E9S84 1994
823'.914—dc20 93-13713
CIP

ISBN: 0-385-46826-1

1 3 5 7 9 10 8 6 4 2

To my husband, Inge, with love

The Sugar Pavilion

One

WHEN THE SHOUT OF WARNING reached the great kitchen of the château, Sophie Delcourt dropped her mixing spoon onto the table with a clatter. It seemed to her that the pots and pans as well as the huge caldrons, the bunches of herbs fringing the beams, and the wide flagged floor all echoed and reechoed what she had long dreaded to hear. It was one of the grooms, waving his arms like a windmill, who was raising the alarm.

"Run for your lives! A mob of Revolutionaries armed with muskets, staves, and pitchforks is storming the gates!"

Sophie reacted with an explosion of rage. "No, we'll stay!" she shrieked. "There are enough of us here to defend the château!"

But nobody was listening. The women servants had already run screaming from whatever task they were engaged in, their only thought to gather what possessions they could from their sleeping quarters and flee. The chef was scooping his best knives into an empty flour sack. The kitchen boys had scattered.

Sophie stood stubbornly for another minute, trying to make herself heard over the panic. Then, furiously, she tore off her linen cap, her wealth of blue-black hair swinging free, and cast aside her apron. Humiliated, she had no choice but to join in the general exodus. Although the drive to the Château de Juneau was two miles long, she had seen for herself in Paris how fast a blood-lusting mob could swarm gates and walls.

Bunching up her skirts, she bounded up the servants' staircase in the wake of the other women. Her teeth were gritted in high temper at having to flee from the Revolutionaries for a second time within a few months. Just to have served the aristocracy in this bloodstained spring of 1793, even in the most humble capacity, was enough to send one to the guillotine. Trained as a confectioner in Paris by her late father, Sophie had been thankful to find a haven in this quiet country château far from the city. But now she was on the run again.

She flew into her small bedroom. The mirror on the wall flashed the reflection of an eighteen-year-old girl of arresting beauty whose black-lashed amber eyes now sparkled with anger under arched brows. Her creamy complexion was presently flushed and she was biting into her lower lip, but her mouth was more provocative to men than she realized. If her chin was too determined for perfect facial symmetry, it also indicated her strong will and driving ambition.

Throwing open a cupboard, Sophie snatched out her traveling bag and proceeded to toss in some clothes, her sewing kit, and a few other items. Sophie did not retrace her steps, but chose instead a quicker route to ultimate escape. It took her from the servants' quarters into the main part of the château, plain floorboards giving way to richly hued Persian rugs. Ancestors of the Juneau family looked down on her as she hurried to the head of the grand staircase. Her heels tapped a tattoo as she descended, her fingertips speeding down the gilded handrail that spiraled gracefully to the entrance hall far below. A couple of footmen overtook her, leaping down the stairs, their liveries and white wigs discarded.

"Don't delay, Sophie!" one shouted. "There's not a moment to lose!"

Both men were out of sight by the time she reached the second floor. It was then that another voice called out.

"Wait! I implore you!"

Sophie halted abruptly. Through the open door of one of the upper salons, the Comtesse de Juneau had come hurrying forward in a rustle of striped silk and a gleam of pearls.

"Madame la Comtesse!" Sophie was dismayed to see that the woman was still not ready for flight. "You should be gone. Your coach will be waiting at the door for you." In other circumstances she would not have spoken so directly, but at this time of crisis all social barriers melted away. "The gates were shut on the mob, but that won't keep them away for long."

"I cannot leave!" The woman was distraught, her face ashen within the pretty frame of her softly dressed hair, and she wrung her be-ringed hands. She was the Comte de Juneau's third wife, the mother of his only child, and devoted to him in spite of the thirty years between them. "As soon as my husband heard the news he had a seizure and collapsed. I cannot leave him."

"Then let me fetch help to carry him down to the coach, madame!" Sophie would have darted off at once, but the Comtesse stopped her.

"No! He's much too ill to be moved. Have you seen my father anywhere?"

"No, madame."

Torn between concern for her husband and her father, the woman was obviously desperate with anxiety.

"Why won't you let me fetch help for the Comte?" Sophie asked again. "Perhaps his condition is not as serious as you fear."

"No. There is no mistake, and I must get back to him." The Comtesse's eyes were brimming with tears, but she tilted her head proudly. "I am resolved that the Comte shall draw his last breath in dignified repose under his own roof in the château where he and his forebears were born!" Her emotion almost overcame her. "Can you understand why this attack should be happening? Even when the Comte was counselor to the King at Versailles he never neglected his tenants or his lands."

"Maybe old enemies have instigated the uprising."

"Perhaps that's it. This is a terrible time for settling old scores and none was more politically opposed to the Comte than Emile de Juneau, the son of his late younger brother, a vicious young man now in league with the traitor Orléans." She swallowed hard. "But I digress, because I scarcely dare voice what I must ask. It's why I called out to you on the stairs."

"Tell me, madame!" Sophie said with compassion. "I'll do anything I can."

The Comtesse flung out her hands in frantic appeal. "Then, for mercy's sake, take my son with you to safety!"

Sophie did not hesitate. "Where is Antoine? In the nursery?"

"No, he's at his father's side. The nursemaid has fled."

"Shall I fetch him?"

"I'll bring him to you." The Comtesse hastened into the salon, pausing only to wipe her eyes before entering. Her extraordinary courage was deeply moving to Sophie, who had also known tragedy in her life. Sadly she pictured the heartrending scene of farewell taking place within the salon, but she had to control her feelings for the child's sake. At all costs he must be spared any indication of what was truly at stake.

The Comtesse emerged carrying her son in her arms. The four-year-old, with his dark eyes and mop of brown curls, was still wearing the blue velvet jacket and breeches the nursemaid had dressed him in that morning. Sophie would have to find him more suitable clothing at the first opportunity. She could not pass him off as a peasant child in those garments. He had no coat, but his mother had wrapped him in a lacy shawl. Although it was late in April, it was an unseasonably chilly afternoon. His round face bore a bewildered expression, but when he saw Sophie he smiled. She had made him sugar horses and little cakes that looked like soldiers and sweetmeats in every color of the rainbow. It was always a treat to visit her in the kitchen, although he had to escape his nurse to get there. His mother spoke in a choked voice.

"I've explained to Antoine that you are going to take care of him for a little while, Sophie." The Comtesse pressed a last loving kiss to the child's cheek, and then she set him down. Obediently he took the hand that Sophie held out to him.

"We're going to start our time together by playing a game of hide-and-seek," Sophie said with a smile.

He gave a skip and a jump. "I like that."

The Comtesse had unclasped her pearl necklace, and now she drew off her rings and bracelets, pushing them into the purse that dangled by its cords from Sophie's wrist. "These should help you to bribe your way through whatever difficulties you may have to face. I've tucked a bag of gold into Antoine's sash. Take the waiting coach and get to England. You'll both be safe there." Her voice broke. "Now go! And may God go with you."

Sophie, seeing Antoine was about to grab his mother's skirt at the sound of her distress, whirled him swiftly to the stairs. "Come on! Let's jump each tread!"

He looked over his shoulder. His anguished mother had returned to the salon door, but paused to wave to him. Reassured, he waved back as Sophie cried out a heartfelt vow.

"One day I'll bring Antoine home again, madame! I swear it!"

The Comtesse, beyond speech, gave a nod of gratitude. Then, with a swish of her skirts, she closed and locked the salon door after her. Sophie was already swinging Antoine from stair to stair.

When they reached the entrance hall, she lifted Antoine up onto her hip and made for the great door, surprised that it was bolted on the inside instead of standing open to the waiting coach. Then a crash against the lock brought her to a skidding halt on the pink marble floor. In the same instant, she heard glass shattering. It was too late for escape in the family coach! The mob must have been advancing on the château from more than one direction. Antoine gave a frightened whimper, his lower lip beginning to quiver.

"That's only the signal for the start of our game," Sophie announced cheerfully, turning to run with him in the opposite direction. "Hold on tight!"

When she thrust open the baize door to the kitchen, she saw that everything was just as it had been left, some pans still simmering, and capons continuing to turn on the clockwork spit. Then, with renewed terror, she heard the yelling of marauders charging through the outer kitchens, cutting off her escape. Immediately she rushed into the nearest pantry where she set Antoine down. Closing the door, she pressed her ear against the panel to listen intently.

"Who are we hiding from?" the child whispered.

Sophie managed to smile, putting her finger to her lips, her ear still at the door. "That's part of the surprise," she whispered back. Her spine stiffened as she heard the invading rabble thunder through the main kitchen into other parts of the château. It was impossible to estimate how many there were, but she guessed it would be a hundred or more. No small gathering would have dared to rise up against the château. Antoine leaned close to her nervously, sucking his thumb. He was frightened by the noise of heavy boots and clattering sabots. Sophie stooped to put her arms around him protectively.

"There's no need to be afraid, Antoine," she said carefully. "You will always be safe with me."

It was a wild promise, but she meant to keep it. As she cuddled him close she breathed a prayer for his parents.

When all became quiet again in the kitchen region, Sophie peeped out cautiously. There was nobody to be seen, although a chair had been knocked over in the rush.

Quickly she turned to seize a loaf of bread from a pantry shelf and some cheese wrapped in a napkin, which she put into her traveling bag. Then she took down a jar of her own sweet wine biscuits and handed one to Antoine before filling his pockets as well as her own.

He munched on the biscuit as she took his other hand and ran out of the kitchen into the cobbled courtyard. From the direction of the stables, the sound of fighting mingled with the neighing of horses and the clattering of hooves. She guessed the grooms were attempting to get away with the horses, but had been intercepted and were now overpowered. Clearly, there was no escape in that direction.

Fearful of making any sound on the cobbles that might attract attention, Sophie kicked off her shoes and pushed them into her bag. Once more lifting Antoine onto her hip, she ran silently across the courtyard into the kitchen vegetable garden and then through a gate to the formal gardens. Not until she reached the shelter of the box hedges did she drop to her knees to regain her breath, seating Antoine on the grass beside her. He was a slightly built child, but heavy enough when she had to run, carrying her hand baggage as well. In the distance she could hear distressing cries from within the château. A more jubilant roar suggested that the wine cellars had been breached by some of the usurpers.

Antoine peered into her face. "Let's go back now."

Putting her shoes back on, Sophie shook her head. "The game is not over yet. We'll hide in the orangery for a while."

She knew that sooner or later the leaders of the mob would discover that the Juneau son and heir was missing. Then the search would widen. She would have to get Antoine away as soon as it grew dark. In the meantime, the orangery was sufficiently distant from the château to have escaped the hunt thus far. It also had the advantage of a secret alcove, installed in some past century for lovers' meetings, where she and Antoine would be safe for a while. She only knew of it because a lusty young gardener had once tried to entice her onto its cushioned bench for two.

Antoine sprang to his feet at hearing where they were to go. The orangery was a warm, sweet-smelling place, the orange trees standing like sentinels of different heights in their square green tubs waiting to be taken outside in the summertime. It was one of his favorite winter playgrounds. As soon as they were inside Sophie breathed a sigh of relief. It would soon be sunset and with the first stars she and Antoine would run to a broken place in the boundary and the thick woods that lay beyond. But her immediate task was to find something to make into a cape for the boy.

He had thrown off the shawl and was skipping in and out among the rows of trees, some so tall and mature that it was like being in the woods already. Sophie pulled away some protective sacking from one of the trunks and held it up. This would do to cover the boy's expensive clothes until she could find something better. Then she searched the shelves lining the walls to see what might be of use: a gardener's knife, a roll of twine, a pocket tinderbox, and a lantern. Suddenly she froze as she caught the sound of shuffling feet and knew that she and Antoine were not alone in the orangery.

"Who's there?" she demanded, concealing her fear.

But it was Antoine, on the far side of a row of trees, who called out the answer.

"*Grand-père!*"

The Comtesse's elderly father, the Marquis de Fontaine, was tall, thin-faced, and frail-looking. He was confused about many things, and not always able to remember the hour or the day or where he was, but he had never forgotten the skills of his youth, when growing orange trees had been his hobby. And as yet he had never failed to know his grandson.

"Is it you, boy?" He looked up vaguely from winding some twine. Antoine climbed onto his knees.

"I didn't know you were playing hide-and-seek too, *Grand-père.*" The child imitated Sophie's earlier action by putting a finger to his lips. "You must be very quiet, but you can tell me a story."

It was a routine familiar to them both. The old man began rambling on about his days as an army officer. There was no telling how much Antoine understood, but as he settled cozily to listen, he took from his pocket and held close the little wooden soldier he always had with him.

Sophie mulled over this new development. She was overwhelmed with relief that the Marquis was safe, but finding him there meant an immediate revision of her original plan. The secret alcove was not large enough to house all three of them. The child's life had priority and the old man would hinder their flight, but she could not leave him to suffer the brutality of the mob and death on the guillotine.

She took note of his clothes, for nothing must mark him as an aristocrat. Fortunately his coat and breeches were of plain brown cloth, his hose woolen and his shoes black-buckled. His green brocade waistcoat was well covered by a gardener's apron, which was also concealing the gold fob watch he always wore. But his cravat and cuffs were of fine Valenciennes lace that would have to be cut away. His white wig must also be discarded. Since the Revolution, wigs and powdered hair had become the stamps of the aristocracy and of the menservants who waited on them.

Opening her traveling bag, Sophie unpacked her sewing kit and waited. Before long, as she had hoped, the old man fell asleep and Antoine, quietly content, became drowsy too. Neither one moved as Sophie's scissors snipped away at the Marquis's lace. When she repacked her bag, she also folded away the Comtesse's shawl. It might comfort the child when he discovered eventually that this parting from his mother was permanent. Now it was time to leave.

Taking the Marquis's hat from its peg, she chose her moment to place it swiftly on his head after whipping away his wig, which she thrust with the lace into the embers of one of the orangery stoves. She did not want to leave any evidence of their having been there. The Marquis awakened immediately and sat forward in a daze, causing Antoine to stir.

"Is it morning?" the old man asked in bewilderment.

"No, Monsieur le Marquis," Sophie replied. "We are going for a walk."

"Are you my daughter?" The old man's fierce white bushy brows contrasted with the mildness of his puzzled gray eyes.

She shook her head and told him her name. Her reassuring tone seemed to put him at his ease. Antoine, rubbing his eyes, slid from his grandfather's knee.

"Where's nurse?" he asked in a yawn.

"We don't need her when I'm looking after you," Sophie said

cheerily as she removed his gilt-fringed sash and put the hidden bag of gold into her purse. Then she added the sash to the stove. After wrapping the sacking about him, she fastened it with a brooch from her own bodice. "When we get outside I want you to take hold of your *grand-père*'s hand. And remember," she added with a smile as she put her finger to her lips, "we have to be as quiet as mice."

He nodded, smiling back at her. To her relief, the old man allowed her to usher him out of the orangery and docilely followed the way she led. The path between the sheltering box hedges stretched like a long pale ribbon in front of them. When they had passed through several small groves with fountains, they came to the broken section of the wall. The Marquis halted stubbornly.

"What's afoot?" he demanded belligerently.

Sophie thought longingly of the shelter of the thick woods on the other side of the wall, but with Antoine by her side, this was still not the time to speak of the plundering mob. Then she had a flash of inspiration. "The château has fallen to the enemy, *Général*. We are in flight!" To Antoine she whispered, "Now we have a new game to play."

The boy beamed and took the toy soldier from his pocket to become part of this new venture. The Marquis straightened his shoulders upon being addressed by his former military rank and glanced about warily.

"Then keep alert, mademoiselle, there may be musketeers pursuing us. The Austrians are a cunning lot! Over the wall with you!"

After making sure there was nobody on the other side, Sophie assisted the Marquis over the treacherous rubble. Antoine went nimbly ahead and gave an excited shout, forgetting the need for quiet.

"Look! There's Bijou!"

Sophie saw the Comtesse's chestnut mare standing saddled and bridled under the trees, her well-groomed flanks gleaming in the twilight. Sophie could only suppose she had been frightened by the uproar in the stable and had galloped away in the melee.

Antoine ran toward her. Many times he had ridden beside his mother on his own little pony. Sophie hastened across the lane, intending to catch up with him, but at her approach the horse moved restlessly. Immediately she slowed almost to a standstill, fearful that the horse might bolt, and let Antoine go to her on his own.

"You can be *Grand-père*'s war-horse," Antoine chatted, reaching up to pat the mare companionably. The horse knew him and became more settled, although she might have shied away from Sophie were it not for the sweet wine biscuits she held out on the palm of her hand. She and Antoine fed Bijou several of these biscuits before Sophie could fasten her hand baggage and lantern to the saddle with twine.

The Marquis mounted from a flat-topped boulder. Then Sophie set Antoine up in front of him before taking the bridle to lead the horse along a little used track through the woods. During her early days at the Château de Juneau, she had come here to grieve privately for her father's untimely death. Later, she had continued to visit the woods when she needed some respite from the hubbub of the kitchen regions. The sun had set, but the path was still visible in the twilight and she could see her way through the trees.

"Walk faster!" the Marquis ordered sternly, seeming to suppose she was a corporal at the horse's head. "We must put as much distance as possible between us and our pursuers!"

These were her sentiments exactly. The route was rough underfoot and overgrown in places, but it was the one least likely to be followed. As darkness began to envelop them, Sophie lit the lantern and trudged on. By now Antoine was asleep, wedged against his grandfather, who was nodding in the saddle.

She walked most of the night. Having long since left the area that was familiar to her, she paused whenever there was an open space or a lake amid the trees, to take her bearings from the stars. She had been taught just enough astronomy to locate the North Star, and it was to the north that the Channel coast and freedom lay.

When at last Sophie began to stagger with tiredness she deemed it safe enough to stop. She chose a grove with a stream running through it. Antoine did not waken when she lifted him down and wrapped him in her cloak. The Marquis dismounted, tethered Bijou, and settled down to sleep under a tree. She supposed that in his army life he had slept out-of-doors many times and found nothing unusual in doing it again since the past was now more real to him than the present. After tucking the Comtesse's shawl around the boy for extra warmth, Sophie attempted to sleep herself, only to discover that her mind was too alert for repose.

She found herself going over the events that had brought her to the

Château de Juneau and to this lonely place in the woods. She had grown to womanhood in the large apartment above her father's shop and the atelier where all his confectionery was made. Her mother's death after six weeks of illness, coinciding with the fall of the Bastille, had signaled the end of those secure, contented years. Her father became heavy-hearted and morose, even as his clientele changed. Foreign diplomats had left the city after the arrest of the King and Queen, the aristocracy had scattered, and there was nobody left at Versailles, where his confectionery had always been in demand.

Henri Delcourt was in no mood to deal with the Revolutionary officer who had come swaggering into his shop after inciting a mob to shout for the death of the royal family.

"Get out of my shop!" Henri had ordered in a rage. "Only true patriots are served here!"

He had been struck down and kicked viciously in the head and ribs, dying even as he was thrown out onto the street. A cart took his broken body away to one of the communal graves dug to accommodate the victims of mob violence. Sophie, who had been on an errand when the incident occurred, arrived back to find the entrance barred to her home. Many of the bystanders were quick enough to tell her what had happened, but none had followed the cart to let her know where she might have mourned at her father's last resting place.

She had only the garments she stood up in at the time, although in her purse was payment of the sizable bill she had been sent to collect. That night she stayed at the home of a childhood friend, Marie-Thérèse, and her husband, Maurice. The next morning Maurice learned that there was a warrant out for her arrest, a trumped-up charge accusing her of being involved in subversive activities with her father against the ruling National Convention.

"It's an attempt to justify your father's murder," Maurice explained. "Marie-Thérèse will pack you some clothes and necessities and I'll help you to get away from the city." When leaving, Sophie had embraced both her good friends in gratitude.

Her decision to take refuge in the village overlooked by the Château de Juneau was made for two reasons. It lay many miles from Paris in a district that had remained trouble-free, and the Comte had been one of her father's customers over many years, which made her certain that she would stand a good chance of getting work in his

11

employ. When she arrived at the château the housekeeper had known her by name and took her immediately onto the staff, saying that the Comte had missed his favorite confectionery since the troubles in Paris had put an end to deliveries.

It was Sophie's making of the Comte's favorite candies that had brought her more in contact with the Comtesse than was usual in a grand household. Her stay at the château had been a period of security, when Sophie had been able to build up her life again. She realized now that she had been foolish to suppose it would last. Her eyes closed at last and she slept.

After little more than two hours Sophie was awakened by the first light of dawn. Reassured that she had not miscalculated her bearings to any degree, she managed to move without disturbing Antoine. After washing her face and hands in the chill stream, she unpacked her sewing kit and stitched to the underband of her skirt the Comtesse's bracelets and all but one of the rings, which she kept in her purse together with a few of the gold coins in case of emergency. The pearl necklace and the rest of the money she fastened into the hem of her petticoats. She had heard that the Marquis never carried money on his person, so there was no fear of his suddenly producing a handful of gold. Now it was time to waken her companions.

Her concern was that the Marquis would have forgotten that they were in danger and start demanding a return to the Château de Juneau, but fortunately that did not happen. Finding himself in the woods reminded him of countless other dawn awakenings on campaign, and he accepted the breakfast of cheese and bread that Sophie handed to him, assuming her to be a camp follower. Antoine was remarkably good, whatever qualms he might have felt were overcome by her promise that he should ride on Bijou again.

When they were ready to set off, Sophie seated herself sideways on the horse behind the Marquis. Before long they left the woods and turned northward at a crossroad, riding through the countryside. They had not covered many miles when there came the sound of horsemen behind them. Sophie glanced back in terror, fearing that some of the mob had tracked them down. Instead it was a troop of soldiers with the red, white, and blue cockades of the new Republic on their hats.

Her urgent hope that the soldiers would ride by was dashed when the sergeant regarded the three of them keenly as he drew level and then wheeled his horse across Bijou's path, causing the Marquis to rein in automatically.

"That's a fine mount you have there, old fellow," the sergeant said, resting his hands on his saddlebow. "How did you come by it?"

The Marquis regarded him blankly, unable to adjust to this curious questioning by a stranger, and Antoine shrank back shyly. Sophie spoke, deciding the truth would be most acceptable in these times when many peasants traded in goods looted from noble houses.

"Finders keepers!" She quoted the adage pertly in the manner of a lively country girl. "We found the horse ownerless and wandering."

"Did you indeed? And where was that?"

"Just back in the woods there." She jerked her head in the direction from which they had come. "I guess it's an aristocrat's horse, but that gives me more right to the animal than its owner. I saw no harm in making use of my good fortune."

The sergeant held her gaze, assessing her account. "Neither was there, but now the three of you must dismount. I can tell you this is far too good a horse to pull a cart or plow or whatever you and this simpleminded old fellow had in mind. I'm commandeering it for the army." He signaled to one of his men. "Take charge of this riding horse, Corporal."

Sophie did not dare make any protest and slid obediently to the ground, telling the Marquis to dismount. To her relief he obeyed her, and she lifted Antoine down before untying her baggage and the lantern. The sergeant spoke again.

"What have you in there, young woman?" His voice took on an amused edge of sarcasm. "Anything else you found wandering?"

She opened her traveling bag for his inspection. Seeing nothing of interest, he swung his horse away with a nod, and the troop of soldiers moved after him in a clatter of hooves. Sophie watched them go, grateful to have escaped so lightly. The loss of Bijou was a disaster, but at least she had not been ordered to produce any papers or answer any probing questions.

It was then that her two companions reacted to the horse's abduction with unwitting recklessness. Antoine had not comprehended at first that Bijou was to be taken away, but as his mother's horse disappeared into the distance he burst into tears. Throwing himself

13

down on the road, he kicked and drummed his feet in temper. At the same time the Marquis let forth a great shout, shaking his fist after the soldiers.

Sophie clapped a hand over his mouth and they staggered together as he tried to fend her off. Some of the soldiers in the rear guard turned in their saddles, but all they could see was a demented old peasant hitting out at the young girl, roaring and stamping.

"Listen to me, Monsieur le Marquis," she implored, dodging his blows and hoping he would understand. "It is the Revolutionaries from whom we are fleeing. They broke into the château yesterday afternoon and your daughter asked me to take Antoine to safety in England. That's where I'm taking you as well, if you will continue to allow me."

The old man became still, leaning a hand on her shoulder for support after the exertion of their short struggle, for he was out of breath. "I'm honored, mademoiselle," he said with stiff formality. Then his voice became querulous. "Where's my daughter?"

Sophie drooped her head. "I fear the worst."

Her anguished tone penetrated his confusion and tears rolled from his eyes. He spoke slowly. "May God receive her soul."

"Amen," she said quietly. Then she saw, as he turned away, that he had lapsed into his own world again.

When Antoine had been pacified with the last of the wine biscuits, Sophie picked up her traveling bag and they set off again. That night was spent in a deserted cottage, their supper some food Sophie purchased in a village they had passed through. While there, she also bought a homespun outfit for Antoine from a secondhand clothes stall in the marketplace as well as a long waistcoat in the old-fashioned style to replace the Marquis's green brocade one. With his fob watch in his pocket, the gardening apron could be discarded, although he seemed loath to see it go. At another stall she had found some good quality shirts and underlinen. Since the coarse red hands of the woman selling the wares looked incapable of such good needlework, Sophie supposed the items to be looted merchandise. She selected enough to give the Marquis and Antoine a change of linen. Lastly she bought a couple of cooking pans and utensils for wayside meals, which made her traveling bag much heavier.

The next day proved difficult. Antoine became fractious, bored with walking and being carried. He was missing his mother, his nurse, his pony, and his toys. Sophie became anxious about the Marquis, who was unused to so much exercise and had slowed down to such an extent that they were covering little ground. Her reckoning was that there was another forty miles or so to go before they reached the coast, but as yet, although she had called at several farms, she had been unable to secure any form of transport. Eventually she was offered a bony old nag and a small cart in which the Marquis and Antoine could sit as she drove. She paid for it gladly.

They had been staying at inns whenever possible, until one evening they were having supper in a taproom when she heard talk of a party of aristocrats, a husband and wife with three children, who had been arrested there. Mention was made of the children going with their parents to the guillotine.

"That's common sense," one brutal-looking laborer remarked. "If there's a plague of rats, only a fool would leave the nests undisturbed."

Sophie's blood chilled at the merciless words and she glanced protectively at Antoine, who was spooning up broth. She made up her mind there should be no more staying at inns. In the future they would sleep side by side in the cart and keep away from places where they might be betrayed.

From then on Sophie kept to lanes and avoided all the main traveling roads, lengthening the journey considerably. The nag plodded steadily, but its pace was slow and often it had to be rested.

There were many setbacks. Sometimes Sophie reached a dead end and had to retrace several miles. Often she had no clue as to where she might be, and she had to wait until nightfall to look at the stars.

Then on a cloudy day, Sophie glimpsed the glitter of sea in the distance. She laughed joyously for the first time on the perilous journey. When she had driven as near as possible, she leapt down from the cart and ran with Antoine to the grassy edge of an incline to gaze at the waves slapping against the rocks some distance below. The crisp wind, flicking white caps on the water, whipped their hair and flattened her skirts against her legs. To the west she could see a fishing hamlet nestling no more than half a mile away. Sweeping Antoine up in her arms, she pointed to the horizon.

"England lies there! That's where we're going to stay until France is herself again and you are home at the Château de Juneau once more." Her heart had expanded with relief that at last their haven was only a few sea miles away.

"What's England like?" Antoine asked uncertainly.

"It will have trees and birds and animals and places where you can play just like home." To herself she added that it was a foreign land on which France had declared war only two months before. Now Britannia, under George III, was allied with Austria in a coalition of nations resolved to defeat the French Republic on all fronts. Sadly, Sophie knew there could be no future for her beloved homeland until its present evil leaders were defeated and deposed.

"Will there be soldiers in England?" Antoine asked, hugging his beloved toy warrior to him.

"Lots of them. But they'll have scarlet coats instead of blue. I'll take you to see them march by."

"I'll tell *Grand-père*. He'll want to see the soldiers too when we get to England."

Sophie lowered Antoine to his feet, and as he went running back to his grandfather, she looked again to the horizon, wondering what awaited her in England. She hoped to secure employment as a confectioner, to settle somewhere she could care for her two charges, and, perhaps with time, to find love.

Two

AS A PRECAUTION, Sophie went alone into the hamlet to make her inquiries about getting a boat for England. She glanced about observantly in the narrow cobbled streets. The only soldiers she saw were drinking wine in a tavern. Making her way to the little quay, she found some fishermen selling their fish to the housewives. She approached one man, older than the rest, who was mending his nets.

"Do many boats go out from here?" she asked as an opening, holding back her hair in the wind.

He glanced at her shrewdly, summing up her presence as a stranger to the hamlet. "Would you be interested in a voyage?" he replied.

"I might be."

"Then it's my sons you want to see." He nodded toward two strong-looking men stacking lobster pots. "That's Jacques in the gray coat. Tell him I sent you."

Both brothers were weather-tanned and broadly built. Neither paid any attention as she approached across the cobbles, but they must have seen their father direct her to them. Without looking up from his task, Jacques spoke first.

"Don't stop here. I'll meet you behind the church at the end of the street in five minutes."

She found the church. It was closed, as was to be expected, for priests and others in religious orders were being hounded and persecuted under the Republic. Jacques soon appeared, to find her waiting among the tombstones.

"How many in your party?" he asked without preamble.

"Three. I have an old man and a child with me."

"You're in luck. My brother, Gaston, and I are crossing tonight to Shoreham-by-Sea. There's almost a full load. You came just in time, but it won't be cheap."

She settled half of what he asked, the rest to be paid before boarding.

He gave her directions to the cove, and the time at which he and Gaston would set sail, warning her not to be late.

Sophie left the hamlet thankful that escape had been arranged, but with no joy in her at the prospect of leaving her native land. It was her reluctance to leave France that had made her seek sanctuary in the countryside after fleeing Paris when she could easily have gone to England. Like thousands of other people, she had thought that eventually the storm would blow over and the monarchy reestablished in a constitutional form. Instead, in January this year, the King had been guillotined.

She had bought food for their supper, including a hot pie, but the Marquis ate little. She was concerned by his increasing physical weakness, but she promised herself that on the morrow, when they were safely in England, she would find comfortable accommodation where he could rest and recover.

As darkness began to fall, Sophie untethered the nag and led him into a meadow, which sloped down to a little stream. He had served them well and had reached the end of his strength. She had purchased some sugar pieces in the hamlet for this moment of farewell and let Antoine feed them to the poor animal. Then she patted the nag's neck, hoping he would draw his last breath in this quiet meadow. Antoine cried as much as he had done when Bijou was taken away.

When they reached the windblown venue, a group of émigrés had already assembled. Gaston was directing them down a flight of steps cut in the rock to where Jacques was waiting in the fishing boat to hand his passengers aboard. Sophie was amazed to see in the subdued glow of the lanterns that several of them, men and women alike, were still painted and richly dressed. They objected strongly at being told they would have to carry their own belongings. It was noticeable that the sensible refugees were plainly clad and raised no objection, only thankful to be getting away. Among these was a girl about Sophie's age, who looked so nervous that Gaston guided her down the first few steps as if he thought she could not manage on her own.

When it was Sophie's turn to pay the balance of their fares, she added something extra, with the request that Gaston take the Marquis directly to the vessel. He lifted the old man and carried him down effortlessly as she followed with Antoine, who turned out to be the only child on board. He sat on Sophie's lap, wrapped in the warmth of her cloak, and was asleep even as the sail was run up to flap noisily and then billow taut in the wind. The Marquis sat slumped against her left side, murmuring to himself now and again. On her right, crammed against her with no room to spare, was the nervous girl, who had pulled her hood forward as if to discourage anyone from speaking to her.

As the shore began to slide away some of the women wept. Several men shook their heads sadly. They were leaving behind not only their country but, for every passenger except Sophie, a privileged way of life that would never come again. The twinkling lights of the hamlet faded as the bow of the fishing boat rose and fell in the choppy waves. It was not long before seasickness added to the misery of many on board and a cold spray flicked into everyone's face.

Sophie soon became aware that her nervous neighbor was shaking with fright. "There's no need to be afraid," she said soothingly. "We are safely away from France. As for the sea, these fishermen know how to handle their boat in far rougher weather than this."

The girl turned her desperate, tear-stained face to Sophie. "How kind of you to show concern. I've always hated the thought of being on the sea and it's even worse than I feared."

"Are you feeling ill?"

"Only from the thought of these awful depths of water beneath the keel. I know I'm a coward, but I can't help it."

"Don't worry. Some people feel the same about spiders. I have a friend who is terrified of frogs." Sophie kept talking, introducing herself and giving the names of the Marquis and Antoine.

"I'm Henriette de Bouvier," the girl said in turn. "Like you, I've no close relatives left in France. I was orphaned as a child and responsibility for me passed to a branch of the family who have all been arrested and sentenced to death." She heaved a deep sigh. "A servant hid me and took me to her village home. She and her husband both support the Republic, but not the bloodshed. They brought me all the way to the coast, hidden under the kindling in their wagon. I'll be forever in their debt. They would not take as much as a sou from me, because they said I might need all I had for my passage to England. And they were right. I'm left with an almost empty purse."

"What are your plans when you get to England?"

"I'm going to Brighton. According to the fishermen, it's not too far from where we shall land. It's a resort patronized by the Prince of Wales and was very popular with fashionable visitors from our country before the Revolution. My uncle and aunt often stayed there, and it's where they settled after fleeing from France."

"I'm sure your uncle and aunt will welcome you."

"I hope so." But Henriette sounded doubtful. "They never did care for anyone but themselves, and I doubt they'll be pleased when I arrive without a sou. What shall you do when you get to England?"

"Find a place to stay for myself and my companions. Then I'll look for work."

"Work!" Henriette exclaimed incredulously. "Whatever would you do?"

Sophie gave an amused little laugh. "Exactly what I've been doing since I was old enough to sugar petals and grate chocolate blocks." She explained how she came to learn her craft, and related the circumstances that had brought her to the fishing boat.

"Tell me about Paris and your life there," Henriette requested eagerly. "I was never in the city and I expect I'll be an old crone before I get there now."

"It may not be that long," Sophie said hopefully. Then she told Henriette how she had learned her skills in confectionery and how her father had taught her the languages he had at his command. Serving so many of the foreign embassies, he liked to pay his customers the compliment of addressing them in their own tongue.

"Do you speak English, then?" Henriette wanted to know.

"I have some mastery of the language."

Henriette gave a wail. "I can't say a single word in any tongue but my own."

"Educated people in England all speak French, and in any case you'll learn soon enough."

"Did you ever go the Palace of Versailles?"

"Yes. From my early girlhood my father always took me with him on his important deliveries. He said his customers liked to have their caskets of confectionery delivered with some ceremony, and he wanted me to carry on his tradition."

"Did you ever see the Queen?"

"Many times. There was never a more gracious lady than Marie Antoinette, except my own mother. But it was not only the rich whom we served. My father's shop was exclusive in its own way, but he always had a range of sweets for more moderate purses, and until the hungry came onto the streets in their thousands, he never let anyone begging for food go away empty-handed."

While speaking, Sophie could visualize the atelier, and the mingled aromas of caramel and vanilla and spices seemed to be in her nostrils once again. She pictured her father, immaculate in his wig and well-cut clothes, coming from the office to inspect and taste and generally make sure that she and those working with her were producing confectionery to the standard of which he was so justly proud.

Henriette had leaned across to peer at the boy asleep in Sophie's arms. "Do you suppose that Antoine would have been at Court when he grew up if the Revolution had never occurred?"

"I'm sure of it. His father was once on the King's Council and a very powerful man. He would have wanted the same for his son and heir."

Immediately Henriette lowered her voice and spoke directly into Sophie's ear, even though not a word of their previous conversation could have been heard by anybody in the noise of the wind and waves. "In that case, I think you should be very careful about using Antoine's name in England. From what you've told me, he has surely inherited his father's title by now, and if it was a politically instigated uprising against the château, he might have enemies who will not rest until they have eliminated the last of the Juneau line."

Sophie held the child a little closer. "But he will be safe in England!"

"I pray that he may, but in a smuggled letter received some weeks ago, my uncle wrote of two émigrés, known to my family, who were murdered there. And each of them was the only surviving member of a distinguished lineage."

"I thank you for your warning." Sophie recalled the sinister words of the ruffian in the taproom at the inn, but before she could say anything more, there was an outcry from some of the passengers, which increased as Jacques moved along the boat, bawling his announcement.

"The sea is getting rough! A storm is in the offing! We'll have to turn back!"

Some of the women screamed and became hysterical at the prospect of returning to dangers from which there might be no second chance of escape. Men bullied, implored, and still failed with mutinous threats to sway the fishermen. One shrieking woman threw herself on her knees and begged Jacques to reconsider. His reply came so quickly that Sophie was certain that he had only been biding his time.

"If you will all open your purses and jewel boxes," he shouted, a hand cupped to his mouth, "and make it worthwhile for my brother and me to risk our lives, we'll face the storm and get you all through!"

It was pitiable to see how people responded. They could not get their valuables out quickly enough. Jacques went from passenger to passenger, demanding more of each one than he was offered. Purses were emptied into his greedy palms and jewelry sparkled in the lantern light as it changed hands. A widow, who had bribed her way out of prison, had nothing left but her wedding ring. He took it from her finger, insisting that her neighbors, both strangers to her, make up the difference. Henriette was panic-stricken, clutching a gold locket she wore on a chain round her neck.

"The only jewelry I have is this locket with miniatures of my parents! I can't give it up and yet I have only a few livres left in my purse! What am I to do?"

Sophie saw that the moment had come to make use of the Comtesse's jewelry. "Slip the locket under your neckline and leave everything to me."

Jacques reached Henriette first, and Sophie spoke for her, producing the diamond ring she had kept in her purse all the time. "This is enough to cover all four of us in extra fares."

22

He examined it in the lantern light, swaying on his feet with the undulating movement of the boat. "Very well, but I want the old man's watch too. Oh, I know it's not on show, but he'll have a good one."

Sophie protested furiously, but to no avail. In the end she had to tell the Marquis what was wanted. It saddened her to see how meekly the old man took his beautiful fob watch from his pocket and held it out to the fisherman, who grabbed it from him.

When Jacques had moved on, Henriette spoke emotionally to Sophie. "I can't thank you enough!"

"We're all in this crisis together," Sophie replied.

"Nevertheless, I see your action as a seal on our friendship. Is that impertinent of me?"

Sophie shook her head with a smile. "It's heartening that we should have become friends at this darkest of time. You must try to sleep now if you can."

The storm Jacques had forecast failed to materialize. Instead the wind dropped to a crisp breeze, and the skies cleared. Sophie supposed the threat of turning back was a trick played on many a boatload of hapless victims. She dozed fitfully, and as dawn filled the sky, she saw the coast of England close at hand. There were gentle green hills, hedgerows snowy with May blossoms, the rugged whiteness of low cliffs, and long smooth beaches. Here and there she could discern thatched farmhouses and cottages with flowering gardens. Once, a grand mansion came into view. The whole vista was peaceful and beautiful in the early morning light.

The other passengers awoke, their spirits revived as they realized that the perilous voyage was almost over. Sophie had decided that from now on her mother's maiden name, Dubois, should be Antoine's surname instead of Juneau, and she would refer to him as her nephew. Henriette's warning had been most timely. As the boy yawned and rubbed his eyes, Sophie gave him a hug.

"It won't be long before we go ashore, Antoine!"

In spite of their more cheerful mood, it was a sorry-looking group that disembarked when the fishermen brought their boat alongside the old quay at the Sussex harbor town of Shoreham-by-Sea. Dampened by spray, cold, hungry, and bedraggled, some with only the smudged remains of paint on their faces, they mounted the seaweedy steps. Glancing up, they saw no welcome in the curious eyes of those who had gathered to stare down at them from the seawall.

Sophie was the last to disembark with her two charges, for the Marquis was exhausted and had to be carried again. By the time Sophie had ascended the steps, holding Antoine by the hand, she saw that there were some on the scene offering to do what they could for the new arrivals. A local squire had sent three of his carriages to convey any aristocrats in need of assistance to his nearby home. Another gentleman had been hoping to find a certain French family of his acquaintance among those present, but his disappointment did not stop him from shepherding several émigrés into a quayside tavern to arrange their transport to London. Two prim, soberly dressed spinsters, who looked like sisters, had come with an urn on a handcart and were pouring tea for all the new arrivals. Henriette had already drunk hers and was standing with some fellow émigrés, one of whom was trying to make the driver of a hackney cab understand where they wished to be taken. Sophie would have gone to translate, but Gaston had set the Marquis down on a bench, and she ran to save the old man from slipping sideways. As she seated herself and put a supporting arm about him, too concerned to notice anything else, a large clergyman bore down on them, his black cloak billowing.

"Mademoiselle! My felicitations on your safe arrival in this fair land. I don't speak French, but I hope to make you comprehend my meaning."

Sophie looked up quickly. "I understand you very well," she replied in English.

He clapped his big hands together in relief. "We can communicate! How splendid! I can see this gentleman is far from well. How may I address him?"

It was no time for formal presentations. "This is the Marquis de Fontaine, and I'm most worried about him."

"With just cause, Mademoiselle Fontaine," the clergyman replied, assuming she was the Marquis's daughter. "I'm the Reverend John Barnes and rector of a nearby country parish." Turning, he called to his wife. "Mrs. Barnes! There's a good deed to be done here. One of our French brothers is in need of succor."

Mrs. Barnes—a tall, thin woman—came hurrying forward, bringing a cup of tea. "The poor gentleman! Our rectory is at your disposal, mademoiselle. Is this your little boy?" She reached out to pat Antoine's head, but he drew away shyly and clung to Sophie's skirt.

Sophie was persuading the Marquis to sip some of the tea. "The boy is my nephew and I'm—" Then she broke off with a cry as the Marquis raised a feeble hand and inadvertently sent the teacup flying. She dabbed at his soaked waistcoat with her handkerchief as she declined Mrs. Barnes's offer. "I appreciate your kindness, but I think it best if I take accommodation in the tavern across the way. The Marquis can't go any longer without rest and medical attention."

"He shall have both at our country home, which is no more than a couple of miles from here," the Reverend Barnes insisted genially. "Our coach is waiting to convey you there."

"Do heed the Rector's advice," Mrs. Barnes urged, poking her head forward in emphasis like a pecking hen. "The tavern is a noisy place of disorder and drunkenness."

Sophie was uncertain why she would be hesitating when this couple were so well meaning. The peace and quiet of a country rectory would be so much better for the Marquis than the tavern. Yet it was almost against her will that she gave a nod. "Very well, I accept your kind invitation and thank you for it."

"Good!" The Rector rubbed his hands together. "Fetch our coachman, Mrs. Barnes. He and I will give the Marquis a bandy chair to the coach."

As she set off to do his bidding, Henriette came running up. "I'm sharing a hackney carriage to Brighton with some people. There's another for hire and you could come too."

Sophie shook her head, explaining the offer she had received. "But as soon as the Marquis has recovered, we'll travel on to Brighton and find you."

"Remember the address that I gave you! If you should forget, you can always look in the resort's visitors' book, which is kept in one of the libraries. According to my uncle, it is signed by everyone of rank and importance upon arrival in Brighton. My name and place of residence will be there."

Sophie smiled. Henriette had spoken as an aristocrat, never doubting her own importance on the social scene. "I'll remember."

They kissed each other's cheek and Henriette stooped to embrace Antoine before running back to the waiting hackney carriage. She waved from the window as it went bowling away along the sea road in an easterly direction.

Nobody could have been more solicitous than the Rector in seeing the Marquis settled comfortably in the coach, which was shabby and not at all clean. It made Sophie wonder what conditions she would find at the rectory, but perhaps the carriage was not under Mrs. Barnes's jurisdiction. The Rector had taken the seat next to the Marquis. Sophie was opposite them, beside Mrs. Barnes, with Antoine seated once again on her lap.

"So you will be going to Brighton," the Rector said as the coach drew away from the quayside. "It is very popular with a certain section of the English aristocracy and you will meet many of your fellow countrymen and women there."

"I've been told the town has royal patronage," Sophie remarked.

"Indeed it has. The Prince of Wales visited it a few years ago to take the benefits of the seawater. He took such a liking to the place that he has since turned his first habitat there, which was originally a farmhouse, into a fine residence. It's known as the Marine Pavilion."

Mrs. Barnes scowled. "He's a spendthrift and a womanizer."

The Rector sighed piously, rolling up his eyes. "Judge not, my dear."

All conversation came to an end as the carriage turned into a lane as rutted and full of potholes as any that Sophie had been through in France. All five of them were tossed about the carriage and she could see why the Rector had taken charge of the Marquis, who might easily have slipped from her grasp.

Sophie looked out of the window again. There were woods and meadows, but not a sign of habitation. She clutched at the handstrap as once again the wheels lurched in and out of a pothole. "Is it much farther?" she asked. "Surely we have covered more than two miles since leaving Shoreham?"

"It won't be long now," the Rector replied amiably. Yet he exchanged a glance with his wife that seemed to convey a message.

Sophie was becoming increasingly uneasy. All along, the couple's excessive geniality had grated on her, but she had told herself she was being ungracious when they were being so solicitous of the Marquis's welfare. She had also had time to notice that the Rector's linen was grubby and there was dirt under his fingernails. His wife no longer looked about sharply as she had done on the quayside, but she seemed extremely tense, sitting quite rigidly. More and more certain that these people were not whom they claimed, Sophie decided she would pull the check string to stop the coach as soon as a cottage came into sight. Then she would remove herself and her charges from this couple's company. Across the fields, she glimpsed a farmhouse and a barn, the first habitation she had seen. She wished it were nearer.

"This is a very long and deserted lane," she commented.

"That's why we came this way," Mrs. Barnes snapped, her whole manner changing. At the same instant, her husband leapt to his feet, signaling for the coach to stop and letting the Marquis slump helplessly to the floor.

"What are you doing?" Sophie cried, her worst fears confirmed. This was no man of the cloth glowering at her with an ugly expression on his face, the bulk of his body between her and the Marquis.

"Making you pay for the nice little ride we've given you! Hand over your purse and valuables to my wife. I'll see what your Pa has in his pockets."

"Don't you dare touch him!" Sophie ordered fiercely, trying to loosen Antoine's arms a little from about her neck, for he had burst into noisy sobs at the angry voices and was clinging to her fearfully. "Surely you know that émigrés get robbed on the voyage over!"

"Not all of them and I'll wager you've still plenty tucked in your stays and up your skirt. Get to work, wife!"

The coachman had opened the door. Barnes snatched the sobbing Antoine from Sophie's arms and tossed him to the fellow, who took him yelling from her sight.

"Don't hurt him!" she screamed as she fought off Mrs. Barnes's attack, but then Barnes himself caught Sophie about the waist and flung her back onto the seat, where he held her while his wife's thieving hands ripped open her bodice and delved into her chemise. Desperately Sophie kicked and screamed, but she could not escape his grip. The pearl necklace and the coins were soon discovered and ripped from the hem of her petticoat.

"Let us go!" Sophie implored. "I'll give you everything we possess!"

"Shut up!" Barnes snarled. To his wife he added, "Look in her waistband. You should find something there."

The woman tore at Sophie's waistband. Then the Comtesse's rings and bracelets were revealed in a sparkle of rubies, emeralds, and sapphires laced with diamonds. The two thieves' triumphant glee was matched by that of their gloating accomplice in coachman's garb, who peered through the open door and congratulated them. Sophie could hear Antoine sobbing hysterically somewhere outside.

"Now we have nothing left. So let us go," she demanded fiercely. "The Marquis's pockets are empty."

"So you say!" Barnes yanked her to her feet, twisted her round, and thrust her toward the doorway. She just had a glimpse of Antoine, lying in the bushes where the coachman had tossed him and crying convulsively, when something bludgeoned her on the back of her head and she slipped into total blackness.

Three

WHEN EVENTUALLY Sophie's eyelids fluttered open, the darkness was still there, but it was full of stars with a risen moon. There was a searing pain in her head, and for a few moments she could not remember where she was or what had happened. Then she heard a horse clop its hoof restlessly.

"Bijou," she whispered, thinking herself back in the forest.

There was the rustle of a coat's silk lining as somebody dropped down beside her. "Thank God you're alive!"

A man's deep voice, full of relief, sounded as surprising to her as if an English oak had spoken. He was leaning over her, holding a lantern, but careful not to let the gleam go into her eyes. In its glow she saw an extraordinarily firm and handsome face, the forehead wide as were the cheekbones and the jaw, the nose straight, with curved nostrils. Greenish eyes were set deep under dark, straight brows that echoed the color of the thick, curly hair just visible beneath a high-crowned, narrow-brimmed hat. The wide, grimly set mouth was warmly sensual, and indented at the corners as if well used to mirth. All this registered in a flash of clarity before her clouded senses drew her away once more. She thought he asked her name, but she had no voice to answer him.

When Sophie next became aware of her surroundings, she was lying at the side of the lane, something soft folded under her head, and she was wrapped like a cocoon within her own cloak. There was

29

no sound of the horse she had heard earlier and for several terrified moments she thought she'd been abandoned and left to die. But as she cried out, she heard hoofbeats returning. Then the man dismounted and was again at her side. In the same instant, memory of the brutal attack flooded back with nightmare clarity.

"Antoine!" Frantically she struggled to sit up, unable to free her arms from the folds of her cloak. The man pressed her back gently but firmly.

"If it's the boy you are calling, he is all right. I've just taken him across the fields to a farmhouse. He was lying with his head on your arm when I sighted you both, and judging by the tearstains on his cheeks, I'd say he'd cried himself to sleep. He didn't wake and I left the farmer's wife putting him to bed."

"What of the Marquis de Fontaine?" The question tumbled from her in French, for she was unable to concentrate on another language in her dazed state. He replied in her own tongue without any accent that she could discern.

"It's very bad news, I'm sorry to say. Prepare yourself, mademoiselle. The elderly gentleman is dead."

She closed her eyes again and tears flowed from under her lids. To have brought the Marquis so far only to lose him overwhelmed her with grief. "He came through so much in France," she whispered brokenly, causing the stranger to bend his ear closer in order to catch her words. "It's cruel that he should lose his life here."

"What happened? Can you tell me? I don't want to move you yet. I'm waiting for help, which is why I'm still letting you lie here. You need to be lifted as gently as possible, and the farmer and his sons are on their way here at a run."

"You're being very kind," she murmured weakly.

"I'm glad I came along. I was riding to Shoreham by a short cut from the tollgate road or else you might not have been found for several hours. It's a lonely route. Was the Marquis your father?"

"We were not related. I only helped him to escape."

"And the boy?"

Almost automatically she repeated the story she had decided on. "Antoine is my nephew. Are you French too, monsieur?"

"No, but I had a French grandmother married to an Englishman, and my brother and I grew up in their house after our parents died.

I'm Tom Foxhill of London and not of these parts, but business brings me to the coast sometimes. Do you feel able to tell me your name now?"

He just caught what she said in reply before springing up to hail the farmer and his two burly sons, who had arrived with lanterns bobbing. "Over here!"

"How is the young woman now, sir?"

Tom Foxhill left her briefly to speak to them. Although he and the farmer lowered their voices, it was apparent from the snatches of conversation that reached her that these men would also be collecting the Marquis's body. Then Tom returned to her.

"We're going to move you now, Mademoiselle Delcourt," he said. "I promise you it will be a far gentler ride than if I'd carried you or taken you on horseback."

A blanket was brought and Tom lifted her onto it. She almost screamed from the additional pain that shot through her head, but bit deep into her lip to check herself. Then the farmer gripped one end of the blanket, and Tom took the other, and they carried her in this makeshift stretcher across the fields in the direction of the farmhouse.

The farmer's wife, a red-haired, freckle-faced woman, held the door wide as Sophie was carried through to a large kitchen with a long central table. The rich smell of boiled mutton blended with the sweeter scent of apple logs blazing on the hearth. The woman, already greatly flustered, threw up her hands in dismay at the sight of the blood on Sophie's ashen face and hair.

"Oh, you poor young thing! What a state you're in!" She took up a lighted candle. "I'll lead the way. Mind the step, Mr. Foxhill. And you too, William," she added to her husband. "I don't want my patient tossed to the floor."

"We've carried her across a plowed field," the farmer stated impatiently, "so it's not likely to happen in the house where I've lived since a boy."

She ignored him, still talking as her feet clacked along the flagstones of a black-beamed passage, her candlelight flickering over plastered walls. "I've made up the bed with clean linen, Mr. Foxhill, and put ready warm water and salve and everything else I'll need to clean and bind up the young woman's head before I settle her between the sheets."

In a small bedchamber, Sophie was lowered onto the bed and then the farmer left the room. With her eyes clamped shut against the pain, she whispered, "Where's Antoine?"

Tom answered her again in French, for as yet she had not spoken a word of English. "He's asleep in the next room. Mr. and Mrs. Millard's little daughter is sitting with him."

"He'll be frightened if he doesn't see me when he wakes!" Sophie became agitated.

"Don't be concerned. I'm sure Mrs. Millard will keep an eye on the boy after she's attended to you. I'll ask her to bring him to you if he should stir before morning."

Mrs. Millard was shuffling her feet nervously. "Don't she speak English? Oh, my! One of these French folk, is she?"

Sophie whispered again to Tom. "Please tell her I can speak her language."

Tom conveyed this information and the woman expressed relief. Then he leaned over Sophie again as she opened her eyes and looked up at him. "You must be as quiet as possible until the pain in your head has gone." He grinned broadly. "I cracked my head once after a fall from a horse, so I've some idea of what you're going through."

Sophie wanted to answer him, but the throbbing in her head was so excruciating that she seemed to have lost the power of speech. The odd thought tumbled through her brain that he was a man to fear as well as trust. Then he turned for the door and paused there.

"Farewell, Mademoiselle Delcourt. May your new life in England be free of all further trouble."

His footsteps receded down the passage. When Mrs. Millard had laid out all she would need for her nursing task, including one of her own voluminous nightgowns for Sophie to wear, she unfolded the cloak the young Frenchwoman was wrapped in and shook her head at what she saw. Sophie Delcourt's clothes were cut about and torn, her shoulder and arm were bruised black where she had fallen, and her breasts were exposed. No wonder Mr. Foxhill had wrapped her up like a parcel.

"Do you hurt anywhere beside your head?" Mrs. Millard asked tactfully.

"I was not raped," Sophie managed to whisper. Then pain shut off her mind again.

32

DURING THE TIME she was bedridden, Mrs. Millard washed and mended Sophie's garments and put them in a drawer ready for when she could dress again. She also took care of Antoine, dressing him in clothes and boots her sons had worn at his age. He was out on the farm all day, happy to be with the animals, and allowed to help Josie, the Millards' ten-year-old daughter, with simple tasks. Sophie learned that Tom Foxhill had paid for her accommodation and left her ten golden guineas to tide her over when she and the boy left the farm. He had also written down his London address in case she was in need of further assistance. Since she had not changed her mind about going to Brighton, she doubted if she would ever see him again, but she planned to accept the money as a loan and repay it as soon as possible.

To Sophie's regret, the funeral of the Marquis de Fontaine took place before she was able to attend. A doctor had attributed the cause of death to a bludgeoned skull. The murder was duly reported to the local magistrate, but there was little hope of an arrest or of Sophie's possessions being recovered, for the criminals had vanished without a trace. She told no one of the jewels that had been lost, for fear that people might ask questions about herself and Antoine that she would not wish to answer. The boy's safety counted above all else. Her name as well as his were sent by the magistrate to London, for all French émigrés had to register upon arrival. He was listed as Antoine Dubois.

Sophie would have liked a white lily, symbol of the old France, to be placed on the Marquis's coffin, but such an exotic bloom was unobtainable locally. Instead, Josie was sent to the village to buy a length of white ribbon, the color of the House of Bourbon. Sophie made it into a cockade, which she fastened to a bunch of flowers picked from the farmhouse garden. This was placed on the coffin as a last tribute to a brave soldier of France.

As Sophie's painful headaches began to subside, Mrs. Millard allowed her to sit by the open window in the kitchen while everybody else was out of the house. "You don't want their noise yet," she would say.

Gradually Sophie was drawn into the family routine. The Millards were as quarrelsome and argumentative and as attached to one another as any French farming family, but there all similarity ended. Here food was in abundance. Large joints of beef turned on the spit, dripping fat onto slices of boiled Sussex pudding, made of suet and flour, which fried in the pan beneath. Hams and sides of bacon hung from hooks in the storeroom; milk, cream, and cheeses filled the shelves in the dairy, and the cupboards were well stocked. Whenever Sophie watched the menfolk piling up their plates, she thought of the starving peasants in her own country.

Her first outing, apart from a visit to the Marquis's grave, was to the village with Mrs. Millard in a wagonette. The time had come to replace the clothes she and Antoine had lost in the theft. At the market, comparing prices carefully, Sophie bought the materials she needed with some of Tom Foxhill's money. Neither her shoes nor Antoine's were wearable anymore, the soles having been worn through in their travels, so she ordered new ones for them both from the local cobbler.

In addition to sewing their new clothes, Sophie found time to help Mrs. Millard with household tasks. She had already gained some insight into English cooking, and was amazed by the number and variety of sweet and savory puddings. Now she took a hand in their making, certain that any knowledge remotely connected with her own craft would be of use to her in this new land. She found many of the puddings heavy fare, but Antoine tucked in, wanting to be like the farmer and his sons. He also copied them in shoveling in his food, all the fine French manners he had been taught quite forgotten.

LATE ONE AFTERNOON a horseman rode in through the farm gates and dismounted outside the house. Sophie, baking bread, dusted some flour from her hands and went to the door. At the sight of Tom Foxhill on the doorstep she flushed with pleasure, for while she had thought much about him during her convalescence, she never expected to see him again.

"Mr. Foxhill! What a surprise!"

Had she but known it, he was far more taken aback than she. Her beauty, now unblemished and restored to health, stunned him with its bloom and freshness. Yet as his gaze traveled over her face, he was aware that the curious elusiveness, which previously he had blamed on the shock and pain of her ordeal, was still with her, and it only added to her fascination for him.

"Good day to you, Sophie. May I call you by your Christian name? It's how I have thought of you ever since the night I left you here."

"Yes, indeed. Come in." She opened the door still wider, uncomfortably aware of the cotton kerchief that covered her hair unflatteringly and of her coarse linen apron.

"You're looking very well! Quite different from the last time I saw you!" He removed his hat as he entered, and she took it from him to hang on a peg. His height was such that he automatically ducked to avoid a beam. "Mrs. Millard must have taken good care of you."

"She did indeed. All thanks to you, Mr.—er—Tom. Please sit down. I must take the last batch of bread from the oven, but first I want to thank you for rescuing Antoine and me that night in the lane."

He took a seat on a bench by the wall. "There's no call to mention it. My only regret is that I didn't arrive on the scene in time to prevent the attack and save the Marquis from death."

She opened the oven door in the brick hearth, blinking at the heat, and set the loaves on the kitchen table. "My only consolation is that the Marquis didn't know what was happening, or even that he had left his beloved France. Had he been spared, I believe that when realization dawned, he would have died from a broken heart." She looked at Tom once more across the table. "You left money with Mrs. Millard to pay for my convalescence and as a most timely loan for me. Words can't express my gratitude and I'll repay you at the first opportunity."

"That's not necessary."

"I have your address," she said firmly, settling the matter, and she wiped the table clean with vigorous strokes as if to emphasize her resolve not to be under any obligation.

"How's Antoine?" he asked, watching her every movement and silently summing her up as strong-willed and resilient. Clearly she had not been broken by whatever she'd had to endure in her escape or by the ordeal that had followed. In fact she showed an undaunted spirit and determination. He admired her for it, just as he admired everything about her. Although he had not originally intended to return to the farmhouse, he had been unable to forget her. In earlier times he might have thought she had cast a spell over him, but he was worldly enough to know that what emanated from her was witchery of another kind. Yet emotional entanglements, at least those of long duration, were not for him. It had been folly to come back, but somehow he had been unable to stay away.

She was replying to his question. "Antoine is very well and as happy as could be on the farm." Her task finished, she began to untie the knot of her kerchief. "I've no need to set the table yet, but I hope you will stay and take supper with us."

"I accept gladly."

With a little feminine gesture she touched her luxuriant hair, as if to ensure it had not been disarranged from its pins, and thrust the kerchief into her apron pocket. "Are you on your way to the coast again?"

"I am." He moved farther along the bench so that she could sit beside him. "But I'm in no haste," he added. "Traveling on a fine night never troubles me."

"So you're either an astronomer or you have the eyesight of a night owl," she declared lightly.

He smiled to himself. A night owl. She had come closer to the truth than she realized. "Something of both, I suppose," he answered jokingly, "but if the stars fail me, there is always my tinderbox to illuminate a signpost and my lantern to reveal potholes."

"I used those same methods during my escape from France."

"I should like to hear all about that if you feel able to tell me."

Sophie looked down at her hands for a moment, needing to gather her defenses. She had the uncomfortable conviction that if she were not careful, Tom would see through the story she had made up to account for Antoine's parentage, but for the time being, until she could be sure of his safety, she would have to keep the truth from Tom and everyone else.

"My father, a widower, was murdered by a Revolutionary," she began, "and I left Paris to work as a confectioner in a château many miles away. When the mob came, I took the Marquis and Antoine, who was with me, into hiding. The boy's mother—my sister—had given him into my charge when her own fate was sealed." She paused involuntarily, almost in tears, suddenly overcome by the image in her mind's eye of the Comtesse's anguished face.

"The guillotine?" he questioned compassionately.

She drew her breath and continued. "Yes, but it's too sorrowful a tale for me to be able to talk of it yet." While this was a true representation of her feelings, it was also an effective way to keep probing questions at bay. To her relief, Tom respected her wish to keep the details to herself. Yet she went on to talk freely about the rest of her journey to England. His rescuing her seemed to have created a bond between them, which she could feel as if it were a tangible link as they sat turned toward each other on the bench. It was a bond given strength by the way he looked at her, letting her deep into his eyes, and she was aware of a warmth stirring in her heart. She seemed to be coming alive again after the grief and shock that had somehow left her feeling drained of all that made her human. Perhaps talking it out had been what she needed to draw her back fully into the everyday world again.

"So now you know exactly how I came to be lying in the lane that night," she concluded.

"I'm honored that you've told me all this," he said, smiling seriously.

"You're easy to talk to—a patient listener," she replied, returning the smile.

"I'd like to be more than that to you."

Although his remark pleased her, she chose not to explore its significance. Instead she suggested a walk. "It's too fine a day to sit indoors."

They set out together, taking a sunny path through the woods and talking easily.

"I'm an importer of high quality wares and works of art from the Far East and the continent," Tom said, "which is why I travel a great deal. I keep my eyes on all the overseas markets, whether in St. Petersburg, Vienna, Florence, or anywhere else. Before the Revolution I was often in Paris."

"Where is your outlet for all that you buy?"

"I've a shop in St. James's Street in London. I had established myself there when my older brother, Richard, came out of the army and agreed to join me in the business. He's become an expert in paintings and antique glass. At the present time he also manages the shop, which releases me for buying overseas."

"It all sounds most interesting," she commented, wanting to know more, but he forestalled her.

"I've talked too much about myself. Tell me what you think of English country life? Have you been well received? I mean outside the farm, in the village, where even somebody from the next hamlet is considered a foreigner."

She was able to tell him that everyone had treated her kindly, possibly out of sympathy for the hardships she and Antoine had already endured. "So everybody has been very friendly in a genuine wish to help us forget our first unhappy experience. I appreciate that so much."

They talked on. Once they rested on a fallen tree trunk and Sophie heard her own laughter ringing out at something amusing Tom had said. In surprise, she realized that she hadn't sounded so carefree for a long time.

When they returned to the farmhouse, Mrs. Millard was home again with the children and Antoine met his rescuer for the first time.

Supper was the usual noisy meal, not only with the clatter of cutlery but with the men's boisterous talk of fishing and shooting. As Sophie was left to chat with Mrs. Millard about the day's happenings, she was aware how often Tom's eyes turned her way. She felt extraordinarily happy, as if she were on the brink of something unknown and wonderful. She could not imagine why she'd had misgivings about him at the time of her rescue and decided it must have been her natural fear of everybody and everything at that time of crisis.

During the meal, Tom spoke briefly of going to Shoreham to meet incoming cargoes destined for his business, but dealing in works of art was not a subject of much interest to farming men and the conversation soon swung to other subjects.

After supper, the Millard men kept Tom talking over flagons of ale while Mrs. Millard and Sophie washed and dried the dishes. Then Antoine was put to bed, and it took longer than usual to settle him down after such an exciting day. When Sophie finally returned to the kitchen, she found Tom waiting to say farewell. She put a shawl about her shoulders and went with him to the gate.

They stood together, silhouetted against the pale glitter of the stars, as she looked up into his face.

"Sophie," he said huskily.

It seemed to her afterward that they moved toward each other in the same moment as if the tender catch in his voice were a signal each had recognized instantly, for it had not been in her mind even if it had been in his. Suddenly she was in his arms, her shawl falling away, as he crushed her to him. His mouth devoured hers with a passion she had never experienced before and she responded ecstatically, gloriously imprisoned in his embrace.

Breathlessly they drew apart, still holding each other. Joy was coursing through her veins. He apologized at once, even though her smile should have told him that there would be no foolish show of outrage on her part.

"Forgive me, Sophie," he implored. "I had no right to take advantage of you. Such a kiss should be the seal on a promise made and shared."

She understood. In France no kiss was exchanged before a betrothal, and he was making it clear that here in England it was the same. Although she was relieved to know he attributed nothing binding to their kiss, his next words sent a chill through her heart.

"There's much I should have told you about my life. It's full of comings and goings, meetings and partings. As you know, my business takes me far afield." His eyes glinted as if with some secret satisfaction. "Often there is danger involved in my travels, which allows little if any chance for lasting relationships. And yet I know, as you do, that there is something special between us, something that we both recognized in the first seconds of meeting each other. All I can say is that I'll be back, Sophie."

All her newfound happiness exploded into pain. She had not looked for or wanted any commitment from him, but earlier, for a little while, he had made her believe that after all the chaos of her life, doors would open again, even to love. Now he had made it clear that she should raise no false hopes.

"Why should you come back?" she queried coolly, withdrawing from his embrace. "You've seen for yourself that Antoine and I are no longer any cause for concern. Consider yourself set free of whatever responsibilities you supposed still existed. I'm afraid you've misread my appreciation of your aid in my hour of need. I only came to the gate to wish you a safe journey. Farewell, Tom. I doubt our paths will ever cross again."

She turned to move swiftly up the path, but angrily he caught her by the arm. "Hell's bells, Sophie! I'm being honest with you and you're kicking me in the teeth!"

Coldly she jerked herself free. "Your meaning was very clear. Look for conquests elsewhere! You'll never come and go as you please with me!"

Exasperated, he set his fists on his hips and glowered after her. Who would have believed how quickly they could ignite each other's temper? He had been going to ask her to show some patience and understanding of his erratic life-style and to trust that in the end all would be well, but she had refused to listen. Even as she was shutting the farmhouse door behind her, he gave a shout.

"You're going to see me again whether it suits you or not!"

Sophie went straight to her room feeling hurt and humiliated. Tom must have thought she was flinging herself at him by talking so freely about her escape. Then letting him kiss her as she had done, making no protest and even responding, had done the rest. All her original doubts came flooding back. She had not been mistaken after all. Every instinct had warned her that he was a man of whom she should be wary. Now she knew why. He had spoken of danger as if it were his mistress, and she had lived with peril too long ever to become involved with a man who thrived on it.

IN THE MORNING Sophie spoke to Mrs. Millard about leaving. During the night, as she lay awake, she had realized how comfortably she and Antoine had settled into this haven, but now the time had come for her to strike out on her own. At all costs she wanted to be gone before Tom took it into his head to return.

"I'll be pleased and sorry to see you go," Mrs. Millard said in her forthright manner. "You've been good company and it would have suited me well to keep you on as a house help, but it would only lead to trouble. You're too handsome a wench and your speech with that pretty accent would charm a bird out of a tree. Both my lads have been making sheep's eyes at you, and I don't want no family feud as to which of them should wed you."

Sophie, who had had to repel several unwelcome advances from both young men, thought to herself what a relief it would be finding herself free of them. "My stay here has surely been longer than expected. I must owe you more than what Mr. Foxhill paid for our keep."

"He wanted to settle the difference with me yesterday, but I told him you had more than offset it with all the work you've done. Shall you go to London?"

All along Sophie had avoided discussing her plans. "No, I'm taking Antoine to Brighton. I'll write to you when I'm settled there."

"No letters, please!" Mrs. Millard shook her head determinedly. "If the lads know you are there, they'll go chasing after you. Brighton is far too near to take that risk. Only me and Mr. Millard will know where you've gone."

So the date of Sophie's departure was soon settled.

Four

IT WAS A GLORIOUS MID-JUNE MORNING with a cloudless, periwinkle-blue sky when Sophie and Antoine left the farm sitting beside Mr. Millard on the high seat of his cart. His sons were elsewhere and Josie had been sent on an errand, none having been told of the departure. Antoine had hurled himself to the ground in a tantrum upon hearing he was leaving the farm, but dried his tears when Mrs. Millard produced a military cape she had made as a parting gift for his toy soldier.

The hedgerows were decked with dog roses and in places along the road the trees that grew on opposite sides had linked their foliage to make a shady green tunnel. Buttercups and clover and oxeye daisies made a haze of gold, purple, and white across the undulating countryside. Sheep sprinkled the green hills like thistledown.

Although it was an enchanting ride, it was also a noisy one, for Mr. Millard's cart was full of pigs that he was taking to market. This indirect route was not his usual one, but enabled him to let his passengers alight at a crossroads. There he gave Sophie directions.

"It's no more than a mile from here to Brighton. Just follow the southbound road. Good luck to you."

For a while Antoine skipped at Sophie's side along the dusty road. They were both lightly dressed in cotton clothes. Her gown was striped yellow and white, and she carried her cloak over one arm. The rest of their possessions were in an ancient hold-all Mrs. Millard had given her. In the heat, Antoine soon slowed to a walk, talking to his toy soldier in its new cape. The child's French was now interspersed with English, which he pronounced in Sussex dialect. Sophie smiled to hear him.

Finally, they came over the crest of a hill and Brighton lay before them. Protected by the grassy slopes of the Downs, the sunbathed town, with its russet, crimson, and gray roofs, faced a promenade and a beach of shingle with pearly sands encroached by a gently incoming tide. The sea was in a different mood from the night of their crossing. Today it lay smooth as silk and sparkling with sun-diamonds. Sophie was seized by a sense of destiny. Here she would carve a new life for herself! With hard work she would reestablish the name of Delcourt and all it had come to mean in its heyday in France.

As Sophie and Antoine entered the resort, she was struck anew by its seaside charm. Clearly many of the houses were new, but they blended with mellower buildings and some ancient ones of local flint, which huddled together in narrow lanes. There was no shortage of taverns and plenty of chophouses offering good meals, while from coffeehouses there drifted the aroma of roasting beans. The number of libraries surprised Sophie, and she peeped into each one. Although a lot of people were choosing books, the sound of rattling dice and the slap of cards could often be heard from the open windows above the reading rooms, indicating that many of the libraries offered other amenities as well.

The print shops had the most colorful windows, displaying many vividly tinted political and satirical cartoons.

"Look, Sophie," Antoine said, pointing to one of the cartoons, "that funny man has a big tummy."

It was a ferocious caricature of the Prince of Wales, who was shown plotting with the Tory opposition party of the House of Commons while through a gap in the curtains behind them the Whig Prime Minister and some of his party were lining up to kiss the hem of the King's robes. It summed up immediately for Sophie the political division between the royal father and his son.

There were many other cartoons whose meaning was beyond the grasp of a foreigner, and also domestic scenes depicting the Prince and Mrs. Fitzherbert, the Roman Catholic widow whom he had secretly married—or so it was rumored here and abroad. Sophie could remember first hearing this tale in Paris, but neither of her parents liked gossip in any form, and the relationship was never discussed in her home. All the cartoons cruelly showed Mrs. Fitzherbert to be fat as a barrel with a large hooked nose, even as the Prince was wild-haired and grossly thighed. In one cartoon she was rocking a cradle while the Prince gazed devotedly at the baby within.

As Sophie glanced at the various drawings, she remembered being told once that Mrs. Fitzherbert had stayed with the Comte and Comtesse at the Château de Juneau when escaping from the Prince's ardent wooing of her. As the heir to the Throne of England, he was not permitted to marry a Roman Catholic, nor to wed at all without the King's permission, so there could be no future for them together. Maybe, in that case, these cartoons were only vicious speculations.

Having looked in one print shop, Sophie had no interest in seeing another, but Antoine dragged on her hand at every one, saying he wanted to look at the funny ladies and gentlemen.

In the busy streets, gleaming carriages and "high-flyer" phaetons driven by young bloods went bowling past, taking precedence over lumbering wagons and tradesmen's carts. Everywhere, scarlet-jacketed soldiers from the great military camp on the slopes of the neighboring Downs served as grim reminders that England was at war with France.

Not since Paris before the Revolution had Sophie seen so many fashionably dressed people at leisure. Now and again she caught a snatch of conversation in French, but she did not see anyone she knew.

Then she and Antoine came to a broad stretch of green lawn spreading north from the sea, and when she inquired of a man pushing a barrow, she was informed it was known as the Steine. The lawn was flanked to the east and west by fine residences, with yet another library nestling among them, and a large tavern named the Castle Inn. But dominating the whole scene was a pleasing mansion faced with cream glazed tiles that gave it a glistening iridescence. It had a central domed bay fronted by Ionic pillars and on the entablature were eight statues. It reminded Sophie instantly of a French château, which gave it an immense appeal. This was most surely the Marine Pavilion, seaside home of George, Prince of Wales. This was where she would seek work!

44

Lawns and blossoming flower beds made an enchanting setting. Although this side of the mansion contained no main entrance, it was designed to present a charming frontage looking east to the Steine. From a distance the tall windows flickered her reflection as Sophie took Antoine's hand and followed the low railings around to the front of the Marine Pavilion. Now she could see that it was E-shaped with a semicircular drive and ornamental gates. She also located the servants' entrance, set unobtrusively into the side of the building. To pacify Antoine, who was tired and hungry, she lifted him up to pull the doorbell there. A footman in a fustian jacket opened the door and grinned at her appreciatively.

"Yes, miss? What can I do for you?"

"I'd like to see the steward."

"If it's about work, you're out of luck. Nobody else is being taken on this season. The Pavilion has all the maidservants it needs."

"I'm a confectioner."

"Are you now? Well, as the head confectioner is nearby in a store-room"—he jerked a thumb over his shoulder—"I'll speak to him for you, but don't raise your hopes."

He went away down the corridor, but soon returned. Sophie felt a lurch of disappointment as he shook his head sympathetically. "Sorry, no luck!"

"I shall reapply," she said firmly.

"That's the spirit! I'd like to see you here myself. You'd brighten the place up no end!" The girl was really strikingly beautiful, and he was enjoying himself immensely. "Come back next spring when the Pavilion is being made ready for the Prince's return to spend the summer here. Most of us come down from Carlton House—that's his London home—but local staff are taken on as well."

"Thank you for your advice."

"But you should be prepared to wield a duster and a broom. I ain't never seen a female confectioner in a kitchen yet."

"Then it's time things changed." There was determination in her smile, which made his grin still wider.

"Maybe you're just the one to do it." He watched her as she turned to leave and called after her before shutting the door. "Make sure you bring your best references when you come back."

References! Sophie had not thought about the fact that she would need endorsement of a good character to enter royal employ. Somehow and somewhere she would get it!

When she and Antoine reached the promenade, they could see fishing boats drawn up on the shingle and nets, emanating the smell of fish and tar and salt, drying in the sun. Moving on, the two of them settled on another part of the beach to eat the picnic Mrs. Millard had prepared before they left that morning. There was a slice of her good meat pie, bread that Sophie had baked the day before, hard-boiled eggs, and a wedge of farm cheese. There was much to watch as they ate, for they had apparently settled on the stretch of beach reserved for ladies' sea bathing.

Most of the women arrived with personal maids to help them undress in the so-called bathing "machines," which were rectangular wooden huts set on four wheels, six feet in diameter. Each hut had a door to the front, facing the sea, and another to the rear, which the bather entered fully clothed. To protect the modesty of the bathers, a horse, harnessed to the machine by chains, drew it hub-deep into the sea. As the occupant emerged from the front door, clad in her voluminous flannel bathing garment, and hesitated timorously on the steps of the machine, she was seized by a stoutly built female "dipper," similarly attired but with a straw hat, who promptly ducked her under the water. As the bather surfaced, shrieking and spluttering, she was ducked again. It was all part of the service, and only after her second ducking was the bather allowed to splash about on her own under the watchful eye of the "dipper," who made certain she didn't drown.

As soon as Antoine had finished eating, he began scooping up the sand to make a little castle while Sophie packed up the remains of the picnic. One of the dippers, who had seen her bather safely back into a machine, came up the shingle, her ankle-length flannel skirt dripping, to where she had left a clay pipe and tobacco on an upturned wooden box that served as a seat. As she sat down and lit her pipe, Sophie went to speak with her.

"Good day, madame. I'm new to Brighton and I wonder if you could tell me where I might find reasonable accommodation."

The woman, her face and forearms bronzed by the sun, regarded Sophie in a friendly manner. "You're a Frenchie, I can tell. I've dipped many of your aristocrats, not just since they became refugees, but before the troubles, when they came to enjoy the pleasures of

Brighton." She shook her head. "These are sad times." Then she called to one of the other "dippers" who were chatting together on the beach. "Clara Renfrew! Do you want a French lodger? She speaks English."

The woman who came sauntering across was in her mid-thirties, big-bosomed and wide-hipped, with a good-humored, thickly freckled face and soft brown hair tucked under her hat. Her eyes, shaded by the straw brim, were bright and lively.

"Is it bed and board you want?" she asked Sophie. "I've a spare room. What's your name?" When she had heard it she nodded toward Antoine. "Is that your lad? How old is he?"

"I'm his aunt and he had his fifth birthday last week."

Clara Renfrewn pointed to a tousle-haired boy paddling at the water's edge. "That's my Billy. He's six. The boys should get on well together. Do you want to see the room now, Miss Delcourt? Martha Gunn—that's her with the pipe—will take over for me for a while."

Antoine caused a hitch by refusing to leave his castle, kicking up the sand in his temper. Sophie thought it must seem to him that he was always being dragged away from anywhere he was happy. Clara beckoned to her son and told him to help the little French lad build a proper castle. Antoine, pleased to have young company, smiled at his new friend.

"We can leave them here," Clara said. "Several of us have young children and we all watch out for each other."

With that, she led Sophie up onto the promenade and along the road by the sea to her cottage on the outskirts of the town. Sophie spoke of her intention to find work locally and her need to engage someone to look after Antoine during her working hours. Clara was sympathetic to Sophie's setback at the Pavilion, but not surprised.

"It does no harm to aim high," she said, "but the Prince is so good to all those who work for him that his servants never want to leave. You may have to wait a long time for a vacancy. In the meantime there's plenty of other places where staff are always needed. As for the little lad, if you come to live with Billy and me, I'll look after him for an extra sixpence a week. I'll have him with me on the beach in summer and when autumn comes I'll be at home again. I'll teach him to swim if you like."

"That would all be splendid, Mrs. Renfrew."

"Call me Clara. There's no need to stand on ceremony."

She then explained her circumstances. Five years ago her husband, Jim, had been swept off his fishing boat in an unexpected squall, leaving her with two sons. The elder, named Daniel, had recently joined the army as a drummer boy. With no income, she had rented Jim's boat to another fisherman, who fished off the coast some distance away.

"If it hadn't been for the boys I'd have taken the boat out myself. I used to fish with Jim sometimes before they came along. So instead I took up dipping to bring in some money."

"It must be very cold sometimes to stand waist-deep in the waves."

It was, Clara admitted, "But it's surprising how soon we all get used to it when the season comes round again."

A winding lane, branching off from the sea road, led to the Renfrew cottage, which stood quite a distance from the other dwellings they had passed along the way. It was a long, low building made of knapped flints that shone amber and ebony and pinkish-brown in the sun. Its thatched roof hung low over its windows. A grove of trees acted as a windbreak and gave additional privacy as well as charm to the setting. Clara opened the wooden gate. She grew vegetables in her front garden and a path to the rear led through the grass down to the beach.

"Do you ever walk along the shore to the bathing machines when the tide is out?" Sophie asked.

"No. I get enough of the beach when I'm on it all day. In any case this is a rocky stretch along here and not easy going. Billy likes to look for tiny sea creatures in the rock pools, and he's the only one who ever goes down that path."

Inside the cottage everything was neat and clean. Sophie liked the bedchamber offered to her, although it faced the lane and not the sea, which she would have preferred. Clara's terms were moderate and there was a spare bed in Billy's room where Antoine could sleep. Everything was soon settled. Sophie paid for the first week in advance. Then she unpacked, storing the few clothes she possessed in a chest of drawers and hanging her cloak on a peg. Clara brought her an ewer of water for the blue-patterned basin that stood on a washstand in the corner. Finally, after putting a comb to her hair, Sophie rejoined Clara, who had passed the time by making a list of all the places she could apply for work.

"Before we go, I'll show you the rest of the estate," Clara said jokingly.

Outside she pointed out the privy and then led the way to a flint-walled building that stood among the trees. It consisted of an ancient kitchen, a storeroom, a deserted stall that would have stabled a horse, and a laundry that also doubled as a bathhouse. There was a copper for boiling clothes, wooden tubs, jars of homemade green soap on a shelf, and a pump.

"When I've been with the sea and sand all day," Clara said, "I come in here first in the evening and strip off, then hang up my dipper garments and dowse myself with fresh water. That's why I keep a cotton robe on the peg there for going back indoors to dress. You might like to do the same after a day's work."

"I'm sure I will. I might even have a dip in the sea first if the tide is up. It would be a new experience for me."

"Do you swim?"

"No."

"Then I'll teach you as well as Antoine. In the meantime, if you do go bathing, keep to the shallow water. There can be strong currents around the rocks along this part of the shore."

They walked back along the lane together. Then Clara made her way back to the bathing machines and Sophie set off into town. She went into every confectionery shop, but nobody needed extra hands. "If you had applied before the start of the season," she was told several times, "there might have been a place for you."

Outside the last of these shops Sophie consulted Clara's list again. With no luck so far, she would have to turn to the kitchens of the inns. She decided to try first at the Old Ship Inn, which Clara had marked as being the most important one in town, with seventy bed-chambers and grand assembly rooms where the Prince of Wales often held private balls.

Bypassing the main entrance Sophie went through the wide gateway to the cobbled stableyard. The door to the kitchen stood open as did its windows, and the clatter within was very familiar. It was such a hive of activity that she was able to enter without anyone glancing in her direction. Unlike the old-fashioned kitchen at the Château de

Juneau or the Millards' farmhouse kitchen with its open fire, here at the Old Ship Inn revolutionary new cast-iron ovens had been installed, with the fires shut away behind doors and dampers controlling the temperature. Saucepans of soup steamed on the range, puddings tied up in white cloths boiled on another, and capons and joints of meat turned on clockwork spits at the fireplace. Here, as in France, the cooks were men, each in his white apron and a cap that flopped down over one ear like a full moon. The head chef, sighting Sophie as he turned from one of the ovens, called out irately.

"Why are you standing there, girl? Get an apron on!"

"I'm applying for confectionery work," she replied.

"Fiddlesticks! I don't want a confectioner, but we need another waiting maid. Do you know how to wait at table?"

Sophie, who had been waited on at table since babyhood, smiled to herself as she answered, "Yes, I do."

He promptly snapped his fingers at one of the waiting maids, bringing her to a standstill. "Polly! Get this girl rigged out for the dining room. There's no time to waste!"

The snub-featured girl led Sophie at a fast pace to the linen room, where she pulled open drawers to snatch out what was needed. "Make haste!" she urged, tossing Sophie a blue cotton gown.

Quickly Sophie cast off her own gown to don the new one. Polly laced it up the back for her and tied the ribbons of the starched white apron while Sophie tucked her hair into a frilled white cap. "Is the kitchen always so busy?" she asked.

Polly shook her mob-capped head, tendrils of yellow hair dancing. "It's exceptional today. The Prince and Mrs. Fitzherbert are bringing a party of newly landed émigrés and Mr. Hicks, the proprietor, was only notified twenty minutes ago."

"Does the Prince go down to the beach to meet the émigrés' boats then?" Sophie questioned as they left the linen room.

"Sometimes, if he is not doing anything else. Mrs. Fitzherbert is often there. A while ago she went to Shoreham-by-Sea to meet a party of émigré Catholic nuns and brought them here to meet the Prince and to stay until they had recovered from their ordeal. They've opened a school now somewhere north of London under the Prince's patronage, even though he is Church of England like me. But then

Mrs. Fitzherbert is a Catholic and that didn't stop him marrying her."

"But is that true? Perhaps it's only speculation."

Polly halted and set her hands on her hips. "We in Brighton know that they're wed and so does most of England, but for the Prince's sake she never lets on, which is why they have separate houses here and in London." Polly set the pace again. "Come on! We can't stay chatting. We're laying up the tables for fifty. Numbers are judged by the size of the sighted boat. You'll soon learn the procedure."

In a private dining room of some grandeur, the waiting maids were unfolding snow-white damask cloths with a snap that sent them billowing over the tables. Cutlery was clattering into place and wineglasses were polished. A head waiter in his serving coat and breeches spoke sharply to Polly and Sophie.

"Where have you been dawdling? Put out the napkins!"

While they were carrying out their tasks on opposite sides of the tables, a large, red-faced man came striding into the room to check that everything was nearly ready. Sophie guessed this was Mr. Hicks, the proprietor, when he beckoned to her authoritatively.

"The best silver salts aren't here! Those presently on the tables won't do! Take a tray and fetch them from the housekeeper, girl!" He then went charging out again. Polly gave her directions.

"Who are you?" the housekeeper asked as she unlocked a cupboard to get out the required salts. When Sophie explained how she was drawn into work at the inn the woman gave a nod. "You certainly walked in on the right day. A girl was sacked for thieving yesterday, so you've a chance of being kept on. I'll fill the salts before you take them and then they'll be ready."

Sophie kept her eyes on the shining salts, fearful they might slide off the slippery tray as she made her way back to the dining room. Then suddenly they skidded about as her tray rammed against the unexpected barrier of a high-cut, double-breasted coat of crimson velvet, which protruded rotundly over a large paunch. With a gasp, her gaze flew to the bloated, floridly handsome face of the tall, broad-shouldered man with fashionably frizzed brown hair whose vigorous way she had blocked. Involuntarily she spoke in French.

"Your pardon, monsieur!"

His gray eyes twinkled good-humoredly as hastily she drew back a pace, able to see now that he had been escorted from the main entrance by Mr. Hicks, who was glaring furiously at her. Instantly it dawned on her that this was the Prince of Wales himself! Again her upbringing came to the rescue and she dipped into the deep curtsy that French protocol had designated to the royal princes of the House of Bourbon. Immediately the Prince leaned forward to support her tray with both hands, ensuring that none of the salt was spilt.

"So you are one of the émigrés welcomed to these shores since political strife has afflicted your marvelous country?" he remarked graciously as she straightened. "How long have you been in England?"

He was smiling at her, spinning the web of his enormous charm, which was as much a part of him as the blood that flowed through his veins. Sophie, returning his smile, could understand why his faults might be forgiven when he gave so generously of the warmth of his personality. "I landed from France a few weeks ago, but I've been in Brighton for less than a day."

"Is that so?" He raised his eyebrows. "And you have found work here already! Such diligence is to be commended." Then he switched to English for the benefit of the man at his side. "When the French company arrives, you may wait on them, mademoiselle. It should please you to hear your native tongue spoken again by fellow countrymen and women."

He moved on and she stood aside quickly. Mr. Hicks gave her a curt nod to endorse the royal usurping of his authority and darted after the Prince, who wanted a glass of wine while he waited for the arrival of Mrs. Fitzherbert and the new émigrés.

Polly was excited to hear about the encounter. "Good old Prinny! He knew you'd get the boot if he didn't speak for you!"

"None of the French princes would have done that!" Sophie declared, remembering the disdain with which she and her father had been treated many times. "Why did you call him 'Prinny'?"

Polly shrugged. "It's just an affectionate term that has come about because people like him! Prince—Prinny. Simple as that!"

The émigrés were to be received in a room adjoining the dining room, where refreshments were to be offered after the Prince's speech of welcome, dinner to be served later. Sophie stood with Polly and several other waiting maids by the wall. Then they heard the sounds of arrival, and Maria Fitzherbert led the newcomers into the room.

Sophie had no eyes for anyone else. Polly had been filling in details while the two of them stood side by side. This plumpish but dignified woman with an abundance of soft golden hair beneath her huge, gauze-trimmed hat had captivated the most eligible bachelor in Europe despite the competition of many who were younger and more beautiful. She had been his wife for eight years, holding him without effort against all odds, and yet still her marital status was officially ignored.

She had a marvelous ivory-pale skin and long-lashed, clear topaz eyes. Her nose, which was sharply aquiline, would have marred her looks if it had not added character to her face, while her smile was like a ray of sunshine. Most noticeable of all, there was a quality of tranquillity about her, so that even in her busy ushering of people into seats, helping the infirm, and holding a baby for its mother, who was feeling faint with exhaustion, she seemed to make the atmosphere calm and serene. Among the group were a Duc and Duchesse and their two daughters, with whom she was well acquainted, but she shared her attention equally with all. Finally she caught the eye of the Prince, who was conversing with the Duc.

"Everybody is ready now to hear you, sire," she said in her soft voice. Then gracefully she took a chair, the azure silk of her skirt settling gently around her.

The Prince made a sincere speech of welcome in flawless French, assuring the company that help would be given and travel arranged according to their individual needs. It struck Sophie that in spite of his being somewhat overweight he was lithe and elegant in his stance and movements, his legs hard-muscled in doeskin pantaloons and high boots. There was also a flamboyance about him, which added to his striking personality and suggested that he was a man with many facets to his character, able to dazzle with his favor or withdraw at a whim. The number of times she had had to deal with people of wealth and absolute power had given her an insight into how easily they could switch moods, not caring who suffered as a consequence. Yet this Prince had shown her great kindness, which she would never forget. Also weighing heavily in his favor in her eyes was the fact that he had risked everything to marry for love alone.

When the applause had died down the Prince made his departure, pleading another engagement. Only Maria knew that he was off to see his architect, who would be waiting at the Marine Pavilion with new plans for further alterations. Her cool glance told him that she thought he should have stayed and that irritated him. He could never accept being in the wrong about anything, and she should be satisfied that he was meeting the cost of the émigrés' accommodation at the Old Ship and any other expenses involved. No doubt she would snap at him later. For all her serene appearance, she could be as sharp-tongued as any wife when angered.

Why shouldn't he please himself sometimes? Maybe he did drink more heavily than Maria wished and was not always as thoughtful as he should be. And perhaps it had been annoying to her when he and his friends made a wager about one of them riding a horse up her staircase. But it was no fault of his that the animal had balked at descending again. Yet it was then that Maria—the dear girl!—had let her sense of humor come to the fore, even though it was another hour before the horse was finally coaxed downstairs by a blacksmith called in to assist. In the same way she should look on the credit side of their union and count her blessings at having a good husband with a true heart instead of casting frosty looks whenever she wanted to put him in his place.

Yet her love for him and his for her were never in doubt. No woman could be more generous and loving than she, no wife more caring and devoted. He had been violently attracted to Maria from the moment he had first glimpsed her with her late husband, and had loved her ever since gazing deeply into her eyes through her widow's veil one night at the opera. He had been twenty-two and she twenty-eight. She was his life's passion. And from what he had observed of other marriages she could consider herself highly fortunate to have such a husband—one who was far more faithful than most.

The Prince turned his mind to the plans he was about to study. His seaside palace had been changed enormously to his own specifications since the days when it was a simple farmhouse, but it had yet to come into its own. It was as if he held a priceless jewel in his hands, one that only awaited cutting and polishing to reveal its true brilliance. Visions of how it might be were constantly dancing through his mind. Surely it should capture all the marvelous colors of the sea, the gold of the sun, the silver of the moon, and the fierce blues of the summer sky? He wished he were not so heavily in debt. The interest on what he owed was horrendous in itself, and some of his creditors had begun to press him most seriously, much to his annoyance. Maria also had expensive tastes, and recently he had had all the rooms on the ground floor of her Pall Mall house refurbished to match the splendor of his own vast alterations to Carlton House. But a woman of beauty deserved the best, and he liked her to have everything she wanted. Once the two of them had tried to economize, but he did so poorly at it that he had seen no point in continuing. The Marine Pavilion should be transformed whatever the cost. Since he could not meet his debts, it was better to go on spending as if he did not owe a penny. That had always been his policy. And in any case, it was only his father's constant refusal to grant him an income sufficient to meet his needs that had brought him to these straits. But the King had been parsimonious all his life, except in begetting legitimate offspring. A faithful husband, he had been responsible for his wife, Queen Charlotte, bearing nine sons and six daughters.

With a sigh, the Prince let his unfocused gaze drift with the passing seashore. Two of his brothers had died young, but the rest of the brood had survived wretched childhoods punctuated by harsh beatings for the boys, as well as a strict regime of lessons—particularly in his case—without respite for exercise or play. One of his brothers, Augustus, Duke of Sussex, suffered from a breathing complaint and been whipped every time he developed a wheezy chest. As for the girls, their lives may have been easier, but the King was far too possessive of them for their futures to look particularly bright.

On reflection, it was no wonder that when he and his brothers reached young manhood they had each broken free to sow the wildest of oats, mixing with the wickedest company, rampaging and womanizing, falling in love and out of it, gambling recklessly, risking their necks racing their high-wheeled curricles, doing anything for a wager, the more outrageous the better. A smile broadened into a grin across his sensual mouth. What good times they'd had! Naturally he and his brothers had eventually settled down—in his case as a result of Maria's good influence—but he still enjoyed a good jape, and a wager was irresistible. It pleased him that his male siblings were fond of

Maria and treated her as their sister-in-law, which indeed she was in the eyes of the Church.

At the same time, the King's obdurate ways remained anathema to him. The Prince did not wish his father ill, but at the same time he could not help yearning for kingship. For a short while, six years ago, during his father's strange illness, when the doctors deemed recovery unlikely, he had been poised gloriously on the brink of becoming Regent. But it was not to be. The King's pain and curious delusions subsided, and all was now as it had been before.

With a gleam of shining leather, the Prince swung his high-booted feet up onto the opposite seat of his carriage, his long legs crossed at the ankles. His thoughts turned to the pitiable state of the émigrés he had just left. They had lost relatives, châteaux, lands, and fortunes, retaining nothing except what they could carry with them. The country they had left behind was now in the midst of a bloodbath. War with France had been inevitable once the notorious Robespierre called the head of the guillotined Louis XVI a gauntlet flung down as a challenge to all the kings of Europe.

The Prince sighed. The ruination of France by its present rulers was a great tragedy. For as long as he could remember, he had been an ardent Francophile. He loved the language and had acquired many beautiful pieces of French furniture as well as works of art. It was his deepest regret that he had been unable to visit the country he had long admired before the collapse of the House of Bourbon, but as heir to the Throne he could not leave the British Isles without the King's permission, and that ban had prevented him from following Maria to France when she tried in vain to quell the flame of his love for her.

His carriage had entered the gates of the Marine Pavilion. The Prince glanced at its classical west front before going indoors. It could not be faulted, and yet the whole frontage needed changing. He believed that if he had not been born a prince he would have become an architect, for his head was always full of ideas. As it was, he had to use architects as tools to fulfill his own creative ability. At times he felt a kinship with Louis XIV of France, who had never stopped building throughout his long life. It was likely, the Prince thought as he strolled through the spacious hall, that he himself would do the same throughout the years to come.

SOPHIE HAD SERVED glasses of Madeira to those who wanted it. Then, during the dinner, she went many times to the kitchen, taking away dirty crockery and carrying clean plates back. It was late when she set off wearily for her new home, thankful that before she left the housekeeper had engaged her as a regular waiting maid at the Old Ship. The walk in the fresh air relieved her tiredness. When she arrived, Antoine, already bathed and ready for bed, was seated at the table with Billy, both of them enjoying their supper. As soon as Antoine saw her he insisted on telling her all about his day, but settled contentedly when she tucked him into bed.

Over a well-cooked supper, Sophie explained where she had been and what work she had found. Clara refused to let her help with the washing-up, saying she had seen enough dirty dishes that day, and Sophie was glad to retire to her room. The bed had been made up in her absence with exceptionally fine linen. She was certain the lace trimming was French and decided it must be an heirloom that had been spared for her. She appreciated its lavender-scented smoothness as she slid between the sheets. Not since her last night in Paris had she slept in such luxury.

With her hearing made keen over the past few weeks for any cry from Antoine, Sophie woke with a start after a short sleep and sprang from her bed to pull open the door before she realized it was not the child she had heard. Angry voices, a man and a woman, although deliberately subdued, emanated from the kitchen.

"Why shouldn't I rent a room if I wish?" Clara's voice was unmistakable. "She's French and a stranger! There's nothing to fear!"

Sophie closed her door and returned to bed, not wanting to eavesdrop. The likely explanation for the quarrel seemed to be that Clara had a lover who came by night. It was no business of anybody except the widow herself. Sophie drew the bedclothes up around her ears and soon slept again.

Five

SOPHIE HAD HOPED that by securing employment in the kitchen of the Old Ship she might eventually be promoted to confectionery work. But the present confectioner had been there fifteen years, and he, aided by his apprentice, guarded his position carefully, producing whatever was needed for the dining room and for the grand banquets and buffet suppers served in the assembly rooms upstairs.

She was interested to see the sugar sculptures made by the confectioner. Although they were adequate, Sophie knew they could not compare with those she and her father had produced. But then, French confectioners were world-renowned for their skill with sugar. Here, as in France, this decorative confectionery was in constant demand, the subject matter sometimes allegorical, sometimes representing national events, and sometimes commemorating special occasions such as a marriage or a christening.

Whereas the sweet-pudding chef steamed and baked puddings and produced a variety of fruit pies, the confectioner had his own more delicate chores. This encompassed making jellies, fruit molds, concoctions of cherries and other berries encased in chocolate, syrup, or caramel, all kinds of sweetmeats, which were made entirely of sugar, and candy, which included other ingredients such as nuts, liqueurs, and so forth. He also preserved fruits to be attractively presented out of season, and he sugared violets and rose petals for ornamentation.

Ice cream in many flavors was also made by the confectioner, but it was a laborious task, always assigned to the apprentice, for the ingredients had to be churned around in a container packed in ice delivered daily from a local icehouse, which in its depths kept ice cut from the rivers in winter and stored underground between layers of straw right through the summer.

Harry, the sweet-pudding chef, was friendlier than the confectioner. He and Sophie often discussed French cuisine, and after he had tried out a lemon syrup, clear as sunshine with a tantalizing tang that lingered on the tongue, he used it regularly. It was also at her advice that he began adding a dash of cognac to his chocolate sauce.

Her own duties as a waiting maid involved long hours of work. When she was on the early shift she had to be at the Old Ship and in her serving clothes by six o'clock in the morning. There were always guests taking breakfast prior to catching the mail coach, which departed for London from outside the inn nearly every morning. There was an equally busy time when the late afternoon coach arrived. Also, there were breakfasts to be served on the promenade, where tables were set up for those who wished to view the Royal Navy preparing for battle with the French.

Sometimes Sophie was assigned to waiting in the taproom. The Old Ship had been a tavern since the sixteenth century, and many local patrons continued quaffing ale there as their forebears had done. Brighton folk still called it an inn, although its status had been elevated over the past thirty years.

"My grandma can remember when Brighton was no more than a fishing village," Polly told Sophie one day. "Then a Dr. Russell—a real crackpot! my grandma says—started telling the grand folk that seawater would cure all ills. So they came flocking here to drink the seawater and bathe in it! You'll find some guests will still ask for it mixed with milk and so forth. Anyway, that's what brought the Prince of Wales here. He came to cure the swollen glands in his neck, and he stayed to enjoy himself. By that time lots of noble folk had built houses here, but it was royal patronage that really changed everything. Brighton never looked back after the day good old Prinny set foot here!"

Sophie served a cross-section of the community in the taproom. In a selected area the well-to-do took their liquid refreshment, while in the evening the humbler section provided some noisy fun. A drunken actor from the theater might recite a poem, or a street entertainer strike up a tune on his fiddle, and there was always a united chorus of singing on popular nights. Sophie heard old Smoaker Miles, a male dipper, recite his oft-told tale of how he had saved the Prince of Wales from drowning.

"I pulled him out by his ear! He was angry, right enough, but I told him I weren't going to be hanged at the King's command for letting the heir to the throne drown at Brighton. Then Prinny threw back his head and laughed! He don't let nobody but me dip him ever since!"

Martha Gunn, who liked her glass of ale, was also pleased to relate her own stories of the famous people she had dipped. When Clara could get a neighbor to mind the children in the evening, she would meet Martha and her other friends there, for that section of the taproom was as popular with women as it was with the men.

Among them all, Sophie would sometimes serve fellow émigrés. These were mostly servants who had accompanied their masters into exile, often to find that there was a sudden reversal of roles. A former château footman explained matters to Sophie one morning when the taproom was almost deserted and she had time to spare.

"The aristos have no idea how to handle money," he said with a shake of his head. "In France they never had to work for it like you and me. It grew on trees as far as they were concerned. Now, with few exceptions, they're in a state of penury that seems unreal to them."

Sophie sat down on the opposite side of the table and leaned her chin on her hands. "I've been told that they plague the banks trying to raise money on properties in France that have been lost to the Republic."

The footman nodded. "They can't conceive that they no longer have any claim to the châteaux and lands that were in their families for generations. The British Government gives them a pension on which you and I could manage very well indeed, but they start off by squandering it all the first day, as if their coffers will be magically refilled on the next. If it weren't for me," he added, sticking a broad thumb against his chest, "and others like me, there'd be hundreds of aristos begging in the streets."

"But what can you do to help?"

"I've put my master to giving riding and fencing lessons to the children of English squires and my mistress to dressing hair. They're both doing well." His freckled face was as pleased and proud as if he were speaking of his own offspring. "I have to keep an eye on the purse for them, though. When my mistress was going to give her first dinner party in England, she rushed out and bought the best linen and silver for the occasion, only to have nothing left for food!" He shook his head at such folly. "Now she consults me first about any expenditure. I even sell what valuables she and the master have left, because there are so many charlatans advertising for anything the émigrés have to sell and then paying them a pittance." His eyes twinkled. "I tell you, nobody tries those tricks on me!"

Sophie grinned at his wiliness. "Why has the British Government been so generous to our nobility, do you think?"

"Apart from it being a case of blue blood helping the blue blood, I'd say it was because the British fear that the poor helpless, homeless creatures would be dying in the gutters if some provision weren't made for them." He gave a guffaw. "The likes of you and me will always survive on our own merits, because we've never known what it means to be idle."

Afterward Sophie thought again about the crime that had been committed against her and her charges. It might be to the good if she gave a further report herself at Shoreham-by-Sea. That evening at supper she asked Clara, who knew of the attack, where she could make contact with the proper authorities, but the widow was not encouraging.

"Let matters lie. The murder will have been investigated."

"Yes, but because I was unwell at the time no details were ever taken from me. If I gave them now, the harbor authorities could watch out for the Barneses."

"That's a vain hope. Villains like Barnes would certainly change their guise before working the same area again."

Sophie was surprised by Clara's attitude. "Maybe so, but other landing places could be alerted."

"Do you suppose that criminals haven't been taking advantage of émigrés since long before you came to these shores? With landings taking place on beaches and harbors and quays all along the coast there will always be victims, no matter what precautions are taken."

"Unfortunately I'm sure that is true, and my friends at the farm weren't optimistic either, but I want the Barneses brought to justice!"

"Naturally you do and I support you in that, but I don't want outsiders tramping into my home to question you." Clara put down her knife and fork, looking distressed. "I've always kept out of trouble. It would shame me and start neighbors gossiping if Keepers of the Law were seen at my door."

"But I would go to them. They wouldn't come here."

Clara shook her head, her cheeks quite flushed with agitation. "You don't seem to realize that whenever a thief, male or female, was arrested who resembled your description in any way, you would be fetched to make an identification. If you insist on going ahead with your report I'll have to ask you to leave my house."

Sophie was dismayed. "Don't say that, Clara! You know how happy Antoine and I are to be here. It's been the boy's first chance to put down roots again, and the last thing I want is to unsettle him again."

"I don't want you or the boy to leave," Clara conceded, although her expression remained stubborn, "but you must make a choice."

Sophie was angry, but she had to consider Antoine's welfare, which forced her into a compromise. "I give you my word that I'll never cause you trouble or embarrassment, but I reserve the right to find a means of bringing those villains to justice without involving you in any way."

For a few moments Clara hesitated and then she gave a nod. "You're too honest ever to make a promise you didn't intend to keep. You may stay and I'm glad of it." Then she and Sophie smiled at each other in mutual relief that their friendship had been left undangered by the dispute.

Still, the matter lingered in Sophie's mind that night when she went to bed, making her restless with a recurring nightmare that she was once more being pursued. Never having lived by the sea before, there were nights when the pounding of the waves on the shingle penetrated her sleep and brought on the nightmare, causing her to cry out as she awoke. Fortunately Clara, who slept at the opposite end of the cottage, never heard her, and only a heavy thunderstorm could wake the children sleeping in the neighboring room.

"Are there any subterranean tunnels in this part of the coast?" she asked Clara one morning at breakfast.

"Yes, but none just here that I've ever heard of. Why do you ask?"

"Now and again, when the tide comes in at night, there's an echoing rumble, almost as if the sea is penetrating inland."

"Old cottages like this are full of eerie sounds." Clara took up the teapot and poured Sophie another cup. "I suppose I'm so used to them I don't notice anymore."

Sophie accepted the explanation. She was still a newcomer and naturally it would take time for her to adjust to new sounds as well as to new customs. Yet there were some sounds that were unmistakable, Clara's whispers and the gruffer tones of her nighttime visitor that, after a time, faded away to the far end of the cottage.

CLARA SOON FULFILLED HER PROMISE to teach Sophie and Antoine to swim. She taught the boy when business was slack at the bathing machines, while Sophie's lessons took place whenever they could be fitted in with her work. Sometimes she and Clara went down to the sea in the early morning. The water was always fresh, but Sophie never minded, plunging straight into the waves and giving Clara no need to duck her. She was quick to learn and when nobody was about, she could swim in her shift instead of a thick serge bathing garment.

When Sophie came home late from the Old Ship she frequently took a swim, and often, when the day had been warm and sunny, the sea was as warm as a bath. On these occasions she left her shift on the shingle and enjoyed the experience of swimming without anything to hamper her speed.

AT THE FIRST CHANCE AVAILABLE, Sophie went into Thomas's Library in the Steine to look for Henriette's name in the visitors' book. From the start she had decided not to call on her friend until she had work and accommodation, for she would not have wanted Henriette to feel under any obligation to help her. According to Clara, new arrivals had to pay a fee to enter their names in the exclusive book, and only people of consequence could sign. As in the fashionable spa of Bath, Brighton had a Master of Ceremonies who supervised all public social events and ensured that those whose names were in the book did not fail to receive an invitation.

After running her finger down several pages, it seemed to Sophie that most of the British and French aristocracy must be crammed into the hotels and rented properties of Brighton, or else staying as guests of those with residences of their own. When she finally found Henriette's name, the address was different from the one her friend had given her. Now she had only to wait for her first free half day to see Henriette again.

THERE WERE PLENTY of entertainments in Brighton for those with the time and money and inclination: horse racing on the Downs, cockfights, pugilists' mills that sometimes lasted for thirty rounds or more, curricle races on the sands with noble young bloods risking their necks, plays at the theater, concerts, and card parties. On Sundays there was tea at the Old Ship assembly rooms, a social highlight of the week, and a ball there every Thursday.

The Prince and Mrs. Fitzherbert rarely missed a ball at the Old Ship and were usually in the company of rakish friends, including one or another of the Prince's brothers. Once Sophie peeped through a crack in the door to watch them go up the curved staircase to the splendid peach-pink and silver-gray assembly rooms. The Prince was slightly drunk, but merry as could be and full of talk and laughter, the diamond star of the Order of the Garter ablaze on his chest. Mrs. Fitzherbert had sapphires in her golden hair, in the lobes of her ears, and around her neck. Her voluptuous bosom was enhanced by the décolletage of a pearl-pink gown of gossamer silk that billowed soft as spiders' webs with every graceful step she took. She was smiling happily as she chatted to the lady mounting the stairs at her side.

Sophie found work as hard on the ball nights as when there was a banquet. She and the other girls ran up and down the stairs with laden trays until she wondered that her feet did not drop off. If the tide allowed, she would walk along the dark, quiet seashore on her way home, wading at the water's edge, her shoes in her hand. The lights of the town twinkled beyond the deserted promenade and a canopy of stars shone overhead. Unless the moon was up, it became even darker as she left the town behind.

Along this section of the shore great rocks, embedded in the sand and shingle, loomed like giant sentinels, reminding Sophie of the woods at the Château de Juneau. Instead of the rustle of trees, there was the soft whisper of wavelets, but the same sense of tranquillity prevailed. After a hectic evening's work, it was bliss.

One night when Sophie reached the rocks, the incoming tide caused her to hitch up her skirt and petticoats. It was then that she heard the creak of rowlocks as a boat drew near the shore. Not wanting to be seen in disarray, she took shelter behind a jagged rock from which she could watch without being seen. She would wait until the fishermen had unloaded their catch and left again. But why would a boat put in here away from the town and amid dangerous rocks?

Although her eyes had adjusted to the darkness and there was a sliver of moonlight, she could not see the boat at first. Then a lantern light blinked, and she saw its black shape form on the water, followed by another, and soon a third. Sophie began to be afraid. These were not fishermen. Now she could see oars rising and falling. There were twelve men to each of the long, sturdy vessels. A tall, cloaked man was standing in the bow of the first of the boats and it was he who held the lantern. He let its light blink again, and in reply, another light shone through the tamarisk hedge that bordered the shore.

Smugglers! Sophie felt a chill run down her spine. She recalled the grisly stories she had heard in the Old Ship's kitchen of how they did not hesitate to slit the throats of those caught spying on them. According to what she had been told, smuggling had gone on along the south and east coasts for centuries. In the past, English wool had been smuggled out to avoid the export tax, and in more recent times, it was the heavy import tax on tea, lace, spices, and brandy that had kept the midnight trade flourishing.

Sophie stayed as if transfixed, not daring to creep away lest she should be seen. The cloaked smuggler in his thigh-high waders was the first to jump ashore. He wore a wide-brimmed hat and the lower half of his face was covered by a kerchief knotted at the back of his neck.

"Quick!" he ordered in a harsh whisper. "The wagons will be waiting!"

Oars were stowed and smugglers in all three boats sprang out, some wading through the water, to unload their cargo. Brandy kegs were passed from one to another with a rhythmic speed born of long practice. By now at least a score of men had come running in silence down the path to the beach. Not a word was spoken as they carried away the kegs. It was impossible to discern the faces of either the smugglers or the shoremen, for most wore tricorn hats pulled well down and some had knotted kerchiefs as well. The man in the cloak did not join in the unloading until he had lifted a heavy box from his boat, which he dropped onto the shingle not far from where Sophie was hiding. She stared at it in frightened fascination. The dark wood of the lid was inlaid with mother-of-pearl and she wondered what it contained.

When the last keg had been borne away, the smugglers returned to their boats and began to take up their oars again. Only their confederate in the cloak was not boarding. As the boats moved out to sea again, he came back to his box. After checking the silver lock, he swung it with a grunt onto his shoulder. Sophie gasped involuntarily as his glittering gaze turned sharply in the direction of the rock behind which she was hiding, almost as if he sensed her presence. His free hand whipped a pistol from his belt and she heard it cock. She pressed herself back against the rock, holding her breath, and heard the pebbles rolling under his heels as he approached. Then came a pause as he stood listening.

It seemed an interminable time before he finally turned away, but later she supposed it was no more than a minute. When she dared to look again, he had thrust the pistol back into his belt and was making for the path. There he vanished into the darkness. The beach was as deserted as before. Already the advancing waves had covered the grooves in the shingle made by the keels of the boats.

Sophie let her forehead sink against the rock. By now the sea was swirling about her thighs, the current tugging at her skirt, but still she did not move. She wanted to allow the smuggler plenty of time to get well away before she left the beach.

Finally, she crossed the shingle as quietly as she could. At the head of the path she paused to listen and to put on her shoes. All was peaceful, but she ran the rest of the way to the cottage, her wet skirts flicking drops of seawater in a trail behind her.

As usual, Clara had left a candle lamp burning in a window. When Sophie slipped through the gate, she saw the curtain of her friend's bed chamber fall back into place. The widow had said more than once that she liked to know when Sophie was safely home.

In the outside washhouse, Sophie removed her wet garments and dropped them into a tub. It was something she often did at night, and there would be no evidence on the morrow of seawater to start the widow questioning.

Naked, Sophie put on the cotton robe she kept on a peg. As she filled the tub with water, she wondered, in the light of what she had witnessed on the beach, if Clara suspected that smugglers might be operating along this part of the coast.

After hanging up her clothes on a line, Sophie entered the cottage by the kitchen door and, as always, went to check that Antoine was sleeping peacefully. He had kicked away his covers, for the night was warm, but she rearranged the sheet over him. She wished she had more time to spend with him. He still cried for his mother sometimes when he was put to bed, and Sophie encouraged him to talk in the French of his parents and his home. She did not want his memories to fade. Although the Comtesse's shawl had been lost, he still had the toy soldier his mother had given him.

In her own room, Sophie sat down on the edge of the bed and realized she was still ashiver inside from all she had been through. Undoubtedly the smuggler in the cloak had been a local man since he had left on foot. He could easily be from a nearby farm; maybe a miller from one of the mills. Was he someone who drank at the Old Ship? He might be among those customers whom she served, for many who smuggled at night were respectable citizens by day.

It would be unwise to report what she had seen to any ordinary individual, and Clara would be furious if she produced another reason for Keepers of the Law to come to the cottage. There were a couple of revenue men in the district, who came into the taproom from time to time. Their duty was to prevent smuggling wherever possible and to arrest those involved in the crime. Often smugglers protested that they were Freetraders, claiming a citizen's right to trade as they wished, but this argument never carried any weight in courts of law.

Perhaps, without revealing herself as the source of information, she could alert the two revenue men to the danger, and they could call on the Dragoons or some other cavalry unit at the Brighton camp to help them set an ambush. It seemed the only solution.

Six

ON SOPHIE'S FIRST FREE HALF DAY, she set off to see Henriette. She had recovered from the shock of seeing the smugglers and was sleeping better. If the tides still rumbled under the cottage she did not hear them, and the crash of waves on shingle no longer disturbed her rest. Only a cry from Antoine or the occasional arrival and departure of Clara's midnight visitor still awakened her. She was settling down and her mind was more at ease since she had slipped an unsigned report into the pocket of a revenue man while serving him ale one evening in the taproom. She hoped he would act on what she had written.

In the Steine, a pig race was being run. Young noblemen were forever organizing such events, and a crowd of spectators had gathered. The jockeys were unfortunate footmen chosen by their masters to compete. The Prince, according to Clara, used to be the ringleader of such japes, but the wilder diversions of Brighton no longer held such appeal for him.

Henriette's address was that of a sizable terraced house near the Promenade Grove, where there was music by day as well as dancing by night. When Sophie tugged the bellpull a French maidservant, looking harassed and cross, jerked open the door and seemed to take some satisfaction from informing her that Mademoiselle de Bouvier was not at home. Sophie then gave her name and asked if it would be possible to see Henriette's aunt instead. With a toss of her head, the maidservant went flouncing off to make the inquiry, and Sophie thought she must not be far from giving notice if even such a simple errand was such a trial to her. Before long the maidservant returned.

"Madame will receive you," she said sharply, leading the way into a walled flower garden. There the Baronne de Bouvier, a haughty-looking woman with thin features and narrow eyes, sat in the shade of a leafy tree. A parasol and a wide-brimmed chip straw hat, tied with rose satin ribbons under her chin, gave her pale complexion additional protection from the sun.

"Pray sit down, Mademoiselle Delcourt," she said loftily, indicating with her fan the cushioned chair beside her. "Henriette has spoken of you." She raised a hand in a gesture of regret. "How I miss the delicious confectionery from your father's shop. There is nothing to compare with it here."

Sophie thanked her and explained the reason for her visit. "So do you expect Henriette home soon?" she asked.

"I regret to say she is working for her living." A shudder emphasized the Baronne's disapproval. "I never thought any member of my family would be reduced to such circumstances."

Sophie was well pleased that Henriette had shown the initiative to secure employment for herself. She was about to ask what work it was when the Baronne continued speaking.

"I only wish my health could match my niece's." The woman's voice was full of self-pity. "I have suffered beyond belief in the winters of this rain-soaked country. My strength is quite sapped. If it were not for the social life we maintain, keeping to the ways of old France, I could not exist." She continued to bemoan her own troubles and was full of complaints about everything English, including the tax on hair powder, which she declared was a vicious penalty on émigrés such as her husband who wished to continue to grease and powder their hair as they had done at Versailles instead of following the new fashion of wearing it naturally. "This nation has no heart and would see us all in the gutter," she exclaimed belligerently.

Sophie, who had been steadily losing patience, could not resist a response. "I disagree with you, Madame la Baronne. The people of these isles are kindly disposed toward us, and I take no account of the few exceptions." She rose to her feet, unable to tolerate the visit any longer. "If you'll kindly give me the address of Henriette's place of work, I'll bid you good day and go now to see her."

A few minutes later Sophie was being greeted by Henriette in joyful astonishment.

"My dear friend!" she exclaimed happily. "I'd begun to think I was never going to see you again! How are you? And Antoine and the Marquis? Have you just come to Brighton?"

Sophie gave her the sad tidings of the Marquis's death, told her of Tom Foxhill's rescuing her and Antoine, and explained all that followed.

"What adventures you have had!" Henriette declared excitedly. "I'm eager to hear whatever else you have to tell, but first I must introduce you to my employer, Comtesse de Lombarde." Companionably she slipped her arm through Sophie's and led her to the stairs. "How did you find me here?"

"I visited your aunt."

Henriette rolled up her eyes expressively. "She never stops moaning despite the fact that it was an English lord who took pity on her and my uncle in their previous cramped lodgings and is letting them live rent free in his seaside residence. Now and again he sends them meat and game from his estate, and they receive the British Government's allowance for émigré aristocrats."

They were halfway up the flight when a white-wigged gentleman in well-cut but shabby clothes met them on his way down. He bade them good day and continued on his way out of the house.

"That is the Comtesse's brother-in-law. He lives here too and is writing his memoirs for a London publisher. Lots of émigrés are getting into print, and one is the editor of a French émigrés' newspaper that gives us all the news of what is happening in our homeland."

"So what are you doing?" Sophie was eager to know. "Is your work domestic in this house?"

Henriette shook her head. "I sometimes think that life as a servant would be easier on my hands than my present employment." Ruefully she displayed sore and blistered fingers. "But domestic work is barred to anyone of noble lineage by the elite of the French community. The men may be bookbinders, tailors, dancing masters, restaurant owners, teachers of chess, the French language, and anything else at which they excel, while the ladies may dressmake, sell their own homemade cosmetics, instruct in etiquette and music and so forth, but none of either sex may be a servant. A certain aristocrat in dire straits who became a footman was stripped of his Order of St. Louis!"

They had reached a door on the landing and there was a chatter of female voices within. "This is the atelier where I'm confined to my task."

Henriette threw open the door and Sophie paused on the threshold in surprise. About twenty women, young to middle-aged, were seated around two tables. At one, plaited straw was being made into wide-brimmed hats and at the other the trimmings of ribbon and fabric flowers were being added. All present wore aprons to protect their gowns. Their fichus and—in the case of the married women and widows—the lacy caps perched on their wide coiffures were pristine, giving them such an air and style that they could as easily have been playing cards or attending a Parisian salon. Some wore a thin scarlet ribbon around their necks, vivid as a blade's cut, out of respect for those whose lives were lost at the guillotine.

"Madame la Comtesse de Lombarde and ladies," Henriette said, "allow me to present Mademoiselle Delcourt, daughter of the late Monsieur Delcourt, the confectioner of Paris."

There was an immediate murmur of recognition, and the Comtesse, a woman with patrician features, welcomed Sophie on behalf of the company present.

"What do you think of our millinery?" she asked.

"The hats are charming," Sophie declared, admiring some that were finished and ready for packing. "I've seen them being worn in the town, but I had no idea they were made locally."

"Our designs are created by a fellow émigré. They caused such a stir among the English ladies that orders are coming in from as far away as London and Bath." The Comtesse waved a hand toward the trimmed hats. "Please try one on, mademoiselle."

Sophie chose a wide-brimmed hat with bunched red ribbons and turned to a mirror on the wall. There was a ripple of applause, for it suited her well. Henriette suppressed an envious sigh. Sophie had such a dramatically beautiful face. How Tom Foxhill must have marveled, she thought romantically, when his lantern showed him such a lovely girl lying in the dust.

Sophie returned the hat to the table. "One of these will be my first purchase as soon as I can afford it," she said, smiling. "Pray accept my felicitations, Madame la Comtesse and ladies, on your success."

Then she wandered round the tables, talking to the women, for all wanted to know how she and Henriette had met. In turn, she heard their tales of escape and of encounters with kindness as well as cruelty. Not all boatmen, it seemed, robbed their passengers. There were also those more compassionate, who had taken several of the women with their husbands and families across the Channel without charge. Most of those present had been well received in England, but one woman of rank had arrived destitute with her young children, and they had almost starved as she begged for food from door to door, only to be turned away.

At the Comtesse's invitation, Sophie drew up a chair beside Henriette, who had resumed the task of stitching plaited straw into a wide brim. As the other women chatted among themselves, the two friends had a chance to talk quietly together. Henriette spoke gloomily about her chances in the marriage market.

"My uncle and aunt want to be rid of my company and are hoping to make a suitable match for me, but it's far from easy. All the eligible Frenchmen are after English women with fortunes."

"You wouldn't want a mercenary husband in any case, would you?"

"I suppose not," Henriette conceded, "but I dread being left on the shelf."

"There are plenty of Englishmen," Sophie encouraged, smiling at the idea that this pretty girl was so concerned about her chances of marriage. "What about all the handsome officers at the Brighton camp? They're swarming all over the town."

Henriette shook her head sadly. "That wouldn't be allowed for me. My aunt says too many younger sons go into the army because they lack any prospects in civilian life. I don't believe you have any idea how much competition there is among Frenchwomen wanting to hook an English gentleman."

"I don't believe I have," Sophie admitted dryly.

"Do you have a beau?" There was a wistful note in Henriette's voice.

"I haven't met a man I like well enough. In any case when I'm not working I like to spend my time with Antoine. I owe it to his mother to continue his lessons and to make sure he doesn't forget our language or his heritage."

"What of Tom Foxhill?"

Sophie was taken aback. "Why should I think of him?" she exclaimed defensively. "His path and mine are unlikely to cross again. I'm grateful for all his kindness, but it wasn't a relationship I would want to pursue."

"Why not?" Henriette was curious.

Sophie shrugged deliberately. "I can only say that I found him to be restless and volatile in his nature. I've not forgotten that such men instigated the Revolution, and I've witnessed enough examples of their ruthlessness to be wary of one of their nature. Such a man would make a turmoil of my life all over again."

"He sounds like a dashing, romantic figure to me," Henriette sighed dreamily.

"I only think of him as my good Samaritan. Otherwise he could complicate my life, and I won't allow that."

She appeared so decided that Henriette did not pursue her questioning.

THE MEETINGS of Sophie and Henriette were not to be as frequent as both would have wished. Sophie's duties alternated between late and early shifts, but even when she and Henriette finished work at the same time, they moved in entirely different spheres. The French aristocrats tried to create little centers of Versailles in exile, holding salons, card parties, gaming sessions where the stakes were low and no longer in gold, and—when finances allowed—private balls, which gave girls such as Henriette a chance to exert their charms on all the marriageable men. Since Sophie was not of noble birth, she could not be included, despite Henriette's entreaties to her aunt.

"Are you mad?" the Baronne had retorted. "It's more important than ever before that those of our station close ranks and maintain our standards!"

"It was those same standards that reduced us to exile!" Henriette gave back angrily.

The Baronne struck her viciously across the face. "You sound like a Revolutionary!" she hissed. "Never dare to speak thus under this roof again or out you go!"

Henriette bit deep into her lip to stop the tears of pain as her aunt stalked away in a furious rustle of silk. She wished she could leave, but she lacked Sophie's dauntless spirit. Henriette felt shame at her own weakness, but she knew nothing could induce her to face life on her own. Her only escape lay in marriage. Her friendship with Sophie, however, remained as strong as ever. It was as though the nightmare they shared had made them as close as sisters.

SOPHIE WAS ALREADY AT WORK one hot July morning when a discovery was made on the beach. It was not long before the news reached the Old Ship. Polly imparted it to Sophie as they passed each other with laden trays.

"I just heard some gents talking at that table in the window. Two revenue men have been washed up on the beach with their throats cut!"

Sophie felt the color drain from her face. Luckily Polly had already continued on to the kitchen with her load of empty dishes. Automatically Sophie set down pots of hot chocolate or tea in front of those who had ordered them. Several customers had left their own tables to question the two gentlemen seated at the window.

"I don't know the details," one of them was replying. "We stopped on our way here to watch the two bodies being dragged out of the water. The fishermen engaged in the task seemed to recognize them, so perhaps they were stationed locally."

Somehow Sophie got through the rest of the morning. She was deeply distressed, certain that her anonymous information was in some way responsible for what had happened. Although there was general speculation in the kitchen that the two revenue men had happened by chance upon smugglers at work, Sophie was certain she knew otherwise. Instead of calling in reinforcements after receiving her note, the two revenue men, perhaps hoping for promotion, had lain in wait by themselves to catch the villains red-handed, and their courageous foolhardiness had ended in tragedy.

Sophie felt a desperate need to get out into the air, the weight on her conscience almost more than she could bear. As soon as all the tables were laid up again for the dining hour, she gained permission to take a break.

After walking on the promenade, she was about to cross the sea road on her way back to the Old Ship when she sighted a company of twenty horsemen approaching and stayed to watch. Uniformed in dark blue with tricorn hats, they were immediately recognizable as revenue men. No doubt the murders had brought them in force to Brighton. The officer at their head, sitting straight-backed on a gray horse, wore a black hat cocked at the front, his top boots as polished and shining as his silver buttons.

Sophie wished Antoine were with her. Several times she had taken him to see the Dragoons in their plumed helmets, silver lacings, and fur-trimmed pelisses. This band of men presented a far more somber spectacle, but the jingle of their harnesses and the gleaming scabbards of their cutlasses still gave them a military air.

At the precise moment that the officer in the lead drew level with Sophie, he turned his head and his stern blue eyes looked straight into hers. With his thick wheat-fair hair, his broad shoulders and austere features, he possessed an air of absolute authority, as if a sense of justice and a dedication to duty dominated his life. Only his need to look ahead again broke the contact between them. Sophie remained where she was, gazing after him until he turned with his company away from the sea and out of sight.

The horses' hooves clattered over the cobbles of West Street as Rory Morgan led the way to the billet that awaited his men. Donald Pearce, his second-in-command, who could handle a cutlass almost as well as his Captain, glanced at the female passersby as they rode along.

"So far the young women of Brighton appear to be as pretty as I've always heard. But then you know that, Captain Morgan, having been stationed here before."

"I've never been disappointed," Rory remarked dryly. In his mind's eye he held an image of the enticing girl on the promenade, whose blue-black hair had danced in the warm sea breeze. Her large-eyed oval face had the kind of foreign beauty that suggested she was one of the many hundreds of émigrés who had made homes along the coast. Unless she was only visiting Brighton. He would have liked to know. Yet what would be the point? He was here on a grim mission and would not rest until it was brought to a satisfactory conclusion. It would do no harm to remind his second-in-command that they would have no time for gallivanting. "I advise you to remember, Mr. Pearce, that we are in Brighton for the sole purpose of bringing to trial the murderer, or murderers, of Deane and Barnley."

"Yes, of course, sir."

"I knew them both. They were good men."

"As you say, sir."

At the Old Ship, Sophie returned to her chores. She thought it no wonder the ranks of revenue men had been so smart and trim when their officer clearly set such a high standard. Somehow she would have to inform him of what she knew. How to do that without upsetting Clara remained a problem she would have to solve quickly.

Passing a window less than an hour later, Sophie saw the officer again. He was standing on the promenade with some local officials, who were pointing in one direction and then another as they answered his questions. She lingered to watch until the weight of her tray reminded her that hungry customers were waiting. When she passed the window again, he and those with him had gone.

As it happened, this was the last tray Sophie ever carried as a waiting maid at the Old Ship. When she returned to the kitchen to collect another order, Harry was using a prong hooked through its cloth to lift a large pudding out of boiling water. Suddenly the knot gave, and before he could step back, the water surged up over his hands and forearms even as the saucepan tipped and crashed down at his feet.

Even as he screamed in agony, Sophie was rushing toward him. Seizing the shocked man about the waist, she drove him ahead of her to the nearest sink.

"Put your hands and arms on it," she ordered, beginning to swing the adjacent pump. As he obeyed, groaning with pain, she called out for ice. She had suffered burns herself in the past and knew that nothing eased the pain better than cold water. Then she instructed one of the other waiting maids, who had just come on duty, to take care of her customers.

Afterward Sophie marveled to herself at the way everyone had obeyed her. It was after Harry had been led away by the housekeeper that the head chef came across to Sophie, who had untied her soaked apron and was putting on a fresh one.

"Harry has a high regard for your cooking knowledge," he said, "and I've seen you giving him a quick helping hand when you thought me out of the way." He half smiled, showing that he was not displeased. "So until Harry is fit to return to work, I'm willing to give you a trial with the sweet puddings. But remember that I want no encroaching on the confectioner's territory. Leave him to do the cakes and ices and fruit molds and sweetmeats. Understand?"

"Yes, Chef," she nodded in eager agreement.

That evening when Rory came alone to the Old Ship, he took a glass of Madeira in the taproom before sitting down to supper in the dining room. After oysters followed by roast Southdown lamb, he was served a feather-light pudding with the most delicious hot wine sauce he had ever tasted.

Sophie went home again by way of the seashore, confident there would be no smugglers with so many revenue men in the area. The sea and sands stretched silver beneath the moon. As usual, she was barefoot, and when she reached the rocks, the pools around them were tepid to her toes. Her thoughts were full of the new routine into which she had slipped since the unfortunate accident a few hours before. She would visit Harry on the morrow. He would be pleased that she was holding his job temporarily, but she wished such work had come her way by any other means.

She neither saw nor heard the man in the moon shadows until she was seized by the shoulders from behind and turned about to be thudded back against one of the seaweed-covered rocks. Even as she was about to scream, a large hand clamped over her mouth.

"In the name of the Law, be silent!" the man barked. "I intend you no harm."

She stared at him above the barrier of his hand, unaware how large and sparkling her eyes appeared to him in the moonlight. She recognized him as the officer whom she had seen twice already that day. The phrase of third time lucky leapt unbidden into her mind and was dismissed almost as swiftly. As he removed his hand, she spoke angrily.

"Why did you frighten me so? Surely you saw me in the moonlight long before I reached this spot. You could have stepped forward!"

He had recognized her, but made no acknowledgment of it. "You might have run away. I'm Captain Morgan of the Excise Service, and I want to know why you're on the beach at this late hour."

"I often walk home along the shore after I've finished work at the Old Ship."

"May I ask what you do there?" His interest, if truth were known, was as personal as it was official.

"I did wait at table, but from today I became a cook."

"I've heard that the French excel in that field and I think you are one of the émigrés." She nodded and he smiled. "May I ask your name, mademoiselle?" When she had told him he questioned her again. "Since you say you walk this way often, have you ever seen anything to suggest that smuggling boats were being run in anywhere along this section of the shore?"

Still taken aback by the way he had frightened her, she hesitated a moment before she countered his query with one of her own. "Why should the Gentlemen risk operating where there are rocks?"

"Precisely because other boats keep away. And let me inform you there is nothing gentle about these criminals whether they are known as Gentlemen, Freetraders, Owlers, or any other nickname. I'll remind you that last night they took the lives of two men who have left widows and young families."

"I know!" Her cry was full of anguish.

His eyes narrowed. "You spoke from the heart. Were you acquainted with either of them?"

"I served them with ale several times in the taproom at the Old Ship."

"I think you could tell me something that you're holding back. Am I right?"

She wished she knew how far she could trust him, but she also had to remember her promise to Clara. She played for time. "It's getting late and my landlady will be concerned about me. I'll come to your office tomorrow."

"That won't be necessary. I shall be interrogating all the staff at the Old Ship in the morning. My two men were last seen alive in the taproom there. I want to know if they were heard to say anything that might help us find their killers. Where do you live?"

"At a cottage that lies a good distance beyond all the rest in the lane near here."

"Mrs. Renfrew's cottage?"

"How do you know that?"

79

He smiled. "I haven't been idle since I rode into Brighton this afternoon. As soon as I learned where the bodies were found and had inquired from fishermen about the play of the tides, my men began to question people living close to the places where the murders were likely to have been committed. Mrs. Renfrew was not at home when my man called, but I saw her going in a few minutes afterward with two little boys and I went myself to speak to her."

"One of those children is my nephew."

"She told me she had a young émigré living with her. Needless to say I hadn't expected to meet you in these circumstances. Luckily it's not a night of smugglers' moon or I might easily have taken a shot at you!"

"But surely this is such a night?" Sophie queried, looking up at the almost full moon.

"No. Quite the reverse. Clearly you haven't been in Brighton long enough to know that a smugglers' moon means a dark night. It's an expression used all along the south coast. The Excise Service and the moonlight are the smugglers' most dangerous enemies."

"Then why did they—" she broke off abruptly, but not before her unguarded exclamation was noticed.

"Yes?" he prompted. Although she shook her head quickly, as if there were nothing more to add, he continued to regard her with interest. "Well, we can talk more tomorrow. Now I'll see you safely home."

"I can make my own way, thank you."

"No, I wouldn't hear of it." He began to walk with her across the shingle. "Mrs. Renfrew told me that she's a dipper. Do you ever go in the water yourself?"

"She taught me to swim."

"Swimming is an exercise I enjoy too," he said with a nod.

Sophie was thinking she would never again swim at night unless there was plenty of moonlight. Shivers ran down her spine at the prospect of the smuggler with the mother-of-pearl box suddenly looming over her in the darkness.

She and her escort had reached the path up which she had seen the kegs being carried away. It was steep and he took her elbow, although she had climbed it many times alone. At the top, a gap in the tamarisk hedge gave way to the lane. She came to a standstill, making it plain that she was determined to go the rest of the way on her own.

"The cottage is in sight now," she said, pointing out the lighted window showing through the trees. "Good night, Captain Morgan."

"I bid you good night too, Miss Delcourt."

She half turned to go and then paused. "You called me 'mademoiselle' before. Out of interest, do you speak French?"

He smiled slowly. "I've had some schooling in your language. I thought to make you feel at home. And, perhaps, more at ease with me."

She returned his smile and went away down the lane. Clara was watching for her at the window and was already in the hall when she entered.

"Where have you been? You're so late! I was worried. There are revenue men all over the place."

The woman was in such a state of agitation that it took quite a while before Sophie could calm her down. Before undressing that night she sat at the side table in her room and, with a pen and paper, worked out all she wanted to tell Captain Morgan in the morning. Then she put the paper to a candle flame.

Seven

SOPHIE WAS EARLY TO WORK the next morning, wanting to get well organized for her new role in the kitchen. In the average household, most people of leisure dined heartily at three o'clock on several dishes. If dinner was to be served at the more fashionable hour of six, it was customary to keep hunger at bay with a very large breakfast, and the custom of drinking tea and eating sweet cakes in midafternoon was beginning to take hold. A late supper was always served, whatever the hour of dining, and was usually a cold collation. On the whole, this was the pattern of meals at the Old Ship.

Sophie was glad for all the knowledge she had gained from Mrs. Millard about traditional English puddings, but she intended to be creative whenever possible. She thought it strange that her fellow workers spoke of "the pudding course" even when the dish served was the lightest sweet soufflé. In France all such dishes were known as *les desserts,* but the dessert course in England was the fresh fruit served at the end of a meal, often with bowls of nuts in season and candies. She decided that in order not to confuse anybody in the kitchen she would always refer to puddings, no matter how delicate the dish she was preparing.

She had Harry's apprentice, an amiable fourteen-year-old lad named Josh, to help her. Josh had an honest, open face and was a willing worker, which made her forgive his boyish clumsiness. He grated lumps of chocolate for her, broke and crushed sugar blocks, beat egg whites, and carried out many other such tasks. He was lining pudding basins with white cloths and she was filling them when Mr. Hicks came in and clapped his hands for attention.

"One moment, everybody, if you please. Captain Morgan of His Majesty's Excise Service has arrived to question all employees about the murder of the two revenue men who were known to some of us." He held up his hand reassuringly as there came a murmur of unease. "Suspicion hasn't fallen on anyone here. That's not the officer's purpose in coming. Mr. Barnley and Mr. Deane were in the taproom on the evening of their deaths, and the officer hopes to gain information that might lead to the arrest of the murderers. You'll all be called individually."

Sophie was surprised that an Excise man should be in command. Normally the duties of that service were confined to the harbors, overseeing the collection of taxes on imported and exported goods, and issuing trade licenses. This particular officer, however, must be experienced in dealing with smugglers to be put in charge of this investigation.

When her turn came to be interviewed, she tapped on the door of the private room where the interrogation was taking place, and Captain Morgan's voice bade her enter. She found him writing at a desk, his quill pen scratching in a notebook. He spoke without looking up. "Be seated."

She settled herself in a chair opposite him and folded her hands in her lap. His unpowdered hair was dressed as before, with a formal roll over each ear and tied back in military style with a black bow at the nape of the neck. It was likely that his rank came from service with the army, which would explain why both he and his men had such a disciplined air about them.

Sophie's gaze went to the Captain's hands. They were strong and broad, with well-shaped fingers and square, clean nails. She thought they looked as capable of tenderness as they did of violence in the cause of duty. Her eyes flicked back to his face, which was set in concentration. He was a very strong-looking man and an extremely attractive one. She was again aware of being drawn to him, as when she had seen him riding by her before.

He put down his pen and looked up, catching her gaze. A broad smile spread across his face. "It's you, Miss Delcourt! My apologies!

I thought the taproom waiting maids were coming in next. How are you this morning after the fright I gave you last night?"

"I suffered no ill effects."

Although she smiled, he could see that unlike the night before, she was now fully in control of herself and what she intended to say. "I'm glad to hear it. Now I have to ask you a few routine questions." He turned to a fresh page in his notebook and began writing. "I know your name and address. When and where did you arrive in England?"

When these facts had been recorded, he put aside his pen and linked his hands in front of him on the desk. "Before you tell me anything more, I've decided to explain to you why catching these murderers is so important. Have you ever heard it said that if every fisherman who smuggled—or acted as a pilot—was clapped into prison, there'd be hardly any fish for sale along the entire south coast?"

"Yes, I have." She guessed how frustrating his task must be. "So how do you deal with them?"

"We make arrests whenever we catch them red-handed, but they can be as slippery as the eels they snare in their legitimate trade, and they get plenty of help from otherwise respectable citizens, who want to continue buying from them. Tax-free goods have been, and ever will be, an irresistible temptation. In the past, I've found pulpits and church lofts stuffed with tea and mansion cellars full of illegally imported kegs. The rich, with their own powerful influence and their friends in high places, are far harder to catch for purchasing contraband."

"And what of the murderers of the revenue men?"

"Ah," he said gravely, "those men are in a different category altogether. There are plenty of fishermen-smugglers who would use a firearm when cornered, but the ones I'm speaking about now are totally vicious and bring in contraband on a very large scale. Sometimes they operate in gangs of sixty or more. They are utterly ruthless and terrorize ordinary citizens into storing their goods for them. They show no mercy to anyone, male or female, who crosses them, and are equally brutal to any of their own kind whom they suspect of informing against them. Although we have broken up most of these gangs, there is one in particular, known as the Broomfield gang, that has

outfought and outwitted us on far too many occasions. I have reason
to believe they have been operating in this area."

"But would they have dared to land with so many Dragoons stationed here?"

"It is a measure of their audacity and cunning."

"And you think they are responsible for the two murders?"

"The manner in which the crime was carried out has the stamp of
the Broomfield gang." He spared her certain gruesome details, which
were not for any respectable young woman to hear. "So, Miss
Delcourt, you must realize just how important it is that you tell me
anything at all that might prove helpful."

She inclined her head. "Only if you give me your solemn word that
you will never reveal the source of your information. It's equally
important that if you should ever want to question me further you
would come to my place of work. I must respect my landlady's wish
that no outsider ever call on me at home."

He put down the pen he had taken up. "I agree to your requests.
What you've just asked is not so uncommon as you might suppose."

"That's why I hoped Mr. Barnley and Mr. Deane would act on
the information I gave them anonymously." Her voice caught. "I
believe that inadvertently I brought about their deaths."

Rory Morgan leaned back in his chair and spoke quietly. "Go on."

When she had told him everything, she sat with her head bowed.
He left his chair then, and came to put a hand on her shoulder. "You
are in no way to blame for what happened. You did your duty as a
law-abiding citizen even as they carried out their duty to the best of
their ability. I thank you for all you've told me."

She looked up at him, still distressed. "I abhor violence. I thought
I'd left it behind when I escaped from France, but it was waiting for
me and those in my charge as soon as I stepped onto English soil."

"What happened?" He listened attentively to her account of the
attack and her rescue. Returning to his desk, he wrote down her
descriptions of Barnes and his accomplices.

"As you are so often at harbors and patrolling the coast in your
work," she concluded hopefully, "I thought the name 'Barnes' might
mean something to you."

He shook his head. "I know of other such crimes against newly
arrived émigrés, and a good many arrests have been made, but the

Barnes trio is unknown to me. How did the Marquis come into your care? And the boy? Was he orphaned?"

She gave him what details she could without contradicting his belief that Antoine was her sister's child. "So you see, England is a haven to me, but I'll not be satisfied until I can be sure that Barnes is not preying on other victims."

"You can rely on me to do whatever I can to ensure that he and his accomplices are caught."

Sophie nodded gratefully. "It's a relief to know that. Perhaps in turn, by keeping my eyes open, I could play a small part in helping you to bring the Broomfield gang to justice."

Immediately he showed his keenness. "Would you indeed? I must say that when I visited Mrs. Renfrew's cottage, I thought to myself that anyone living there would have an unimpeded view of the shore for a considerable distance in either direction. I could supply you with a spyglass, but I should want you to keep possession of it to yourself."

"And what would I be looking for?"

"A farm gate left wide at night to give no hindrance to trundling wagons or galloping horses. A marker, not normally to be seen, floating offshore. Footsteps in the sand that weren't there the night before, the sails of a windmill set at a certain angle at times of a high tide, and so forth."

"What would a marker look like?"

"It could be a small buoy. Most likely a few cork floats, which are less easily seen from the land. The latter are used mostly when the smugglers have collected kegs, either from France or from a schooner lying offshore in deeper water, and are not sure if it is safe to bring them ashore. The kegs are submerged with weights on a rope under the markers and drawn in when the smugglers are certain there are no revenue men about."

"Let me have that spyglass."

He admired her spirit. In spite of all he had told her, and her own experience of violence, she still wanted to help. Taking a spyglass from his pocket, he invited Sophie to the window. There he showed her how to extend the spyglass and put it to her eye. As she looked through it, a ship leapt into focus on the horizon, its sails curved like petals. It was a fine sight.

When Sophie lowered the spyglass and closed it, her gaze remained on the horizon. "The seamen on that ship can see France on their port side."

"Do you get homesick?" Rory asked sympathetically.

"Sometimes," she admitted quietly, touched by his understanding, "even though I was lucky to escape with my life."

"Remember the new regime can't change Paris or the landscape or the skies of France that you knew."

She turned from the window to look questioningly at him. "You sound as if you know what it's like to be exiled."

"No, but I remember how often my thoughts turned to England when I was in India."

"When I return to France," she said firmly, "as I hope to do one day in a better future, I'll never leave it again." She put the spyglass into the pocket of her skirt and smoothed her apron back over it, saying she would find a good hiding place for it in her room at the cottage.

"I appreciate your cooperation," he said. "I shall need to see you from time to time to hear if you've noticed anything."

"I'll call in at your headquarters."

Rory shook his head. "I'm not often there. In any case, I wouldn't want anyone to know I've enlisted your help. It would allay any suspicion on that score if we met socially. Are you averse to mixing business with pleasure?"

She hesitated. "I hope you haven't used the spyglass as a means to an end. I should feel very foolish."

"Not at all." He was vehement. "The smallest grain of information can set a trail to an arrest. That is entirely divorced from my personal wish to become acquainted with you."

She could tell he was speaking truthfully, and it was her own wish to see him again too. "I have a free half day now and again."

"How soon? I'd like to take you to dancing and supper at the Castle Inn."

"Next week."

"Not before then?"

She reminded him that in the meantime he would be as busy as she. The arrangement was made, and well pleased, he opened the door for her and she returned to the kitchen.

When Sophie arrived home that night, Clara was just coming out of the boys' bedchamber.

"Clara," Sophie began, "we were all interrogated at work today by the Excise officer who called on you."

"Captain Morgan? Oh, yes."

"I told him about Barnes. No, don't frown! He has given me his word that he would always contact me at my place of work. He has also invited me out."

"That's all right, then," Clara said amiably, "but if he starts courting you seriously, don't expect to use my parlor."

Sophie burst out laughing. "You matchmaker, Clara! I'll make sure he stops at the cottage gate."

"No, down the lane." Clara wagged her head sternly. "I don't want that busybody, Mrs. Furlow, peeping through her curtains and spreading talk about men going past on their way to this house."

"Don't worry," Sophie said reassuringly. "It shall be as you wish."

That night she heard again the far-away rumbling she could not identify. Throwing back the bedclothes, she padded across to the window. There was only the moon-silvered lane and the motionless trees to be seen. In spite of what Clara had said, it must be the waves that caused the curious vibrations. Perhaps she couldn't hear them at the far side of the cottage.

Sophie went to the drawer where she had hidden the spyglass and took it into the boys' bedchamber, where the window looked out to sea. She put the spyglass to her eye, but there was nothing untoward to be seen when moonlight broke through the clouds. Mystified, she went back to her own room. Soon afterward she heard Clara's nighttime visitor arrive.

IT WAS A RELIEF to Sophie that she did not have to fend off advances from the men in the kitchen of the Old Ship. With the exception of the head chef, who had appointed her and kept his distance, the rest were too hostile to consider her anything but an unwelcome female usurper in their midst. Their attitude was that a woman could cook in her own kitchen or as a domestic servant, but the important preparation of food was, by long tradition, an exclusively male domain. She knew this dated from the time when kitchens throughout Europe were made so unbearably hot by the great open hearths that the men were naked while they cooked, but times and the cooking apparatus had changed since then.

Henriette offered to lend Sophie a gown for her evening with Rory. The Castle Inn rivaled the Old Ship as a fashionable venue in Brighton. It had its own grand ballroom, and the Prince of Wales patronized it as well. Nothing in Sophie's wardrobe would be suitable to wear.

"There's a collection of gowns kept at the Comtesse de Lombarde's house," Henriette explained. "Mostly they're for those of our age, because we're the ones hoping for husbands and we can't wear the same garments for all the social occasions we attend. There's also a box of silk flowers and sashes we use as accessories, or you may have some of your own."

Most of the gowns were in the current fashion for soft fabrics. There were diaphanous muslins, filmy lawns, and silk gauzes. With simple frill-edged fichus and softly gathered skirts, the style was fairly easy to make, even for those French ladies who had never made a gown before, especially since all of them had been taught as children to embroider and sew.

Sophie tried on several of the garments before finally making her choice. Then Henriette expressed her concern over Sophie's lack of chaperonage.

"Chaperonage?" Sophie echoed in disbelief. "As far as I'm concerned, that's a thing of the past. It ended with all else of the life I'd known on the day I fled."

As Sophie left with the borrowed gown wrapped in a linen cloth, she thought to herself that Henriette's innocence of the ways of the world was as remote from her own outlook as it could be.

CLARA WAS DELIGHTED to see the borrowed gown and offered the loan of some gold earrings. Sophie accepted with pleasure. "These are lovely, Clara!" Sophie held the earrings to her lobes as she looked in a mirror. "Are they an heirloom?"

"Yes," Clara said quickly. "They suit you well."

Sophie had arranged to meet Rory at the Castle Inn. In her borrowed gown of pale green lawn, the gold earrings, and her cloak about her shoulders, she was given a lift by a neighbor in his wagonette to the Steine, where the Castle Inn stood adjacent to the grounds of the Marine Pavilion. She saw at once that Rory, in his best uniform, was waiting for her at the entrance. Unexpectedly, she felt her heart lift at the sight of him. He came hastening to meet her and lead her inside.

"I've been looking forward to this evening, Sophie, and hoping all the smuggling activity wouldn't cause me to be called away." He took her cloak and handed it to a woman in attendance. "How have you been since I saw you last?"

"Extremely busy, but I'm sorry to say I have nothing to report."

"No matter. It's early days yet."

"Are you making any progress?"

"No, clues are still evading us. But we'll talk no more of it this evening. We're here to enjoy ourselves."

They had reached the ballroom. Like the one at the Old Ship, it was long and rectangular in shape, which suited most dance formations, and it was brightly illuminated by hundreds of candles in glittering chandeliers. Mirrors on the walls reflected a gathered assembly of women in fashionable pastel gowns, the men in strong crimson, King's blue, green, claret, and black. All the fashionable younger men wore their hair in the new shorter, unpowdered styles, except the Dragoons. Magnificent in their dress uniforms, they kept to their powdered hair as did every Frenchman present, although for them it was a symbol of continued loyalty to the House of Bourbon.

The orchestra in the gallery had struck up for a country dance and Rory led Sophie forward. Although the dance itself was unfamiliar to her, the steps were so similar to old French measures that she picked them up immediately. She felt extraordinarily lighthearted as she and Rory took their turns rotating between the two lines of dancers.

At supper time in the adjoining assembly room, Sophie cast a professional eye over the buffet table. Rory would have fetched her anything she fancied, but she wanted to compare the confectionery centerpiece of the Castle Inn with that of the Old Ship. Not surprisingly, the main piece was a turreted and castellated castle, which she knew had been built up by the skillful use of sugar over wire and pasteboard. Although well executed, she thought the confectioner at her place of work outdid his rival with the centerpiece of a galleon in full sail that graced similar functions at the Old Ship.

While they ate their supper, Rory asked about her life in Paris before the Revolution and what she thought of living in England. She in her turn learned of his childhood in the country of Surrey and how he had joined the army, following in his late father's footsteps, and been wounded in a skirmish in India while serving with the forces of the East India Company.

"I was ill for a long time. After being shipped home I was invalided out of the army because it was thought I would never recover." He smiled at her concerned expression. "It's hard to believe now, isn't it? Our family doctor sent me to Brighton for the sea air. Since I thrived in it and my career in the army was over, I joined the Excise Service. It has kept me by the sea and I wouldn't have it otherwise."

He went on to tell her that he had three sisters, two of whom were married. His widowed mother lived with the third in a small coastal town some miles away. He was intrigued by Sophie's account of her training in confectionery.

"You must have been working while your childhood friends played."

"I was allowed time for education and recreation, but making sweetmeats was like another game to me." She made one of the vivacious little gestures that were part of the fascination she had for him. "Maybe the use of gold and colors in the work caught my fancy."

"You should have a confectionery shop of your own," he said.

"That's what I would like one day. In the meantime, I have a long way to go. I intend to apply for work at the Marine Pavilion next spring."

"I wish you luck, Sophie."

When the dancing began again Sophie did not notice the tall, vigorous man, his dark hair short-cut and curling, who appeared on the threshold of the ballroom. With a swirl of green velvet coattails, he shepherded a lively party of people to an alcove set with gilded chairs from which they would have a good view of the festivities. As he bent to retrieve a fan dropped by one of the women, Sophie caught sight of him. In a flash, a shiver of danger ran up her spine, then in the next instant, she gave a little gasp of surprise.

"There's Tom Foxhill, who rescued Antoine and me!" she exclaimed, thinking almost in despair that no man should have such power to excite even from a distance. The trouble was, he was too handsome for his own good or for any woman's either.

Tom, sighting her at the same moment, felt a surge of relief charge through him. After weeks of trying in vain to trace her, he had found her again! Her partner had led her out of the dance, and she stood with her head high, startled recognition blazing in her amber eyes. They could have been alone in the spacious room, so magnetic was the gaze that passed between them.

Deliberately he swung away the chair that blocked his way and set off toward her. It was uppermost in his mind that they had parted on a quarrel at their last meeting, and he guessed it was also in hers, but at least she had not turned away and was even smiling slightly as he approached. When he reached her he bowed.

"Your servant, Sophie."

"So we meet yet again in unexpected circumstances," she said calmly. "Let me present Captain Morgan. Rory, this is Mr. Foxhill, my good Samaritan."

Tom, after exchanging a few words with Rory, turned back to her. "I'm so pleased to see you again. When I returned to the farm you'd been gone some time. But we can't talk here. I'd be honored if you'd both join my party."

It was not what Rory wanted, but the matter was out of his hands. The Foxhill party included some well-to-do young men and their pretty flirtatious women. There was witty conversation, but it galled Rory that he should be seated away from Sophie while she and Tom Foxhill sat together. Since they were already engaged in conversation, he invited one of the young women to dance and led her into a cotillion.

Tom had expressed his thankfulness to Sophie for acknowledging him in spite of the angry words exchanged at the farm gate. Sophie shrugged. "I don't bear grudges and the matter is closed."

He decided not to pursue the point. "What made you decide to come to Brighton?"

"I've a friend here."

"The Excise officer?"

"No, I've met Rory since. It was a fellow émigré, Henriette de Bouvier, who suggested I come here. Thankfully all is well now. I have employment and comfortable lodgings." She told him about her work and her living arrangements with Clara, and asked how long he would be staying in town.

"Not as long as I would wish now that we've met again. I came down to the seaside with the friends at this table"—he was reminded to glance in the direction of one of the young women, whose hard look told him he was neglecting her—"and we're staying here at the Castle Inn. I leave for Holland tomorrow. Amsterdam is the place to buy splendid pieces imported from the Far East."

"You mentioned your frequent comings and goings to me last time," she stated without expression.

"Don't suppose I've forgotten," he commented dryly. "Since then I've been thinking about opening a branch of my London shop in Brighton. I'd gain a rich clientele both in the season and out of it."

"You'd have no difficulty in buying stock cheaply from the émigrés in this town." There was an edge to Sophie's voice.

He raised an eyebrow quizzically. "I'd buy from them at a fair price and sell at the same standard too. Fleecing the unfortunate is not my habit."

She flushed. "I'm sorry. Did I sound as if I were accusing you of being a charlatan? I was thinking of others. I know of your generosity."

He grinned. "I wasn't offended. It would take more than that for us ever to fall out again, but I admit to being ruthless in business on occasion. We all want to profit from our labors—just as Captain Morgan expects a good bounty when he unearths contraband and hauls in the wrongdoers. I'll also remind you that not all your fellow émigrés are impoverished. Some came away with a king's ransom in jewels."

"But most had to leave everything behind, and others lost whatever they had on their journey." Sophie was remembering the theft of the Comtesse's jewels, about which he knew nothing. Then she changed the subject. "How were the Millards when you saw them again?"

"All well as far as I could tell, but they claimed to have no idea where you had gone. And I hadn't been the only one making inquiries. Mrs. Millard told me a Frenchman had called not long after you left."

"But nobody of my acquaintance knew I was there!"

"He wasn't asking for you. He had heard indirectly of the death of the Marquis de Fontaine and wanted the local details. Mrs. Millard didn't grasp his name, saying the pronunciation was beyond her, but she understood that he was the old gentleman's widowed son-in-law."

Sophie felt a spurt of excitement. Antoine had an uncle in England! Although this man was not blood kin, it was still good to know that her charge had a living relative. Perhaps there were others with whom the boy could be reunited one day, not that she would ever relinquish her guardianship of him until she had fulfilled her promise to his mother. "Did Mrs. Millard say anything more about this man? Where he was staying or if he had any family with him?"

"No, she said nothing of that to me. When the Frenchman left the farm, he asked directions to the Marquis's grave as he wished to pay his respects. Mrs. Millard did mention that he had inquired about any persons with the old gentleman and wanted to know where they might be found. But, of course, she didn't know. Why didn't you want Mrs. Millard to receive an address from you after you had settled?"

"Is that what she said?" Sophie commented. "It wasn't my idea at all, but her wish."

When she had explained Mrs. Millard's reason, Tom smiled wryly but made no comment and they talked on. He told her he had supplied the Prince of Wales with some fine furniture for Carlton House as well as for the Marine Pavilion. Quite often the Prince would accompany him to auctions. Whenever Tom acquired anything of particular beauty, whether a painting or some other work of art, he always gave his royal patron the first chance to buy it.

As the evening wore on, Sophie danced with Tom, and then with Rory and other men in the party. When the ball drew toward its end, she and Rory bade the other guests good night and Tom accompanied them to the hallway. When Sophie went to collect her cloak, he spoke in confidence to Rory.

"I didn't want to spoil Sophie's evening, but there's something she should know. Perhaps you could choose the right moment to tell her, because I feel sure it's bound to cause her distress. That countryman of hers, who visited the farm, desecrated the Marquis's grave. Equally sinister, a white cockade, which Sophie had made and which the farmer's wife had secured there, was kicked aside and ground into the mud."

"Then it's as well Sophie wasn't at the farm when this happened," Rory said at once. "She's been through enough already. Part of my work is to watch for enemy infiltrators, such as that fellow, but they arrive as émigrés and that makes it a hard task."

"It must be. Ah! Sophie is returning."

At last, taking his leave, Tom expressed the hope that they would meet again soon.

"If you open a shop in Brighton, I'm sure we shall see each other now and again," she answered casually, not wanting him to see that in spite of herself she was remembering the kiss they had shared at their previous parting. By the way he was looking at her, she knew he was thinking of it too.

When they had gone outside, Tom went to stand on the steps and look after them, hands resting on his hips, elbows jutting, and feet set apart in an unconsciously aggressive stance. The chandelier behind him threw his long shadow across the cobbles. He wanted Sophie and he meant to have her. That was settled in his mind, as if she had already agreed, but he was under no false illusion. It was going to be difficult. She was as determined a person as he was himself, and she had put up strong barriers against him, but nothing would make him give up the chase, and he would not let her slip away from him again.

Sophie and Rory strolled the sands on their way back to Clara's. She was full of chat about the enjoyable evening, and he decided to wait until another day before repeating what Tom Foxhill had told him.

"Once we leave the beach," she said after a while, "you won't be able to come with me beyond where the lane branches away from the sea road. My landlady has made a very strict rule that I arrive home unaccompanied. She has a fear of gossip."

He was puzzled. "Mrs. Renfrew seemed a bold, outspoken woman to me, not the type to worry about idle talk."

"I believe I know the reason." Sophie's eyes twinkled. "But I'm not sure I should tell you."

He laughed. "Why? Is it scandalous?"

"Some might think so. The fact is, I believe she has a midnight lover, which is why she is extra careful to avoid any talk. She has no idea that I always know when he is there!"

"It sounds as though you don't sleep very well."

"I do. But I'm always half listening for Antoine." Her voice dropped a note. "Sometimes I have nightmares about terrible happenings in the past."

"I'm afraid any terrible experience can have that effect. Most men who have been in battle would say the same."

She paused to look at him. "You too?"

When he nodded, she rested her hand against the side of his face. Immediately he cupped her fingers and kissed her palm. She would have withdrawn her hand instantly, but he continued to hold it.

"Rory," she protested, gently but firmly. It would be foolish to let him into her life. There was too much she wanted to do first, and never again would she let herself become vulnerable to any man as she had once with Tom.

He released her hand. "You hardly know me yet," he said quietly, "but I want this to be a beginning between us."

She shook her head, for she could not make any promises. "Only friendship, Rory. That I will gladly share with you, but don't look for anything more."

He frowned. "I spoke too soon. My feelings for you ran away with me. Is there someone else?"

"No." She was adamant, crushing down a sudden thought of Tom. "But surely there is a girl somewhere who loves you?"

"There's nobody." Mentally he dismissed a certain young woman whom his mother was set on having as a daughter-in-law.

"Not through lack of opportunity, I warrant!" Sophie's eyes were full of mirth and mischief, which she hoped would coax him out of those serious moments they had shared.

"That's true," he replied genially enough. "I believe you mentioned friendship, Sophie. We'll keep to that."

To himself he added "for the time being," and thought by the way she looked at him that she might have done the same. Before long they took the path up from the beach, and before parting, they made arrangements to see each other again. After saying good night, Sophie had gone no more than a few yards when she turned and ran back to where he stood. She grabbed a handful of sleeve as if she might shake him into taking full notice of what she had to say.

"Be careful in your hunt for the Broomfield gang!" she implored.

He smiled reassuringly. "I'm always wary, but what made you so concerned for me?"

She was at a loss how to answer him, for she did not know what had stirred the immense feeling of foreboding that had seemed to envelop her in the lane like a cold, invisible mist. Was it that suddenly she had remembered Antoine's mother had had no sister? So it could not have been a son-in-law of the Marquis who called at the farm. Her lapse of memory could only be blamed on the turmoil of meeting Tom again. The revelation, linked to her deepest fears for Antoine's safety, must also have whirled up a terrible concern for Rory.

"I simply felt a need to warn you." She shrugged.

He took her by the arms, looking down into her strained, upturned face, her eyes wide and dark. "I thank you for it. Now let it go from your mind. It's a passing thing, like one of those nightmares. All will be well."

She gave a nod, trying to feel reassured. Then once again she ran down the lane. He watched her until she was out of sight.

SOPHIE HAD CALLED on Harry and his wife several times since the accident in the Old Ship's kitchen. She knew he appreciated her visits and was pleased to discover that his apprentice wished to call on him too. Yet Sophie could not let Harry know how unhappy she was with Josh's work. He had become so thoroughly careless that she'd had to scold him on more than one occasion. Often, when she told him to add a pinch of salt, it seemed that he added a tablespoon or more, causing everything to be thrown away and a fresh start made. Frequently this meant a race against time to get the puddings ready when needed. He always protested that he'd done only what she told him, but he was equally haphazard when adding spices and with the same unfortunate results. Since the responsibility was hers, she was the one who had to face the head chef's displeasure.

Only gradually had it dawned on her that Josh was deliberately sabotaging her work. Exasperated, she had already decided to talk severely to him when he finally played one trick too many by mixing sand into her flour bin. It was lucky for Josh that the head chef was out of the kitchen, for she turned on him and exploded with wrath. He stared at her in half-admiring astonishment at such a fiery display of rage.

"No more!" she stormed. "I've had enough of your stupid pranks! If I hadn't noticed the difference in the texture of the flour, the diners would have been as livid at eating sand in their puddings as I am with you now! I can only suppose you're acting this way to prove your loyalty to Harry, but you're being very foolish, because mine is to him too, whether you understand that or not. Don't ever dare to play such a trick again or I shall box your ears until they're red as beacons! Now throw out that ruined flour and scrub the bin thoroughly."

"Yes, miss." Josh's initial reaction had given way to misery. Shame-faced, he lifted the bin to carry it away.

Sophie was acutely aware of the general amusement at her discomforture. The confectioner and the three underchefs were all loudly expressing their sympathy for Josh's having to work for such a shrew. Suddenly it occurred to her that they might well be at the root of the trouble, either encouraging Josh in his tricks or bullying him into them. When the head chef returned, Josh glanced at her in fear that she would report him. When she simply carried on with her work, his relief was apparent.

During the morning, a local flower seller made her daily visit to the kitchen. With edible flowers used extensively in salads and for gar-nishing, the head chef made his own selection and left Sophie to choose whatever she required for decorating her sweet puddings. She placed the blossoms she had picked in a shallow tray of water kept for that purpose and then decided she would need a few more rosebuds for her Quaking puddings, an old English recipe she had learned from Mrs. Millard, and so-called because it quivered at the slightest movement.

"Wait!" she called after the woman, who was already leaving. But the roses remaining in her basket weren't the right pink, and Sophie returned to the kitchen a few seconds sooner than expected. She was in time to see one of the chefs push Josh out of the way and tilt her table, sending her tray of flowers crashing to the floor and spilling the liquid in her mixing bowl.

"So it was you!" she shrieked furiously. "Not Josh at all!"

The anger Sophie had shown earlier was nothing compared to the tirade she released on the offending underchef. He tried to bluster his way out of it, but Josh, encouraged by being vindicated and seeing he had a strong ally in Sophie, burst out with the truth that all three of the underchefs had been playing tricks on her. The resulting uproar in the kitchen, which included Josh dodging cuffs to his head, brought waiters and waiting maids running to gape. Even the barman from the taproom turned up to see what was amiss. Fortunately Mr. Hicks was out of the building or there was no telling what the result might have been. It was the head chef who finally restored order by sending the onlookers out of the kitchen and then scathingly upbraiding all those under his supervision.

"Now," he breathed dangerously in conclusion, "everybody back to work! Or else—!"

Sophie stooped to gather up what flowers she could salvage while Josh began clearing up the spilled pudding mixture from the floor.

"I'm sorry I wrongly accused you, Josh," she said apologetically.

He gave her a quick smile. "That's all right. I shouldn't have been too scared to tell you what they were doing, but I didn't think, being a foreigner and a female, that you would know how to stand up to them. They said they'd get my apprenticeship terminated if I delayed their getting rid of you."

"Well, we'll just have to present a united front from now on," she declared triumphantly.

"Indeed we will, Miss Sophie."

Sophie did not experience any more direct harassment, although a certain amount of mocking talk continued when the head chef was out of earshot. She ignored it. Although there were times when she clenched her jaw and simmered with anger, never again did she lose her temper.

Almost immediately, Sophie's *oeufs à la neige* had become a favorite among the diners. The secret—as she instructed Josh—was in the dash of rose water she added to the egg whites while whisking. The resulting snowy mounds, floating in a golden sauce, were skillfully set with a bakers' shovel full of red-hot coals, which she held suspended over the dish. The same sort of controlled heat made the caramel bubble and tinge to amber on her *crème brûlée*. As she had always done, she decorated the sweets with fresh flowers, rosebuds and tiny Johnny-jump-ups and pansies, adding to the presentation of a dish just as chive flowers and marigold petals gave color to the chef's salads. Orange nasturtiums set off her *blanc-mange,* which was in such demand by diners that finally the confectioner became incensed,

throwing pans about and shouting that Sophie's *blanc-mange* was causing his fruit molds to go uneaten. It took quite a time for the trouble
to settle down, and then only when Sophie's recipe was withdrawn
from the menu.

"I warned you," the head chef said to her. He would have dismissed her if the rest of her work had not been so good.

"What I made comes more into my sphere than the confectioner's," she answered angrily.

"Agreed," he conceded, "but you are a woman and therefore the
one to give in."

Sophie fumed, but the next day she had her revenge. She created a
steamed pudding, light as gossamer, with a rosy sauce into which she
stirred fresh sweet local strawberries. It became the most popular dish
on the menu, and demand for the confectioner's ices and molds began
to fall off immediately. Later, as strawberries went out of season,
Sophie substituted other fruits with equal success, secretly relishing
her victory in the conflict.

Harry laughed heartily when she told him about it on her next
visit. His mirth pleased both Sophie and his wife, for he was still in
dreadful pain, his hands and arms bound in layers of linen.

"I can't think that the head chef will want me back at the Old Ship
after all you are doing there," he said soberly, anxiety apparent behind
the goodwill in his eyes.

"He will," Sophie countered firmly, "because apart from your being a tip-top pudding chef, I know how he and the other chefs
continue to resent my presence in the kitchen. They wouldn't mind if
I were washing the floor or peeling vegetables, but it's galling to them
that I'm taking a man's place and have the same responsibility.
They're only tolerating me in the certainty of your return. In any case,
I shall leave as soon as you are back because I have other plans ahead
of me. In the meantime, I'm keeping your post for you and benefiting
from the experience."

She could see that Harry was reassured.

Eight

RORY MADE SEVERAL ARRESTS in the neighborhood after discovering contraband hidden in barns and stable lofts, even behind a false wall in one deserted house, but none of those taken into custody could be linked to the two murders. Since the Broomfield gang remained unaware that anyone had witnessed their landing, a secret watch was set up on that section of the beach. Rory kept Sophie informed whenever they were able to meet.

Wherever they went together, whether to a concert or supper at an inn, or even for a walk, Sophie could not rid herself entirely of the uneasy feeling that Tom might intrude on them again. His declared intention to return to Brighton worried her more than she was ready to admit even to herself.

One overcast morning, as Sophie was on her way to work, Rory and his men passed her at full gallop. He hadn't noticed her, and she turned to watch them disappear along the sea road, which had been partially flooded by unseasonably high tides during the night. Later that day she heard that during those same night hours there had been a pitched battle between two rival gangs of smugglers somewhere in the hills, and two wounded men had been left behind. When she next saw Rory he had suffered another setback.

"I'd hoped the two prisoners would turn King's evidence, but both have died of their wounds."

"Do you know if they were members of the Broomfield gang?"

"One lived long enough to tell me it was the Broomfield gang he and his confederates had been fighting. The other man never recovered consciousness. But," he added, "that's the way things go sometimes. My luck will turn sooner or later."

"I hope so," she replied fervently.

They had been strolling along the promenade after Sophie finished work and had paused by the railings. He turned then, looking toward the town while she rested her hands on the top rail and faced the sea. The good weather had returned and the stars were as bright as diamonds. It seemed to Sophie that as many were floating on the sea.

Seeing her serious expression, Rory judged the time and place were right to pass on the information Tom Foxhill had given him.

"Sophie," he said, straightening up as he turned to her, "there's something else I have to speak about and I know it will distress you. Foxhill confided it to me that evening at the Castle Inn and asked me to choose my moment to break the news to you."

"Was all not well at the Millard farm?" she exclaimed anxiously.

"It's not that." Then he told her about the desecration of the Marquis's grave.

She shook her head and twisted her hands together in distress. "Such hatred! Can't even the dead be left in peace by the Revolutionaries? They can't endure anyone escaping their evil net. I knew that the Marquis had no son-in-law but Antoine's father, who is dead!"

Rory put his own hands over hers protectively and stilled them in his grasp. "What are you saying? Was your sister's husband a nobleman?"

She turned her face away, her voice choked. "I've said too much."

"Not enough, I think," he said levelly. "What are you holding back? Surely you can trust me by now."

Swiftly she turned her anguished gaze to his face. "I do! Maybe this is the time for me to tell you everything, Rory. I haven't been entirely truthful with you or with anyone else since I came to England, but it has been for Antoine's sake. He is not my nephew. I had no sister. Even before we reached the French coast Antoine was the new Comte de Juneau." Then she told him the whole story, from the Comtesse's frantic appeal to the discovery of the Marquis in the orangery, and how they had escaped the mob and made their way to the coast. Although she did not go into details about the hardships of the journey, Rory could guess at the difficulties she must have encountered.

"Only Henriette knows Antoine's true identity," Sophie concluded, "and she would never tell. It was she who gave me the timely warning in the boat."

Sophie had introduced Rory to Henriette at the Promenade Grove one evening. She had babbled happily to Sophie, obviously treasuring their friendship, but whether her discretion could be relied upon in all circumstances remained questionable in Rory's mind.

"I remember the Comtesse saying just before we parted that the Comte's own nephew was his most bitter enemy," Sophie went on, drawing her fingers across her brow as if to summon her thoughts more clearly, "but he was so in league with the traitors that he must surely have reached high government office by now, which would keep him occupied in Paris. Perhaps," she gulped, "he has delegated someone to hunt Antoine down!"

Rory put an arm about her, for she was trembling. "I think that's highly unlikely," he said reassuringly. "It was sheer chance that you and Antoine were at the farm in the first place. By traveling with Barnes from Shoreham, you left no trace. Barnes certainly would have covered his tracks. The murder was dealt with locally and the Millards would never have revealed your whereabouts. Nobody could have picked up your trail with the boy. No, it sounded to me right from the start that the Frenchman was an infiltrator whose only intent was to harm this country through spying or sabotage. He must have heard that a French aristocrat was buried in the churchyard and went there just to desecrate the grave. I reported the incident the morning after Foxhill told me about it."

She took heart from Rory's counsel. Perhaps she had let her fears run away with her. "I'm hopeful that you're right," she said, "but I shall continue to be vigilant."

"As is only sensible. I'll walk you home now, Sophie. If it's any consolation, you can consider me Antoine's second protector."

She smiled at him gratefully. "I'm glad I have been able to tell you the truth."

"You can trust me in all ways, Sophie."

"I know that."

Rory saw her right to the gate of the cottage, determined not to leave her in the lane on this occasion. Fortunately, Clara was already in bed and asleep, exhausted after a hot and busy day with the bathing machines. So there was no one to see the kiss Rory gave Sophie before they parted. It was the first kiss they had exchanged.

As ONE WEEK OF SUMMER followed another Sophie continued to meet Rory as often as his duties and her hours of work allowed. Although based in Brighton, the district he had to cover was wide, and sometimes they were able only to exchange a few words at the kitchen door of the Old Ship. It made the time they could spend together all the more valued. Occasionally they were able to have a late supper at one or another of the forty-one taverns in the town. Then they would talk, oblivious to all else around them. It was after one of these suppers that they stood in the Steine among a crowd of people to watch the fireworks display celebrating the Prince's thirty-first birthday. There were festivities within the Marine Pavilion, but the Prince, with Mrs. Fitzherbert and all their guests, streamed out onto the lawn to gaze up at the canopies of rainbow stars cascading down. The crowd cheered him and he waved happy acknowledgment.

"Felicitations, Prinny!" and "Good luck, Prinny!" rose up the general chorus of shouted good wishes. Merrily, Sophie and Rory joined in the roistering chorus as if they too had been born in this town, which owed its prosperity to the Prince's patronage.

Twice when Sophie had worked almost twenty-four hours consecutively, she was given a full day off by the head chef. The first time, Rory rearranged his duties in order to hire a wagonette and drive her, with Antoine and Billy, up onto the Downs to watch a royal review of the troops.

The Prince had designed a new uniform for the Dragoons, of which he was Colonel-in-Chief and a handsome sight himself in tight blue jacket laced with silver, white nankeens, and headdress of black fur with a white plume. There was such splendid marching to a tattoo of drums and swirling of gold-fringed standards that both Billy and Antoine were beside themselves with excitement. After seeing the boys home, Rory and Sophie ended the day by going to the theater.

The next time on the grassy slopes of the Downs Rory took Sophie and the boys to the Brighton races. Again the Prince was present, but this time as one of the crowd, cheering on the horses with the full strength of his lungs, albeit from a section roped off especially for his party. Mrs. Fitzherbert, her flawless complexion shaded by a large hat trimmed with roses as well as by her frilled parasol, watched from his nearby carriage. Sophie, holding Billy's hand, saw how she smiled at Antoine who was seated high on Rory's shoulders. Sophie wished it were possible to present the boy to Mrs. Fitzherbert as the Comte de Juneau, whose parents had once received her.

There was no longer any doubt about the Comte's and Comtesse's fates. Henriette had shown her their names in the London-published French newspaper, listed among the Republic's victims. He was deceased and his wife had been guillotined. The same newspaper had reported the killing of a young French duc in London, the last of his line, whose murderer had written the words *Liberté, Egalité,* and *Fraternité* on a mirror in the victim's blood. Sophie realized that it was now more important than ever to keep Antoine's identity a secret.

Antoine liked to be with Rory. He was an intelligent five-year-old and the loss of his grandfather, even more than his father, had left an empty place in his life. He still threw a tantrum from time to time out of some inner misery that was beyond his own comprehension. He could not endure being teased by other children when he did not phrase his English correctly, and on these occasions he would yell and kick in his frustration. His fights and quarrels with Billy were on a different plane, for the boys were good friends, and Antoine had begun calling Clara "Ma," as Billy did. Sophie would have corrected him, but Clara shook her head.

"Let him be. Neither you nor I can take his mother's place, but the child draws comfort from saying 'Ma' to me."

Sophie thought, as she had done on many previous occasions, how lucky she and Antoine had been to find a home with Clara.

SOPHIE HEARD about the latest wager among the nobility when she was at work. It came from the underchef who most resented her presence in the kitchen.

"Have you heard what's new?" he announced. "Some of those rich nobs with nothing better to do have wagered one another on which female in a trade can run the fastest. There is to be a milliner and a fishwife, a dressmaker, and some others. If they're all Frenchies it'll be a good race, because they can run faster away from trouble than anybody I know."

There were guffaws from the men and sniggers from the apprentices. Sophie's lips tightened as she continued decorating a cream pudding with heads of elderberry dipped in syrup, which gave a delicate, lacy effect. She was well aware that mocking eyes were on her. She never retaliated, for that would have increased the goading, and her silent show of contempt usually made the gibes fall flat. The head chef, although not exactly on her side, took no part in the jesting and exerted his authority when matters threatened to get out of hand. Then for a while she had peace again. At least the experience was standing her in good stead for what she could expect in the kitchens of the Marine Pavilion.

As Sophie turned her attention to her next decorating chore, putting a ring of tiny blue borage blooms on each of a row of puddings tinted with a puree of scented rose petals, she thought about the race and wondered if the prize would be worth the competing. A little extra money would certainly be most welcome. As a woman, her wages were far below those of the men, even though she was doing Harry's full work. When she had paid Clara for her board and lodging, what was left went to necessities. Antoine would need warm clothes for the coming winter and much more in the future.

"What's the prize for this race?" she asked, turning to face the man who had spoken of it.

"The Prince himself has promised twenty guineas to the winner and a new pair of shoes. Why? Were you thinking of entering?"

Twenty guineas! More than she was presently earning in a year! It would meet all winter expenses and leave a nice nest egg for the future. Once she would have spent more on a gown at a Paris dressmaker, but these were different times. She did not hesitate to reply.

"If there's still a place in the race for a cook, I will! As you said, we French are fleet of foot, particularly when it comes to snatching a prize from the English!"

There were derisive shouts, a banging of spoons on cooking pots, and some good-natured laughter. Sophie could tell that no matter what the men felt about working with her, they would cheer for her in the race.

Word of her intention flew through the Old Ship. Within five minutes Mr. Hicks had heard of it and came to the kitchen himself. An entry from his kitchen would bring the name of his hotel to the fore, and whether Sophie won or lost, it could only be to the good as far as he was concerned.

"I haven't applied yet, Mr. Hicks," she said. "I've only just been told about the race."

"Then I'll send a messenger at once with your name and get the details in return."

The messenger returned to report that no cook had yet entered her name, and Sophie was accepted for the race, which would be run through the town the following Sunday afternoon. Everybody wanted to look at the map of the route that had been provided, and Sophie was inundated with advice. She was to have eight fellow runners and it was hoped that a tenth would enroll.

That evening Clara pored over the list of runners. A dipper had entered later the same day, making up the tenth. "That's Amy Wyatt," she said. "Her entry will be taken as a joke, because she's so overweight, but I've seen her run and I tell you she has strong legs."

Sophie walked the route, which started and ended in the Steine, taking in one of the narrow passageways known in Sussex as twittens. She was determined to be fully prepared. The prize was literally a crock of gold to her, and she was desperate to win. Footwear would be a problem. All her shoes had heels, and finally she decided to run barefoot. Late one night she ran the route on her own, becoming alarmed when some drunken fellows began shouting and running after her. But she outstripped them easily and arrived breathless in the Steine.

The windows of the Marine Pavilion were all aglow. As she stopped to lean on the railings and catch her breath, she could see the finely dressed people seated in a salon with peacock-hued walls, their jewels sparkling and fans wafting. Then the Prince came into sight, and standing with his back to the window, he began to sing to the company.

Sophie listened attentively. The Prince's love of music was well known and the ballad he had chosen to sing gave full range to his splendid voice. Then, as he bowed to the applause, it was echoed by several other passersby who had stopped to listen too. Smiling to herself, she set off for home.

The Prince was thoroughly enjoying the evening. Soon he and Maria would lead their guests through to the buffet supper laid out in the next room. He was never happier than when in good company. Lady Jersey had been particularly charming to him, and he glanced at her speculatively once again. He had known her and her husband for many years, but from all he heard the couple went their separate ways. She was a witty, vivacious woman in her forties and a grandmother, but her good looks were unblemished and her mature, full-breasted figure very fine. He had always been attracted to women older than himself, right from his first youthful affair with the actress Mary Robinson. In his wild infatuation he had called himself her Florizel, for she had been playing Perdita in *The Winter's Tale* at the time. The nickname had stayed with him, although none dared use it to his face.

Lady Jersey had seen his look. Oval-faced and large-eyed, she smiled her little catlike smile as she came, in a sweep of peach satin and lace, toward him.

"You sang superbly, sire. I could have listened to you until dawn."

He beamed, always susceptible to flattery. To be liked by men and loved by women suited him well. There was a deeply sensitive streak in him that could not endure being spurned or rejected. "I'm delighted that my singing pleased you. How are you enjoying your sojourn at Brighton?"

"It's very agreeable and I regret that family matters are causing me to leave tomorrow. The season here is more than a match for anything London can offer, invitations to Court excepted."

He was sure she found Court functions as dull as he did himself, even though she was on exceptionally good terms with his mother, but he made no comment. "I must say I never look forward to the summer's end."

"I'm not surprised, when you have such a charming cottage here." Her beringed fingers twinkled as she indicated the sumptuous room.

He laughed merrily. It pleased him to refer to the Marine Pavilion as his cottage, although he doubted that anyone except Maria knew how important it was to him. From the depths of his extravagant emotions he loved his jewel by the sea. "Work will begin on the new extensions as soon as autumn comes."

"I hope I shall be among the first to see the results."

His eyelids dropped sensually as his gaze rested upon her. "You have my word on it, madam."

Maria, seated on a couch in conversation, was like many wives in being able to keep her attention apparently undiverted while making note of her husband's interests in another woman on the far side of a room. How well she knew the signs! The quick laugh, the admiring glance, the light touch on the elbow to guide the woman still farther away. Had she not succumbed herself to the way he had of inclining his head downward to any woman who appealed strongly to him? It was an action both attractive and curiously endearing, and women responded to it like flowers to spring rain.

Maria heard herself chatting easily, but her heart was crying out. Not another *amitié amoureuse!* And not Lady Jersey! The woman was too clever, too devious, and the Prince so easily beguiled!

That night in her house in the Steine, Maria lay awake while her husband, the Prince of Wales, slept solidly beside her. It had been a relief to learn before the evening's end that Lady Jersey was leaving Brighton in the morning. Not that the Prince seemed to have given the woman another thought. On their short carriage drive from the Marine Pavilion he had talked laughingly of the forthcoming race, saying he had already placed a hundred guineas on the milliner, whom he'd been told had a good chance of winning.

"Which one shall you place your money on, Maria?" he had asked.

"I'll wait, George, until I see all the contestants lined up before I place my wager."

"That's my wise darling," he declared approvingly.

Wise? She had thrown wisdom away when she married him, not that she had ever regretted it, in spite of some difficult times. Now turning back the bedclothes restlessly, Maria pulled on a robe and went to sit on the window seat, looking out at the moon-bathed Steine. How different had been wedlock to her two previous husbands, both Roman Catholics like herself, even-tempered, serious, and faithful. Her first marriage in her eighteenth year to a rich, widowed landowner, Edward Weld, came to an end before their first anniversary when he was fatally injured in a fall from a horse. Although he had been much older, she had been happy and content as his wife. After three years of widowhood she married Thomas

Fitzherbert, ten years her senior, a wealthy intellectual who owned great estates, and she had blossomed in the wide social circle to which he'd introduced her. She was with him in a carriage the first time she saw the Prince, who had stared at her as if beholding a vision.

Their first meeting took place in her uncle's box at the opera. She was still in mourning for Thomas, who had died three years before of lung disease, but had been persuaded to attend the performance. The Prince, who had sighted her from the royal box, came to visit in the interval.

"Who the devil is this beautiful girl, Henry?" he demanded of her uncle, whom he knew well. "Present me at once."

It was the start of everything. She was well used to suitors, but nothing had prepared her for the Prince's ardent wooing. She did her utmost to discourage him and avoided him whenever possible, but he could not keep away from her. Mutual friends told her how he wept disconsolately at failing to make her see that he was truly in love at last. Once he actually threw himself down on the floor in despair.

At the peak of his handsomeness, he was hard to deny. His charm, which other women found irresistible, tugged as much at her as it did them, but her will was stronger. Her scruples were unassailable, and her religious faith sustained her. She could not and would not follow the only available path, which was to become his mistress.

Maria turned to look at the man she had shut out of her heart for as long as was humanly possible. When he began to talk of marriage the situation had become even more alarming. She remembered vividly the tempestuous scene that had occurred. As heir to the throne, he was barred from marrying either a commoner or a Roman Catholic, and she was both. To marry secretly, which was what he wanted, would contravene the Royal Marriage Act, and their children would never be acknowledged. But he had shouted that he cared for nothing except her. One of his brothers could produce an heir to succeed him. His duty was only to become king, and what would that life be for him without the only woman he had ever loved, and would love until his life's end. When she still refused, he made an attempt at suicide. It was not a very serious attempt, but at the time she had not realized this. Summoned by his physicians, whom he would not allow to stem

110

his bleeding side wound until he had seen his beloved Maria, she feared from his groans that he was dying and promised she would be his wife. It was when he made a lightning recovery that she saw through his ploy and fled to France, only to be pursued by couriers bearing his love letters.

Yet by then she was unable to deny any longer the love he had awakened in her. Seeing him, as she supposed, on his deathbed had made her realize how much she cared for the emotional, unpredictable prince. At last she agreed to a secret marriage and returned to England only when all the arrangements had been made. The ceremony took place in the drawing room of her London home, performed by a Church of England clergyman who had been released on payment of his debts from a debtors' prison, only to break the law more dangerously by marrying the future King of England to a woman who would never be recognized as his wife.

Maria returned her gaze to the Steine and the Marine Pavilion. She had slept there on a few occasions when the Prince was ill, but never had they shared a bed under its roof. She had steadfastly insisted on maintaining the appearance of their living separate lives. Yet somehow the secret of their marriage had leaked out. Maybe the King and Queen had been the first to hear, but they had never given any sign. As far as they were concerned, the marriage did not exist, but they were always gracious and pleasant to her when she was at Court. In fact she was sure that all the royal family liked her and that they regretted in their own minds the barriers that prevented her being welcomed into the fold.

In bed her husband stirred and raised himself on an elbow. "What is the matter?" he asked sleepily. "Are you not well?"

"I couldn't sleep, George dear."

"Come back to bed."

She obeyed, slipping off her robe and lying down beside him. He put an embracing arm about her even as he slept again. Still she gazed up at the pleated silk canopy. If a crisis was looming again in their married life, she knew from past experience how to deal with it. By never displaying hurt feelings, never showing just how much she cared, she had maintained her dignity at all times, and she knew that her spell over George was not diminished. Had she behaved otherwise, she would have lost the magnetism that had made him chase after her in the beginning and that would bring him back to her again. She had nothing to fear from Lady Jersey or anyone else, no matter what she suffered within herself during his amorous encounters. He had spoken the truth when telling her that he would love her until his life's end.

Nine

ON SUNDAY AFTERNOON Sophie had Rory, Clara, and the boys to cheer her on in the race. Remembering how her petticoats had hampered her movement when she ran from the attack on the château, she decided to wear only a full cotton skirt. None of the other competitors appeared to have discarded their petticoats, and she hoped this would give her a slight advantage. Each woman had to wear or carry something to represent her trade. The fishwife had a fish in her apron pocket, the milliner wore a pretty hat, and the lacemaker a fichu of her own delicate work. Sophie had chosen to carry a wooden spoon, and she saw that the dressmaker had a pincushion dangling from her waist, the tavern waiting maid held an ale mug, the laundry woman a small tub of green soap, and the hairdresser had a comb tucked into her hair. When the glover arrived, her hands in white kid, there was a flurry of new wagers, for she had an energetic look about her and a springy step. People had also decided that Sophie looked a likely winner.

Tremendous cheers, whistles, and laughter welcomed the dipper, who had chosen to appear last. Sophie knew Amy Wyatt and liked her, for she was a jolly woman, but her weight was likely to be her downfall. Yet she was considered the dark horse of the race, for the local people knew how swiftly she could move, and the odds against her decreased as the wagers were made. She waved exuberantly to the spectators and whirled a bathing towel over her head, thoroughly enjoying their enthusiastic reception.

The royal party emerged from the east front of the Marine Pavilion and the competitors lined up quickly. The Prince, always at ease with people, whatever their station in life, came to each in turn, full of smiles and congratulating all on their good spirit in entering the race. He fired the starting pistol himself, and the runners bounded forward to a thunderous roar from the crowd.

The glover was in the lead with the milliner, a spritelike creature, close behind. Sophie, reserving her strength as Rory had advised, let another two get in front of her and was aware of Amy keeping at her side. Spectators lined the route, people having halted their carriages to clap and cheer the women racing by. It was a moderate distance for any man used to sport, but for women who did not normally run any distance it was a taxing test.

They pounded into Castle Square, feet flying. Flag-holders waved them past the west front of the Marine Pavilion to take a twitten into the Steine and the winning post. The lace-maker had already dropped out and the waiting maid had tripped and fallen.

Sophie and Amy began to increase their speed as they approached the twitten. Suddenly it dawned on Sophie that the dipper intended to sprint ahead, and with her bulk she would prevent any other runner overtaking her in the narrow way. The milliner and the fishwife were now neck and neck in the lead.

Then Amy began to shoot forward, but Sophie kept pace. The front-runners were overtaken, and the twitten was now only a few yards away. Summoning up all her strength, Sophie hurled herself forward. She had to enter the twitten in front of Amy or her chances of winning would be lost. The dipper seemed to sense Sophie's purpose. Unexpectedly, she threw out an arm and gave Sophie a great shove that sent her reeling. She collided with the runner behind her and they both fell. The nearby spectators roared their disapproval of the dipper and then cheered as Sophie scrambled up and raced on. But the moment was lost. Amy was ahead in the twitten and there was no getting past her.

Sophie gathered speed, and spurred by anger, she watched for the moment when Amy would turn out of the twitten for the final sprint to victory. When the moment came, Sophie put her head down and dived like a bullet under the dipper's arm and took the lead. A crescendo of cheering rent the air as she passed the winning post and reached the Prince where she came to a halt, swaying and gasping for breath. Amy came a close second, with the rest of the runners struggling behind. The Prince congratulated Sophie.

"Well done, Mademoiselle Delcourt. I've spoken to you before, have I not?" He prided himself on never forgetting a face, especially a pretty one, and this was a most memorable visage.

"Yes, Your Highness. At the Old Ship when I had salts on a tray."

"I remember. You've run a splendid race. Who would have thought that a cook would be the fastest? Allow me to present you with your greatly deserved prize." He handed her a purse. "The new shoes may be chosen at your leisure from the cobbler in Great East Street."

Sophie curtsied. "Thank you, sire."

Mrs. Fitzherbert came forward then, expressing concern. "Your foot is bleeding badly, Mademoiselle Delcourt. It must be seen to without delay. Come with me. I shall have it bathed and bound up at once."

Seeing that the lady intended to take her into the Marine Pavilion, Sophie hung back, for she had glanced down at her foot and seen it was bleeding profusely. "I shall get blood over the carpets, madame."

"So you will." Mrs. Fitzherbert turned to one of the Prince's equerries, who promptly summoned two footmen from the Marine Pavilion. One brought a linen towel to wrap loosely around Sophie's foot, which had begun to throb painfully. Then they made a bandy chair of their arms and carried her by way of a glass door into a smallish room with colorful Dutch flower paintings on the ivory silk walls. She was lowered onto a burgundy-red chair and the housekeeper, who was already waiting, placed a stool covered with towels under her injured foot. A basket with bandages and other necessities was positioned by a maidservant within the woman's reach, and another maid came with a bowl of water, which she held in readiness.

"Is it a bad cut?" Mrs. Fitzherbert asked the housekeeper.

The woman examined the sole of Sophie's foot carefully. "It's quite deep, ma'am. I'd say it was made by a piece of glass, but there is nothing embedded."

"That's good." Mrs. Fitzherbert sat down to watch the proceedings and smiled at Sophie. "Do you remember where you sustained this wound?"

"I've no idea," Sophie answered, trying not to wince as the house-keeper began to clean it. "All I thought about was winning the race."

"Did it mean so much to you?"

Sophie nodded. "I have an orphaned nephew in my charge, and he deserves the best I can do for him."

"Since I can hear you are French, my conclusion is that there is some tragedy behind the little boy's being in this country with you. The Prince and I have been most grieved by the fate of our many friends in France. Some of those friendships went back to my girl-hood, when I was a pupil at a convent school in the Faubourg St. Antoine in Paris. I had such a happy time there."

"I've passed the convent many times, but now that the present National Convention has abolished Christianity in France, I fear it is no more."

Mrs. Fitzherbert sighed sadly. "I'm sure you're right. Where did you live in Paris?"

They talked on, drifting into French. Sophie spoke of her father and all that had happened in Paris, but did not mention Antoine again, and Mrs. Fitzherbert did not ask. Sophie's foot was bound up neatly and then she was ready to leave. The housekeeper and the maidservants went from the room.

"Thank you so much for having my injury treated, madame." Sophie wished more than ever that she could have revealed Antoine's identity to this kind-hearted woman, but the favors that would be bestowed on the boy as a result might be as dangerous as a dagger at his throat. She had become more protective of him than ever since Rory told her about the desecration of the Marquis's grave, but if ever Antoine were in desperate need, she was sure Mrs. Fitzherbert would prove a good friend. "I'm certain my foot will soon heal."

"It will take time. Be sure to rest or else the wound will keep reopening and then it might become inflamed. You shall ride home in my carriage."

Sophie could see through the window that although the crowd had dispersed, Rory was still standing by the railings. There was no sign of the boys and she guessed they had gone home with Clara.

"Thank you so much, but I've a friend waiting for me. That is he by the railings."

Mrs. Fitzherbert followed the direction of Sophie's gaze. Then she summoned a footman, and a few minutes later Rory was being shown into the room. He bowed to Mrs. Fitzherbert and she asked him about the progress of his investigations. He replied optimistically, and Sophie could see he was impressed, not only by the beauty of the Prince's wife but by her warm disposition as well. Then he lifted Sophie up in his arms and carried her out through the main entrance to the waiting carriage.

When Clara saw the elegant equipage arrive at her gate, she hurried outside just as Rory was lifting Sophie from her seat. "When you have taken Sophie inside, Captain Morgan," she said, "you'd better stay for a cup of tea."

Sophie guessed that in spite of Clara's aversion to officialdom in any shape or form, she had taken a liking to Rory at the race.

Before he left, Sophie asked his advice about bankers to whom she might entrust her prize money. He gave her a name and advised her to keep the money in a safe place until she was fit to go into town.

"Remember you'll only do yourself harm if you don't rest your foot," he said.

Clara reassured him. "I'll see to that."

At first Sophie's foot was too painful for her to move about, but by the end of a week she was able to hobble and could endure her idleness no longer. She asked a neighbor, Mr. Pomfret, if he would take her to the beach in his donkey cart. He agreed, asking a fee of a penny a trip, which was reasonable enough. She managed to hop and hobble to his cart at the cottage gate, he lifted her into it, carried her onto the beach by the bathing machines every morning, and carried her up again in the evening.

Seated on an upturned box, Sophie was able to be near Antoine and Billy while they played together and also to help Clara and the other dippers by taking the money from those who came to bathe. Her bandaged foot was protected by a large boot that had belonged to Clara's late husband. The effect was comical and she laughed at the good-humored quips of the dippers and the boys' teasing when she hobbled about.

Sophie was as happy as could be to have this unexpected break from work. She had heard that a retired cook had been called to the Old Ship to take her place temporarily, and so she knew she would not be missed. She loved the sight and sound of the sparkling blue sea, the cry of the sea gulls, the chatter of the dippers, and the fashion parade of the ladies who came to bathe. So many enormous hats trimmed with rainbow gauzes, silken flowers, and masses of ribbons, so many soft, abundantly gathered gowns that swept the beach and sent out little clouds of sand as the ladies mounted the steps of the bathing machines. And what a different picture when those same modish creatures reappeared on the other side to descend into the sea in their shapeless bathing attire. At times their garments floated up around them on the surface of the waves, giving them the appearance of bobbing water lilies.

Clara had lent Sophie an old straw hat, but the sun and the sea air still managed to give a golden tint to her skin. Tom, spotting her one day from the promenade, thought her a beautiful sight. He leapt over the railings, landed with a scattering of shingle, and hurried over.

"Sophie! What are you doing here? Have you left the Old Ship?"

She was astonished to see him suddenly standing before her, but before she could speak there were screams of outraged modesty from the bathers, who crouched down in the water to avoid being seen, and great shouts from the dippers, who descended upon him, some dripping from the sea, like avenging Furies.

"No men allowed here!"

Tom, realizing his error, retreated hastily to a flight of steps and called to Sophie.

"Come up onto the promenade. I want to talk to you!"

Amused, Sophie took pity on him and called Billy to her.

"Go and tell that gentleman, who was here on the beach just now, that I have an injured foot and can't go up there to him. Say that I'll be going home in a donkey cart about six-thirty and he can speak to me then."

Billy did as he was told. Sophie saw Tom give the boy a coin and Billy returned excitedly with sixpence in his hand. "Look what I got and the gent says to forget about the donkey cart. He'll be waiting for you in a hired carriage and will escort you out to supper."

"Will he indeed!" Sophie exclaimed. "He's taking a great deal for granted!" She looked toward the promenade but Tom had already gone.

When Mr. Pomfret arrived and carried Sophie up to his donkey cart, Tom was waiting on the promenade. He greeted her cheerfully and scooped her from the man's arms to seat her in a curricle.

"I'm looking after you now," he said.

"I'll bid you both good evening then," Mr. Pomfret said in the satisfied tones of the well tipped and touched his forelock to Tom.

Sophie sighed with mock exasperation, for he was so transparently happy to have her company that she had to forgive his high-handedness in altering her arrangements. "You haven't even asked me whether I might prefer to go home, Tom!"

"I'll take you there later." His glance fell on her boot. "What in hell's name is that?"

"A fisherman's boot, of course. Surely you've seen one before?"

"Yes, but not on a woman."

She laughed and slipped her bound foot out of it. "There! Is that better?"

"Not much." He sprang up into the seat beside her and took the reins. "I'd prefer to see your toes."

She gave him a sideways glance. The sight of her toes was not for him, nor was any other part of her that was normally hidden. "You know I can't go anywhere for supper like this! My skirt hems are dusty with sand, my hair is windblown, and this hat is only fit for a scarecrow!"

"On you it looks like a milliner's delight."

"Don't tease!" She pulled the hat from her head. "Why are you back in Brighton?"

"I heard from an agent about a property he thought might interest me."

"How did you find me on the beach?"

"I happened to see you on my way to the Old Ship. I'd expected to find you there."

"Have you been to the Millard farm again by any chance?" she asked soberly. "Rory told me what you learned there."

"I thought you might ask me that when I saw you again, so I made a point of calling on my way to Brighton. There's been no repeat of that foul incident, and Mrs. Millard tends the Marquis's grave regularly."

"She promised me that she would." Sophie had been looking down with an unfocused gaze at the hat she was turning slowly by its uneven brim. "It was thoughtful of you to let Rory choose the right time to tell me."

"I was grieved to hear that it had happened in the first place." Then he changed to a more cheerful note. "I've good news from the farm this time. One of the Millard boys is betrothed and his brother —in Mrs. Millard's words—is courting one of the village girls, so perhaps it won't be long before they are suitably married and you're able to visit the farm."

"I hope so." Sophie raised herself and looked around. "Where are we going?"

"To sup alfresco on the Downs."

She laughed, throwing back her head. "Then I'll not be out of place in my present attire."

They talked all the way to the place on the hillside he had chosen for their picnic. When they arrived, Sophie waited in the carriage while Tom spread a rug on the grass and set the picnic basket by it. Then he returned to carry her to the rug and put her down carefully.

"It's lovely here, Tom," Sophie said appreciatively. A grove of trees was at their back and the grassland dipped and rolled before them to the town, which was just visible, spread like a multicolored carpet. And beyond lay the sea, blue-green as antique glass in that final hour before the sinking sun dyed it another hue.

"Your ill luck turned out to be my good fortune," Tom said. "But for your accident, you would have been at work and I'd have been wondering how and where I might spend some time with you before leaving again tomorrow."

"So soon?"

"I'm afraid so. I've business commitments I have to meet." Tom lifted a linen cloth from the picnic basket. "Let's see what the Castle Inn has prepared for us."

It was a superb spread with a bottle of good wine. Sophie was hungry, having had only a snack on the beach at noon. Both she and Tom did justice to the good food. While they ate, they talked of many things. She was particularly interested to know more about the unusual treasures that passed through his hands in the course of his work. He told her about a Japanese cabinet, lacquered scarlet and gold, in which he had found an ancient fan, and how on another occasion he had discovered an exquisite miniature of a woman painted on ivory, the sitter unknown to him until one day he came face-to-face with her in her old age and was able to return it to her possession.

Sophie listened in fascination as he described his two trips to the Orient, transporting her so vividly from the quiet Sussex Downs to those Far Eastern climes that she was almost able to hear the tinkling of strange musical instruments, taste the foods, and inhale the perfume of exotic flowers. By now the sun was setting and the sea had turned to burning gold.

"I've talked too much," he said with an apologetic grin. He was sitting with one knee updrawn, his arms resting across it.

"No! Not at all, Tom," Sophie declared. "I can understand so well why sometimes you keep an item you had intended to sell because of its beauty or its special interest. I would be the same."

"I'm not always so lucky. Once the Prince of Wales noticed a table in my shop that I had no intention of selling, and he decided he would have it. It's an age-old tradition that one must never deny royalty when they wish to purchase, but I was hard put not to refuse."

"Why was it there and not in your home?"

"For display purposes. I hadn't known the Prince was in London at the time." He watched her packing away the remains of the picnic. In spite of the interest she had shown in all he had to say, there was an invisible line she would not allow him to cross. He was enthralled by her. She was in his blood, in his breathing, in his flesh. His voice broke from him. "Sophie—"

"Yes?" She had closed the picnic basket and, alerted by his change of tone, looked up at him and the expression in her large, lash-shadowed amber eyes warned him to be careful. The empathy they had shared was already spiraling away. Immediately he revised the tender words he would have spoken.

"I hope you'll let me escort you again when I'm in Brighton."

"My social arrangements depend so much on my work," she said evasively. Everything from his good-natured spontaneity in arranging the outing to his attractive physical presence had threatened a revival of the feelings she had crushed down after the clash between them at the farm gate. She reminded herself severely that Rory's steadfastness was what mattered to her above all else. The thought of him was stabilizing. "This evening has been enjoyable," she continued, "but I think it would be best if we just exchange news whenever we chance to meet. I'll always be glad of anything you can tell me about the Millards and also how you are progressing." She paused and briefly her gaze softened. "I do wish you well, Tom."

He thought to himself that she might as well have slammed a door in his face. But she had misjudged him badly if she thought she could change whatever had already begun to develop between them.

They rode back into the twinkling lights of Brighton, and at Clara's cottage, Tom lifted Sophie down from the curricle but she would not let him carry her indoors.

"I can manage the path," she said. "Farewell, Tom. Have a safe journey back to London."

He stayed by the gate until she reached the door and went in with a final smile over her shoulder. Then he returned to the Castle Inn.

To his disappointment, he found the next morning that the premises he had come to view were not suitable. This visit to Brighton had been far from successful.

As SOON as Sophie returned to work, she sent a bank draft to Tom, repaying at last the ten guineas she owed him. She also went to the shops to buy a gift for Clara out of her prize money and a toy each for Antoine and Billy. From the cobbler she ordered the other part of her prize. When Rory next took her dancing, she wore her new shoes, which had red heels and shining buckles.

Ten

IT WAS BILLY'S BOASTING that he would be starting school at the summer's end that made Sophie give thought to Antoine's education. There was no way she could afford the kind of school he should attend when the time came. If the Comtesse's jewels had not been stolen, there would have been no problem. Antoine could even have gone on to the university afterward. But it was pointless to consider what might have been.

"Do you suppose there would be any chance of Antoine's being allowed to start at the Free School with Billy in the autumn?" she asked Clara one day. "He knows the alphabet and can read and write a little in English. He's quick to learn, and my time for teaching him is so limited."

"There's no harm in asking," Clara replied. "But he might have a tough time of it from the other children—his being French and talking comical sometimes."

"I know. That's what makes me hesitate. Perhaps in another year he will be more adjusted."

As it turned out, the matter was settled by Antoine himself. "Billy's going to school. I want to go too!"

Carefully Sophie explained that it would not be easy for him either in the lessons or with the other boys, but he stamped his foot in determination.

"I'll hit them back if they hit me! And I will learn!"

Sophie took him with her to the Free School in Duke Street. The teacher, Miss Stanton, was a sensible, intelligent-looking woman and Sophie liked her at once. As they talked, Antoine wandered about the empty schoolroom looking at everything. He lifted the desk lids and then put a finger into an inkwell to see if it was full. It was, and Sophie had to wipe his hand clean.

Miss Stanton prevented further exploration by giving him a book to read aloud. He managed well but haltingly. He also gave correct answers to two of the three simple sums she chalked up on the blackboard.

"So, Antoine," she said, replacing the chalk, "why do you want to come to this school?"

He looked at her solemnly, chastened by not having managed the third sum. "I must know everything for when I go home again one day."

"Home?" she queried.

"To France, madame."

Sophie felt very proud of him. He had obviously taken to heart all she told him about his parents and his grandfather. Not that she ever spoke of their titles or of the chateau as such. Neither did she ever mention the attack by Barnes and his accomplices, and fortunately Antoine's enjoyment of his time with the Millards seemed to have erased that experience for him.

Miss Stanton raised her eyebrows slightly at the child's answer. He was certainly bright and precocious. She expected difficulties, but they could be overcome.

"You may come as a pupil to this school, Antoine," she said, "but the children call me 'Miss' and not 'Madame.' Will you remember that?"

He jumped up and down in excitement at being accepted. "*Oui,* madame! Yes, Miss!"

Miss Stanton assured her that no bullying was allowed at the school, and as the woman was obviously a disciplinarian, Sophie knew Antoine would be in good hands. Since their arrival in Brighton he had run wild every day by the bathing machines like a little suntanned sea urchin, and an orderly routine would be good for him.

SEPTEMBER BROUGHT AN END to the season of the bathing machines. Horses drew the lumbering huts to a field on the outskirts of town, where they were lined up in rows for painting and renovation during the winter. Their departure from the shore coincided with the start of the school year.

Sophie and Clara went with the two boys on their first morning and saw them to the door. Sophie was thankful that the nest egg of her prize money had enabled her to send Antoine off well clad and stoutly shod on this new adventure. He liked best his cap with a shining brim and a tassel hanging from the middle of the soft crown, for it was exactly the same as Billy's and those worn by all the other boys. Miss Stanton came to meet the new pupils.

"I'm here, miss!" Antoine announced, doffing the treasured cap as Sophie had taught him. "Now lessons can begin."

"So they can, Antoine," Miss Stanton replied dryly. She thought that if she had not known he was the nephew of a confectioner's daughter she would have thought his youthful arrogance inbred.

From everywhere in Brighton visitors began leaving, at first in a trickle as the weather remained summery and then in a steadier flow. Coaches laden with baggage rolled off along the London road. The aristocratic émigrés remaining in the district counted themselves fortunate if invited to London by English acquaintances for part of the winter season, or to spend Christmas and New Year's Eve at one of the great country houses.

At the Old Ship, Harry was expected to return any day, although no definite date had been fixed. So it was a surprise to everyone when he appeared one midmorning dressed in his best. Sophie was glad for his sake, even though it meant she would have to return to waiting tables.

"Good to see you, Harry," the others were saying. "Welcome back!"

"I'm not coming back," he announced. There were shouted questions and he held up his hands for silence. "I'm starting work tomorrow. I'm to be head chef at the Castle Inn!"

There was a general chorus of good-humored booing that he should be going to work for the Old Ship's rival, followed by warm congratulations. He came over to Sophie and gave her a wink.

"Now your job is safe here. What's more, your wages will take an upturn when you're on a permanent basis. But if there's ever a vacancy for a confectioner at the Castle Inn, I'll let you know."

Sophie thanked him for his thoughtfulness, but in her own mind she hoped her next move would be to quite another location.

LATER IN THE MONTH Sophie, tears swimming in her eyes, took a narrow scarlet ribbon from her drawer and tied it round her neck, her face grave. She had no mourning clothes, but Clara had lent her a black fichu and cuffs, which she attached to her gown. The previous evening, news had been received that Marie Antoinette had been guillotined. France's loveliest queen was no more.

In the days that followed, it was noticeable how much mourning apparel there was to be seen. There were few, if any, émigrés who had not suffered personal bereavement already, and those who had emerged from black redonned it now. The fact that many English visitors had already departed for the London season made the émigrés' state of mourning all the more apparent.

At the Marine Pavilion, the Prince was deeply shocked by the news and canceled all immediate festivities as a mark of respect for the tragic queen. He was wearing a black velvet coat and breeches as he signed the papers his secretary placed before him. There were also vast bills that he should have settled, many with letters pressing for payment. He glanced through a few of them. Maybe he had not needed those diamond shoe buckles, but they had caught his fancy and the craftsmanship was superb. There was also a bill from Tom Foxhill for an exquisite Chinese clock hung with gilded bells, and more accounts from other agents who had offered him works of art he had found it impossible to resist. The disadvantage of being a collector with a true eye for the magnificent and the exquisite, who reveled in having beautiful objects all around him, was that his income would have to be inexhaustible if debts were not to be incurred. The Prince sighed. Unfortunately that rightful privilege of a munificent income due to a prince of his standing would not be his until he was King.

"I'll settle this bill," he said, sorting it out from the rest of the pile, which he brushed aside. "Take these away."

It was Tom's account that he held in his hand. He liked the antiques dealer and enjoyed his company. Moreover, the amiable fellow outstripped all others in obtaining rare porcelain and other objets d'art from the far-off land of China to satisfy his growing passion for chinoiserie. The Prince smiled to himself. Earlier in the century, some while before he was born, there had been an opening up of trade with China, and the fashion for all things Oriental had swept through Europe, even influencing the furniture made by Chippendale and other English cabinet-makers. Although the mode had waned in popularity over the years, he himself had rediscovered it. How he admired the brilliant use of color, the exquisite workmanship in ivory, gold, and enamel, as well as the painted scenes, both quaint and exotic, on everything from tiny snuff bottles to whole dinner services. The overall richness of chinoiserie appealed to him so much that he was contemplating adding Chinese pagodas to the Marine Pavilion, even though they would add astronomically to the cost of the renovations he had already ordered.

The secretary withdrew, but hardly had the door closed when it opened again and Maria entered, dressed for traveling. As always, the Prince took pleasure in her appearance. The gleam of her golden hair, her lustrous, beautiful eyes, and the luminous quality of her rose and white skin remained untouched by time.

"So you are about to leave, my dear Maria," the Prince said. He rose from his desk to put his arm round her waist. She was like him in having put on much weight since their marriage, but he loved her ample curves and always admired her figure.

"You will try to let nothing delay your coming to our country retreat," she urged.

"You may count on it. Just as soon as I see the scaffolding go up here and the work begin I shall leave."

She was strongly tempted to advise him yet again to curb his excessive expenditure on the Marine Pavilion, but a quarrel was the last thing she wanted at the moment of departure. He did get so inordinately irritable whenever she reminded him of his colossal debts.

"Very well, George dear. I shall look forward to your coming."

"As I will to seeing you again." He embraced her closely and they kissed. Then he escorted her out to her waiting coach.

As Maria was borne away she wished, as she had done many times before, that she could make George see the danger in his continued extravagance. He believed that eventually Parliament would be compelled to settle his debts as it had done previously, but she was certain that some condition would be imposed this time to bring him to heel, and that thought worried her constantly. In the past, George had listened to her wise counsel on many matters. Once she had even brought about a reconciliation between him and the King after a bitter estrangement, which had earned her the Queen's gratitude. Now father and son would soon be at loggerheads again, and nothing would ever change that state of affairs. The King and his heir rarely saw eye to eye on anything, even to favoring rival political parties. Yet Maria had great sympathy for her George, for surely there was no more difficult role for any intelligent prince with energy and strong ideas of his own than to be condemned to wait for the Throne.

LATER THAT DAY, the Prince donned his uniform of the 10th Light Dragoons. The jacket felt decidedly more comfortable since the tailor had let out the seams. When a needle and thread could no longer extend the wearing of this uniform, it would be folded away into storage as was every good garment he discarded, for he was a hoarder as well as a collector, always reluctant to throw anything away.

The Prince stood regarding himself in a full-length mirror as his valet adjusted the silken cords that held his Hussar-like cape across one shoulder. He was aware of the dashing figure he cut as he strode from the room. His horse had been brought to the main door, and with his equerries behind, he rode out of the gates.

Normally, when he strolled the promenade or rode by in his carriage, he received little attention from the local people, who were used to his presence in the town. But when he appeared in some style, such as today, they gave him unabashed cheers. He acknowledged them with a salute and a smile, basking in their goodwill, and pleased to know that he held a special place in the hearts of the Brighton people. It was the same with his soldiers. How glad he would have been to lead them into battle against the French! He would have led every charge! But there again he was thwarted by his obdurate father, who had refused him—as heir to the Throne—permission to serve abroad. A fearsome quarrel had resulted. The Prince frowned at the memory of it now. How different everything would be when he was king!

At the camp of the Dragoons, which the Prince visited whenever he could, he had every comfort. His tent was large enough to be divided into spacious sections, and was hung throughout with chintz printed all over with the three feathers of the Prince of Wales. He dined merrily with his officers in the dining section, drank several of them under the table, and a while later was himself carried senseless to bed.

The following morning he left his horse to the care of an equerry and rode home in a carriage. His head ached abominably and he wished Maria were waiting at the Pavilion to bathe his painful temples with rose water as she had done so many times before. On second thought, perhaps it was as well that she was away. She had become more and more exasperated with his drinking, which meant she would probably have left him to suffer without her administrations. It would not have been the first time.

In his disgruntled mood, the Prince was less than pleased to learn he had a visitor. But when informed it was Lady Jersey, he brightened considerably. She was just the company he needed! A charming woman with a soft voice who would politely ignore the bloodshot state of his eyes and would entertain him with the latest gossip at Court.

"This is a delightful surprise!" he exclaimed in welcome as he entered the circular salon where she awaited him in a huge plumed hat and a gown of russet silk and velvet. "I hadn't expected to see you again until I returned to London. What brings you back to Brighton at the time of the autumn exodus?"

"My concern for your cottage, Your Highness!" she declared, her tone light, her eyes dancing flirtatiously. "Everybody returning to London has some different tale of what you intend to do here, and I had to be sure you weren't going to give it a thatched roof and have a well dug in the middle of the east lawn."

He guffawed, leading her to a sofa and then sitting down beside her. "Have no fear of that! I compare my cottage to an exotic butterfly still waiting to emerge from its chrysalis and spread its wings."

"Splendid!" She clasped her hands together in her enthusiasm. "It's as if you had taken the words from me, sire. I came hoping to persuade you myself to think along those lines. I see the Marine Pavilion as an oyster about to spew forth pearls if you would only prise it open with all the force of the marvelous imagination and taste you have shown at Carlton House."

He slapped his knees as he laughed in delight at her advice. What a treat it was to receive this encouragement to disregard his debts and have a free rein! What a change from the carpings of his father, the reproaches of his mother, the censure of Parliament, and the dire warnings of his wife. Once Maria had been as carefree with money as he, but more recently she had changed, to become increasingly anxious about what she now called his spendthrift ways. In contrast, this full approval was as sparkling as champagne. He would have a bottle opened for the two of them.

"How right you are, madam!" He sprang to his feet, headache forgotten. "Come with me. I'll show you the plans Mr. Holland had drawn up to my specifications. You shall tell me what you think of them."

"Gladly!" With a little throaty laugh she swept to her feet at his side.

As they went from the room together, she cast him a sideways look and, glimpsing his animated expression, was well satisfied with the impact she had made, apparently by being there at just the right time. She hoped that all she had gushed out would prove to be the thin edge of the wedge she intended to thrust between him and Mrs. Fitzherbert. After all, it was at the request of his mother, the Queen, that she had come to Brighton for this very purpose. But she must go carefully. She knew he had been attracted to her for some time, but seduction was not necessarily in her immediate plans. The Prince had an erratic conscience, and Mrs. Fitzherbert always drew him back to her like a magnet. That must not be allowed to happen this time. Although no woman had ever managed to separate them, Lady Jersey was wholly confident in her own particular powers. A careful campaign of hints and lies and persuasion would open the way to tearing asunder the bond between the Prince and his morganatic wife. It was politically essential that he be free of her. Divorce was out of the question, of course, since the marriage was legally invalid in any case. But Lady Jersey knew that plans other than hers were being made in a high circle for his future. She was only laying the foundation. Not that the task would be arduous. The Prince's natural charm and handsome looks would be a temptation to any woman.

In the library, the Prince unfolded and spread out the architect's plans for her inspection. "There! Now you can see for yourself how my cottage will be when this next stage is completed."

She leaned over the drawings and showed knowledgeable interest, which she knew pleased him. Although the Queen had emphasized what a service would be rendered to the nation by the destruction of her son's marriage, Lady Jersey had her own fiercely ambitious reasons for achieving that end. She foresaw herself becoming a formidable power at Court, and the idea was intoxicating. It made her smile radiant as she complimented the Prince on the forthcoming changes to his beloved cottage.

"I've only one small reservation about what is to be done here," she said, indicating a particular section of the plans.

Immediately the Prince was keen to know what that might be, and as she explained, their heads close together, he became intensely aware of her warm flesh beneath the velvet and the rustling silk of her gown and the delightful bouquet of her perfume.

The curved wings designed for the Marine Pavilion were never added. Henry Holland suspected that Lady Jersey had not cared for them, but that would never be known. Neither was any mention of Chinese pagodas ever raised again.

THE TIME that Maria and the Prince spent at their country retreat went by all too quickly for them both. They strolled through the autumn woods, carpets of russet and gold at their feet, dined alone by candlelight, sometimes on pheasant the Prince had shot himself, and took drives in the countryside, even having picnics on balmy days. The only company who ever shared their time was a little boy, fostered by the couple who kept their house for them. The Prince and Maria were very fond of him and took a dedicated interest in his welfare. The only thing that marred the visit for Maria was the way George kept quoting Lady Jersey on what she thought of this and that.

They traveled separately back to London in the old pretense that no longer deceived anybody, but kept up the appearance that Maria had maintained from the start. The Prince had given her a splendid house in Pall Mall near his own Carlton House, but previously she'd had her own home in Park Street. It had been Thomas Fitzherbert's London residence, where he and she had lived during their marriage. He had bequeathed it to her together with a generous income for life.

As the door of the Pall Mall house closed behind her, Maria

paused in the entrance hall. The crystal chandelier, glittering in the wintry sunshine coming through the fanlight, shot myriad sequins all around her. A gilt-framed mirror above a side table held her image as if in a portrait. She looked into her reflected eyes and saw the question lingering there. How long was it going to be before George shook himself free of Lady Jersey?

AT BRIGHTON, it was not only the Marine Pavilion where workmen were busily employed, for many other buildings were in the process of being erected or extended to meet the ever-increasing demand for apartments and individual residences. There were a number of invalids who lived there permanently, but the colder months had brought a new wave of people in poor health, who had taken their doctor's advice to spend the winter in a milder clime. This meant that the Old Ship was as busy as ever, for in addition to the new guests with their attendant nurses, and often mothers and sisters as well, there was a coming and going of merchants and businessmen concerned with the development of the town. The balls at the Old Ship and the Castle Inn continued uninterrupted, as did the many other entertainments attended by those people of substance now residing locally all the year round.

Sophie had supposed that Rory would have more spare time come winter, but that was not the case. Although gales and strong winds buffeted the Channel from time to time, sending huge waves snarling over the shingle and battering the cliffs, there were long, quite balmy periods when smugglers could run their boats inshore with ease. Rory was responsible for the breaking up of a gang that had troubled the coast east of Brighton for a considerable time. The ringleaders were hanged in chains, some side by side with highwaymen who had suffered the same fate, but Rory had little faith that the gruesome sight would act as a deterrent. The war with France had increased the demand for illegal French goods since they were virtually impossible to obtain legally. And the lure of the money involved ensured the continuance of the crime.

To her great surprise, Rory invited Sophie and Antoine to spend Christmas with him at his sister's home. She was both pleased to be asked and disappointed at having to refuse.

"If only I could, Rory! But the head chef would never release me at such a time. I've already made so many plum puddings for Christmas Day that I can smell the spice in my hair even when I've washed it."

"Your hair has the scent of flowers, Sophie," he said softly. He had walked her home to the cottage gate as he had done ever since Clara invited him to tea, although the invitation had never been repeated. He and Sophie had been to the theater, and the powerful drama had held her enthralled.

"Dear Rory," she whispered, touched by his compliment. It was a dark night with a rough wind that sent the triple shoulder capes of his greatcoat flapping and its skirt beat about her as he held her to him.

"There's one way by which you could spend Christmas with me."

"How?" she asked, puzzled.

"By giving in your notice at the Old Ship."

"You know I can't leave there yet."

"You could if we became betrothed. Then you and Antoine could stay on with my mother and my sister Ellen until we were married. Just as soon as it could be arranged. I love you, Sophie!" His voice throbbed. "I want you for my wife!"

Her eyes searched his face. They had become very close, and she loved him in a deep and gentle way, for he was all she admired in a man. She answered him truthfully.

"I'm very fond of you, Rory, but I have to settle my life before I can think of marriage to you or anyone else."

He crushed her closer to him. "Is it Antoine? Have no fear on that score. I'm fond of the boy and he will be as my son."

She wrenched herself from his arms and stepped back a pace to stand with her hands clenched at her sides, her cloak whirling in the gusts sweeping off the sea. "It's killing me to hurt you, Rory, but that would never do. You would want Antoine to think of you as his father, and since he already loves your company it would only be a matter of time before his filial loyalty was entirely centered on you. It would make an Englishman of him, and that can't be! I have to keep him French in his mind and in his heart, always endeavoring to make him realize that his roots are not here, but across the Channel!"

"Do you believe his mother would have put your promise before his happiness?"

"No, but he is happy at the cottage. He has Clara and Billy as well as me."

"He still doesn't have a father. When are you going to tell him the truth?"

"Before Antoine started school, I told him his parents were no longer at the château, but in Heaven. He said at once that they would be with his *grandpère* and that they would be happy to be together again. Children can accept the death of a parent, but never desertion. To a degree, I've taken his mother's place, and I intend to give him the love and care she would have given him until—please God!—he can return home as a man one day."

Rory's face had become strained and angry. "Are you saying I must wait for you until Antoine comes of age?"

She bridled. "No! I'd never ask anyone to wait for me!"

It was rare for him to lose his temper, but he could feel the anger rising in his chest. "Anyone? Is that all I am to you?"

"Don't misconstrue my words! Why can't I make you see that the promise I made to take Antoine home again governs my life for more reasons than one. The whole future of France lies in his hands and those of children like him. Not to reestablish the old regime, but to preserve what was good and mold it with true justice and freedom and liberty, to give back honor to my poor bloodstained country again." She covered her eyes with a trembling hand, fighting back tears. "Nothing will make me forget that responsibility."

All his anger went from him. "Then let me share it."

"Oh, Rory!" She shook her head at his persistence. "Haven't you listened to anything I've said?"

"Every word. But I remain unconvinced by your argument, even though I understand why you've made such a stand over the boy."

She gazed imploringly at him. "Then please show that understanding by letting the subject rest between us."

He said nothing, not wanting to distress her further, but she knew his mind, as well as his love for her, remained unchanged.

It was impossible for Sophie not to consider how she might have reacted if it had been Tom who proposed to her. She decided that she would have been surprised, even pleased, but most of all triumphant that she had gained the upper hand, for she would most certainly have refused him.

SOPHIE AND RORY exchanged Christmas gifts before he left. He gave her a fan and she had found a book written by a traveler in India, which pleased him immensely. She missed him over the Christmastide, although she had a merry time with Clara and the boys after working hours. As Christmas Day had not fallen on a Sunday, the shops opened and trade continued as usual, but children sang carols in the streets and the church bells rang. Sophie was among the working folk who snatched what time they could find for brief moments of worship at the back of St. Nicholas's Church, where only people of leisure could attend the full services.

Rory returned to Brighton two days after Christmas, but had orders to leave with his men for Dorset, where three revenue men had been killed and five injured in a pitched battle with smugglers. These sea criminals were becoming more desperate, for with the British Navy blocking French ports, their sloops were being challenged, and although fast, they did not always get away. Many were now using small fishing boats to avoid notice at sea, and their contraband was becoming all the more valuable when it landed safely. Rory had been expecting another posting, since he and his men had already captured many of the local ringleaders. The Broomfield gang had eluded him by moving on to operate elsewhere, but he was determined to bring them to justice.

"At least we can see the New Year in together," Rory said after telling Sophie about his posting.

Although she had known he would probably be leaving Brighton at an early date, the news still came as a blow.

There was to be a ball at the Old Ship, as there would be at the Castle Inn where Rory wished to take her again. Sophie had little hope of the head chef granting her request for a free evening, but he hesitated and then nodded.

"You worked very hard over Christmastide. You may leave after the three o'clock dinner."

On New Year's Eve, once more in a gown borrowed through Henriette's kindness, Sophie danced every dance with Rory, and this time there was no Tom Foxhill to interrupt their time together. The year 1794 was an hour old when Rory set her on his horse, swung himself up behind her, and took her home.

"Please don't run any risks in Dorset," she urged when they made their farewells by the cottage gate.

He surveyed her teasingly, wanting to reassure her. "You worry too much about me."

"How can I not? You're the kindest, dearest man I've ever known."

It was not quite the kind of answer he would have wished from her. He would have preferred her to cry out that she loved him too much to be able to live without him, but Sophie always spoke from the heart and would never say anything she did not mean.

"I shall write to you regularly," he promised.

"As I will to you." Abruptly she buried her face in his shoulder, anguish tearing through her voice. "Is there to be no end to partings in my life?"

He stroked her hair and then put his fingertips under her chin, tilting her face upward. "You must have realized that sooner or later I'd be moved on."

"Yes, of course. I was prepared."

"Then why should you be so distressed now?"

"Because once again you're riding into danger. Because I don't know when I'll see you again."

"I'll always come back to you." His voice thickened with desire as he caressed her. "Nothing shall keep me from you until my dying day!"

She jerked back at his words, her eyes wide with fright, her pupils dilated. "Don't speak of death!"

"Sophie, my love!" His mouth found hers and he kissed her with a greater depth of passion than ever before. He believed she loved him more than she knew and he was filled with hope for the future.

When finally he rode off, Sophie stayed in the hall and listened until the hoofbeats faded from her hearing.

SOPHIE WAS SUBDUED in spirit for the next few days, and in no mood for tittle-tattle from Polly, who was quick to repeat any salacious gossip she overheard at the tables. Sophie frowned when the waiting maid came to nudge her sharply with her elbow.

"Want to hear the latest?"

"No, Polly."

"You will when you know what it is! There's trouble between Prinny and Mrs. Fitz!"

"That can't be. You're mistaken." Sophie moved away impatiently.

Polly followed her. "Well, according to what I've heard with my own ears only a few minutes ago at two different tables, he's seeing far too much of Lady Jersey and not enough of his wife!"

"I don't believe it," Sophie said crossly.

Polly smirked. "That's up to you. We'll know the truth all right when we see which lady comes to Brighton for the summer."

The Prince made two flying visits during the months of February and March to see how the alterations to the Marine Pavilion were progressing. Each time he came on his own, but the rumors persisted.

At the cottage Clara continued to receive her lover at irregular intervals. Sophie was tempted sometimes to say that there was no need for such caution as far as she was concerned, but she did not wish to embarrass Clara, who obviously thought her secret was safe.

Eleven

IT WAS DURING one of the Prince's fleeting visits that Tom traveled to Brighton. Although the appointment he had to keep was at the Marine Pavilion, his most important aim was to arrange a meeting with Sophie. Remembering her evasive attitude the last time they were together, he decided to issue an invitation she would be unable to refuse. After booking in at the Castle Inn, he sat down at the table in his room and wrote her a note, which he sealed and dispatched with a messenger.

Sophie was extremely busy in the kitchen of the Old Ship when the note was delivered to her. She had never seen the handwriting before, and she broke the seal almost impatiently. Her frown lifted as she read it through.

"Tell Mr. Foxhill," she said to the waiting messenger, "that I accept his invitation and will meet him tomorrow at the place and hour arranged."

Throughout the rest of the day her thoughts turned constantly to what she had agreed to do for Tom at the Marine Pavilion. Getting the two hours off work would present no problem, because Josh was more than able to carry on in her absence. She wished she had a new cloak to wear on such an important occasion, but that was an expense she could not justify.

At midmorning the next day Sophie left the kitchen and changed into her best gown, made of soft crimson wool, which she had brought with her to work. Then she stood before the mirror and lowered Clara's new Sunday hat onto her head. It was pale gray with a sprightly little plume and suited her well. Clara had also lent her a pair of kid gloves, saying that nobody should call on royalty in knitted mittens such as Sophie usually wore in cold weather.

"It's Tom's day, not mine," Sophie had said. "I don't know if I shall see the Prince, but I owe it to Tom to look my best if we should be received together."

The air was crisp and cold as Sophie set off for the Marine Pavilion, and the lowering clouds seemed almost to touch the sullen, olive-hued sea. She sighted Tom before he saw her. He was waiting by the main gates, tall and lean, one gloved hand resting on his silver-topped cane. Even in repose, he seemed to exude vibrant energy, reminding her of a sleek jungle tiger. She felt her pulse begin to race at the prospect of the turbulent atmosphere they seemed to create when in each other's company. Ah! He had seen her. As she expected, he greeted her appreciatively.

"It was good of you to come at such short notice, Sophie. I returned from abroad only yesterday and had no means of making my request sooner."

"That's of no consequence." She glanced about as if suddenly suspicious that she had been cajoled into coming on false pretenses. "I had expected to find a porter here carrying the Sèvres wares you mentioned in your message."

"They were delivered about ten minutes ago and are awaiting us."

"Why are you so sure I can be of help in identifying them?"

"When this pair of special vases came into my possession I remembered that at the Castle Ball you spoke of the number of times you went to Versailles with your father. Since I was told the vases came from there, I hoped at once that you would be able to authenticate them for the Prince and for me."

"But I may not be able to do that! I wasn't everywhere in that vast palace!"

"These are said to come from a particular apartment. When you see them you have only to say yea or nay. I assure you that these vases once seen could never be forgotten."

"But why couldn't I have inspected them before they were brought here?" Sophie persisted.

He raised a quizzical eyebrow at her. "If you had any idea how carefully such items have to be boxed you wouldn't ask that question." He swung open one of the ornamental double gates and stood waiting for her.

She hesitated, knowing that in England not even a doctor entered a great house by the main entrance. "Aren't you making a mistake?"

"No," he said, amused. "I'm privileged in this respect. Allow me to offer you my arm."

She tucked her kid-gloved hand in the crook of his elbow. "Suppose my entrance by this grand route is not acceptable?"

"It will be," he said confidently and began leading her up the drive.

"In what capacity?"

"Porcelain adviser to His Highness."

A little laugh escaped her at his audacity. "That's still in the sphere of trade."

"Yes, and thank Heaven for it. I could never lead an idle life and neither could you, I'm sure. We're well matched, wouldn't you say?"

She was saved from answering by the main door being swept open, the footman on duty having seen their approach. Tom led her through the portico and into the entrance hall. It was as warm as she had been led to expect and she was glad that her cloak was taken from her. Tom was well known to the Prince's staff and another footman came forward to lead the way into a magnificent corridor, almost as wide as a ballroom, that was in itself a grand reception area.

As Sophie was shown into a side room ahead of Tom, she saw that a Persian rug had been spread over a table to protect its surface and the box of Sèvres wares placed upon it. Tom took a key from his pocket, turned the lock, and raised the lid. Carefully he removed some of the packing.

"So far so good," he breathed. "This pair of vases has had a hazardous journey, but there appears to be no noticeable damage as yet."

"No broken pieces, do you mean?" Sophie asked, finding herself as anxious as he that all should be well. It had been the chance to see something familiar from France and perhaps even to handle these special vases that had prompted her to accept Tom's invitation.

"That's right." Tom continued the unpacking, his expression concentrated. "Now we must hope there's no cracking either."

Sophie held her breath as, with extreme care, he lifted out the first vase and stood it on the table, still wrapped in sapphire silk. Then he took out the second one, also still in its silk. The vases were about fourteen inches high as far as Sophie could judge. Tom gave her one to cradle in her arms and he picked up the other. The footman, who had stayed to clear away the packing, opened a door for them into a large salon and then closed it again, leaving them on their own.

It was a sumptuous room hung in sea-green damask. Gilt, surely the most ostentatious and dazzling of ornamentation, shone like trapped sunshine from all sides. It blazed from the griffin firedogs, the arms and legs of stools, tables, and chairs, the ornate candelabra and the handsome pedestal clock that Sophie knew could only have come from France. There was also a drop-leaf secretaire that had the appearance of being molded in gold and inlaid with ebony. Even the pier table on which Tom had placed the wrapped vases had a frieze of acanthus leaves as delicate as gold lace.

"I'd like you to unveil the vases if you would, Sophie," he said very softly, barely breathing the words.

If he had asked her to undress, there couldn't have been a more intimate note in his voice. She flushed in spite of herself, all her nerves atingle, as once again the very air seemed to pulse between them. Yet she had to take what he had said at face value. Maybe her own heightened senses had made her suppose more than he intended.

"I hope these vases are not lost among the magnificent furnishings of this room," she said evenly as she went toward the pier table.

His expression was confident. "No fear of that. You'll see."

Then he drew back a few steps, as if to give her more room. Silently he watched her reflection in the tall pier glass above the table. He wanted to see her expression when she first looked upon the vases, and he was as aware as she that there was something sensual in the way the soft silk drifted about her fingers as she unwrapped the first one. Her face, framed by her hair and the brim of her hat, was flushed but composed.

Just as the silk was about to fall away from the first vase, Sophie looked up and met Tom's eyes in the mirror. It was an electrifying moment, his desire for her was so stark in his gaze that she recoiled involuntarily. With her heart crashing against her ribs, she acknowledged the full strength of his feeling and knew how easily she could be drawn by his magnetism to forget the promises she had made to herself.

Swiftly she looked down again at the vase of Sèvres porcelain that had now been revealed, letting the sight of it sweep her back to the task she had to do. She caught her breath. It was exquisite, gracefully egg-shaped and girdled in laurel leaves of chased bronze and gilt that made it perfect for its present setting. It had an inward-curving neck covered with dots of turquoise and gold and a wide, trumpetlike mouth. On its white ground was an exquisitely painted Chinese scene with figures, foliage, and flowers. Gently she turned the vase around by its scrolled handles to look at the group of exotic birds on its opposite side. Then slowly she turned it back again. As she unwrapped the silk from its mate, she kept a firm hold on the feelings that had overtaken her before.

"Well?" Tom said quietly.

Sophie turned to face him. "Yes," she said with a catch in her voice. "I have seen the vases before."

"At Versailles? Whereabouts? Tell me if you can remember. It's important that I know, and it's not for the money involved. The Republic is selling off many such cultural treasures to raise war funds, and world markets are being flooded with them. Naturally the value goes up on anything known to have been the personal property of the late King of France, but it's the aesthetic aspect that I care about. Since I was almost sure this was the case with the vases, I wanted them to be in the hands of a true collector, who would revere and appreciate them properly. You've made that possible." Tom flung his arms wide. "I could have sold them anywhere, but I brought them here."

A deep voice spoke from the doorway. "I'm relieved that you did, Tom."

They spun around and saw that the Prince had entered the room without either of them noticing. Immediately Tom bowed and Sophie dipped into a curtsy. The Prince strolled across to them, his greeting cordial. There was speculative interest in his eyes as he looked from one to the other of the handsome couple whose discourse he had interrupted.

Tom stepped forward. "Pray allow me to present Mademoiselle Delcourt to Your Highness," he said. Again, Sophie curtsied and the Prince himself raised her up.

"We meet again, mademoiselle." Democratic in his ideals, he did not consider it in the least odd that a cook should appear with Tom Foxhill under his roof. "Are you still at the Old Ship?"

"Yes, sire."

"But today you're here because you know more than Tom about what he has to show me. Is that right?"

"I know something about these vases," she said reservedly. Then she moved away from the table, realizing she had been blocking his view of the Sèvres masterpieces.

The Prince was without guile in many ways, his emotions too near the surface. Any unscrupulous dealer could easily have taken advantage of his immediate and enthusiastic reaction to the vases, but Tom had already set a price in his mind. Not that it would be mentioned. The responsibility remained with an equerry to quibble about the cost on the Prince's behalf should the figure be considered exorbitant.

"These vases are superb, Tom!" the Prince exclaimed, picking one of them up. "Asselin was the artist of this chinoiserie scene if I'm not mistaken."

"That's correct, sire," Tom said. "Fallor painted the birds on the back while the painted ground decoration is Taillandier's work."

"The Sèvres factory had so many fine artists," the Prince remarked with a sigh. "I wonder where they are now."

"One can only hope they have survived to carry on with their fine work."

"Yes indeed." The Prince continued to study the vase that he held.

"Mademoiselle Delcourt has confirmed that they came from Versailles. I was told they were displayed in the Hall of Mirrors."

Sophie intervened swiftly. "They were never there!"

Both men turned to look at her. Tom spoke first. "Was I misinformed?"

"Very much so."

The Prince carefully replaced the vase on the side table and turned again to Sophie. "Would you be prepared to tell us where the vases stood, mademoiselle?"

"Yes, sire. I first saw those vases when I was a child."

"Bless me! How was that?"

"Queen Marie Antoinette was very fond of children, and when she saw me one day with my father she spoke to me." Quietly Sophie explained the purpose of their visits to Versailles. "I was only eight at the time, but she said that in future whenever I was at the château I should bring her a casket of her favorite bonbons. After that she received me many times."

"So you are saying that these vases are hers without any shadow of doubt?"

"Yes, sire. They stood on the red marble mantel of the fireplace in the Gilded Cabinet of her own apartment. That is what makes them unique."

"Then, mademoiselle," the Prince said with feeling, "these vases shall have pride of place whether I have them here or in London. I've been told that no soldier met his death more courageously than the late Queen of France at the guillotine."

Tom could tell by Sophie's expression that the Prince had won her over completely. The future King of England was capable of enormous kindness and generosity toward others, even moved to tears on occasion by the plight of the unfortunate; but he could be equally ruthless and selfish and stubborn if the mood took him, which made life difficult for those around him. Tom had seen both sides of the Prince's character, but continued to like him immensely. He was glad Sophie had been treated with such consideration.

Then, their business concluded, the Prince drew Tom into talk of horse racing, about which both of them were knowledgeable enthusiasts. Sophie listened quietly, soon gathering that Tom's friendly acquaintanceship with the Prince had its roots in the rakish outer circle of pugilism and racetracks and gambling, which still held the heir to the Throne in thrall.

Tom was in high spirits when he and Sophie left the Marine Pavilion. He had made a good sale, found the right home for his two precious vases, and the Prince had given him an excellent tip for a horse in the next Newmarket races.

"Where did you get those vases in the first place?" Sophie asked.

"From a French source. Many émigrés come claiming that what they have to sell is from Fontainebleau or Versailles or one of the other French palaces, but the exceptional beauty of those vases made me believe that they had actually graced the Hall of Mirrors." He gestured carelessly. "In reality, I got the feeling that there was something unique about them. That sort of thing does happen in my trade. But that they should have been the Queen's personal property had never occurred to me."

Sophie glanced at him as they walked along. "Of course by rights the vases should now belong to the new uncrowned King of France, even though he—the poor orphaned child—has been left in that terrible prison without anyone to comfort him."

"Knowing the Prince of Wales as I do, I'm certain he would return the vases as a gift if ever the young boy is set free."

"If," she echoed with deep sadness. "I fear for his life too."

Tom was of the same opinion, having reasons of his own, which he did not want to discuss. "I appreciate what you did for me today."

She paused for a moment. "I suppose many such treasures of France pass through your hands."

"More than you would suppose."

She sighed. "Each one a dire loss for my country's heritage."

"I fear it is. When I'm able to open a shop here in Brighton, at least you'll be able to see some of them."

"Have you found premises yet?"

"No. When I do you'll be the first to visit."

At the Old Ship he thanked her again, and she recalled a snippet of information about the vases that she had not remembered before.

"I heard once it was the Queen herself who ordered those vases from the Sèvres factory."

He was pleased. "I shall tell the Prince the next time I see him."

"At Newmarket?" she queried with a smile.

"That's right." He grinned at her. "I'll place a wager on your behalf."

"Why should you do that?"

His greenish eyes roved warmly over her face before he answered her. "The Prince told me there is a horse running called Good Fortune. It's what you and I are both seeking. Farewell, Sophie. May it not be long before we meet again."

When Sophie was back in the kitchen and had given an approving nod to the work Josh had done in her absence, she wondered if she would visit Tom's shop when the time came. The display of his stock would be a sight to see, yet could she risk even the slightest further involvement with this man? The deep look she had surprised in the mirror revealed all she had feared since meeting him. But he could not know how desperately she wished to avoid the kind of emotional involvement he held for her.

How different were the warm and tender feelings Rory could arouse in her without any dangerous upsetting of her equilibrium! It was odd to think that it was Rory with his perilous work who represented stability to her, whereas Tom, who had a conventional role in life as a dealer in fine wares, personified total disruption.

That evening, to soothe her jangled nerves, Sophie reread the letters she had received from Rory. He wrote little about his work, but all he told her was full of interest. Each time he closed with reference to his unchanging love and his hopes for their future together.

When she had put the letters away again in a drawer, she thought how well she understood him. He was thirty years old and weary of having no place of his own. What he wanted was a wife and family as a haven from his dangerous and demanding job. But how could she fulfill his dream when there was a driving need in her to reach the peak of her profession, to recreate and reestablish the Delcourt confectionery as a blazing memorial to her beloved father and a retaliation against the regime that had destroyed so many innocent lives.

Would Rory ever wish to share her strong, unswerving purpose? Somehow she doubted it. He had once said that she should have a confectionery shop of her own, but perhaps he had pictured her in a pretty apron serving candy out of jars to local people in a quiet village, ready to let an assistant take over whenever he came home.

Her gaze softened. Dear Rory. She doubted he would be willing to allow her the time and freedom she most certainly required. Although he was the most understanding of men, she didn't think he could ever understand those needs.

Twelve

IT WAS ANTOINE who discovered the metal object in the cottage garden when searching for a ball that Billy had thrown to him. Sophie, coming from the washhouse with clean laundry, found them examining it.

"What's this, Sophie?" Billy asked, showing it to her.

With her free hand Sophie took it from him and saw at once that it was a strange kind of lantern with a long spout through which the light would be revealed. Then it dawned on her what it must be.

"Where did you find this?"

"I didn't. It was Antoine. In the bushes by the steps down to the cellar."

"It's a lantern. Put it back there, Billy. Perhaps your mother uses it when she fetches potatoes or her preserves from the cellar."

The boy did as she asked and then he and Antoine went back to their game. In her room, Sophie folded away the clean clothes while considering Antoine's discovery. She knew from what Rory had told her that it was a smuggler's lantern. The long spout directed a beam of light to either ship or shore with no telltale surrounding glow. It was just such a light she had seen that night on the beach. But why did Clara have one? Could the widow's lover be one of the Gentlemen? Clearly the lantern had been forgotten or else it would never have been left about.

When Sophie looked again, the lantern was gone. Many things

began to fall into place. There were the many luxuries Clara seemed to have, such as the golden earrings and kid gloves she had lent Sophie, her fear of gossip, her aversion to Keepers of the Law, and her always wanting to see that Sophie came safely home. Perhaps she simply wanted to be sure her lodger came home by the land and saw nothing that might be happening on the beach. Sophie felt herself to be in an invidious position, bound by her promise to the widow and yet duty-bound to help Rory. She decided to speak to Clara as soon as the proper moment presented itself.

It came one evening after a wet day when Clara sat by the kitchen table darning one of Billy's socks. Sophie, after hanging up her damp cloak, sat down opposite the widow at the table.

"Let's have a nice cup of tea," Clara suggested.

"I'll make it in a minute, but first I want to ask you something." Sophie was afraid that if she didn't speak at once she would lose her nerve. "Are you involved with the Gentlemen?"

A flicker of surprise showed in the woman's eyes, but her amiable expression did not change. "What sort of question is that? There's been no sun today or else I'd have said it had addled your reasoning."

"I want an honest answer. Do you rent your boat to a smuggler? Is that the true source of your income?"

Clara put down her darning, but still she bluffed. "Fish fetch a good price and the fisherman who has my boat allows me a percentage on each catch. It's not much, but it makes a difference to the way Billy and I live."

"Particularly when the catch includes contraband!"

Clara had turned quite white and there was fear in her eyes. "I don't know what has given you these mad ideas."

"Antoine found a smuggler's lantern in the bushes by the cellar door."

Clara managed a derisive little laugh. "So that's what this is all about! Yes, I have one. Billy found it on the beach one day. I use it sometimes in the cellar."

Sophie thumped a fist on the table. "Stop lying to me. Billy had never seen it before. You use it from a window to summon your smuggler into shore. Is he one of the Broomfield gang?"

Terror swept over Clara's face and she sprang to her feet, causing her chair to fall back with a clatter. "No! I swear it! As God is my witness I'm telling the truth!"

Sophie had also risen. "But you are working with a gang!"

"Only with my partner. He just brings me a box of tea now and again."

"So he is a fisherman by trade. I always thought it surprising that there was so much expensive tea in this cottage!"

Clara wrung her hands agitatedly and her voice rose in panic. "What are you going to do? Denounce me to the revenue men? Do you know what would happen then? It's hanging for smugglers and prison for receivers. Would you see little Billy left alone in the world with nobody to care for him?"

"Calm yourself, Clara. We don't want to wake the children." Sophie righted the widow's chair. "First I'll make that pot of tea. Then we'll talk, and afterward I'll tell you what I intend to do."

There was boiling water on the range. Sophie made the tea and set cups and saucers on the table. Deliberately she had chosen china of Chelsea porcelain that was another luxury not normally to be found in a fisherman's cottage. Clara was seated again, subdued and dejected, all her natural ebullience gone. Sophie did not speak until she had resumed her seat and poured the tea.

"I've no wish to pry into your private life," she said, setting a cup in front of Clara, "but is your partner also the man who sometimes visits you at night?"

"So you know of that too, do you?" Clara said bitterly. "Yes, he is. How did you find out about that?"

"I sleep more lightly than you've realized. I heard you arguing the first night I was here."

"He didn't want me to rent you a room. He was afraid that something of this kind would happen, but I liked the idea of having company and thought it would be good for Billy to have another child around."

"I'm surprised you haven't married again."

"I'd have married this man if it were possible, but it's not what you're probably thinking."

"That he is married already?"

"He is single right enough, but he's a Frenchie like you. He won't leave France and I won't leave here." Clara saw how astounded Sophie was, and in spite of her misery she smiled wryly. "You never thought of that, did you? It was another reason why I decided to have you in my house, you and the boy having the same nationality as Pierre."

"How did you meet?"

"On a smuggling mission with Jim. I told you when we first met that I went out in the boat with my husband before the children came along. He and Pierre, both fishermen operating their normal business on opposite sides of the Channel, cooperated in smuggling as their fathers did before them. I don't suppose you ever thought of hereditary camaraderie in smuggling, but that's how it is with the Renfrew and Froment families."

"So it is Pierre who has your late husband's boat?"

Clara nodded. "It was larger and better than his, and so we made the agreement I've told you about. There are certain dates and tides when I can expect him. At first it was to bring me my percentage, but he'd always fancied me and I was lonely." Clara took a sip of tea. "I loved my Jim, but he never looked at me as Pierre does. Maybe I shouldn't say this to you, seeing that you're not a married woman, but it was never the same in bed with Jim as it is with Pierre." She set down her cup. "So now, tell me your verdict. Do you intend to have me arrested and a trap set for Pierre?"

Sophie gave her a long direct look. "One answer from you first. Is Pierre Froment an enemy of England?"

"If you mean does he support the new Republic, I can tell you that he does, but only because he knows on which side his bread is buttered. Living in Dieppe, he never saw the late King or troubled himself about politics. With fishing and smuggling neither he nor his kin ever went hungry, and they just wanted to get on with their lives. It's still that way. All that worries him about the war is whether British ships will eventually interfere with his smuggling. But I tell you this," she added, wagging a fierce finger, "if I thought him a spy, which you are supposing, and much as I love the fellow, I'd have given him away to the authorities myself! Remember that my elder boy, Daniel, is in the army and no spy's work is going to harm him if I can help it!"

"Then I'll accept your judgment of Pierre Froment, but before I give you my decision, what would you say if I told you that I believe I've seen the Broomfield gang in operation?"

Clara gasped in horror and clapped her hands over her ears. "I don't want to hear! You're not to say another word about those devils! Nobody wants to know about them!"

Sophie gripped Clara's wrists and pulled down her hands. "I do! In exchange for keeping my mouth shut about you and your Frenchman, I want him to tell me anything he can about that murderous gang!"

"But he has nothing to do with them!"

"Since he and they are in the same business, he must hear about them from time to time." Sophie's voice became threatening. "That's my ultimatum! Take it or leave it!"

Clara looked shattered. "You don't know what you're asking. You'd be getting into dangerous waters yourself."

"I'm prepared to take the risk."

Clara heaved a deep sigh. "Very well. Pierre will do what you ask for my sake."

Sophie gave a nod of satisfaction. "I realize that after this evening you will want me to move out of the cottage as soon as possible, but I have to stay until I have the information I'm seeking."

"But I don't want you to go!" Clara exclaimed at once. "What difference does it make that you've found me out? In a way it's a relief. When you kept on about the rumbling you heard I was sure you'd soon start investigating the cellar."

"So it was Pierre moving contraband? But tea comes in boxes. It would only be the rolling of kegs that I heard. Am I right?"

"He does bring me a drop of brandy from time to time."

"A drop! Clara, you're incorrigible!" In spite of herself Sophie burst out laughing. "Judging by the rumbles I heard, there must be quite a stockpile down there!"

A smile crept across Clara's lips. "All right, if you must know, I do sell a keg or two now and again to some of the taverns in the town."

"But how is it distributed?"

"I've a couple of runners who collect and deliver at certain times, but that's all you need to know." Clara left the table to unlock a cupboard and take out a crystal decanter of brandy and two goblets Sophie had not seen before. "I think you could do with a taste of this to help you recover after all you've learned this evening." When they each had a goblet in hand, Clara proposed a toast. "To friendship!"

The superb brandy ran golden over Sophie's tongue. "Do you supply the Old Ship?" she asked.

Smiling, Clara tapped a finger against the side of her nose. "I don't talk about my customers." She tipped more brandy into Sophie's goblet. "This will make you sleep well. I would have had many a wakeful night myself if I'd suspected you were hearing more than you should have done!"

The evening, which had started in high tension, took on a relaxed and quite merry tone. When there came a sudden knocking on the cottage door both women started.

"Who on earth is that?" Clara exclaimed, glancing at the clock. It was after eleven and late for any visitor. "Quick, Sophie! Put the brandy and the glasses away while I go to the door. There's no telling who it might be at this late hour!"

Swiftly Sophie did as she had been asked while Clara went into the hallway. At first she opened the door only a crack. As she was to say afterward to Sophie, her heart seemed to stop when she saw the uniform of the caller in the second before she recognized the tall, smiling man on her doorstep. Then she swung the door wide.

"Captain Morgan! What a surprise!"

"My apologies, madam, for calling at this late hour, but I'm only passing through Brighton. Had there been no lights in the window I would have gone back to the Old Ship where I've taken a room and returned here early in the morning."

"Come in! There's someone here who will be glad to see you."

He entered gratefully, removing his hat and swinging off his cloak to shake the raindrops outside before Clara closed the door.

Sophie, upon hearing his voice, had jumped up from where she was sitting and now stood framed in the kitchen doorway. He moved swiftly to her.

"How good to see you again, Rory!" she exclaimed joyfully.

"I've come direct from London and made this detour before returning to Dorset."

"I'm so glad you did."

"Go into the kitchen, both of you," Clara scolded teasingly. "It's cold here in the hall." Then she made a comical face at Sophie behind

Rory's back, conveying only too plainly her amusement at having an Excise officer under her roof while her cellar was full of contraband. Sophie's eyes danced, knowing that Clara enjoyed sharing the joke as she had been unable to do on Rory's previous visit. Yet it was not a joke against Rory himself, for she and Clara had this evening combined forces to help him catch his particular prey.

Clara, ever hospitable, heated some tasty soup and set it before Rory with plenty of home-baked bread and a mug of ale. He was tired and cold after his long ride, but the hot soup revived him. Yet just looking at Sophie sitting opposite him, her arms resting on the table, would have been tonic enough. He explained that he had been to London to make a report to his superiors, and since he was not yet due for any leave he had snatched this opportunity for a meeting. In all, he made little reference to his work, merely stating that he was kept quite busy at times, which Sophie guessed to be an understatement. Clara remained talking to him until Sophie had cleared the table, and then rose to leave them.

"I'll bid you good night, Captain Morgan," she said, "but do stay another half an hour." Then she left him alone with Sophie, having placed a firm limit on their time together.

Rory frowned as he went to sit beside Sophie, who had moved to the inglenook by the fire. "We should have a roof of our own. I resent being treated like a courting youth."

"You don't realize how lucky we are to have any time together," Sophie remarked cryptically. "It's only because Clara happens to like you. Anyone else in your uniform would be barred." Swiftly she changed the subject. "But tell me what you saw in London. It's a city I've long wanted to visit."

"I spent all my time at the Customs House, but while reading through some reports the account of one particular robbery caught my eye. A revenue man was attacked by local smugglers, who left him for dead. After a time he managed to drag himself to the side of a lane where he hoped to be found. At dawn a coach drew up. A large man and a thin woman alighted and came to him, followed by their coachman. As he lay helpless they robbed him of his watch and rings, emptied his pockets, and did nothing to help him. A shepherd eventually came to his rescue."

Sophie sat with her hands clasped tightly in her lap. "So Barnes and his accomplices are still at liberty."

"There's no proof it was them, but the descriptions fit and all the signs are there."

"Where did this happen? Near here?"

"Not more than twenty miles away." Rory put an arm around her and drew her close. "They'll be caught sooner or later, I promise you."

He turned her face to his and kissed her lips, softly at first and then with increasing passion. "I love you so much," he murmured huskily. "Surely by now you've had time to think over all I said before I went away and all that I've written to you."

"Nothing has changed, Rory."

"Maybe not, but I still believe we can overcome any problems if we set our minds to it."

She put her fingertips gently against his lips. "Don't say any more, Rory my dear. It only makes everything more difficult."

He caught her hand and kissed it. "Then make me one promise and that's all I'll ask of you."

"What is it?"

"Give me your word that if ever your life or Antoine's should be newly imperiled by any threat from France, one that proved impossible to overcome, you would let me take you both away to a safe place. I'd resign from the Excise Service and the three of us could start a new life together in America. What's more, I'd cooperate with you in keeping the boy's sights on France. He could think of me as his joint guardian with you."

"You would do all that for me?" she asked incredulously.

"I'd do anything for you! Give me that promise. You may never have to keep it, but in the meantime you'll know that there will always be an avenue of escape for you and the boy. It will also ease my mind." He took her by the shoulders and looked into her eyes. "Well?"

Sophie realized he had made an offer that was virtually impossible to refuse. Yet she considered it carefully from every angle before eventually she dipped her head in a nod. "For Antoine's sake I give you my word on it."

Swiftly he folded her into his arms and kissed her lovingly. If in some recess of her mind she still cried out against the possible complications of the promise she had made, she refused to acknowledge these doubts, for leaving England one day might be the only way to save Antoine's life.

"In an emergency," he said, still holding her in his embrace, "take a sealed message into the Excise office and state its urgency. It will reach me at high speed. I'll be calling at the office myself tomorrow before I leave and I'll give instructions to that effect."

"I'll remember that."

Rory's half hour had almost run out. He shook his head and sighed significantly as he heard Clara moving about. Although the tide was not right for a visit from Pierre Froment, Sophie guessed that she did not want to take any chances.

"If ever I hear anything about the Broomfield gang," Sophie said when Rory stood by the door, "I will send word to you in a sealed letter, so don't take alarm if one arrives."

"Why did you say that? Have you learned anything that might be helpful?"

"Nothing new, but I'm always hopeful."

Rory took her face gently between his hands as he gazed into her eyes. "Let our final words this time be of us. You are still as free a person in your own right as before I arrived this evening. That's how I want you to be if I am to win you as you should be won."

"I know, Rory. I couldn't have made that promise otherwise."

He kissed her once more, and then was gone. She closed the door and leaned against it, thinking over what had been arranged.

Clara's voice broke into her thoughts. "Has he left now?"

"Yes, Clara."

"Good night, then."

"Good night. Sleep well."

Three weeks passed before Pierre Froment came again to visit Clara. There was nothing unusual about that, for as she had explained, his visits were decided not only by the tides but also the weather. Sophie heard their voices raised in a sharp quarrel, but then all was quiet again.

In the morning Clara gave Sophie a nod. "Pierre will do what you've asked, but it may take time before he has anything concrete to pass on to you."

"I'm afraid it caused trouble between you."

Clara had a little smile on her lips. "I've never seen him so angry, but making up a quarrel is better than anything else I know."

Sophie noticed that the woman sang to herself as she prepared the breakfast.

ALTHOUGH EAGER for her first meeting with Pierre, Sophie had another matter to take care of, for already carpets of crocuses were heralding the spring. Before long, primroses made pale moons of blossom under the trees near the cottage and it was time for Sophie to reapply for work at the Marine Pavilion.

Now and again she used Clara's kitchen to make a batch of sweetmeats for Christmas, for birthdays, and for other special occasions. On the eve of her important day, she spent a long time preparing a sugar concoction. In the morning she placed it in a strong box, setting it off with paper lace, which she had made often enough during the early days of her training.

Clara was full of admiration. "It's fit for a king, let alone a prince!" she declared. "Good luck to you. You deserve it."

"Thank you, Clara."

Sophie's hopes were high as she set off, carefully carrying the example of her work now closed in its box. Much of the expansion of the Marine Pavilion had been completed during the winter, but a large part of the building was still covered with scaffolding. There were no main gates for her this time. Instead she jerked the bellpull at the door for servants and tradesmen. It was opened by a footman in the red and green livery of the Prince of Wales. He wasn't the same man she had seen before. When she had explained the purpose of her visit he informed her that the housekeeper, Mrs. Palmer, always dealt with female applicants for work. She was admitted to the tiled hallway and took a seat on a bench while she waited to be interviewed. Remembering the housekeeper's kindness while dressing her foot raised her hopes this morning. She could hear the familiar sounds of a busy kitchen and the hollow echo of hammering from the section of the building still under alteration. After a few minutes she was shown into the housekeeper's room.

Mrs. Palmer sat at her desk, a pleasant-looking woman with a direct, almost piercing gaze and a neat mouth. Her black silk gown was abundant in the skirt and tight in the bodice. Her fichu and cap were both of fine white lawn.

"Good morning, Miss Delcourt." She gestured with a capable hand. "Sit down. I hope that nasty cut you had on your foot did not trouble you for too long."

Sophie smiled. "It healed in a remarkably short time, thanks to your kind ministrations."

"I'm glad to hear that. Now, have you your references with you?"

"Yes, madame." Sophie handed over two, the first from Mr. Hicks, and the other from Harry, who, as head chef at the Castle Inn, wrote of the time they had worked in the same kitchen. Both gave her an impeccable character and praised her dedication to work. When the housekeeper had read them through, Sophie opened the box, which she had been resting on her lap, and lifted out the sugar concoction. It was in the form of a delicate waterfall spouting from the mouth of a central dolphin.

The housekeeper showed her pleasure. "That's charming! You're extremely talented, but then it's well known that French confectioners are unsurpassed at sugar sculpture. Unfortunately, I've no vacancy here in your particular sphere."

Sophie, numbed by a wave of intense disappointment, answered almost automatically. "Is there no opening for me on the skeleton staff?"

Mrs. Palmer shook her head. "When His Highness pays a quick visit to inspect the building work there is no elaborate entertaining and when he comes to stay, the staff of his London house is installed here. Do you sew, Miss Delcourt?"

"Sew?" Sophie answered dully. "Yes, I made this gown I'm wearing."

"Then I can see you're a skillful needlewoman as well as an artist in confectionery. Those tucks on the bodice are totally professional as are the scallops on the sleeves. I can offer a part-time post as linen maid. It should suit you well since you have a young child in your care and naturally you would not be living in as does the full-time staff."

Sophie found it difficult to concentrate on what the woman was saying. She had been so sure her destiny lay under this roof, so confident that having displayed the sugar waterfall, at least a post as confectioner's assistant would be offered her. She had no wish to return to the Old Ship, even though Mr. Hicks had said he would hold her notice in abeyance. That phase of her life was over. Now she hoped to expand the confectionery skills for which she had been trained from childhood.

Then almost audibly Sophie caught her breath. It was as if, suddenly, she saw how this new development could be used to her advantage. Her chin jerked up on a resurgence of optimism. Perhaps after all she had not been wrong in supposing her future would be shaped in this royal house. Her smile lit up her eyes.

"Yes, of course. The hours of a linen maid would suit me admirably. What exactly would my duties entail?"

She listened attentively to Mrs. Palmer's instructions, and by the time she left the Marine Pavilion her mind was whirling with schemes for the future.

At the cottage, Clara was baking when Sophie burst through the kitchen door with such force that a cloud of flour went flying up into the air.

"I start on Monday, Clara!"

"Well done!" Clara clapped her floury hands.

"Yes! With a thimble, needle, and thread!"

"What?"

Sophie came to a halt and leaned against the table. "As part-time linen maid. It's only for a few hours a day—more when there's company staying. That means I'll have a small but regular income while having enough free time to conduct my own confectionery business. I'll make sweetmeats and sell them to the local shops. Of course, that's if you'll rent me the ancient kitchen in the washhouse building."

"But that hasn't been used since Jim used to cook up his lobsters, crabs, and prawns on the hearth. Some of his old lobster pots and nets are still stored there. It's neglected now and full of cobwebs."

"It won't be when I've scrubbed it from floor to ceiling and given it a coat of whitewash. What do you say?" Sophie waited in anxious suspense. Surely Clara was not going to refuse her!

Then Clara sighed, but she smiled too. "Very well. Do as you like with it. You'll have to get the chimney swept for a start."

"I'll arrange that tomorrow. Oh, thank you for letting me have the place!" Sophie almost skipped out of the kitchen, eager to change into working clothes and decide what she must do to get the old kitchen in order. Clara called after her.

"Wait a minute!"

Sophie popped her head back round the door. "Yes?"

"There's a letter for you." Clara went to the dresser and took down the letter she had propped up by a plate.

Sophie took it from her and studied the handwriting. "It's not from Rory," she said in surprise. "This is from Tom. How much do I owe you?" she asked, for letters had to paid for on delivery.

"It was the same as usual," Clara answered, returning to her baking.

Sophie took the money from her purse and placed it on the dresser. When she broke the seal and opened the letter, a banker's draft fluttered to the floor. Picking it up, she looked from it to the few words Tom had written. Then she clasped it to her, laughing in her exuberance.

"What do you think? Tom promised he would place a wager on a horse on my behalf and it won! Thirty guineas! The money couldn't have come at a better time! I shall take it as his investment in my confectionery business—not that he will know until I can buy him out again!"

Clara shook her head. "Sometimes I think you're too independent for your own good, Sophie. If anyone had wagered on a horse for me I'd have accepted the winnings as a simple bonus."

Instantly Sophie's expression changed and she became very serious. "You don't know what it means to lose freedom or else you would never say that to me. It was taken from me in Paris and I only regained it here. Nobody is ever going to take my independence from me again."

"Not even Captain Morgan?"

"Not even he."

"Marriage is always on a man's terms. You'll soon find that out."

"Not when I marry—if I ever do! I'll be my husband's equal—not his chattel!"

"Brave words!" Clara quipped. "Come, don't look so serious. If any woman can achieve such status you are more likely to do so than anyone else I could name."

"I'll not be swayed from it," Sophie replied resolutely, but her smile came through. She was on the brink of starting a whole new and important phase in her life, and this was no time to worry about something that was not going to happen. "There's something else I have to do before I reorganize the old kitchen."

"I can guess. You want to make a batch or two of sweetmeats in my kitchen to offer as samples to shopkeepers. Am I right?"

"Yes, it's important that I have orders to fill as soon as I have everything ready."

"Maybe I can give a hand," Clara offered.

"I'd appreciate that."

"What will you do if you get swamped with orders as time goes on? When I'm dipping on the beach I'll not be able to help you."

"I've thought of that too. I'll employ Henriette. She'll be thankful to escape the hat-making."

"You seem to have worked everything out on your way home. But isn't she on such a lookout for a husband that she'd be off at any time?"

"As yet there's nobody. Her uncle and aunt forbid her the company of local army officers except widowers of higher rank, none of whom she liked. Young noblemen won't consider her without a dowry, although a few have been attracted to her before either they discovered she was penniless or their own fathers intervened. She was very upset when one brief romance ended."

"Poor girl. I'm sure there's many an ordinary Brighton fellow with prospects who would suit her better than any of those of the upper crust."

"But she wouldn't be allowed to marry anyone associated with trade."

"Yet she's in trade herself making those hats!" Clara exclaimed.

"That doesn't count, because she is only in genteel company."

"Would she be in genteel company with you?"

Sophie laughed. "No, but because I befriended Henriette when she was most in need of help, I'm allowed the privilege of being received in her home and associating with her. I think her aunt might even consider the making of sweetmeats slightly more refined than making hats!"

"She'd certainly have more fun here, I'd say. A nice young woman. Ever since you introduced her to me on the beach last summer, she spoke to me whenever she came down to bathe and liked me to be her dipper. She said I was gentler than the others."

"So she told me once, but I've never thought of dipping as being gentle," Sophie declared with amusement.

"Well, I don't push 'em under by the head. Pressure on the shoulders is my method."

"If all goes well Henriette may not have much time to bathe when summer comes."

"I still think she'd be better off wed to a healthy young fisherman with his own boat than to some overweight nob."

"It doesn't matter who it is if there's love in the marriage and her husband is kind to her. There's been a sad lack of kindness in her life. Now I'm going to survey my new premises."

When Sophie unlocked the door of the old kitchen she was met by the mingled odors of fish and tar, dirt and dust. Nothing had been touched here since Jim Renfrew's untimely death, except that it had become a place for storing unwanted furniture and cast-out domestic items.

Eagerly she entered the long, low-ceilinged room with its flagged floor and cobwebbed black beams. It was impossible to set an age to the flint building, but Sophie took a guess that this part of it might have been a little family home as long ago as the sixteenth century, even though it had been added to and altered at some later date. Jim himself had installed the larger windows that now gave it light. In the old brickwork at the side of the hearth there was a baking oven, and nearby were the caldrons Jim had used for boiling his shellfish. Fishing nets and lobster pots in need of repair were dumped about haphazardly, and Sophie had to climb over some of them to examine a long table that stood under one of the windows. After a good scrubbing it would provide her with a splendid work surface.

She emerged from the building with dust streaks on her face and cobwebs clinging to her clothes, but quite undaunted by the cleaning task that lay ahead. The money from Tom's wager would enable her to have a small boiler installed for clarifying sugar in large quantities, and she could purchase the tools of her trade she would otherwise have lacked. All that remained was to secure her customers.

She spent the rest of the day making a list of all the equipment and ingredients she would need when her kitchen was spick-and-span.

Thirteen

WHEN SOPHIE HAD PREPARED plenty of samples, she made a number of small boxes out of strong white paper, each with an inner lining of fine paper lace.

"These containers were made by young girls in a workroom near the confectionery kitchen at the back of my father's shop," Sophie told Clara. "It was how customers carried small purchases away, although the hard sweetmeats, such as Orange Flower prawlings or Harlequin pistachios were put into a cone of paper tied with a ribbon."

"So what did you have for the best candies?"

"Boxes with exquisitely painted lids or inlaid with bronze or semi-precious stones. There were others covered with satin or velvet in lovely colors and trimmed with sequins, embroidery, or bows. All were lined with fine white linen scalloped at the edges by a needlewoman employed for that purpose. Often a special order would be for a gold or silver casket, and many times a rich aristocrat demanded a jeweled one."

Clara whistled under her breath. "My! That's a long way from toffee apples at a fair! Before you came here I'd never tasted anything like the delicious things you make." She continued to watch Sophie packing the little boxes side by side into a flat-bottomed basket, which had been lined with white linen and a large frill of paper lace, the handle bound with ribbon. "Didn't those rich French folk have their own confectioners to make sweetmeats for them?"

"Of course they did, but their confectioners couldn't match my father's products. Now I have to establish a good selection at a competitive price. Later I can produce more exclusive and expensive candies." Sophie covered the contents of her basket with a spread of white lawn. "Now I'm ready." She took from her pocket a list of the shops she intended to visit. "I'll start at Mrs. Edward's shop first— she keeps a high standard of confectionery—and then I'll go on from there."

CLARA WAS SCRUBBING the flags of the hallway when Sophie came running back into the cottage by way of the back door and almost fell over her.

"Oh, Clara, I'm sorry! I didn't expect you to be here."

Clara sat back on her heels. "Neither did I think I was going to see you again so soon. What happened? Did you spill your basket?"

"No!" Sophie clapped her hands with glee. "Mrs. Edwards took every box. I offered her a candy to taste and she asked to buy all I had with me. She's given me a regular order for delivery every Monday."

"Well done! She knows a good thing when it comes her way. It's lucky you only took half the samples with you."

"I'm going to pack the rest into the other boxes now."

Although Sophie had had a good start, she was not so fortunate with the rest of the places on her list. Even though her wares were well received, not all the proprietors were interested in taking on another supplier, but a number did give her small orders on a trial basis. She was turned away from the shops where the family was employed in serving and producing, for these wanted nothing from outsiders.

Sophie had one box left in her basket when she had finished her rounds and was reluctant to go home with it. Nearby was a coffee-house patronized by the wealthier element of the town. She took notice of the proprietor's name above the entrance and went in. The blended aromas of coffee and hot chocolate made her realize how long it had been since breakfast. She asked to see Mr. Mitchell.

"He passed away ten years ago," she was told. "It's Mrs. Mitchell who is in charge."

When Sophie entered the woman's office, Mrs. Mitchell was standing by the window, studying a file.

"What are you selling, mademoiselle?" she asked in French. "I never refuse an émigré if I can help it, but I have to tell you that I have no need of lace mats, embroidered napkins, or dried flowers."

"I have none of those, madame," Sophie replied in her own tongue. "My confectionery would make a change from the sweet cakes you serve here."

The woman raised her head and looked across at her. "I was told your name is Delcourt. Are you—? No, you couldn't be—?"

"Henri Delcourt of Paris was my father."

Immediately Mrs. Mitchell put down the file and came across in a rustle of dark green silk. "I was saddened to hear of his demise. Are you following in his footsteps?"

"I am, madame."

"How splendid! Sit down. Would you like some hot chocolate?"

"Yes, I would."

Mrs. Mitchell rang a little bell and gave the order to a waiting maid. Then she sat down herself. Sophie held out the box of sweetmeats from her basket. Mrs. Mitchell bit into one and closed her eyes appreciatively. "Paris! I can see your father's shop. It always smelt so delicious. He used to keep a pyramid of bonbons in a crystal dish on the counter. How strange I should recall that!"

"Did you know my father personally?" Sophie was touched by this sharing of memories.

"No, only as a customer, and that's a long time ago. You see, I met my English husband when he was in Paris on business and when I ran away to marry him my family never received me again. Let me try another of those sweetmeats."

Sophie spent a pleasant half hour with Mrs. Mitchell. The result was an order beyond her wildest expectation. When she left it was not to go straight home. Instead she went to have a word with Henriette. The girl's eyes opened wide when she heard Sophie's offer.

"I'd love it! But I've never cooked anything in my life. I was just taught how to run a large household in preparation for marriage and I know how to select a menu for any occasion, but I've never set foot in a kitchen, not even here in Brighton, because my aunt forbids it."

"But there's only one maidservant in your house. Does a local woman still come daily to cook?"

"Which one? We've had a stream of them. It's chaos most of the time, because Aunt Diane still behaves as if she had fifty indoor servants at her command. I've wanted to try my hand with a cookbook, but—as I said—I've not been allowed."

For a moment Sophie felt a surge of impatience at her friend's submissive attitude. Then she reminded herself quickly that it was no fault of Henriette that she had been conditioned to show complete obedience to those in authority over her and to follow customs no longer practical in present circumstances.

"So you see," Henriette concluded wistfully, "much as I would like to become your confectionery assistant, my aunt would never let me work in a kitchen, and in any case, I fear that with no experience I'd be more of a hindrance than a help to you."

Sophie smiled. "I'm willing to take a chance if you are. As for my working premises, from now on they shall be known as the Delcourt atelier of confectionery. I think the new status should eliminate the kitchen stigma for your aunt's benefit. I shall be doing all the complicated work. You'll have the monotonous tasks at first—just mixing sugar paste and so forth, as well as washing up and keeping the place spotless. Does that still appeal to you?"

"Yes! And I'll learn, Sophie. I promise!"

"Then ask your uncle's permission this evening."

"I will. But I'd like you to be there."

Sophie sighed. "It's time you stood on your own two feet."

"Yes, but not this time. I might make a muddle of asking and then Aunt Diane is likely to tell him to refuse me."

Sophie inclined her head. "Very well. I'll come to the house at seven o'clock."

Henriette hugged her exuberantly. "What a dear kind friend you are!"

That evening Sophie did as she had promised. The Baron de Bouvier, tall, thin, and white-wigged, looked down his long, aristocratic nose at her with some disdain. She could tell that he considered her little better than a peasant, but she had never been cowed by such foolish airs, and in a forthright, sensible manner she requested his permission to employ his niece, who stood nervously at her side. His wife was present, listening to every word. When she heard that Henriette was to receive a regular wage higher than her present piecework payments, which fluctuated with the season for straw hats, the Baronne gave her husband an almost imperceptible nod. Money, which once she had spent as if it poured from a cornucopia, had by its present agonizing shortage become all-important to her. By working for Sophie, Henriette could contribute more to her keep. The Baron had observed her signal.

"Very well," he said to Sophie, not having consulted his niece at all on the subject. "Henriette may enter your employment on condition she is adequately chaperoned at all times."

Sophie curtsied as politeness demanded and Henriette left the room with her. In the hallway Henriette danced a jig of triumph.

"You did it! When can I start?"

"As soon as the atelier is ready. I was lucky enough to get the sweep there this afternoon, and a neighbor in the building trade has already started bricking in a boiler. He's also cleared out all the rubbish that was there. All that's left are some pieces of furniture that I'll find useful. The workman says he will finish off the boiler by ten tomorrow morning, but I won't be able to use it until the mortar sets."

"Then I'll come when he goes and help you get the place clean. Surely I can learn to scrub a floor. I've seen women doing it often enough."

WHEN HENRIETTE ARRIVED at the cottage in the morning, Clara took one look at her unsuitable attire and turned out an old cotton garment and a large canvas apron for her to wear instead. There was also a mob cap to cover her hair. Sophie, who had started work in the atelier, was similarly dressed and gave her friend some jesting advice.

"Don't look in a mirror. You might not recognize yourself."

"I don't care if I look like a scarecrow," Henriette declared lightheartedly. "I'm here! Where do I begin?"

Clara came to give Sophie and Henriette a hand, for soot and builder's dust had added to the dirt that had to be banished. First of all the hearth was cleared of the sweep's debris, including a few old nests that had been dislodged from the chimney. Then a fire was lit under the ancient caldron to heat plenty of hot water for the washing and scrubbing. The trio worked hard, vigorously brushing the walls and beams and getting rid of festoons of cobwebs. Henriette screamed every time a large spider scuttled for safety. Then the scrubbing brushes were put into action, and soapsuds frothed over the flagstones until the task was done.

Sophie stood back with her two friends to regard with satisfaction the result of their combined efforts. The whole place smelled damp but clean, and there was a fragrant aroma from the kindling of applewood that was still crackling in the hearth. The walls were a shade lighter with the grime removed and the flagstones would have appeared new-laid if it had not been for the wear of centuries. Even the windows shone, and the top of Sophie's working table was as white as a linen cloth.

"You've done wonders, both of you!" she declared to her two helpers, ignoring how tirelessly she had carried out the hardest tasks herself. "I'm taking us and the boys out to supper this evening."

The three of them took turns in the bathroom, stripping off to dump their working clothes in a tub before pouring warm water over themselves to bathe away the effects of their labors. Sophie, while awaiting her turn, ran down to the sea in her shift and plunged into the waves. The water was cold, but it refreshed and exhilarated her.

Henriette wanted to go home and change, saying that the gown she had arrived in that morning was the one she had worn for hat-making and not fit for going out to supper. It gave Sophie the chance to lend her friend one of her good gowns and then, with the boys in their best clothes, they all set out for a chophouse in Black Lion Street. Antoine and Billy were excited and began pushing each other about exuberantly until Clara took the hand of one and Sophie the other and order was restored.

It was a jolly evening, although not an expensive one, for the chophouse was not among those that catered for the elite. Yet the food was good and plentiful. They all had steak and kidney pudding, the boys' first choice, and it was served with some ceremony. A white napkin was untied and folded back by the waiter to reveal a white suet crust. Then, with the skillful use of a plate, the pie was deftly reversed. The savory aroma of rich gravy and tender morsels of meat immediately made their mouths water. Potatoes and carrots and turnips and braised onions completed the course.

The only awkward moment for Sophie occurred when they were leaving. Clara knew the landlord's wife and stood chatting with her while Sophie and Henriette waited with the boys. Antoine, who had not dined under a chandelier since leaving home, glanced up at one overhead.

"We had lights like that at the château, but ours were much prettier. They had dangling bits that sparkled."

"Bet you didn't!" Billy gibed. "What's 'shatoo' anyway?"

"Yes, we did!" Antoine insisted heatedly. "It's my home in France where I'm going back one day!"

Sophie, after exchanging a dismayed look with Henriette, intervened quickly. "No arguments! We don't want a happy evening spoiled. Be good, both of you."

To her relief they both obeyed her and Clara rejoined them at that moment, eager to pass on some local gossip she had just heard. Later, when Sophie was tucking Antoine into bed, she took the chance of Billy being out of the room to give him some advice.

"I don't think we should speak of the château except as 'home,' Antoine. We wouldn't want to make others feel we were boasting, would we?"

He considered, then gave a nod. "All right," he said, yawning and holding out his arms for a good night cuddle. As he leaned sleepily against her, she tucked back a strand of his hair. It was getting darker and no longer curled as it had done. Soon to be six, Antoine had grown into a sturdy little boy.

Sophie saw he was asleep. She kissed his brow and laid him back on his pillow before drawing the covers over him.

CLARA PUT HER PROPOSAL to Sophie and the boys at breakfast. "Why don't we make a bonfire of all the rubbish turned out of the old kitchen? We could take all the bits and pieces down onto the sands while the tide is on its way out and add some dry driftwood to really get it going."

The boys cheered, waving their porridge spoons in the air and kicking their feet against the rungs of their chairs. Sophie laughingly restored order. The boys were told they could invite their school friends and Sophie went into town to purchase supplies for the atelier. On the way, she called to invite the neighbors to the celebration. At that time of the year the tide went far out and although it would be on the turn, there would be at least three hours in which to enjoy the bonfire. She would have invited Henriette, but knew her friend had to accompany her aunt to a card party that evening.

When she arrived home, the aroma of baking cakes filled the cottage and Clara was already preparing a second batch.

"Would you take the pips from another pound of raisins for me?" she said in greeting. Immediately Sophie put on an apron, washed her hands, and began the task. It had been arranged that Antoine and Billy should help with moving the rubbish down to the beach when they came home from school, but while Sophie was out Clara had had two male volunteers, both neighbors, willing to spare the time as soon as the tide was right.

By dusk at least forty people had gathered for the lighting of the bonfire, which was stacked high, the two helpers having added some large pieces of timber from an old wreck. As soon as a lighted taper was put to the great pile, there was a cheerful crackling and almost instantly blue and gold sparks flew up into the air as the flames seized voraciously on the tarry ropes and old lobster pots. Clara and Sophie passed round the trays of cake. Everyone had been asked to bring a cup or a mug and there was ale for the adults and a drink for the children of diluted red currant juice that Clara had made from her own bushes the previous summer.

It was dark and the stars were out by the time the eating and drinking were done, but the bonfire was still blazing as high as ever. Some of the fathers, who had come with the schoolchildren, had thrown on pieces of driftwood they found on the beach. One parent had brought some fireworks, and there was added excitement when the rockets went shooting high. Quite a number of people, sighting the bonfire from a distance, had walked along the shore to join the gathering, doubling the number.

It was at the height of the fun that Sophie sensed with every nerve in her body that there was another new arrival. She turned her head sharply and saw Tom in his long, shoulder-caped coat standing on the slope of the shingle, illumed dramatically in the red-gold light of the bonfire. His eyes in their shadowed hollows bored into hers across the distance between them. It was a moment akin to when she had met his gaze in the mirror on the day of the vases, but this time she did not recoil, for what he felt for her was no longer a revelation. Instead she felt a curious and dreadful excitement rush through her veins and she stood as if transfixed amid the milling children and adults. Then, as if she had called to him, he began to descend the shingle. He was carrying his beaver hat by its narrow brim and the single buckle of its hatband winked bronze in the fiery glow as he drew near. She braced herself, her pulse racing.

Tom had been watching her for several minutes before she realized he was there and had seen her moving through the gathering, smiling and talking to this person and that. She had sprung away with a laugh to escape a fall of hot ash and had been swift to restrain a child she spotted going too near the blaze. When she turned her head and met his eyes he had felt her beauty fill his heart.

Threading his way through the spectators, he kept his eyes locked on hers. She spoke first, almost huskily.

"What brought you back to Brighton this time?"

There were reasons he couldn't give her, but one that he could. "A need to see you, Sophie."

She raised her eyebrows quizzically. "More vases?" she quipped, the lightness of her tone belied by her tenseness.

"Not this time." Tom cast a glance at the bonfire. "Isn't it early to be celebrating Guy Fawkes night? That's not until November."

"Indeed it is! Even I as a Frenchwoman have learned that, but this evening we're not celebrating the saving of Parliament from that villain's plot to blow it up. The reason is something quite different. I'm starting a new venture. We're burning up all the rubbish from the place that is to be my atelier."

A slow grin of genuine pleasure spread across his face. "You're taking up confectionery again!"

"Yes!" Sophie clasped her hands in front of her, warming to his instant approval. "And thanks in no small part to you for sending me the winnings of that wager at Newmarket. I have written my thanks to you."

"I expect the letter is waiting for me in London. I've been abroad again. In any case, I don't want you to write formal letters to me. I'd much rather you told me all you've been doing and what has been happening."

She looked up as the last rocket exploded overhead in a shower of golden stars. "I haven't time to write long letters."

"So tell me what brought about this change of work for you."

When she had relayed the details briefly, his brows drew together in a puzzled frown. "I don't see why you should still take the post of linen maid. Surely you have enough orders already to show that there'll be plenty to do from now on without giving up part of your time?"

"If I had only myself to think about it would be different, but I can't risk everything when I have Antoine to consider." She glanced around at the crowd of children. "There he is. Antoine! See who has come to our bonfire."

Antoine, sandy and disheveled, had come bouncing up to them, but he remembered his manners and bowed. "Your servant, Mr. Foxhill."

"You honor me, Antoine," Tom replied, smiling with equal civility. "You're having a good time, are you?"

"Yes, sir. I've never been so close to a big bonfire before."

"Did you know that bonfires are lit on hilltops in a chain throughout England whenever invasion threatens?"

"That must be a lot of bonfires!"

"It is indeed."

Then one of the other boys pulled Antoine back into the fun. Tom took Sophie by the hand. "Show me the atelier where you are going to work."

After telling Clara where she was going, Sophie led the way to her new premises. When they reached the building she pointed out each of its sections before opening the door of her atelier.

"Wait while I light the candle lamp," she said.

Earlier Sophie had made a permanent place for the lamp and a tinderbox on a ledge just inside the doorway. When she had lit the wick and replaced the glass she stood aside and Tom crossed the threshold.

He tossed his hat onto a peg and unbuttoned his coat. Then, hands on hips, he strode into the middle of the floor to survey the well-scrubbed room with its sparse furnishings and firewood laid ready on the swept hearth. He gave his verdict.

"This is very good. Plenty of room and windows to give you light.

171

Those wouldn't have been of that size when this place was built. At a guess I'd say it was one of the oldest buildings in the area. Alterations have been made, of course."

"Clara's husband did some of them." Sophie glanced about happily. "I'm so lucky to be able to make this my atelier. Tomorrow I'm going to give it a coat of whitewash."

"I'll do it for you," he volunteered at once. "Would you like some shelves put up as well?"

"You've done more than enough for me," she said firmly. "Clara knows a good carpenter and I'm going to get in touch with him."

Tom was wandering around. "Where did you plan on having the shelves?"

"I thought half a dozen at the side of the table." She indicated the place and then pointed to a windowless wall. "I'll have more put floor to ceiling near this corner."

"Good planning. I'll do them. I'm a better carpenter than you might suppose. On my way here in the morning I'll order the timber to be delivered. What about the whitewash?"

"I have that. I've mixed it already."

"Do you have enough of the right brushes?"

"Clara has some to lend me. But surely you've more important things to do?"

He answered as he continued to wander. "My purpose in coming to Brighton this time was solely to see you. So what could be better than making myself useful on your behalf? I don't have to leave again for twenty-four hours."

She shook her head in wonder. "What a restless man you are, Tom. You're forever either going away or returning. Don't you get tired of traveling so much?"

He had stopped with his back to her in front of an antique cupboard she had scrubbed inside and out. "I suppose I do," he admitted, "but for the present I can see no end to it."

Sophie went across to where he stood studying the carving on one of the cupboard doors. "Couldn't you send out agents to buy on your behalf?"

He flicked a half smile at her. "I do. But there are certain matters that I have to deal with myself." Then he nodded toward the cupboard as if to halt her line of questioning. "This is a handsome piece."

"I thought so too," she said. "It's really too good for storing candy molds and all the rest of my tools of trade, but Clara says it's too large to go into the cottage."

Tom stood back to give his assessment. "It's English oak. Early sixteenth century."

"Could it be sold for Clara?"

He shook his head. "No. The demand these days is for the delicate and elegant. I'd say it was made by a local craftsman."

"That means it could have belonged to the first family who lived here."

"It's possible."

"Then it is something I shall hold in special esteem."

"Esteem?" he repeated on a lower, softer note. "That's how I hold memories of you every time I leave Brighton."

Sophie jerked up her head in what he recognized as a defensive manner, but he saw she did not seem able to draw away. As when he had faced her from the shingle in the bonfire's glow, she remained motionless except for her more rapid breathing. Suddenly both became aware of how very quiet it was in the atelier, the sounds of merriment round the bonfire faint and distant. The candlelight threw their flickering shadows on to the far wall.

Sophie knew she was on the brink of what she had feared all along, but nothing was inevitable if one acted in time. Why was it then that she was doing nothing to stem the growing intensity of feeling rising between them? Every nerve and fiber of her body was aware of the masculine strength and power that emanated from him. There was such desire in his face. As if time had slowed down everything, she saw his arms reach out for her. But at the last moment she threw up her hands to ward him off, hearing in sudden fright the approaching thunder of galloping horses.

"Listen! Horses! Lots of them! Whatever is happening?" Then terror gripped her. "Is it smugglers? Merciful Heaven! Antoine and Billy and all those children are still on the beach!"

Tom was ahead of her out of the door. She ran after him, able to hear screaming now from the direction of the bonfire. As she rushed from the woody grove, she cried out again, for the whole happy scene she and Tom had left was changed completely. Mounted Dragoons were everywhere, on land and on the sands, sabers drawn as they encircled the panic-stricken group. Shrieking women clutched their children while the men threw lighted brands, rocks, and driftwood at the soldiers, whose horses snorted and reared.

Sophie saw Tom go plunging down the shingle, coattails flying, yelling as he went. "It's not the French! Use your eyes!"

Nobody listened, and he came to a skidding halt by the bonfire, drawing a pair of pistols from under his coat and firing them into the air. The explosion brought paralyzing shock, and he used those precious seconds of silence to roar out again.

"It's not an invasion! These are our own Dragoons!" Then to the ring of military men he yelled his demand. "Who's in command here? Let him come forward!"

Everybody had become quiet, except for some of the children, who were still sobbing with fright. Sophie watched as an officer rode down the path onto the shingle, a supercilious expression on his face. Sadly she understood how the general nervousness of an invasion by the French had caused the disastrous panic that occurred when soldiers had suddenly appeared. Tom was now totally in control.

"What's the meaning of this?" he demanded of the officer, the smoking pistols still in his hands. "How dare you intrude on this peaceful group of local people and their children!"

"I was informed," the officer replied coldly, "that a bonfire had been lit to notify us that an enemy invasion had started. I realized the error of this communication as soon as we arrived, but a woman screamed out that the French had come and you have seen the result for yourself." He pointed the tip of his saber at the bonfire. "Douse those flames immediately. There are to be no more bonfires! That's an order. One of this size could have sent a chain of groundless warnings across the country."

He wheeled his horse about and rode back up the path, issuing a snapped command to his troops to withdraw. Sophie leapt down onto the shingle and ran to where Clara, white-faced, was clutching Billy. Antoine stood at her side, far less upset, although he was quick to grasp at Sophie's hand.

"I didn't like the noise, but French soldiers wouldn't have hurt us."

She stooped to hug him to her in order that he not see the glitter of tears in her eyes. Then she rose to her feet and dashed them away with the back of her hand as Tom came toward her. His pistols were once again concealed by his coat.

"Nobody's been hurt," he said reassuringly, "but it's been a sorry end to the party."

She nodded. "But it could have turned out much worse if you hadn't intervened when you did."

People were coming up to thank him and Sophie moved away. Those living nearby had run home to fetch buckets and already the first had returned to wade into the sea and fill them. The tide was now rapidly approaching the bonfire, but nobody wanted the Dragoons to return. There was a hissing and a billowing of steam as water was tossed onto the blaze. People were drifting quickly home with their children. Tom returned to Sophie and advised her and Clara to go home too.

"I'll stay and see the fire out." To Sophie he added, "I'll be with you in the morning."

As Sophie took Antoine's hand and followed Clara and Billy up the path, she wondered why Tom went permanently armed with two formidable pistols.

Fourteen

TOM ARRIVED at seven-thirty in the morning. Sophie was in the atelier, tying on her canvas apron, when he knocked a tattoo on the door and entered carrying a carpenter's bag.

"Good day, Sophie. The wood is ordered and will be here within the hour. I hired the tools I need at the same builder's yard. I'm not late, am I?"

"No, quite the reverse. Henriette hasn't arrived yet."

Swiftly Tom removed his coat to commence work in his shirt-sleeves. "I'll need a ladder for the ceiling," he said as he put on a gardener's apron he had brought with him.

"There's one next door in the old stable. You could leave your coat there to save its being splashed with whitewash."

"I'll do that." But Tom did not go at once. Instead he took a couple of steps toward her. "How are the children this morning? And Mrs. Renfrew? No ill effects from the scare of last night?"

"None. The boys were their usual noisy selves when Clara and I had breakfast with them."

"And what of you, Sophie?"

"All's well with me," she replied.

As he went to the stable, Sophie crossed to the ledge that held the tinderbox and then knelt to light the fire. The flicker of the rising flames reminded her again of the bonfire and the deep thrill of sensuous pleasure she had experienced at seeing Tom watch her from the shingle. She was amorously stirred whenever Rory kissed her, but there was an excitement in Tom's nearness that was a very different feeling and could not be denied.

When the door opened again she gave a start, as if somehow Tom would read her thoughts. But it was Henriette who had arrived, a copy of the London-printed émigré newspaper in her hand.

"Have you read this week's edition?" she demanded at once.

"No, I haven't collected my copy yet," Sophie answered with a pang of foreboding, for she could tell from Henriette's face there was cause for alarm.

"Read that notice! The once I've encircled in ink." Henriette thrust the newspaper at Sophie where she knelt.

It had been folded to a column that listed entries from émigrés seeking news of fellow countrymen with whom they had lost contact. With trepidation she began to read.

> A kinsman wishes to trace Antoine, Comte de Juneau, grandson of the late Marquis de Fontaine. Born June 1788, the boy is of fair complexion with light brown curly hair. He was abducted from his family at a time of crisis by a young woman, believed to have been a servant of the household. A reward of one hundred guineas is offered for information as to their whereabouts.

Henriette looked over Sophie's shoulder as she read. "Fancy stating that Antoine was abducted! Such wickedness after the way you risked your life to save him! I suppose that's to thwart any claim to the boy on your part. You've told me more than once that to your knowledge Antoine has no close kin, so who could have inserted that notice?"

Sophie spoke anxiously. "It's surely the same man who desecrated the Marquis's grave. I—" She broke off as Tom returned with the ladder and hastily tucked the folded newspaper down by the side of some kindling on the hearth. The secret of Antoine's identity was not one she wished to share with him. She rose to her feet and presented

Tom to Henriette, explaining that he had kindly offered to help with the redecoration.

"How gallant of you, Mr. Foxhill!" Henriette exclaimed.

"Not at all. I was glad to be here at the right time."

Sophie could tell that Henriette thought Tom attractive, for she dimpled, chatted about nothing very charmingly, and went almost reluctantly to hang her cloak in the stable.

"Are you all right, Sophie?" Tom questioned, narrowing his eyes at her.

"Yes." Sophie smiled a little too brightly, realizing she had appeared distracted. "I've a lot on my mind at the present time. I'm glad you've made Henriette's acquaintance at last, because I've spoken so often to each of you about the other."

"She's a very pretty girl." Tom propped the ladder into position and carried up a bucket of whitewash, which he hooked to a convenient nail in the beam. Sophie, unable to keep her thoughts from the implications of the notice, absently unfolded pieces of old linen sheets, which she draped over the sparse furniture. Henriette returned and giggled mischievously as she whispered to Sophie. "Now I've met Mr. Foxhill at last! What a handsome fellow! If I hadn't known he always arrived unexpectedly I'd have thought you were deliberately keeping him to yourself!"

"Don't be foolish," Sophie whispered back sharply. "My patience is running thin at the moment."

"Sorry!" Henriette looked chastened. In the surprise of meeting Tom Foxhill, she had forgotten momentarily how worried Sophie would be by that notice. As they could not leave all the whitewashing to Tom, she and Sophie donned mob caps before making a start on the walls. Henriette, who thought such headwear unflattering, managed to coax out a few curls about her face. Tom spoke to her from his ladder as she took up a brush.

"Have you heard yet what took place on the beach yesterday evening, Mademoiselle de Bouvier?"

"No." Henriette was agog. "What happened?"

Sophie explained about the bonfire and described what had happened. Henriette expressed her dismay.

"What a dreadful calamity that a happy evening for the children should have been spoiled in such a frightening way. I have to say I'm thankful I wasn't there. I would have been terrified." She paused in her brushwork and looked up at Tom. "How fortunate you were armed, Mr. Foxhill, otherwise, judging from all Sophie has said, you mightn't have been able to make yourself heard in the panic."

Sophie continued to swish her whitewashing brush up and down, but she listened intently for his reply. It came casually enough.

"I agree it was. But then highwaymen are still a menace along some parts of the London road, and I've become used to being ready to defend myself when I'm traveling."

"But to be wearing pistols in Brighton of all places!" Henriette persisted, her tone becoming more flirtatious, for although he had not stopped work Tom was smiling down at her. "Surely you don't expect to be robbed in the streets here? If you do, I'll scarcely dare to walk alone along the sea lane to this atelier."

"Put those fears at rest. I daresay it's only when there's a smugglers' moon and the Gentlemen are at work that it would be dangerous for a young woman in the lane or any other place near the shore."

"Would she be ravished?" Henriette gasped in a horrified whisper.

"There's no telling what a Gentleman might do."

Sophie intervened. "Get on with your work, Henriette. Tom's teasing you."

Henriette obeyed and for a while there was no sound except the slap of brushes and the crackling of the fire on the hearth.

When Clara had finished her household chores, she carried a tray of refreshments to the atelier. The coat of whitewash had just been finished and everyone welcomed the break. The room was chilly, the windows having been opened wide to let an April breeze hasten the drying of the whitewash, so Tom drew a bench up to the fire. With a three-legged stool placed beside it, all four of them were able to benefit from the warmth. He held up his mug of hot chocolate and read out the humorous poem on it. Henriette squealed when having drained her mug, she found a frog at the bottom, but it was molded in china.

"I meant to drink out of that one myself," Clara apologized. "When my son Daniel was at home he played many tricks on visitors with it."

"Shall you be seeing him again soon, Mrs. Renfrew?" Tom asked.

She shook her head sadly. "He's up in Yorkshire and that's where he'll stay until our soldiers start battling on the continent again."

"That's unlikely to happen for a long while yet," Tom said. "At present it's the Royal Navy that's doing all the work, blockading the continental ports to bring a total cessation of imports to France."

"Will they succeed, do you think?" Henriette asked.

"With the French Navy in its present disarray, there's every chance. Almost without exception the officers in the past were aristocrats, and now that so many of them have gone to the guillotine or fled abroad, the result is a shambles of inexperienced new officers and poorly disciplined crews."

"There have been a number of French ships sunk too," Sophie remarked. "I saw a list in one of the émigré newspapers." She resisted a glance toward the kindling behind which the latest edition was concealed. The audacity of that notice was almost beyond belief. And the accusation of abduction was a blatant threat to her personally. Her enemy seemed to suppose he could resort to the Law of England to lay claim to Antoine if ever he should track them down.

"Back to work!" Tom had already risen and was waiting to replace the bench against the wall.

While he was left to start putting up the shelves and Henriette to wipe the flagstones clean of whitewash splashes, Sophie and Clara returned to the cottage. There they washed and dried the mugs as well as the new utensils Sophie had purchased for her confectionery work.

She was lining everything up ready to take into the atelier when Henriette came in. She was carrying newspapers that had been put down earlier to protect the floor as much as possible.

"Thank you for all your hard work," Sophie said appreciatively. To her surprise her friend, whose color was already high as if from her exertions, flushed even deeper and she looked ill at ease. Sophie thought she knew the cause. "Don't worry if the flagstones are still a bit splashed. That will wear off in time."

Henriette seemed to pounce on the reason offered with some relief. "I hope so. It was careless of me."

Sophie flicked a second glance at her. Had Tom been flirting? Was that why Henriette seemed unusually tense? There had been some bantering between them throughout the morning, but then Henriette was always lighthearted when freed for a time from the restrictions of her home. Clara, who had observed everything, noticed how Henriette avoided Sophie's eyes and turned to the new utensils placed together on the side table.

"What's this for?" she asked, picking up a tin frame that was divided into small squares.

"It's for cutting barley sugar," Sophie replied.

"And this?" Henriette turned a screw set in a small funnel.

"That will make tiny jewellike drops of candy."

Henriette reached out and picked up a syringe with a wide nozzle. "What happens with this?"

"It will make star shapes of marzipan."

Privately Clara marveled at Sophie's patience. Henriette became lively as she listened and handled each item in turn. The last was a hollowed block of wood containing a tool for cutting borders of paper, saving the painstaking care needed to do the task by hand.

"To think of all the sweetmeats I've eaten without the least idea of how they were made or how much goes into the making!" Henriette seized a whisk and twirled it in the air. "I hope I soon become accomplished enough to use all these things."

"You will if you work hard," Clara said uncompromisingly. Although Henriette had shown her mettle by tackling hard tasks, it was difficult to imagine her becoming particularly skillful at anything. The girl would most probably excel at repetitive work, but anything too complicated would be beyond her. "You'll have to be diligent in your training."

"I will!" Henriette exclaimed fervently, her eyes suddenly swimming with tears. "I want to become another right hand for Sophie. It's the least I can do."

Sophie was touched by this emotional outburst, which most surely stemmed from her friend's sheer physical tiredness. Clara, less impressed, picked up the folded newspapers Henriette had placed on a chair and returned them to the atelier, where they could be used for lighting fires. After a few words with Tom, she returned to the kitchen. Henriette was now sitting at the table, waiting to be instructed in box-making, the paper and scissors put ready.

"I'll leave you in charge, Clara," Sophie said as she went out of the

181

cottage with a bucket of hot water and a bowl to wash out and scald the newly built boiler.

She was glad that Henriette would be able to sit for the rest of the working day. Clara had learned how to make paper boxes while they were preparing the samples. Now larger ones would be needed, and the widow, with Henriette under her instruction, could be relied upon to produce what was necessary. Entering the atelier, Sophie saw that Tom had already put up one set of shelves.

"Those are splendid, Tom. Just the right height and width."

"I'll have finished the rest by the end of the afternoon."

"Maybe you've missed your vocation," she joked, raising the lid of the boiler to begin her task.

He grinned across at her. "I'll have carpentry in reserve if ever the flow of fine works of art should ebb."

"Fortunately for you that's most unlikely."

"If it weren't for the fact that I have to leave Brighton this evening I'd have helped you again tomorrow."

She had emptied some of the hot water into the container, and now put a bowl under the tap in the brickwork to draw it off again, cleaning the pipe through which the clarified sugar would run. Then she refilled it and collected kindling from the hearth to light a fire in the boiler for scalding the container. She noticed that Clara had stacked the soiled newspapers out of reach of sparks, but the one with the notice remained safely concealed.

"How do you intend to deliver your confectionery?" Tom asked as Sophie stooped down again to thrust the kindling and some crumpled newspaper into the boiler.

"I'll hire a boy for carrying. As soon as I've built my business up sufficiently, I shall buy a horse and a little carriage. Not a cart, because elegance will count. My father taught me to ride and how to handle reins when in the driving seat."

Tom continued his work as they talked. Sophie took advantage of his back being turned toward her as she returned to the hearth. Quickly she snatched up the hidden newspaper and tore out the notice, which she thrust into her pocket. The rest she used as a taper by pushing it into the flames and then taking it to light the boiler.

"You know," Tom remarked almost casually, "you could hire transport from me."

"Whatever do you mean?" Sophie asked, closing the door of the boiler as the fire took hold.

"The truth is I've missed having my own horse and equipage in Brighton and have been looking out for what I want. I spoke to Mrs. Renfrew when she was in here a few minutes ago, and she is fully agreeable to my hiring her stable. It would mean that you could have the use of the horse and gig for your deliveries. In fact, it's already been arranged and I'll hire an ostler's lad to feed and groom the animal after it's been delivered."

Sophie sauntered across to him. "A gig? I should have thought a high-wheeled, break-neck phaeton would be more in your line."

"I already have one of those in London."

"But you'd find one equally useful in Brighton. Think of the fast speed races you could compete in! Somehow I judge you to be a man who enjoys danger."

"When I come to this part of the coast, it is not for the phaeton races. A gig will suit me well," he replied equably. "So what do you say?" Now he did pause in his work to look at her.

As had happened before, she found it hard to resist his genuine acts of kindness, for they were so clearly well meant. "I believe," she said on a gentler note, "that you're using yet another ploy to be generous toward me."

"That comes into it, but on my oath I meant what I said about wanting my own transport here. You would be doing me a favor by using it in my absence."

She inclined her head. "Very well then. Sixpence a delivery it is and I thank you for it."

"Done!" With a laugh he clapped his hand against hers in the Sussex manner of sealing a bargain. "I have the right horse in mind and I know where there's a suitable gig."

"How do you know that?"

Tom grinned. "Because I ordered it last time I was here. As I told you, I've had such a purchase in mind for some while."

"I'll go and tell Clara I've agreed." Sophie turned to leave, but Tom moved swiftly and caught her by the wrist, causing her to fall backward against his chest. He jerked round and kissed her full on the mouth, taking advantage of her lips being parted on an initial gasp of surprise. Several moments passed before he released her.

"That's a better way to seal a bargain, Sophie," he said softly with intense satisfaction.

She drew sharply away and feigned a casual air to hide the effect his kiss had had on her. "Maybe I was wrong about your true vocation being in carpentry," she said teasingly. "Moving so fast and unexpectedly as you did just then toward me, you could have made a career as a Gentleman. None would have been able to anticipate your movements."

His smile grew a little wider as he matched her jesting tone. "What an idea! That wouldn't be my choice of a career, but a highwayman on the road could offer rewards. I'd be a Robin Hood robbing the rich to give to the poor instead of a fine art dealer frequently impoverished by the failure of the rich to pay their bills."

"That happens to you, does it?" She replied lightly, the tense mood broken.

Tom had resumed his measuring for the next shelf that was to be put up. "Unfortunately it does. Perhaps tailors suffer most of all. Coats are worn out and discarded before payment reaches them. Make sure you get your accounts settled in time."

"Those who buy from me are ordinary local people not accustomed to keeping one another waiting too long for payment."

"Nevertheless, every business gets some bad debts. Just watch out, that's all."

"I will."

She left the atelier then and Tom finished putting up the shelves and a triple row of hooks before he saw her again. He had stopped work only once, when the water in the boiler had begun to steam. After letting some of it scald through the tap, he had raked out the fire to let the rest cool down. He told Sophie what he had done when she came to call him to dinner.

"That's good. I hadn't realized it would boil so soon."

The meal was ready on the kitchen table. The boys were home from school and already in their places, with Henriette seated beside Billy. Tom drew Clara's chair out with great ceremony, which pleased her immensely, and the meal began with smiles all around. Clara asked Tom when he would be in Brighton again, so that she would know when to expect the horse and gig.

"I never know ahead when and where I'll be," he replied, "but the horse and gig shall be brought here this evening. I'll arrange that before I leave town."

The boys could scarcely believe what they had heard. "Is there to be a real horse in the stable, Ma?" Billy exclaimed incredulously.

"There is," Clara replied.

"Shall we be able to have rides?" Antoine asked, his face agog.

"That depends on Sophie. She's the one who'll be hiring it."

The children, becoming as still as if frozen in their suspense, turned their desperately eager faces toward Sophie. She and the other adults burst out laughing.

"La!" she exclaimed. "How well behaved you both look all of a sudden! You must remember that a gig only seats two, but I suppose you could manage to share the space intended for one sometimes." The boys were exuberant but Sophie gave them a little warning frown to be quiet. "Save that excitement for when the horse arrives and be good while at the table. It's lucky I swept out the stable this morning for the delivery of the timber," she continued. "I always thought how content a horse would be in that roomy stall."

When the meal was over Tom offered to escort Henriette home. "As long as I walk on my own when I reach the street where I live," she said anxiously. "I daren't be seen unchaperoned with any man."

"Naturally," he responded.

Henriette turned to Sophie. "I'll be back at the same time tomorrow."

Sophie expressed her gratitude to Tom for all his hard work as well as making the horse and gig available to her.

"Everything I do for you is a pleasure," he replied easily.

When he and Henriette had gone and the boys were putting down straw in the stall, Sophie told Clara she would be away on the morrow.

"Where are you going?" Clara asked in surprise. "I thought you wanted to make a start on the sweetmeats."

"That's true, but I made up my mind today to visit the farm where Antoine and I were cared for after the attack. I intended to take a coach part of the way and walk the rest, but now I'll be able to set off early with Tom's horse and gig. I'll not be many hours away."

"But why now of all times?"

"I have the chance now. When I start my employment at the Marine Pavilion I won't be able to have a day free when it suits me."

"Shall you keep Antoine away from school to take him with you?"

Sophie shook her head firmly. "No, he mustn't miss his lessons. I still have some of those chocolate candies left, and I'll take a box to Mrs. Millard."

Not long before the boys' bedtime, while they were still watching the gate, the horse and gig arrived in the charge of the groom. Clara directed him round the cottage to the stable. Tom's choice was a high-stepping chestnut with a white blaze, and soft eyes, and a look of speed about its strong flanks. The animal was not in the least put out by the boys' cheering as they pranced around him, almost as if he knew they were making him welcome. The gig was crimson with a gilt trim and matching paintwork on the wheels. The seat, upholstered in white leather, had a box behind designed to hold baggage. Sophie saw at once that it would take a good number of stacked confectionery boxes.

The groom unloaded a bag of feed from under the seat and informed Clara that a regular supply would be delivered from tomorrow onward. Upon hearing that Sophie was to drive the gig, he gave her some advice.

"This 'orse is a good un' in the shafts or out of 'em. 'E's been tried out several times as a riding 'orse by Mr. Foxhill. You'll 'ave no trouble with this fine beast unless 'e feels the whip. Then 'e'll go like the wind, gig behind 'im or no. Can you 'andle that?"

Sophie patted the horse's glossy neck. "I've ridden and driven a number of horses in France, a very spirited one among them. What's his name?"

"Star, miss. On account of the shape of 'is white blaze."

WHEN MORNING CAME Sophie harnessed Star to the gig and drove the boys to school as a treat. Then she continued on her way inland. For the first ten miles she followed the London road and then turned off to take a winding route to the Millards' farm. It was a mild, clear day with a soft breeze and a silk-blue sky. Sophie realized it was the first time she had been anywhere completely on her own since leaving the Château de Juneau. Not that she had any regrets about that, for she had grown to love Antoine as if he were truly her sister's son. The boy had some of his mother's sweet disposition, but also the Juneau pride, which made him want always to excel, to get top marks in his schoolwork, and to be the winner in any contest.

As she drove through the village on the final lap of her journey, people glanced at the girl in the spanking new gig, but she saw only one man whom she recognized. He farmed land next to the Millards.

"Good day to you," he called out. "So the little French miss is back again!"

She drew up alongside where he stood. "I trust I find you well, Mr. Bromley. And your wife and family."

"Never better. How's the little lad?"

"Growing fast and doing well at school." A thought struck her. "You called me the French miss. Was that how people used to speak of me?"

"Either that way or as the Fontaine girl!" His pronunciation of the Marquis's name would never have been recognized by any French person. "It took me by surprise seeing you again!"

Sophie smiled. "It's ten months now since I left."

"I suppose you're on your way to see poor Mrs. Millard." He shook his head. "That was a nasty accident."

Sophie felt her blood chill. "What happened?"

"Didn't you know? About a week ago she slipped in the byre and cracked the back of her head on a stone stoop. She's been very poorly ever since."

Sophie bade him farewell and drove out of the village in the direction of the farm. It distressed her deeply to think of that strong, active woman being so badly injured. She wondered how Mr. Millard and the sons were faring. Perhaps there was a new daughter-in-law managing the household. As she turned the horse into the rutted lane that led to the farmhouse, there was no sign of the menfolk, who were most probably in the fields. Sophie alighted, but before she could reach the door, it was flung open and Josie sprang out, having seen her arriving from a window.

"You've come back!" The child hugged Sophie and was hugged in return.

"La! How you've grown, Josie dear!"

"Where's Antoine? Why isn't he with you?"

"He's at school. Why are you home today?"

"The teacher has left to be married and we haven't a replacement yet. Come into the house!" The young girl rushed back indoors, calling out as she went. "Aunt Hannah! It's Miss Sophie!"

The woman who appeared, wiping her hands on her apron, bore some resemblance to Mrs. Millard and had the same reddish hair. The aroma of stewing mutton drifted out from the kitchen and Sophie was reminded poignantly of the night when she was carried into the farmhouse.

"So you're the French miss," the woman exclaimed. "Maggie told me all about you some months ago. I'm her sister, Hannah Harwood. Come in! How good of you to visit her."

"I only heard of her accident when I reached the village," Sophie said as she entered the familiar surroundings. Mrs. Harwood would have shown her into the chill, little-used parlor, but Sophie paused on the threshold with a smile. "I was made to feel so much at home under this roof that I'm much more used to the kitchen."

"Then that's where we'll go after you've seen Maggie. I don't know how far you've come, but you must have dinner with us. It's what Maggie would have wanted."

"I've brought your sister some chocolate candies."

Mrs. Harwood took the box from her. "That's kind of you. I'll mash one up in some warm milk and see if she can take it."

Then Sophie brought out the gift of a shell bracelet she had for Josie and gave it to her. "That's for you."

Josie was overwhelmed with delight. "I've never had anything so pretty!"

"The shells come from the place I'm living now."

Mrs. Harwood gave her niece a little push. "Run off now, child. I'm taking Miss Sophie to see your mother."

When the girl was out of earshot Sophie looked gravely at Mrs. Harwood. "How soon can you expect your sister to make a recovery?"

"The doctor says we must be patient and keep her quiet. So I can't let you stay for more than a minute. I warn you that she looks very poorly."

Although prepared, Sophie was still shaken to see how frail-looking Mrs. Millard had become. She was white as her pillows, her eyes closed. Her sister went across and spoke to her.

"Miss Sophie has come to see you, Maggie."

Mrs. Millard's eyes fluttered open. "How nice," she whispered weakly. "Such a good girl."

Sophie sat on the edge of the bed and took the woman's hand from the patchwork coverlet into both of hers. "I'm so sorry to find you unwell, but I'm sure you'll soon be recovered. Then I'll bring Antoine to see you too."

"Yes, please." The woman's eyes closed again.

Sophie kissed her brow and went quietly with Mrs. Harwood out of the room. In the kitchen where she had spent so much of her own convalescence sitting by the hearth or the window, she was introduced to a shy young woman named Sally, who had married the Millards' elder son and was visibly pregnant.

"What of your husband's brother?" Sophie asked her. "Is he betrothed?"

"Yes, miss. That's why he ain't living at home anymore. His future father-in-law is a butcher and he's gone into the family business. You'll not see my husband today either, because he's gone to market and won't be home till late."

"Unless Miss Sophie can stay the night," Mrs. Harwood intervened hospitably.

"No, I have to get back to Antoine, but thank you all the same."

Mr. Millard was pleased to see Sophie when he came in from the fields. Since revealing her whereabouts was no longer a threat to the domestic peace of the household, Sophie spoke of her work in Brighton and her new venture. Before leaving, she had the chance to speak to Mr. Millard on his own and explain the original purpose of her visit.

"Did your wife ever say what the Frenchman looked like? Was he tall or short? Dark or fair?"

He thought carefully. "He wore a white wig and had fancy manners. My wife ain't much good at describing anyone and she didn't like his bowing and scraping to her. She just said he was ordinary-looking in a foreign way. Why do you want to know?"

"I can't be sure he wouldn't inflict some harm on Antoine and me if our paths were ever to cross."

"Not much chance of his meeting you, I'd say. Maggie didn't take to him, so she didn't give your name or Antoine's when he asked

189

about the young woman and the boy who had been attacked with the old gentleman. She don't have patience with nosiness in anyone. After all, he claimed to be related to the departed and not to you and your nephew. So Maggie said as far as she knew you'd gone to London. I must say that she knew our younger son Joe was in the house and she didn't want him to hear by chance where you'd gone."

Sophie had breathed a sigh of relief. "The Frenchman was truly sent on a wild goose chase, then."

The farmer put his callused hand on her shoulder, his eyes shrewd. "You take care of yourself and the boy. As Maggie said to me after she sent that stranger away, you'd already had a packet of trouble in having to leave France and then being set upon by villains. She didn't want nobody else causing you more trouble."

"You and Mrs. Millard have done so much on my behalf. One day I hope I may be able to tell you the whole story. Could Joe add anything to Mrs. Millard's description of the Frenchman?"

"He only saw the back of the fellow as Maggie closed the door. When you return through the village you could speak to the landlord of the Oaktree Inn. The stranger asked directions from him as to where an elderly Frenchman and his party had been attacked. That's how he found his way to us."

When Sophie reached the inn, she did as Mr. Millard had suggested. The landlord was willing to tell her all he could.

"The foreigner came on a market day when we were all rushed off our feet in the taproom and nobody paid him any attention. All I can tell you is that he was tallish and wore a wig or had powered hair. I doubt if I'd remember him at all if there hadn't been all the talk afterward about the vandalism in the churchyard."

As Sophie drove homeward she decided that her enemy had gained little, if any, information about her personally. The mention in the notice of the possibility of her having been a servant could only have stemmed from inquiries made in the vicinity of the château. The fact that there had been no other aristocrat in the château with the Comte and Comtesse, and that the Marquis was missing as well as the boy, had pointed to a member of the household helping in their escape. It could have been an educated guess that all three had gone to England.

It occurred to Sophie that her enemy might even suppose her to have been the nursemaid who had whisked the two away. Judging from what she had heard from the innkeeper the man had been so sure of finding his prey at the farmhouse that he had spent no time in the village. After his temper had gained the better of him in the churchyard, he'd had no choice but to get away as quickly as possible.

Still, how he had traced her and her companions to the farmhouse remained a mystery. Somewhere and somehow he must have picked up word of the attack. Sophie was certain that if Mrs. Millard had been able to talk, she would have remembered more about the Frenchman's appearance. Now Sophie did not know when she would be able to visit the farm again.

Fifteen

IN THE DAYS before Sophie was to begin her job as a linen maid, she was totally happy to be back into full confectionery work. Wonderful aromas of caramel and lemon, vanilla, orange flower, cinnamon, almond, and chocolate all wafted from the atelier. Clara, who from the first morning had donned a white apron and mob cap to give Sophie assistance, was becoming so absorbed in this new work that already she was thinking seriously of giving up her summer job as a dipper. Like any capable housewife, she could make simple sweetmeats, but she began to take a keen interest in the more complicated work. Under Sophie's direction she soon found herself able to spin sugar into nests or baskets or cradles. The art of bonbon-making appealed to her, particularly knowing the exact moment to add coloring to the sugar syrup before pouring it into the many little molds.

Sophie gave Henriette equal attention and instruction. As the youngest and least experienced, she was the one who had to strain through a cloth bag the clarified sugar that poured from the charcoal-heated boiler. It was a tedious task and had to be done several times, but Henriette never complained. She liked best to dip preserved fruits or segments of orange or caramel in the sugar and put them to set in small ornamental pyramids, which afterward would be placed in spun sugar containers. At first her pyramids were lopsided and often collapsed, but she soon became quite adept. She also liked making barley sugar with Clara. The widow would cut small pieces off the prepared mixture and toss them to her. These would then be rolled out by hand like strips of soft wax before being twisted. Sophie had said that in her father's atelier the women rolled six at a time with each hand, and that was the number Henriette intended to reach.

It was Sophie herself who made the millefruit candy, the multicolored French ribbons, the transparent bonbons that had to be kept at low heat in the old oven in the hearth brickwork until just the right second, and all else presently beyond the skills of her two willing assistants.

The day of her first delivery was one of high excitement. The paper boxes, complete with frills patterned by the new tool, were fitted into light wooden trays, which had been made locally. The neatly packed confections in pastel hues, many decorated with sugared violets or nuts, candied peel, and tiny strawberries of marzipan with angelica leaves, made a pretty sight. There were trays of nougat, chocolate drops, and candies and a variety of lozenges, some of licorice, looking like tiny gems. The trays were all packed into the box on the gig, and then Sophie, in her best gown and wearing a new chip straw hat tied by ribbons under her chin, took her place on the seat. She had trimmed her whip with a bow, its streamers flying. Then with a shake of the reins she was on her way.

Her sweetmeats were well received by Mrs. Edwards, who wanted to have all the barley sugar, which she kept in stock for children. Other shopkeepers were clearly impressed by Sophie's presentation, but none renewed their orders, saying, somewhat condescendingly, that they would see how her confectionery sold before she need call again.

At the coffeehouse there was quite a different reception. Mrs. Mitchell began tasting from each selection.

"These are superb! My customers will revel in them! That candy-coated jelly melted in my mouth!"

Less than twenty-four hours later, a waiter from the coffeehouse tapped on the door of the atelier and entered.

"Miss Delcourt," he said as Sophie came to him, "Mrs. Mitchell needs another two trays of confectionery most urgently. I'll take them with me. She said I'm to tell you that she has already had inquiries from customers wanting to buy some to take home."

When he had departed with the trays, Sophie turned to her two pleased assistants. "It's early days yet, but I'm beginning to believe that Delcourt confectionery has been launched successfully!"

As one week after another slipped by, reorders began to trickle in from the other shops, and the boxes of sweetmeats made up for the Mitchell coffeehouse went as fast as they were put on sale. Clara and Henriette were jubilant, and even Sophie began to wonder if she needed the security of employment at the Marine Pavilion. Then she reminded herself that the new business could prove to be a flash in the pan and she was in no position to throw everything else aside. Having gained a foothold in the Prince's household, she could always strive to become the supplier of the royal confectionery.

ON THE MORNING in early May when the new linen maid arrived at the Marine Pavilion, none suspected she had been up since four o'clock making sweetmeats and had seen her two assistants well settled at their work for the day before leaving home. Sophie was shown into the linen room, where two other maids, both on the staff of Carlton House, were already installed.

"I'm Rose Lewis," one said in a friendly manner, "and this here is Betsy Dawson. We're mending aprons at the moment, but you can have something better for a beginning. Take that top sheet from the pile. The lace needs a stich."

Sophie took the sheet onto her lap and threaded a needle from the sewing box by her chair. It was beautiful lace that had come adrift. Then she noticed that the sheet was embroidered with the three feathers of the Prince of Wales. Betsy spoke up.

"Yes, all the sheets are embroidered like that. If you like you can help make up His Highness's bed with it afterward. That might give you a thrill!" Both young women chortled, watching for Sophie's reaction.

Sophie grinned. "It might! I'll have to see the bed first."

They were relieved. This French girl wasn't going to be hoity-toity as so many of them were. She could take a joke. As they began to chatter on, she learned that the Prince would be arriving the next day. There were only two guest suites and so house parties were always small, although many other people were invited to the functions arranged for entertainment. The Prince reserved one part of the day to himself, never joining his guests in the breakfast room and keeping to his own suite. This custom also kept private his return in the morning if he should have spent the whole night with his wife at her house in the Steine.

"People always have a splendid time here," Betsy said wistfully. "I'd like to change places with one of them ladies just for a day. Mrs. Fitzherbert usually arrives about noon and at table she always sits at Prinny's right hand, which is as it should be in spite of this game they play of her not being officially his wife. It's all such a pity. She'd have made a lovely queen one day."

"I admire her very much from what I've seen of her," Sophie said.

"She's a good, kind woman and no mistake."

When Sophie had finished attaching the exquisite lace, she was handed more ordinary sewing. Mrs. Palmer came in to inspect her work, and before she left, Betsy took her into the kitchen wing to meet the rest of the staff. The impudent footman, whom she had met at the door on her first visit, recognized her and grinned.

"So you're here after all! I'm Nick Barlow. Pity you're not in confectionery and then I'd have seen more of you in the kitchen. Are you coming in to the midday dinner?"

The meal was about to be served in the servants' hall, and those men in shirtsleeves were putting on their jackets, the women checking their appearance to make sure they were neat and tidy. Sophie declined, wanting to get back to the atelier, but there was a delay as a page, who had been out on an errand, suddenly returned with some electrifying news.

"Mrs. Fitzherbert isn't coming back to Brighton this summer!"

"Where did you hear that?" Betsy demanded.

"I met one of the Steine house kitchen staff. He's been laid off indefinitely and has had to get other work. Mrs. Fitzherbert has rented a house called Marble Hill at Twickenham. Think of that! Things must be much worse than we thought." He moved away, answering the questions of others who wanted to hear all the details.

Sophie turned to Betsy. "What did he mean by things being worse?"

"Haven't you heard the rumors about the Prince and Lady Jersey?"

"Yes, but I refused to believe they were anything but gossip."

"Well, in London we've seen the trouble brewing. Now Mrs.

Fitzherbert's absence for the summer shows that matters are really serious."

Sophie was saddened by the news of this split in a marriage that had withstood so much and hoped it would not be of long duration. At the atelier she found all was well and within minutes was at work there again herself. When she told Henriette and Clara what she had heard, Clara spoke grimly.

"Brighton folk aren't going to like that! I know there are a lot of politicians and other high-and-mighty nobs who'll be glad to see Mrs. Fitzherbert out of the way, but it'll be different here. I wouldn't like to be in Lady Jersey's shoes if she starts swanning about at the Marine Pavilion. The ordinary people of this town will make their feelings known. You'll see." She was pouring her own melted apple jelly, made last autumn, into candy molds. When set, they would be sugared and then covered with chocolate. Still holding the jug of jelly, she faced Sophie across the extra table that had been newly purchased for the atelier. "I've something of my own to tell you too."

"What's that?"

"The bathing season opens on the first of June, but I'm not going back to dipping. If you're willing, I'll stay on here."

"But you'd be taking a risk!" Sophie protested.

"I doubt it. I could always go back to dipping if I had to, but I don't think that will happen."

"Then I'll be glad for you to stay on," Sophie declared thankfully. Clara was proving extremely skillful and was totally reliable. "Now that money is beginning to come in I can adjust your wages as well as Henriette's. That is what I promised."

On the strength of Clara's new commitment, Sophie felt able to take on another line of confectionery. When delivering to Mrs. Mitchell, whose demand alone would have kept the atelier at work, she made a suggestion.

"All the shops I supply are steadily increasing their orders, but in addition to what I already bring here, how would you like a special range exclusive to this coffeehouse? It would be expensive, because I'd use the choicest of ingredients as well as liqueurs and cognac and so forth, but I can promise you candies such as my father made for the late King Louis himself."

Mrs. Mitchell's eyes gleamed. "How soon can you let me have the first batch?"

"By the end of the week, but there's one stipulation. If ever I should be fortunate enough to start supplying the Marine Pavilion or have my own shop I would make the same."

"Agreed!"

As a result, delicious new aromas began blending with the rest in the atelier. At last Sophie was able to use her very special skills and each of the exclusive candies was individually decorated.

Sophie's first delivery to Mrs. Mitchell coincided with the news of a great naval victory. The Royal Navy, under Admiral Hood's command, had destroyed six ships that were convoying American grain ships to France. The date that was to become synonymous with the battle was the Glorious First of June. Church bells rang and the Dragoons fired cannons in salute. All Brighton celebrated with the rest of the kingdom. Bunting and flags were still being displayed a week later when the Prince took up residence at the Marine Pavilion. He arrived on his own, and when two married couples appeared to occupy the guest suites, local hopes were raised that Mrs. Fitzherbert might still be coming to Brighton after all. But disappointment came when, during a heavy rainstorm, a yellow coach with liveried postillions mounted on black horses swept into town. Lady Jersey had arrived. On her first outing, taking a stroll in the sunshine with the Prince along the promenade, she was hissed. Two fishermen went further and spat in her wake.

IN A MATTER OF DAYS the hissing spread throughout the town whenever the Prince was seen with Lady Jersey. He was as deeply hurt as he was furious. He had always been the idol of the Brighton people and looked upon them as his loyal friends, rejoicing in the affection and respect they had always shown Maria as well as himself.

Maria! He clapped a hand to his forehead and paced the floor of his Cabinet. His conscience had begun plaguing him so much that it was like a perpetual headache. At times he thought himself mad to have neglected her as he had done during the winter. It was no wonder she had gone elsewhere for the summer. But then, she had always retreated when he had displeased her. She was punishing him far too harshly. Damnation! He would not be punished! Hadn't he enough to endure with his creditors hounding him and debts mounting daily?

There was a click of a handle as the door opened. Relief and pleasure swept over him as Lady Jersey entered. What a desirable woman she was!

"Am I disturbing you?" she asked sweetly.

"Only by your alluring presence, my dear Frances," he replied gallantly.

Frances smiled as she moved gracefully toward him, her soft summer skirt pink with woven rosebuds. There was nothing more rewarding for an older woman than the admiration of a younger man too besotted to remember the number of years between them.

THREE MORNINGS A WEEK Sophie set out to spend her two hours at the Marine Pavilion. As she was always shut away with the sewing maids, coming and going by the servants' entrance, she did not catch a glimpse of the Prince, although occasionally she heard his voice and his laughter. Lady Jersey was staying elsewhere in Brighton, but according to Betsy and Rose she was with the Prince all the time. It did not please Sophie when she had to mend Lady Jersey's silken shawl, which had been snagged by a rosebush in the garden, and was instructed to do it as quickly as possible. When the mending was done, both Rose and Betsy admired the result, the minuscule stitches completely invisible.

"It's better than the haughty bitch deserves," Rose said. "I'm thankful I haven't got to return it to her."

"I'll find her lady's maid," Sophie said, folding the shawl.

Betsy disagreed. "No, you were ordered to finish it and take it straight to Her Nibs."

Sophie was told by the footman, Nick, that the royal party was to be found in the Circular Salon. It was the first time Sophie had been in this room, which was the focal point of the house. The curved ceiling, profusely decorated with flowers and cherubs in delicate hues, rose up through the upper floor, culminating in the dome of the roof and effectively dividing the Prince's suite to the south of it from the guest suites to the north. The Prince was present, having just come in from riding with his two gentlemen guests, whose wives sat with Lady Jersey, all of them conversing together.

Sophie curtsied, holding out the shawl. Lady Jersey cast her a disdainful glance, but the Prince moved swiftly to take the shawl from Sophie and drape it around the woman's shoulders.

"There, my dear lady. You'll not feel a draft now."

Lady Jersey gave him a dazzling smile and raised her hand for him to take into his own. "Thank you, sire. I'm vastly obliged."

Sophie withdrew unnoticed from the room. The Prince had had eyes only for Lady Jersey. It did not bode well as far as Mrs. Fitzherbert was concerned.

THERE WERE MANY NIGHTS when Sophie went to bed early, exhausted from her early rising, the delicate needlework, her hours in the atelier, and the time she always gave to Antoine. Sometimes she believed she was asleep before her head reached the pillow. She was in just such a sound sleep when she stirred reluctantly one night to find Clara was shaking her by the shoulder.

"Wake up! Pierre is here! This time he wants to see you."

Instantly Sophie was wide awake. She thrust her arms into a robe and her feet into slippers. Quickly she ran a comb through her hair and hurried to the kitchen. Pierre Froment was standing with his back to the hearth, tamping tobacco into the bowl of his long-stemmed clay pipe. Clara was clearing away the remains of the meal she had served him, although a decanter of wine and his glass were left for his further refreshment.

"Good evening, Monsieur Froment," Sophie said.

He turned his head toward her. In his early forties, he had a broad nose, ill-proportioned features, and sea-weathered skin, and yet he was not an ugly man. His sharp eyes summed Sophie up immediately and apparently to his satisfaction, for he indicated that she should sit down. When he had lit his pipe and drawn on it, he pulled forward another chair and sat down opposite her, resting one arm on the table.

"So, Mademoiselle Delcourt," he said in French, "you're prepared to step in where revenue men shake in their boots."

"I've good reason."

"But no common sense."

She jerked up her chin. "That is your opinion! Just because I'm a woman doesn't mean I can't be as dangerous an adversary to the Broomfield gang as any man."

"You don't have to tell me what viragos women can be," he acknowledged. "I've witnessed a couple of incidents not far from my village when several aristos were discovered in disguise. It was the local women who used the pitchforks on them."

Sophie shuddered. Clara, although she had no understanding of French, noticed her reaction and promptly gave Pierre a prod in the arm.

"Don't go frightening the girl," she ordered, not realizing how incongruous her remark was in view of the purpose of this meeting. "Speak in English so I'll know what's going on. Be nice to Sophie. Remember that when she found out about you and your visits she could have gone straight to the authorities without speaking to me first. And that would have put your neck in a noose!"

Pierre patted Clara's rump in amorous apology for earning a reprimand and directed a grim look at Sophie. "Clara says I shouldn't frighten you. Does that mean you have no true idea what you might be getting into if I give you the facts you want?"

"I'm well aware," Sophie replied firmly. "Don't keep me in suspense any longer. Tell what you know."

"So be it." He shrugged as if shouldering off any part in her decision. "The Broomfield gang don't come in regularly to the same section of the coast. They have coves and tunnels and beaches that they use in turn."

"Does that mean that sooner or later they will come back to the part of the shore where I saw them?"

"Undoubtedly. I happen to know they've used it before, and therefore they will do so again. But they always have lookouts ready to warn them if there's any danger."

Sophie, although she did not much like the smell of any tobacco, could tell that he was smoking the very best of all contraband varieties. "Where is the Broomfield gang now?"

"Last week they put ashore near Rye. Where they'll be on their next run is a matter of guesswork. At the present time, I still can't tell you anything definite."

"Then why did you want to see me?"

"I had to be sure I wasn't dealing with some foolish girl liable to blab to everyone at the last minute."

"I know Clara would have spoken of me better than that."

Clara set her fists on her hips in an indignant stance. "Yes, I did! What are you saying, Pierre? Didn't I tell you she was a levelheaded young woman?"

He puffed on his pipe, unmoved by her reproach. "Yes, *chérie,* but a man likes to judge for himself, particularly when it's a matter of life and death. So, Mademoiselle Delcourt, tell me yourself why you want to see the Broomfield gang scuppered. You're a Frenchwoman. What happens here is no concern of yours."

"But it is. England is my home now. Moreover, two revenue men were murdered because I gave them a warning after I'd seen the smugglers."

"The fools! Went on their own to stalk the gang, didn't they? Greed killed them. They didn't want to share the bounty for making a catch."

"But their deaths showed that the Broomfield gang was operating over a certain period in this area."

He nodded. "Yes, that happens when there are large shipments to land and disperse."

Sophie spoke out forthrightly. "I believe you decided to see me because there's something in the wind. Am I right?"

He was noncommittal. "Maybe. Anyway, I need not keep you from your night's rest any longer. *Bonne nuit,* mademoiselle."

Sophie did not sleep again with so much churning over in her mind. Pierre had not been gone more than half an hour when she rose from her bed to wash and dress and go into the atelier, where she made an extra early start on the day.

ON MIDSUMMER EVE the Prince received a letter from one of his sisters, who wanted to consult him on some matter. He was fond of all his sisters and although it meant leaving Brighton for Windsor, there was no question of his not going. Yet there was also another reason for this journey. It seemed as if Fate had decided to give him a chance to mend the rift between Maria and himself. His brother William, Duke of Clarence, was holding a dinner party that evening, at his home near Hampton Court, and since he would be staying at Carlton House, the Prince knew he would be expected to attend, particularly since Maria would also be a guest. He sat down and wrote her a loving letter, calling her his dearest love and signing himself forever hers. After he had dispatched it, he heaved a deep sigh of relief that soon the differences between him and his darling wife would be healed. She had forgiven him many times before and she would do so again.

At Windsor, the Prince went first to see his father. As expected, he had to suffer yet another tirade on the subject of his debts. This one proved to be the worst to date. The old man's tongue lashed out and the threat to let him drown in his own folly began to seem a terrible possibility.

"Father, as I've said many times before, if I had an income suited to my position—"

"Bah! If you had fifty times the income it would run through your fingers! You're nothing but a wastrel! All you live for is pleasure!"

"And whose fault is that? You allow me no duties of responsibility! You refuse to let me lead our army! I want to serve our nation. I would dedicate my life to our people. But no! That is denied me. All I have left is the pursuit of pleasure. There was never any to be found in this penny-pinching Court!"

"How dare you!" The King rose up out of his chair, shaking from head to foot, his face becoming so purple that he looked on the point of an apoplectic fit. "When your debts set you before a judge in another kind of court, do not look to me for one farthing to save you! And neither shall Parliament. I'll see to that! The Lords and the Commons are as tired of your profligate ways as I am. Now get out of my sight!"

The Prince found his mother unsympathetic. Although fond of him, she sided with his father in almost everything, and he left her chilling presence as soon as she permitted him to escape. The affectionate welcome he received from all his sisters did nothing to lift his gloom. When he left them he went straight to Carlton House. All the way there he sat with his eyes shut in despair. The magnitude of his debts was notorious. No bank and no friend, however close, would be prepared to make him a loan with no possibility of repayment in the foreseeable future. He was at a loss to know what to do.

He groaned aloud. How wretched he was! How cruelly misjudged and mistreated! And if his financial worries were not enough, he had risked his marriage with Maria through his infatuation with Frances, who had teased and tempted him in spite of himself. Would Maria believe that he was really in no way to blame and still loved only her? She might be too hurt and humiliated to forgive him. Suppose he arrived at the dinner party to find her cool and distant, unmoved by his loving letter? That would be the final straw. He would not be able to bear it. Dread began to overwhelm the joy he had felt in Brighton at the prospect of seeing her again.

When the time drew near for the Prince to leave for William's dinner party, he was in such a state of deep depression that he scarcely knew whether to attend or depart at once for his beloved cottage by the sea. His guests had ended their visit and nobody would be there to disturb him, even Frances had returned to London on family business. The pier glass reflected a tall, still handsome but portly man in dove-gray satin coat and breeches, the Order of the Garter sparkling on his breast, who paced the floor with his head sunk in utter misery.

When the door opened, he thought he was to be informed that his carriage was waiting, but to his surprise it was Lady Jersey who entered. She had discarded her cloak in the hall and came softly toward him, her skirts billowing, her cleavage deep in the décolleté neckline, her pale arms extended.

"My dear George! I was at Windsor and heard from the Queen of the distressful interview with His Majesty. I had to come straight to you! You're not alone. I'm here to show you there is one who will always fight on your behalf."

"How sweet you are, Frances!" he exclaimed emotionally.

Her arms went about his neck, and he wept as he embraced her. Such loyalty! Such compassion! No coolness or retreating in his hour of dire need. She was stroking his hair, whispering between her kisses as she had never done before. He felt new hope, all his troubles seeming to melt away in her fragrance and her seductive closeness. Why should he face Maria's heartless rejection yet again when this lovely creature could see no fault in him?

The interruption of a tap on the door was unwelcome. His carriage was waiting. There was a terrible moment of indecision. Lady Jersey settled it for him. "The carriage will not be needed after all," she said to the footman, "but a letter will be delivered instead."

Intoxicated as much by the spell of her presence as by the brandy he had imbibed, the Prince wrote the letter at her direction and knew a sense of triumph.

William, who had kept his guests waiting as long as he could, had just led Maria on his arm to the table when the letter arrived. They had already decided between them that the Prince had been delayed at Windsor, and she was happy in the certainty that when she returned to Marble Hill she would find he had gone there to await her.

But William saw at once that his brother's letter had shocked her almost to the point of fainting. She was ashen to the lips.

"I can see you're not well, Mrs. Fitzherbert," he said, covering for her against the curiosity of the other guests and escorting her quickly out of the room. In silence and with a violently trembling hand, she gave the letter to him. He was appalled at what he read.

"I'll see you home," he said, full of concern.

"No," she answered bravely, "you mustn't leave your other guests."

"Then I'll call on you tomorrow."

"Thank you, good friend, but I would like to be alone."

When she had gone, William returned to the table. Although he was a jovial man, normally full of laughter and bawdy seafaring stories of his service days in the Royal Navy, he was subdued and only good manners kept him attentive to the conversation. All the time a question drummed in his brain. What was his brother thinking of? George had written to Maria that all was over between them.

MARIA LEFT MARBLE HILL to spend some weeks at the seaside resort of Margate on the east coast. The Prince, who had quickly repented his cruel letter to her, used every means available to try to coax his way back into her favor, but she refused to see him or answer his imploring letters. Neither did his brothers, whom he sent as envoys, manage to persuade her otherwise. News that remorse had made him seriously ill did not send her rushing to him as before.

Gradually it began to dawn on the Prince that this time Maria might forgive him, but she would not return.

Sixteen

IN LONDON, Tom made his way through the narrow, ill-lit streets. His destination was an inn where he had arranged to meet the Frenchman who claimed to be Antoine's kinsman. As he had expected, the address in the newspaper notice turned out to be that of a Royal Mail office where letters were collected. He had then written a letter himself on the spot and handed it in. Now he was following up on the directions he had received in reply.

He smiled to himself as he recalled Henriette's dismay when she returned to the atelier to find him on one knee by the hearth reading the encircled notice, which he had spotted in the process of putting more kindling on the fire. Foolishly she had tried to snatch it from him. It had been so easy to get the whole story from her after that. She had begged him not to give her away to Sophie, and he had promised he would say nothing until he judged the moment to be right. That worried her until he gave her his assurance that he would take the blame upon himself. Privately it had galled him to discover, also from Henriette, that Sophie had confided in the Excise officer while keeping him in the dark, but he intended to nail this Frenchman, whose threatening shadow lay over her and the child.

He reached the Golden Lion, which was a terminus of coaches and therefore one of the busiest taverns in London. The busy courtyard was full of horses. There was noise and bustle, ostlers and porters, touts and peddlers of London maps, and urchins seeking pennies.

In the inn, Tom gave his name at the desk and was directed to a corner table in one of the busy taprooms. To his surprise, he found a woman waiting for him. He saw at once that she was a London whore and guessed she had been recruited to speak on the inquirer's behalf. She greeted him amiably as he sat down at the table.

"Do you want to wet your whistle first?" she asked, indicating her own half-empty tankard of porter.

He shook his head. "I'll wait for a third person to join us."

She laughed convivially, showing bad teeth. "You'll die of thirst before that 'appens. You just tell me what a certain gentleman wants to know. I've money to pay you," she added with satisfaction, seeming well pleased with this unusual reversal of remuneration.

"I'll not deal with a go-between. You must fetch him."

" 'E ain't 'ere."

Tom pushed back his chair as if to leave. "Then this interview is over."

Dismayed, she tugged imploringly at his sleeve. "Wait, sir! 'Ave a 'eart! I'm being paid well to do this. Don't spoil it for me! I was told what to do if you should want to leave."

Tom, who had no intention of going, sat down again. This time he caught the eye of a waiter and ordered ale for himself and another porter for the woman. "So, who gave you these instructions?" he asked when she had gulped down what was left in her own tankard and his order had been served.

She shrugged her shoulders cynically. "Come now, sir. How would I know that? I wouldn't want to anyway. You and 'im are involved in something that's no concern of mine."

"What's he like? You can tell me that." Tom put a five-shilling piece on the table between them.

She looked at it longingly. "If I give you an honest answer that you mightn't like will you still give me the five bob?" To her relief he pushed the coin nearer and she pocketed it swiftly. "I never saw 'im. Madam Rose, who employs me, arranged everything."

Tom thought to himself that the Frenchman was certainly covering his tracks. "So what provision was made for my not wishing to give you the information?"

"The same as if you'd stayed," she answered impudently. "You give me the woman's name and I give you twenty-five guineas now.

206

When the name 'as been checked on the London register of all the French folk that's escaped to England we'll meet 'ere again. You'll get another twenty-five when you've told me 'er address. When she's found you'll get the remainder of a hundred."

"How can I be sure of the final installment?" He had to show interest, even greed.

She leaned forward, her bosom rising up in her tight bodice. "Between you and me, my guess is that the gent will scarper when 'e's got what 'e wants, although that's not for me to say. So you'd better make up your mind to settle for fifty guineas and be glad of it. At least you don't 'ave to hand over 'alf of what you get to your employer like me. So what's the name you're to give me? Maybe you'd best write it down. Some French names are so odd."

Again Tom signaled to a waiter and writing materials were brought. When he had written a name and sanded the ink he handed the paper to her. She studied it, although he doubted she could read. Then she folded it and put it into her purse before taking out a small bag of coins. The guineas clinked as she handed them to him. As he checked the amount, she emptied her tankard and rose to her feet.

"I'll leave you to finish your ale. We'll meet 'ere same time tomorrow."

Tom waited until she went out into the night, then went swiftly after. He intended to follow her to wherever she handed over the name. One fitful candle lamp was suspended from a bracket on the neighboring building, and in its glow he saw her halt as the door of a waiting closed carriage swung open for her. He moved forward swiftly, intending to catch hold and ride on the back of the carriage, but as she put her foot on the step she spoke to someone within, whose hand reached out to hasten her inside.

"I didn't know I was to be met, sir."

The Frenchman was there! Tom changed his tactics and hurled himself at the door even as it swung closed, the horses already whipped up. He looped an arm over the open window and grabbed the handle, all in a matter of seconds. Then a pistol exploded from within, the bullet passing within inches of his face, and the woman screamed. He fell back onto the cobbles. The woman tried to look out to see if he was still alive but was snatched back inside as the carriage sped away.

Picking himself up, Tom swore under his breath at the error he had made. He had thought to come face-to-face with the Frenchman, but he should have been prepared with his own pistol ready. Then he grinned savagely as he remembered what he had written on the paper. It was the maiden name of his late French grandmother.

SOPHIE WAS ASTONISHED at how quickly news traveled on the servants' grapevine and how much they knew of the Prince's personal affairs. Mrs. Fitzherbert's rejection of his overtures was discussed and dissected at length. Loyalty to the Prince was unswerving within his household, although all felt that the sooner he was out of Lady Jersey's clutches and reunited with his wife the better it would be. On the surface the Prince was as hospitable and genial as ever, but his servants knew he was hurt and upset that many old friends and others whose good opinion he prized now declined his invitations, their sympathies entirely with Mrs. Fitzherbert. Yet Lady Jersey still continued to hold sway over him, and her solution to his financial troubles had become well known.

"No," he had roared at her once in the Circular Salon, unaware that the double doors were not quite closed and footmen's ears were primed. "Good God! I'm married already! I'll not be made a bigamist with some foreign bride!"

"Legally you're still a single man. Try to remember that. As for Princess Caroline of Brunswick, she is charming and amusing and greatly taken with the portrait of you that was sent her."

"It should never have been sent! I would have forbidden it. Princess Caroline is my father's niece, for mercy's sake. Can you suppose the King's choice of a wife for me would ever be mine?"

"But such a marriage would be popular here in the kingdom as well as abroad. Parliament is ready to settle every penny of your debts on condition of this match. Your income will be adjusted most favorably and all will be set fair."

"No!"

"You must have an heir!"

"My brothers can supply a string of children for succession to the Throne."

"You have to be sensible. Do you want your creditors to humiliate you in the eyes of all the world? This political marriage would be the saving of you. You've everything to gain and nothing to lose. Mrs. Fitzherbert is never coming back to you!"

The Prince uttered a heartbroken groan and a chair creaked as his heavy weight descended into it. His desolate sobbing was clearly heard before Lady Jersey noticed suddenly there was a gap in the double doors and closed them swiftly.

The general opinion was that she had then held his head to her bosom, her role more maternal than amorous in this present crisis.

At Margate, rumors of a possible marriage between the Prince and a foreign bride reached Maria Fitzherbert, but she paid no attention, for such rumors had cropped up at various times throughout their married life. Her husband was prone to folly, but he would never commit such a heinous sin. It was typical of him to be always wanting his cake and eating it too, and that had made him try to win her back while still remaining in Lady Jersey's thrall. When he threw off the other woman's clutches and came to her unfettered and free, she would be a wife to him once more. A man's nature could not be changed, and she loved him still in spite of everything.

ONE SUNNY MORNING, Henriette arrived for work bubbling over with news.

"At the Promenade Grove yesterday evening I was with Uncle François and Aunt Diane in a party that included such a pleasant man. He danced with me more times than he should have, but since he has a title and is rich and is—as my aunt said—of a sensible age, I was not reprimanded and everybody beamed approval."

"What's his name?" Sophie asked, pleased to see Henriette looking so happy.

"Sir Roland Westonbury. He's a baronet and a widower, about thirty-five. He lost his wife three years ago, so he's out of mourning now. I can't say he's handsome, and he is corpulent like the Prince of Wales, but he's the first man I've ever found agreeable whom my aunt and uncle like too. He's invited the three of us to the Castle Inn ball this evening!"

Sophie wondered if the approval of Henriette's aunt was altogether a good recommendation, but she would not dampen the girl's pleasure. "Is he in Brighton for the season?"

"Yes, he's taken an apartment on the Steine. His London residence is in Berkeley Square and he has a country seat in Gloucestershire!"

Clara spoke from where she was melting chocolate. "Has he any children?"

"No. Aunt Diane asked him that."

"He'll be wanting an heir, then. You shouldn't find him hard to catch, Henriette!" Clara joked.

Henriette blushed. "Don't tease! I hardly know the man."

Yet she could hardly settle to work and talked nonstop about her new acquaintance. Clara was soon bored by the topic and felt quite envious of Sophie when she set out for the Marine Pavilion. By midmorning the widow could take no more.

"Henriette! You've said everything about Sir Roland ten times over. I don't want to hear any more until you have a betrothal ring on your finger!"

"Do you think that's possible?" Henriette was touchingly hopeful. She then pondered aloud and at length how long a couple should know each other before a marriage proposal. Clara noticed that not once did Henriette mention love.

When Sophie's work was done, she left the Marine Pavilion as usual by the servants' door. By now everyone had known for some time that she also made confectionery, and there had been a number of requests that she bring some in for the staff. She planned to do that on the Prince's birthday in August.

To her surprise she found Tom waiting for her in the gig. "Good news!" he greeted her, springing down from the equipage. "I've purchased premises in Brighton at last. That's where I'm taking you now!"

He explained on the way that the property had belonged to a recently retired cabinet-maker and consisted of a small shop with a large showroom and a workshop to the rear. It had not been decorated for some years and would need considerable renovation before it was fit to house and display Foxhill wares.

In Middle Street Tom drew up outside the bow-windowed shop. Gates at the side led to the stable and the workshop. The cabinet-maker's trade sign, of a chair, still hung suspended over the shop's entrance.

"I'll be changing that," Tom said with an upward nod toward the sign before unlocking the door and letting Sophie enter ahead of him.

"What shall you have instead?" Sophie asked, loosening the ribbons of her hat to let it dangle against her back as she glanced around the shop. It was clean and empty except for a fitted bench of polished wood on which Tom put his hat and gloves.

"In London I have the sign of a mother-of-pearl box. I shall have the same here."

Sophie froze, the image of the smuggler with the mother-of-pearl box flashing instantly into her mind's eye. Was it Tom himself whom she had seen that night on the beach? She wanted to dismiss the idea, to cry out against her own suspicions, but shocked as she was, she was able to see in retrospect that many things had begun falling into place. There was his avoiding the main road on the night he had found her, his frequent comings and goings, and, as she knew from that evening of the bonfire on the beach, the way he went about well armed. Then there was the abundance of French wares that passed through his hands! Who was to say that he did not bring them in tax-free?

"Are mother-of-pearl boxes plentiful?" she questioned carefully, hoping desperately that his answer would dispel her fears. Otherwise she would certainly have to confront him. Nothing could make her keep silent!

"Plentiful? No, far from it," he replied. "The kind I seek are very rare and uniquely beautiful. They were made in China about two hundred years ago. I was lucky enough to get hold of one to sell to the Prince of Wales some time ago."

"When was that?" She was avoiding his gaze, deliberately looking about at the shop.

"Let me see." There was a short reflective pause. "It was sometime last summer."

Then she knew, as surely as if he had confessed, that he was the smuggler she had seen. With her thoughts in a wild turmoil, Sophie wandered slowly through the open double doors that led into the showroom, the leisurely tap of her heels echoing in the cavernous space. Here all the windows were shuttered except one at the far end. It gave enough light for her to see that the building was old and might originally have been a barn. An ancient wooden gallery with a strutted balustrade ran round the walls. Her instincts were compelling her to put some distance between Tom and herself before she confronted him. She began to mount the narrow flight of curved steps that led to the gallery, her skirts rustling in the stillness.

From on high, she paused to look down at where he stood with his face upraised to her.

"Where is the Prince's mother-of-pearl box now?" she asked very directly.

"At Carlton House," he replied easily. "Why?"

She turned away to stroll along the gallery. "Does His Highness realize that you sell him smuggled wares?"

She heard him draw in his breath sharply, but when he spoke, his voice was unruffled and smooth.

"Whatever put that notion into your head?" He gave an easy laugh. "Are you thinking about those Sèvres vases I sold His Highness? I told you at the time I'd bought them from an émigré."

She paused to look down at him, her eyes sparkling and angry. "No, it's not the vases, but something that happened before then! I was on the beach that night when you brought the mother-of-pearl box ashore!"

He stared hard at her, his face tightening. Then he turned for the steps and she felt the gallery shake as he took them two at a time to reach her. She spun around to face him when he drew level.

"You've made an extraordinary allegation," he stated crisply. "I think you should elucidate."

"The Broomfield gang came ashore that night! You were with them. When the two revenue men had their throats cut, I made up my mind not to rest until you'd all received justice for your crime!"

Fury blazed through him. "I am no murderer and never have been!"

"You're still tainted by the company you keep! I know what I saw!"

"So what do you propose to do now?" he demanded fiercely. "Do you have some proof of my supposed activities to offer a judge?"

"None except my word as a witness," she retorted triumphantly.

"So you will point to me in the dock and say you recognized me instantly in the full moonlight?"

"There wasn't much moonlight," she admitted, her voice faltering, "and your face was half-covered by a kerchief."

Tom's eyebrows shot up in angry mockery. "Indeed? In that case, I don't think you'd be able to make your accusation stick. At best, you could denounce me to Captain Morgan. I'm sure he would believe you, but he would want to know why you hadn't told him to arrest me before now."

She became flustered, no longer sure of her ground. "Heaven knows I've never wanted to think of you as a criminal! You've only to tell me truthfully that you obtained the mother-of-pearl box for the Prince by honest means!"

"I paid a good price for it."

"That doesn't answer my question! Were you on the beach that night?"

Tom sighed heavily. "I was, but any situation can be more complex than at first appears. Maybe you should give some consideration to that possibility. I suppose I could be called an independent Free-trader."

Her face was anguished. "So you are a member of the Broomfield gang!"

"I sail with them, but I'm not one of them. There's a difference."

"I see none!" She threw up her hands in exasperation. "You're mad! That can be the only explanation." Her voice shook. "Mad as the Revolutionaries murdering innocent people, and whatever you say, there's blood on your hands, however indirectly it came there! I hate men like you!"

He shrugged impatiently. "Then there's nothing more I can say, since your mind is made up against me. So what's your next move?"

"What can I do?" Unconsciously she was wringing her hands in despair. "You're tearing me apart! My first loyalty is to Rory and the vow I made to justice, but how can I even try to send to the gallows the man who saved my life and that of my nephew?"

"Don't you mean the young Comte de Juneau?"

With a moan Sophie clasped her head with spread fingers, drooping like a broken reed, her elbows tucked tight into her body. "So you have that knowledge to hold over me too," she cried. "How did you discover the truth?"

He moved closer, but made no attempt to touch her. "On the day of the whitewashing." Then he explained how Henriette had found him reading the newspaper notice and how he had drawn the whole story from her.

Sophie rocked slightly. Now she understood why Henriette had been so flushed and embarrassed when she came into the cottage from the atelier. "She broke her promise to me!"

"You must excuse her. Henriette means well, but she was no match for me." He lowered his voice questioningly. "Why didn't you tell me everything? I thought you trusted me."

She flung up her head, anguished and wild. "I've never trusted you! And all that you've just said only confirms how right I was!"

"That's where you're wrong! It's yourself you don't trust, because in your heart you know that we were meant for each other! You've only refused to acknowledge it because it doesn't fit in with all your neat little plans about how your future should be." He reached out and gripped her supple waist, drawing her close. "I've never wanted any woman as I want you!"

His arms were about her before she could break loose, the back of her head cupped in his hand to prevent her jerking away. She tensed, but he kissed her tenderly, as a man might kiss a beloved bride on their wedding night. She felt she was sobbing inside from rage and frustration and despair because he was creating a fiery harmony between them that she found impossible to resist. It was as if their hearts were beating simultaneously, their blood flowing the same course, their limbs exulting in the pressure that made her helpless in his embrace. Tremor after tremor passed through her, but when he lifted his mouth from hers and would have kissed her temples and eyes, she moved sharply back. He spoke softly.

"Let us go on from here. Be tolerant of my adventurous ways, Sophie. So much could be ours."

But reality and reason had returned to her. She spoke with painful intensity, standing very stiff and calm. "You ask too much. This is a time for speaking frankly. Through the shared knowledge of our individual secrets each of us is in the power of the other. I have sworn to see the Broomfield gang arrested if the chance should come my way, but no matter what I feel about your way of life, I could never betray you. Can I rely on you to promise the same?"

"I'll tell you something first. I made it my business to follow up the address given in that newspaper."

Stress swept color high in her cheeks. "You saw my enemy?"

"Not quite. I had written offering to meet him, mentioning that I had taken a young woman and a boy to the Millards' farmhouse and knew their whereabouts."

"You did that! Tom, how could you?"

She was stunned that he, either through thoughtlessness or bravado, should have betrayed her. In a surge of rage and fear and temper she tried to wrench herself free of his grasp, but he was equally determined not to let her go.

"Listen to me!" he roared.

"Let me go!" She fought him like a wild cat, both of them shouting, and as they swayed and struggled neither noticed the creaking of the gallery boards underfoot. Then, as they staggered together, there came an ominous vibration and he released her, his hands flying up in the air as a board fell away underfoot. She cried out in alarm, thudding back against the wall. Tom had fallen forward, one leg out of sight in the gap.

"Stay where you are," he shouted when she reached forward to help him. Before he could recover, there was a splintering as the next board loosened under his weight, followed by another that broke away behind him to go thumping and booming onto the floor below. She cried out frantically, thinking he was going too, but he remained head and shoulders in the gap, supporting himself precariously with his arms. She could see his muscles straining, and careless of her own safety, she flung herself flat and grabbed handfuls of his coat while the struts of the railings began to follow those that had gone with the boards, setting off a chain reaction as they leapt and tumbled into space.

Tom was trying to get a foothold on the wall to lever himself up. "Get back!" he barked. "If any more boards go you'll fall and break your neck!"

There came more ominous splintering. For her sake he gasped his decision. "I'll have to drop. Draw back now! Now, I said! While there's still time. Hang on to whatever you can find."

She obeyed him reluctantly, scrambling to her feet and sliding her back along the wall, watching as he lowered himself from her sight until only his hands showed, the knuckles white with strain. As he disappeared three more boards vanished too, and then others followed until in seconds the gap had reached to within inches of her feet, huge clouds of dust ascending.

"Are you all right, Tom?" she called out desperately as she edged her way along until she reached the gallery window and perched on the ledge. From there she could see the length of the showroom. "For mercy's sake, answer me!"

To her immense relief a figure rose from the debris, stumbled a few steps, and then straightened up. Facing her in silhouette against the sunny interior of the shop, Tom ignored her anxious inquiry.

"Stay exactly where you are, Sophie. Don't move! You're safe on that ledge. There's a ladder in the workshop."

He dashed across to the pair of tall doors that led into the stable-yard, flinging them wide to let a rectangular patch of sunshine fall across the floor. His shadow disappeared. Looking around, she could see that the supporting brackets had given way in several places. Tom was soon back with the ladder, which he propped exactly in front of her.

"Now, Sophie! And as quickly as you can without causing any vibration."

She bundled up her skirts and lowered her foot onto the top rung. Then she was descending swiftly and surely. He swept her into his arms before she reached the floor and whirled her back into the shop. As he let her down, she saw he was covered with dust and his cheek bleeding.

"As I had been about to say before that untimely interruption," he said as she felt in her pocket for a handkerchief to dab the blood away, "I wrote to the inquirer of that notice only stating that I knew of your whereabouts, not that I would reveal them. You should have understood that!"

"You frightened me!" she said accusingly. "You must realize that I go in constant fear of being betrayed by some chance remark. Why couldn't you have made yourself clear?"

"You didn't give me time. Hell's bells! What a temper you have!"

"So what happened?" she demanded impatiently, sitting down on the bench. Now that they were both safe, she became aware that her legs were shaking. But Tom was not ready as yet to disclose what had taken place.

"I could almost feel pity for your enemy for having an opponent like you, Sophie. He doesn't know what he's taken on."

"So let me know about him."

Tom sat down on the bench, half turned toward her, and gave her a full account of the whole incident. "I blame myself for the mistake I made," he concluded. "I should have understood that a man so determined in his quest would brook no interference. Henriette said you believed him to be kin to Antoine's father."

"Yes. The Comtesse de Juneau spoke of a certain Emile de Juneau, her husband's nephew, who had always been bitterly opposed to him. I believe he is my enemy. Whether he's in this country himself or has sent a hired assassin is impossible to say."

"I'd wager it's this Emile himself who's here. His wish to maintain secrecy gives that away. He would have to avoid being recognized by royalist émigrés while an agent would not."

She made a small uncertain gesture with her hands. "I've wondered if there's more to all this than merely eliminating the last member of the main branch of a long and aristocratic line."

"Inheritance?"

With a nod she stood up and moved away to look unseeingly out the bow. She was in profile to him, the sunshine etching her lashes, her brow, and the lovely curve of her lips.

"Many great estates have fallen forfeit to the Republic," she said thoughtfully. "Suppose Emile wants to ensure that the Juneau château and all its vineyards and lands come to him. If there were no other living heir, the claim of a close relative of rampant Revolutionary ideals, who had been shunned by the Juneau family in the past, would surely constitute a strong case. How easily he could promise to share the income with the tillers of the soil, how cunningly he could divert most to himself."

"You speak as if you knew him personally."

"I've had plenty of time to think about him and try to discover the motive that prompted such hatred. Envy is a common root. Greed is another. Emile knows, as we all do, that eventually France must end her wars and settle down again. It may take many years before it is safe for émigrés to return home, but the Comtesse said that Emile de Juneau was a young man. No wonder he wants to secure a fortune while he can. All would be lost to him should Antoine go back one day." Abruptly Sophie flung her forearm across her eyes. "Until today I had avoided speaking of my enemy by name. Somehow that always kept a safe distance between us. Now he has drawn near and taken on flesh and shape and form. If I feared him before, I fear him now a thousand times more."

Tom rose to his feet, but knew enough to keep his distance. She was too overwrought to tolerate his touch. Instead he spoke in measured, reassuring tones.

"Try to remember that your enemy still has no idea where you and the boy might be. He can't seek information openly when he has to avoid recognition himself, and that leaves him with all of England to search. You have every advantage. Before long he'll have to give up and return to France."

"But that might only delay the outcome. I will never stop fearing him." Sophie turned to Tom again. "You risked your life in London for Antoine and me. I—"

"As you risked yours for me just now."

She dismissed his interruption with a sweep of her hand, seeing no comparison. "It means my debt to you increases daily. All I can do in repayment is to protect you from the authorities with my silence."

"It should be enough, but I want more from you."

"No!" She raised her hand again, anticipating what he would say next. "Don't confuse gratitude on my part with any sentimental attachment you imagine I might feel."

"There's no point in arguing about that," he conceded dryly. "I'll be leaving Brighton later today, but I'll be back as soon as the builders put up the scaffolding here. That gallery must have been there since the place was built. What I wanted to say is that I regret what happened up there and I'm thankful you came to no harm."

"It was an experience," she remarked, dismissing it lightly.

"One that I wouldn't want to happen again. The gallery will be the first thing torn down."

"Shall you replace it?"

"Yes, I will. And, by the way, I shall continue to leave Star and the gig in Mrs. Renfrew's stable, so you'll still be free to drive whenever you wish."

"But you have stables of your own now."

"I'll have other transport there. I'll probably get a breakneck phaeton as you first suggested."

His continued kindness was like a dagger in her heart. If only things were different! "Why didn't you tell me the truth about yourself that day at the farmhouse?" she burst out. "Maybe together we could have found a means to help you overcome this senseless obsession for excitement. Since you already have a good business in London, there can be no other reason for you to keep such dangerous company."

"You think that now, but your reaction would have been the same as today. Then I might have lost you altogether. When I first saw you lying bruised and bleeding in the lane I felt pity, but when I raised you on my arms and looked into your face I knew love."

Sophie turned her head away defensively. "Don't try to win me with soft words. That evening at the farm gate you made it very clear that you would only seek me out when it suited you."

"You flew into such a huff, you gave me no time to ask for your patience."

Her eyes flashed at him. "I think I have shown patience, but that finally ran out today."

"Then why are you so concerned for me?"

"I hate waste," she stated bluntly. "Even your life shouldn't be thrown away, but put to good purpose instead."

He burst into a shout of laughter. When it subsided, his grin was still wide.

"You dare to speak of waste, Sophie. You're guilty of wasting time by refusing to acknowledge what there is between us."

She simmered, rising to her feet and opening the door of the shop to leave. Defiantly she looked at him.

"If there is a man for me, there's only one I'd name. That's Rory Morgan. Nobody else."

Tom was taken aback. "Don't you dare!" he roared.

She gasped, her eyes wide. "Whatever makes you think you can dictate to me?"

"In this case it is my right!"

"Your conceit is insufferable! Let's make sure we don't see each other again for a long, long time!"

Sweeping out of the shop she slammed the door after her.

She was at work in the atelier an hour later when a package was delivered to her with a note.

Lessons have been paid for in advance with Sergeant Jones, Rtd.,
of No. 15, Black Lion Street, for you to be taught how to use the
enclosed. You must be able to defend yourself and the boy in an
emergency.

Tom

Inside was a pistol. Tentatively she curled her finger around the trigger, disliking the weapon, yet thankful for the means to meet Emile de Juneau on equal terms if a confrontation should ever occur. Not for the first time she thought to herself that Tom was the most exasperating of men, infuriating her at one moment, then undermining her anger with kindness at the next. By this fait accompli he had ensured against her refusing in the heat of the moment to accept either the pistol or the lessons. With time to consider, she knew she would make use of his thoughtful act for Antoine's sake, if not for her own.

Sergeant Jones proved to be a burly, red-faced fellow who had lost a leg in the early days of the war when there was some fighting on French soil. He was an excellent instructor. As soon as Sophie had become proficient in handling and loading the pistol, even able to clean it thoroughly in army style, he set up a target against the sea on a deserted stretch of beach. When her bullets went wide, there would be no chance of anybody coming to harm. Sometimes he treated her with courtesy and at others like a raw recruit, forgetting to control his language. But she was quick to learn and had a true eye. Before long she was earning a few reluctant words of praise. At the end of the last lesson, he nodded approvingly.

"You've become a good shot, miss. I'll tell Mr. Foxhill the next time I see him."

Tom liked the letter Sophie wrote him. Sensibly she had accepted the lessons and the pistol as they had been given quite divorced from personal feelings. Yet the sooner she put Morgan out of her life the better. One of the reasons he had engaged Sergeant Jones was to make sure she did not seek instruction from the Excise officer.

Seventeen

WHENEVER SOPHIE PASSED Tom's premises in Middle Street she looked to see if the alterations had been started, but nothing had been done. She concluded that he was abroad and the builders had instructions not to begin until he could be on the spot himself.

She and Clara had hired a girl between them to watch over the two boys during the summer when they were not in school, but on Sundays they arranged picnics and outings as a family. Antoine no longer missed Rory; he was now too busy with his own life and his friends, which was all to the good.

As the summery days continued to slip by, Sophie half expected Tom to arrive unannounced at the atelier or to meet her at the Marine Pavilion, but he did not come. She happened to be thinking about him when Henriette tentatively broached a request.

"I know you're busy from morning to night, Sophie, and I'd never ask if it could be done any other way."

"What is it?" Sophie asked amiably. She had just received a box of bonbon wrapping papers, which she'd had printed with fortunes and romantic phrases. In France these novelties had been popular from the time her father first produced them, and for this reason she'd had them done in French.

"My uncle and aunt wish to give a dinner party for Sir Roland. They seem to think it will provide him the opportunity to propose to me. Would you cook a truly splendid feast for us, one that will put Sir Roland in the most contented of moods?"

"But are your kinfolk agreeable?"

"Oh, yes. I've told them nobody can cook like you, and I can say that from experience."

"That's very complimentary!"

"My aunt wants the expenditure limited, but I'll make up the difference with my own money, and there are good wines that were left in the cellar by my uncle and aunt's benefactor."

Sophie regarded her very seriously. "Is Sir Roland the man you really want with all your heart?"

Henriette lowered her eyes for a moment and then raised her head quickly. "Yes, he is. He's considerate and rich and I'm fond of him." Her voice became choked. "I like working with you, Sophie. You know I do. But I have to get away from my uncle and aunt. I'm so wretched under their roof. All I want from life is a husband and a home and children. That's why I'm asking you to help me with this special evening."

Sophie smiled. "Then I will, with pleasure. Tell me what your kinsfolk wish to spend and we can plan the menu between us."

It was decided there should be two removes, which was the term for the serving of courses in England, each always consisting of a variety of dishes. As there were to be only ten guests, there would be a limited number of entrees, whereas a banquet at the Marine Pavilion would include thirty-six entrees along with scores of other dishes. After the removes, Sophie's sweetmeats, with fruits in season, would be served with a choice of Madeira or red or white port.

Henriette clasped her hands. "It all sounds wonderful!"

Although Sophie could barely spare the time, she gave meticulous care and thought to the preparations. She bargained with a local fisherman to provide his best prawns and lobsters on the day, and from another she ordered plaice. She drove out to a local farm to buy Southdown lamb direct, as well as veal and beef, because it was cheaper than going to a butcher. Sophie knew that the Baronne was taking advantage of her willingness to do her best for Henriette, but that did not lessen her determination to produce a truly wonderful dinner. Fresh salads, herbs, and vegetables presented no problem since Clara grew a variety herself. She told Sophie to take whatever she needed and refused payment. It was her contribution to Henriette's gambler's throw.

"I hope Henriette does become Sir Roland's wife," Clara joked. "It will give my ears a rest from her wedding plans."

"I wish I could be sure she wasn't trying to convince herself as much as us that he is as good a man as she could wish him to be."

"Ah!" Clara remarked enigmatically and said no more.

On the day before the dinner party, Sophie inspected the Bouvier kitchen and dining room. She and Henriette went through the linen and selected a fine damask cloth trimmed with heavy lace.

"Scaffolding is going up at Tom's shop," Henriette said as she folded the rest of the cloths away. "I caught a glimpse of him through the bow window when I was on my way to collect a fan I'd had mended."

Sophie drew in her breath. So he was back! Then, deliberately putting him out of her mind, she went to give instructions to the maidservant and Clara, who had volunteered to help in the kitchen and prepare the removes for the two French footmen whose services had been hired for the evening.

That night after spending several hours at confectionery work, Sophie continued late in the cottage kitchen, finishing off the puddings and dealing with anything else that could be made ready in advance. Clara helped, for in any case Pierre was expected. He arrived soon after midnight when both Clara and Sophie had sunk into their chairs and were having a cup of tea. He greeted Clara with a kiss before acknowledging Sophie's presence.

"I wanted to see you," he said.

"You've news!" Sophie tensed.

"*Oui*, but you'll have to use your own judgment as to whether it will be helpful to your cause."

"Tell me!"

Pierre sat down leisurely, never seeming to be in a hurry about anything. Sophie linked her hands in her lap and waited.

"I ran my boat in on business at Sidlesham a couple of nights ago," he began. "The miller at the tidal mill there told me he was having to line up four wagons for a large shipment that will be coming in shortly." Pierre paused. "Now, in my trade nobody shows himself to be too inquisitive. It's not wise. But a nod is as good as a wink among the Gentlemen, and I would say that it's the Broomfield gang who'll be bringing in the consignment. To my knowledge there's nobody else who could operate on that scale nowadays. Many smuggling ships have been mistaken by the Royal Navy for American vessels running cargos of wheat into French ports, and when a warning shot across the bows failed to have effect, the Gentlemen's ships were pursued and sunk."

"Where is Sidlesham?"

"It's a small village in West Sussex about thirty-five miles from here."

"When is the Broomfield gang expected?"

"Nobody could say for sure. My guess would be the next moonless night."

When Sophie went back to bed, she agonized over what she should do. She did not want Tom to be caught by Rory in the ambush, and yet she dared not warn him in case he in turn should alert the Broomfield gang. She would have to find some way to keep Tom with her until the danger was past. At least she knew he was in town.

In the morning Sophie made two important calls. She went first to the Excise office where she handed in her urgent letter to Rory. Even as she drove off again, a revenue man on horseback overtook her on his way to deliver it at speed. Next she went to Tom's shop in Middle Street. The whole building was encased in scaffolding and work had begun on the roof.

The bell on the shop door tinkled as she entered and a tall, broad, and well-dressed man came from the showroom where the gallery was in the process of being knocked down. He closed the double doors to shut out the noise and she saw at once that this could only be Tom's brother. The likeness was more in build and height and color of hair than in features, although there was a similarity around the eyes and the unmistakable, well-cut Foxhill mouth. Sophie introduced herself and expressed her certainty that she was addressing Richard Foxhill. His smile lit up his gray eyes.

"Tom has spoken of you many times, Mademoiselle Delcourt," he said warmly. "It's an honor to meet you."

"I have to speak to him."

"He's not here."

She wondered how much Richard knew of his brother's activities.

Tom had always spoken of him as being reliable, conscientious, and hardworking. This recommendation, combined with the serious look about him, made it hard to believe he could be involved, however indirectly, in the smugglers' trade. And yet they were partners in the business.

"Then if you have no objection I'll sit and wait on this bench for his return."

"There'd be no point. I'm afraid I misled you. He's been out of the country for some while."

Suddenly she felt sick with fear. Tom was already in France! She should have come here first, before sending that letter to Rory. It had been Richard and not Tom whom Henriette had glimpsed through the window, and it was easy to see how she could have made that mistake. "I must get a message to him!"

"That would only be possible if you took ship to St. Petersburg."

A gush of relief made her tremble. She smiled thankfully. "My message has lost its urgency. I hope he has a successful buying trip, which I presume it to be."

"It always is when Tom goes far afield." Richard saw that she was moving to the door and went to hold it for her. "It would be a great pleasure for me if you would have supper with me one evening."

"I should like that very much."

Later that morning, she transported her own cooking pots, prepared vegetables, and other necessities to the Bouvier house in the gig. Clara and Henriette were left to carry on without her in the atelier, although Henriette was too excited to be of much use. It made Sophie consider what she would do if the girl's hopes were fulfilled and a marriage was forthcoming. The business was gaining a sound footing, and perhaps it was time to take on a young apprentice.

The dinner was to be served at the fashionable hour of six o'clock. Sophie had everything under control in the kitchen and went to make a final check on the dining table. The centerpiece of roses was charmingly arranged, the glasses for white wine had been placed upside down in individual silver containers holding crushed ice, and every knife, fork, and spoon was perfectly in place. All these preparations had been organized by Henriette, who was well trained in this sphere of housewifery. The Baronne had done nothing and was now awaiting the arrival of the guests. The Baron had approved the selection of wines, making only one change.

In the kitchen, Sophie and Clara were making last-minute preparations when they heard the guests being welcomed. The two of them, helped by the maidservant, handed through the dishes of the first remove, some of which would be kept warm over candle-lit hot stands. There were oysters garnished with lemon and served with a sauce *poulette*, lobsters on beds of crisp lettuce, prawns arranged to form a pink cascade, plaice enhanced by cream, chicken pie with a golden crust, braised pigeons, and roast duck with an herb stuffing. Salads pretty as flower gardens and summer vegetables would complete both removes. The *potage de poissons à la Russe* steamed gently in a silver tureen.

It was not as a formal French dinner would have been served, with each course announced as it was brought in, but this was the British custom and Henriette had been desperate that nothing appear odd or out of place to the guest of honor. Her fears had also put a brake on what Sophie would have prepared if the choice had been entirely hers, for she had gathered that Sir Roland was a conservative man with a dislike of all things "foreign." Obviously Henriette held a strong attraction for him since he seemed able to overlook her French blood.

Sophie wiped a tiny splash of sauce from the rim of a dish with a clean napkin and nodded to Clara and the maidservant. "All is ready. In a moment one of the footmen will go to the door of the drawing room and announce that dinner is served. Now don't look so worried. All will go well!"

Her words proved to be right. The serving and clearing away of the first remove went without a hitch. Then the second remove was borne into the dining room by the footmen. This time there was fillet of veal with mushrooms in a rich sauce, roast sirloin, a pudding filled with tender chunks of beef in a special gravy, and tiny lamb chops served with mint. A Chelsea porcelain dish shaped like a bunch of asparagus was used to hold the vegetable it mimicked. And at this stage of the meal the sweet puddings were introduced. Sophie had excelled herself, but her pièce de résistance was an old French recipe dating from the time of Madame de Pompadour and said to be her favorite. Heart-shaped and tinted pink, this delicious blending of cream, eggs, sugar, and subtle flavorings was decorated with violets Sophie had picked and candied herself in the spring.

Finally the cloth was drawn and fresh fruit was served, the center-piece being one of Sophie's sugar creations, a basket-weave casket filled with a selection of her own best candies. All that remained was the tray of tea to be served in the drawing room. Only when she had seen this carried in did Sophie finally look at the clock. It was twenty minutes to midnight and the gentlemen, having finished their port, were rejoining the ladies. Now, Sophie hoped, was the time when Sir Roland could suggest to Henriette that they stroll in the rose garden. The balmy air would welcome them and the glow of the waning moon should do the rest.

Sophie surveyed the kitchen, which was surprisingly tidy. The two young women at the sink, whom she had hired at her own expense to help with the washing up, had kept pace from the start. The final task was to put all the leftovers in clean containers in the pantry.

Clara was beaming as the remains of the dessert were brought into the kitchen. "I bet that was the best dinner ever served in this house. The footman told me I should have seen how they tucked in! Even the Baronne de Bouvier had a little taste of almost everything."

This was certainly a compliment. Sophie was longing to know if Sir Roland, lulled by good food and wines, had cast Henriette any senti-mental glances. She was on her way into the pantry with a bowl of leftovers when there came a heavy tread along the passageway. As she was emerging again, the green baize door of the kitchen was flung open. To her astonishment it was the Prince who entered, his face crimson from the amount he had eaten and imbibed. His brocade waistcoat was taut across his paunch.

"Splendid repast!" he announced loudly. "I've come to congratu-late the chef!"

Sophie, who had not been told he was a guest, curtsied quickly. The startled young women at work followed her example and bobbed.

"I'm honored to know that it pleased you, Your Highness," Sophie said.

"So it's you again, by Heaven!" he blinked at her in recognition. "I meet you everywhere! You're the expert on French porcelain. What are you doing here?"

"I prepared the dinner, sire."

"It was a feast." The Prince gave his smile that never failed to charm. "If courtesy to my host and hostess did not prevent it, I'd have you installed as head chef in the kitchen of the Marine Pavilion tomorrow. Good night to you."

The baize door swung shut behind him.

"Did you hear that, Sophie?" Clara exclaimed. "The First Gentleman of Europe would have liked you to cook for him!"

Sophie laughed. "But I'm a confectioner, not a cook. I would have preferred praise for my sweetmeats."

Then the baize door burst open again and Henriette came rushing across to embrace Sophie.

"I'm betrothed, Sophie! Sir Roland and I are to marry in the autumn!"

"That's wonderful! I'm so happy for you!" Sophie exclaimed as she hugged her exuberant friend.

"You're to be my bridal attendant! I'll have no one else. And Antoine shall be my page. Come and meet my future husband."

"Not now, Henriette. Not in these clothes. I'll want to look my best. Go back to him now. He'll be wondering where you are."

Henriette needed no further urging, staying only long enough to receive Clara's good wishes before dashing back to the drawing room.

FOR DAYS Sophie heard nothing from Rory. Although he had promised her before leaving Brighton that he would send word immediately if he were ever injured in any affray, she could not help being anxious about him. Henriette came daily to the atelier, although it would be only a matter of time before social engagements with her betrothed began to cut down and eventually eliminate her working hours. Sophie went to ask Harry at the Castle Inn if he knew of a confectioner willing to take a chance in a new business.

"You've come to the right person," Harry said, beaming. "I've a nephew who's just finished his apprenticeship in confectionery and is ready to make change from the master he's had for seven years. He's a good lad and could live with my wife and me."

"Where is he now?"

"In Reading, but as soon as he hears from me that you have a job to offer him he'll be in Brighton before a chef can fry an egg! His name is Robin Brown."

Robin was well named, for he was quick and perky, with sandy hair and a ready smile. He had been well trained and after he'd been a week in the atelier Sophie wondered how she had managed without him. It made her realize how often she'd had to remind Henriette of her chores and how much instruction she'd had to give both her assistants while still concentrating on her own work. Robin knew what had to be done and did it well.

"Will I be able to stay on here, Miss Delcourt?" he asked anxiously at the end of his two weeks trial.

"Yes, Robin. You are now a full-time employee of Delcourt confectionery, sweetmeats fit for a king!"

"You should use that slogan."

Sophie raised her eyebrows. "It only tripped off my tongue, but I think you are right!"

She took a design to a local craftsman, who stamped out a hundred and fifty medallions, each bearing her surname and that of Brighton in a semicircle above the slogan. Such trade coins were an advertising novelty, for they were easily passed around, often circulating out to far distances. Sophie and her assistants were examining the medallions that had just been delivered when Richard appeared in the doorway of the atelier.

"Good day, Mademoiselle Delcourt. I trust I find you well."

"Yes, indeed. Come in. You're most welcome. Is Tom back in Brighton too?"

"No. And I'm sorry to say it's for a most unfortunate reason."

Sophie felt her heart miss a beat. "What's happened?"

"He came home from Russia with a high fever. The next day he was delirious, and he is still having lapses when he doesn't know where he is." Richard saw by Sophie's expression how anxious she was. "Try not to worry. He is well taken care of, and the best doctor in London calls on him daily. If it were not so, I wouldn't be here to check on the building work on Tom's behalf."

"Is there anything I can do to help?"

"Write to Tom if you can find the time. He'll be glad to hear from you, I'm sure, because it's certain he will be bedridden for some time to come." Richard glanced about the atelier. "I'd appreciate being shown around if you're not too busy."

"It would be a pleasure."

He had noticed the medallions and picked up one to read it. "May I take this and hand it on?"

"Yes, do."

Her employees had returned to their tasks and Sophie explained to Richard the various stages of the sweetmeat making. They came finally to Henriette who was wrapping bonbons in the tinted papers with the romantic French phrases that were proving a neat success. Richard was intrigued, not having come across them before, and Sophie left him talking to Henriette about the French poets from whom almost all the phrases were taken.

Richard leaned forward, resting both hands on Henriette's table. "You've a happy task preparing bonbons for lovers," he remarked with a smile.

"Yes, I have." Henriette took one at random and translated as she read it aloud. " *'Your true love is nigh.'* That would be a nice prediction for anyone."

"I agree." He picked up one himself and did the same. " *'The stars should be your pearls upon a string, the world a ruby for your finger ring.'* "

Henriette nodded approval. "Just think what a wonderful gift that would be." She held out her own left hand as if displaying an imaginary ruby ring. Her own betrothal ring had been left at home while she was at work.

He translated another. " *'I swear allegiance to your lips, your eyes, your hair.'* "

"Such lovely words." She spoke almost wistfully, then quickly changed the subject. "How are the alterations progressing in Middle Street?"

Sophie had returned to her own work, but she glanced a couple of times over her shoulder in Richard's direction. He was still in conversation with Henriette, who was steadfastly wrapping bonbons as she chatted.

Then at last he made a move. "It's been a pleasure to meet you, Mademoiselle de Bouvier."

Henriette watched him return to Sophie. What a fine-looking man he was! Her fingers grew still at her task. When he followed Sophie out of the atelier, he looked back over his shoulder at her, interest lingering in his eyes. Henriette returned his smile, but she felt more like crying. He had no idea what he had done in that quarter of an hour when he stood by her table. By reading aloud those tender phrases in his deep and articulate voice, he had made her realize how unlikely it was that Roland would ever say such words to her. Sighing, she forced herself to accept the adage that half a loaf was better than none.

Before taking his leave, Richard invited Sophie to dine with him at the Old Ship, and she accepted. For propriety's sake they sat at a table in the main dining room. Sophie thought to herself that had Tom been well and in Richard's place, dinner would have been served in a private room. She came to the conclusion that since Richard appeared to be the opposite of his brother in every way, he could know nothing of Tom's dangerous sideline. Once she was tempted to voice her concern about it to him, but held her tongue. He had enough to worry about with Tom being ill and, for that matter, so did she.

When Richard returned to London, Tom's fever was still high. Their aunt had regimented the two nurses of her own age into night and day shifts, making sure he was never unattended. Richard waited until his brother took a turn for the better before returning to the shop at Brighton and reporting to Sophie again. Before he left, Tom spoke weakly from his sickbed, heedless of the nurse in the room.

"I'm starved for the sight of a pretty woman, Richard. Tell Sophie to have her portrait painted and you bring it to me."

"Sophie is too busy to sit for a likeness."

"Tell her!" Tom half rose from his pillows, and then fell back again, mumbling incoherently. Patiently the nurse bathed his forehead. There was no denying that she and her companion were extremely plain.

Richard did not pass on the message, because he doubted that Tom would remember the request he had made.

SOPHIE MET SIR ROLAND with Henriette at a formal tea party to which she had been invited by the Comtesse de Lombarde, head of the millinery atelier. Henriette's spirits, never low for long, had revived since meeting Richard. As she firmly reminded herself, she was no longer on the shelf, had captured a title as well as a future life of luxury, and only a fool would ask for more. So it was with pride and satisfaction that she presented her betrothed to Sophie whom she introduced as her dearest friend. When her aunt beckoned, Henriette left Sir Roland and Sophie to converse on their own.

Though red-faced and overweight, his manner was affable enough. "When I first met the Baronne," he said, "she told me that her niece was instructing you in the fine art of confectionery."

"Did she?" Sophie commented dryly.

"I thought it most admirable of the dear girl to share her talents but—and I know this will come as a heavy blow to you—I feel the time has come for Henriette to concentrate solely on her trousseau and our future plans."

"I quite understand. I knew that sooner or later she would be leaving the atelier."

Before the party broke up, Henriette had a quick word with Sophie, apologizing for never having corrected the deception her aunt had created.

"I was so afraid of losing him, Sophie! Please forgive me."

"Of course I do!" Sophie said with a smile. "Just be happy. That's all I want for you."

On her way home Sophie saw a crowd gathering to read a news sheet that had just been placed in a window. She supposed it to be a war bulletin or perhaps word of some new development in France. It was only a matter of three or four weeks since the chief instigators of the Terror had ended on the guillotine themselves, bringing that horrific spate of bloodshed to an end. It was with a sense of disbelief that she read their Majesties' announcement of the betrothal of their beloved son, George, Prince of Wales, to Princess Caroline of Brunswick.

How could he? As Sophie moved away, her heart went out to Mrs. Fitzherbert, once so loved and now so cruelly cast aside. The poor woman! Sophie could have wept for her.

At Marble Hill Maria Fitzherbert was not at home to visitors. She maintained a dignified silence and hid her tears from the sight of others.

Eighteen

AS SOPHIE HAD HOPED, Rory came himself to report on what had occurred at Sidlesham. His arrival was announced by Billy, who popped his head in at the atelier door.

"Captain Morgan is coming up the lane!"

Although she was in the middle of making liqueur rings in brandy, Sophie flung off her apron and cap and rushed to greet him. Rory was on foot and had almost reached the cottage gate as she came running into his arms.

"You're safe, Rory!" she exclaimed thankfully. She clung to him like a child finding a safe haven, and with her eyes still closed in relief, she felt him put his lips to her brow. Not until she leaned back to look into his face did she realize something was wrong.

"What is it?" she asked anxiously.

He sighed and put his arm about her shoulders as he led her away from the lane and down onto the beach. "A great deal went amiss, Sophie. My men and I watched and waited night after night in the vicinity of the Sidlesham mill, but the smugglers kept away."

She shared his bitter disappointment. "Oh, Rory. I'm so sorry. I know the information was given to me in good faith."

He shook his head. "No, Sophie. You were duped."

"I can't believe that."

"I can prove it. You see, I had set a trap at a certain section of the coastline where there's a natural inlet from the sea. I was convinced that was where the gang would come ashore next. But when I received your urgent message I drew my men away to Sidlesham. Can you guess what happened?" He halted for she had come to an abrupt standstill, her expression fearful.

"Don't tell me they landed at the place you'd left unguarded!"

"Exactly." A muscle flexed in his jaw. "I almost had them in my grasp!" He clenched a fist in front of him and then let his hand fall open to his side. "It's becoming more and more difficult for these criminals to land large shipments, and they needed to be sure I was well away from the area on a false trail. You were the one who did that for them."

She uttered an unhappy cry. "I wanted to help and I made a terrible mistake!"

He took pity on her then, drawing her into his arms. "The blame is mine, not yours. I should have gone by my own judgment instead of letting myself be influenced by the urgency of your message. Who gave you that false lead?"

"I can't tell you."

He held her back from him by the arms, his eyes hard. "But I demand it! That person is an ally of the Broomfield gang and must be rooted out. Who are you shielding? A man or a woman?"

"However much you question me I'll not give you an answer." Her face was taut and determined.

He threw up his hands in exasperation and stepped back. "Won't your pride allow you to admit a mistake? I thought you wanted retribution for the murder of those two revenue men."

"That's unfair! You know I do. But I can't tell you what you want to know without implicating someone innocent of the trick that was played on you."

"How can you be sure of that person's innocence? Those who associate with smugglers become tainted by them."

"Then that taint is on me too."

Rory stared at her appalled. "Do you know what you're saying?"

"Only too well."

"This can't be. I don't know what company you've been mixing with, but you must extricate yourself at once. You've enough trouble keeping watch over Antoine without bringing more down on yourself.

Clearly the time has come to change your surname and your place of abode. Marry me now, Sophie!"

She shook her head. "You should be arresting me, not proposing marriage. I've placed you in an invidious position, Rory. If I'd been anyone else you would have interrogated me, even imprisoned me on the strength of what I've said."

"Then absolve yourself by revealing your source of false information. By turning King's evidence you'll be able to talk freely as a witness in court without fear of punishment for your involvement."

"You're asking the impossible!" She was still convinced that Pierre had intended well, but even if she had thought otherwise she still had Clara to shield. She faced the hard fact that she should end her relationship with him.

"We've been drifting apart, Rory. What I once thought might one day be possible, now can never be, in view of what has arisen."

His face became rigid with anger. "What has happened to you? Do you suppose I would desert you because you've fallen into the wrong company? On the contrary, I'll not rest until I've cut you free!"

"I can free myself at any time, but I'll still maintain my silence."

"Then do that! I'll accept those terms."

"You're not thinking clearly. What of your career? If ever my link with the Gentlemen should come to light, your relationship with me could ruin you."

"To hell with my career! Nothing matters to me except you!" He crushed her to him and kissed her passionately, aroused and shaking with desire. When he forced himself to cease his kissing, she remained within his embrace and let her brow rest against his shoulder.

"You shouldn't love me so much," she whispered.

"How can I help it? Remember that I'm a patient man and I'm waiting for the day when you'll feel the same love for me."

She knew there was nothing she could say that could sway him from cherishing that hope. Although patient, he was also determined, and in that they were somewhat alike.

AFTER THE FIASCO of the false information, Sophie told Clara she wanted no more dealings with Pierre. The woman said very little, but it was clear she was troubled.

The night came when Sophie heard Pierre knocking sand from his boots on the stoop. Then came his tap for admittance. It became more impatient, but still the bolt was not drawn back for him. He began shaking the door by its handle. Sophie slid from her bed and stood by her own door. The candle lamp was alight in the kitchen, showing that Clara was about, but the smuggler's demand for admittance was being rigidly ignored. Finally he aimed a great kick at the door that split the wood, but it was done vengefully and not to force admittance. Gravel crunched beneath his feet as he went away again.

Slipping on a robe, Sophie went to the kitchen. Clara sat sad-faced and dry-eyed at the table. She spoke in dull tones without looking in Sophie's direction.

"I could have forgiven Pierre anything except helping the Broomfield gang. I never said it to you, but as everything worked itself out, I became more and more certain that he had deliberately misled you. That's why I kept the door barred against him. He'll know why and he'll not be back." She passed a trembling hand across her eyes. "Make us a pot of tea."

A cup of tea was fast becoming the English panacea for crisis, and Sophie herself now welcomed the prospect of the comforting drink. She and her friend had both severed all links with the Broomfield gang, Clara by finishing her affair and Sophie herself by rejecting Tom.

"My only regret is that I have inadvertently brought about your present heartache," Sophie said when she and Clara were seated with their tea.

"It's not so much as you might have supposed." Clara shrugged wearily. "I've thought for a long time that I ought to end it. Ever since the increasing clampdown on smuggling, I've been worried about the kegs of brandy passing in and out of my cellar. I have to think of Billy. So it's as well for my sake that matters came to a head." She became more cheerful. "I don't need a smuggling sideline now in any case. I've a good job in your atelier. My days of breaking the law are over."

"That's a relief for me to hear. I hope so much that my business will continue to prosper. If people start ordering from me after they've left Brighton for the London season, I'll know that I'm truly established."

"Why don't you take Prinny a box of your sweetmeats? He knows you now."

Sophie gave a quick shake of her head. "I'd never do that. It would not be correct. In any case I wouldn't want to win his custom that way. At the present time he thinks I'm a good cook and a linen maid and an authority on porcelain. But one day—oh, yes, one day!—he'll discover Delcourt confectionery for himself, and then he'll order from me."

SOPHIE HAD WRITTEN TO TOM, as Richard suggested, to wish him a speedy recovery. "He's going to pull through, isn't he?" she asked his brother, desperate for reassurance.

"If he follows medical advice all will be well." Richard's mouth twisted in a wry smile. "But you know Tom as I do. He doesn't suffer patiently."

"Would it help if I went to see him?"

"He's very proud. I'm not sure that he'd wish you to see him in his present stricken state. But do keep writing." Richard took Sophie's letters with him whenever he went to check on Tom's progress.

Sophie wrote about whatever she thought would be of interest to him, from happenings in Brighton to her thoughts and opinions on various matters. She mentioned her wish to find a small house of her own one day because, grateful though she was for all Clara's kindness and the good friendship, there were still times when she longed for the quietude of her own home.

These days Sophie saw little of Henriette, who was entirely occupied by social events with her betrothed. It was only when there were fittings for their respective gowns for the wedding day that they were able to have a little time together. A French dressmaker, who lived locally, had been entrusted with the task, and the results promised to be the height of elegance. Henriette had chosen a self-patterned cream silk for herself and a rose silk for Sophie, both in the newest, increasingly simple style. There was less bulk to the skirts and waists were higher, although the fichu remained. Their hats were to be huge-brimmed, worn at an angle to set off their faces, and trimmed with silken gauze. At the final fitting of his attire Antoine was delighted with his own splendidly cut coat and breeches of crimson velvet.

"Is this what I would have worn at home in France?" he asked Sophie when they were alone.

"For formal occasions, yes."

But the novelty of being dressed up soon wore off and he was glad to be back in his everyday garments. Going to Gloucestershire for the wedding was what he looked forward to most, because he and Sophie would be traveling by stagecoach to London and staying overnight at an inn. In the morning one of Sir Roland's own coaches would arrive to take them the rest of the way. Henriette had hoped to be married in London at the height of the season, but Sir Roland, being a widower, had decided the ceremony should take place quietly in the family chapel at his country seat. A grand ball for eight hundred people was to follow the next day.

"Think of it, Sophie," Henriette exclaimed, clapping her hands. "I shall be the focus of everyone's attention! The new lady of a great house! All the county will be there to meet me."

ONE MORNING at the end of the Brighton season, Henriette came to say farewell. Sir Roland had left for Gloucestershire already and now the time had come for her to follow with her aunt and uncle. They were to stay as guests of an earl and his wife on a neighboring estate until the wedding day.

"I shall miss you, dearest Sophie," Henriette wept as they embraced, "but Sir Roland has promised we shall come back to the seaside every summer."

"In the meantime, there are only three weeks until your marriage and then we shall be together again."

"That's right!" Henriette dried her eyes, all smiles once more. "Your gown and Antoine's velvet garments have all been packed most carefully and will be awaiting you when you arrive. Au revoir, my dear friend."

Sophie waved her off as she was driven back into town in a new apple-green phaeton by a liveried coachman.

Rory had also been invited to the wedding, but duties prevented his going. Antoine was wild with excitement as he and Sophie set off together from Brighton. He would have preferred to ride on an outside seat on top of the coach, but Sir Roland had paid for the best seats and those were inside. The boy cheered as a blast was blown on a long horn by the guard and the horses clattered through the streets. As they passed Tom's new premises, Sophie saw the scaffolding had been taken away and a hanging sign depicting a mother-of-pearl box twinkled in the sunlight over the entrance.

The coach kept up good speed, changing horses twice. There were four other inside passengers, including a fellow Frenchwoman with whom Sophie conversed. They passed through Cuckfield and Crawley, Reigate and Croydon, as well as many villages before arriving exactly seven hours later at the White Horse Inn in Fetter Lane. Sophie and Antoine were equally thrilled to see the City of London at last. The hustle and bustle of the streets reminded her nostalgically of Paris. So many coaches and carriages, carts and barrows, bawling peddlers and ragged beggars. Everywhere people of fashion could be seen among the throng of those going about their daily lives.

The courtyard of the White Horse was surrounded on three sides by the building itself, with tiered galleries giving access to accommodation. Ostlers came running to take the horses' bridles and porters to unload the baggage. Sophie stepped down first and Antoine came springing out after her. Even as she took the boy's hand, she saw Tom leaning his weight on a cane as he came toward her. Her heart contracted at the sight of how thin and pale he had become, his eyes sunken, his cheeks hollowed. Before she could even greet him he burst out at her in fury.

"At last! Why haven't you been to see me?"

"Tom, please! We can't discuss that here. How are you?"

"How do you expect me to be?" he shouted.

She saw he was beside himself, and people were glancing in his direction. "Wait here while I see to our luggage," she said to Antoine.

Tom snapped his fingers. "My servant is here to do that for you. You'll both come back to my house for the night."

"Indeed we shall not! I'll not be harangued for as long as it suits you!" Sophie's patience was running out. "Antoine and I need a good rest before we travel on tomorrow."

"Does it mean nothing to you that I've met every Brighton coach for three days? All because Richard left London without telling me which day you'd be traveling to the Westonbury wedding!"

"I'm sorry you did that, but please allow me to take Antoine into the inn now without further harassment."

"I'll come with you." Tom beckoned to his servant, who had already collected her baggage. There was a crowd of newly arrived passengers at the reception desk, but Tom, with his authoritative air, received immediate attention and Sophie was handed her key. She wanted to say goodbye then, but Tom insisted on staying to have supper with her.

Sophie's accommodation was entered from the lowest of the three tiered galleries and consisted of a bedchamber with a four-poster for her and a truckle bed in a connecting boxroom for Antoine.

"Why is Mr. Foxhill so cross?" the boy asked as she poured water from the ewer into a basin to wash his face and hands before supper.

She answered truthfully as she always did. "He doesn't want me to marry Captain Morgan. I once threatened that I might do so, and I suppose he thinks I've been spending time with Rory, instead of coming to London to see him."

"I wouldn't want you to marry Captain Morgan either."

"Whatever do you mean?"

He screwed his face up as she wiped a wet flannel over it. "I like Captain Morgan very much. It's not that. But he's always away, isn't he? I'd like you to marry someone who'd be living with us all the time. All the boys at school have fathers at home except Billy and me."

She handed him a towel, thinking sadly that the boy was missing a father far more than she had realized. "I don't suppose things would be any better with Mr. Foxhill. He would be away just as much, and in any case he's never mentioned marriage to me."

"Well, he wouldn't be angry about Captain Morgan if he didn't want to marry you himself, would he?"

"I'm not sure. Now let us go downstairs to the dining room. I'm certain you're hungry and I know I am."

Tom was in a calmer mood when he rose to his feet as they approached the table. When they were seated he spoke in French to Antoine.

"I was remiss in not addressing you before, Antoine. You must forgive me. I trust my anger didn't alarm you."

"No, sir. Ma Renfrew shouts at me and Billy all the time, but it doesn't mean anything."

"Indeed?" Tom raised an eyebrow. "I'm relieved that you take such an attitude, although I think Sophie knows I never indulge in idle talk whatever the volume of my voice. Now what would you like to eat?"

The boy's presence limited the conversation over supper. When the meal was over, Tom saw Sophie and Antoine to their room. He unlocked the door and returned the key to Sophie. As the boy entered, Tom blocked Sophie's way by reaching out an arm to rest his hand against the jamb.

"Why didn't you send me a likeness of yourself?" he demanded fiercely. "There are enough artists in Brighton during the season. Richard would have paid for it on my behalf. I kept waiting and waiting, thinking that he was leaving you to surprise me with it."

She was bewildered. "What are you talking about?"

"I sent you a message that I wanted a portrait of you."

"I know nothing of that," she protested.

"Weren't you told, then?"

"Maybe you imagined it," she suggested gently. "After all, Richard said you were very weak for quite a time and not always lucid at first."

"All the more reason for you to have visited me."

"I did offer early on, but you were too ill for visitors. Later I was rushed off my feet with work, and by then I knew that you were out of danger." It was difficult to remain composed, for his face was intense and she was affected by the force of the passion that emanated from him. It seemed to sear her flesh and drive into her bones.

"Do you think Morgan isn't gentleman enough to bow out if you told him that it's me you really love?" His voice was raspingly harsh. "Of course he would. Self-sacrifice for the happiness of the woman he adores would be well in his line!"

She flushed. "But not in yours, of course."

"Not when it would be going against all that draws us together. You know that I've loved you since I first saw you. Nobody has the right to come between us!"

In spite of herself, she was becoming agitated. "You shouldn't presume to know my feelings. I'm my own person and intend to remain so for the rest of my life. Please let me pass now, Tom."

He did not move, but caught her off guard with the sudden tenderness in his eyes and tone. "You are my heart, my soul, and my breathing. I need you to live."

Frantically she pushed him aside and rushed into the room, slamming the door behind her and turning the key in the lock. She stood trembling and upset, her hands covering her eyes, and heard his footsteps move slowly away along the gallery. It was quiet, and when she let her hands drop, there was no sign of Antoine. She went to the doorway of his little room and saw that he was already fast asleep in bed. She folded the garments he had discarded and put them on a chair. Then she lay down on the bed in her own room and gazed upward at the canopy as she thought over all that had passed between Tom and her. She could not deny that the wilder side of her nature, which was kept under restraint by self-discipline and responsibilities and commitments, had never failed to respond to him. It rose up and fluttered inside her like a trapped bird, only to be subjugated again by her own firm will. In one sense, she would never be free of him. Not that she would ever let him know it. He had been right in supposing that Rory stood between them. Rory had become her steadfast shield against the tumult that Tom could so easily arouse in her ordered life. In spite of her tiredness, it took Sophie a long time to get to sleep.

In the morning there was just time to take Antoine to see the Tower and London Bridge before the Westonbury carriage arrived to take them to Gloucestershire. The wedding was as quiet as Sir Roland had wished it, with only family and close friends filling the box pews of the family chapel, but the ball the following evening was a spectacular affair with the great house full of lights and music and garlands of flowers. Sophie was glad to see that Henriette was receiving all the attention for which she had hoped. If the girl's bubbling spirits were more subdued since her wedding night, it only gave her a new dignity and nothing could dim her charm.

When the time came for parting, Sophie and Antoine waved as their carriage pulled away. Before Henriette vanished from sight, Sophie was glad to see Sir Roland come to his young wife's side and put an arm about her. He might not be Henriette's ideal in every way, but Sophie was sure he would be as kind to her as he knew how.

"I think Henriette would have liked to come back to Brighton with us," Antoine said as he and Sophie settled back in their seats.

Sophie thought it a discerning remark for one so young. "I daresay she did for the moment, but she'll soon settle down and be happy."

The carriage was taking them all the way to Brighton, with one overnight stop at a country inn, so there was no chance of another meeting with Tom. They arrived home to the good news that a first order had been received from London. Within an hour, Sophie was in her apron again and at work in the atelier.

"The Prince of Wales's marriage is the one I'll want to hear about next," Clara remarked, "although goodness knows when that will be."

The Prince was equally in ignorance. His bride's departure from her homeland had been delayed several times already through the difficulties of travel created by war with France, and the severe winter weather on the continent. Mrs. Fitzherbert had been seen again in London society, and, judging by what was relayed through various grapevines to Brighton, her serene countenance gave no hint of how she felt with regard to the forthcoming marriage of her husband to another woman.

Not that Brighton saw much of its patron. The people's continued hostility had made the Prince so angry that he kept away. Once, in a temper, he had declared he would turn the Marine Pavilion into an army barracks, but everybody knew he thought too much of it ever to do that.

In late November Rory stopped for a short visit on his way to London. He had been assigned to work at the Customs House for an indefinite period because he had particular knowledge that could help the authorities solve a tax fraud being perpetrated by a number of importers.

"It will mean a lot of slow and careful work," he explained. "None of them must get wind of it. If I'm successful, it will mean promotion. I have my eye on an important administrative post at Shoreham that covers the whole of Sussex. The man who holds it now is soon due for retirement."

"That's splendid."

"But there's something I have to do first."

She did not have to ask what it was. "You'll take up your coastal patrols again until you've caught the Broomfield gang."

"That's right. I never leave a task unfinished."

In all, Rory spent three days in Brighton before carrying on with his journey to London. Antoine was particularly sorry to see him go. Whenever Sophie was otherwise engaged, Rory had given him his first lessons in fighting with a rapier. Although his was only a home-made one with a blade of wood, his instructor had the real thing.

"Captain Morgan said that if I'm to be a true French gentleman one day, I must be able to use a blade," Antoine told Sophie.

"Indeed you should," she agreed. Privately she thought that he ought to learn to ride too, but such instruction was not yet affordable.

It continued to frustrate Sophie that there was so much she did not know about Emile de Juneau, and she decided to make another visit to the Millards' farm. She found Mrs. Millard fully recovered physically and pleased to see her, but certain periods in the woman's life remained blank in her memory, and the incident with the Frenchman was among them.

The journey would have been quicker if Sophie had been driving Tom's sprightly horse, but she'd had to hire cheaply a nag and a cart for her deliveries and for any other occasion when she needed transport. After the confrontation in his shop, she had decided that she could no longer make use of Tom's horse and gig. When Clara had questioned her decision, she had replied that she wished to make room for the pony and trap she intended to buy as soon as she could afford them.

Nineteen

IN DECEMBER 1794 the Prince married by proxy his still-absent royal bride. Mrs. Fitzherbert let it be known she had resumed the state of widowhood and withdrew from society to reside quietly at Marble Hill in the countryside at Twickenham. It was as if the nine years of her marriage to the Prince had never been. Sophie felt deeply sad for both of them. They had shared a great love in the face of countless difficulties, and it was a tragedy that it had foundered on his debts, on politics, and through the acknowledged influence of Lady Jersey.

To Sophie's disappointment, only a few more orders for her confectionery came from London, but local sales continued to keep her and her two assistants fully employed. She saw no sign of Tom at his shop and the shutters remained in place.

Then, as spring rippled out carpets of daffodils, business began to pick up decisively, and Sophie took on a young apprentice named Oliver. On the second day of April, Princess Caroline of Brunswick landed at Greenwich, where she was met by Lady Jersey. When Sophie called in at the Marine Pavilion two days later to see when she would be needed for linenwork again, the whole place was buzzing with the news of the disastrous meeting between the Prince and his bride. The grapevine had done its work again.

"She's one of those women who always look a mess whatever she wears. Not like Lady Jersey who would look elegant in a sack. We heard that as soon as Princess Caroline entered the room, a stricken look came over poor Prinny's face! He hated her on sight! After the presentations, he moved away to the side of the room and swallowed a stiff drink. Then what do you think the Princess said in her heavy accent? 'I didn't expect him to be so fat! And he's not as handsome as his portrait!' "

Sophie listened in dismay. The tragedy, which had begun with the rejection of Mrs. Fitzherbert, was deepening. How was it to end for the unfortunate Princess and foolish Prinny? "Is Princess Caroline so very plain?"

"No. Not that she could be called pretty either. The truth is she's just not his cup of tea. She's proud of her bosom and shows far too much of it by day as well as evening, but then, there is nothing ladylike about her. One of the maidservants told me Lady Jersey had to speak to the Princess about bathing more often. Think of that!"

Sophie shook her head hopelessly. It was well known that the Prince was extremely fastidious.

When she arrived home, a letter from Rory was waiting for her. He wanted her to leave at once for London to see how fine the city looked with all the decorations that had appeared for the royal wedding. His sister Ellen, who was to have a well-deserved rest from looking after their mother, would be there too. Not only did he want Sophie to meet her, but they would be company for one another while he was at his duties. Clara encouraged Sophie to go.

"You've worked hard for so long and never had a holiday. I know how protective you are toward Antoine, but I'll look after him just as if you were here."

"No, I can't leave him. Not even with you."

"Why ever not?" Clara looked hurt. "In my opinion, you fuss too much in any case. It's very hard for me not to be trusted to take care of the boy."

"My good friend, it's not that. Please believe me."

"Then go! Or else I'll believe that some special danger lies over the child." It was a shot in the dark, the voicing of a long-held suspicion, and Clara saw she had at last uncovered the truth. "Don't you think you'd better tell me about it?"

Sophie gave her all the facts. When Clara asked why she had not been told before, Sophie explained. "At first I had to be so careful that no chance remark would give Antoine and me away. Later, when I'd learned how well you can keep secrets, I often thought of telling you, but I kept my own counsel out of habit."

"I'm glad you have told me at last, although I knew almost for certain you had a special fear when you took those lessons with Sergeant Jones. Leave your pistol with me if that will give you peace of mind. My Jim taught me how to handle one when we used to go smuggling together." Clara pointed to Rory's letter. "You write back now and catch the evening mail. Then tomorrow Captain Morgan and his sister will know when to expect you."

Rory and Ellen were both at the White Horse Inn to meet Sophie when she arrived on the stagecoach. It was impossible not to remember her previous arrival there, and she was unable to stop herself glancing about as if Tom might suddenly come storming forward again. But it was Rory who came to kiss her hand.

"Welcome to London, Sophie. I would like to present my eldest sister, Ellen."

At the age of thirty, a year younger than Rory, Ellen Morgan had the same wheat-colored hair as her brother, but there the likeness ended. Her eyes were a smiling gray to his stern blue, her features as gently molded as his were austere.

"I'm so pleased you decided to come, Mademoiselle Delcourt," she said enthusiastically as the three of them left the inn yard. "I've been looking forward to this meeting."

She was like the rest of the Morgan family in wanting to see Rory settled with a wife, and she was certain this young Frenchwoman had captured his heart. For herself, she had suffered too much after being jilted on her wedding eve to consider marriage again. The man had been her life's love and no other suitor had ever interested her. Nowadays, her mother's whims and cantankerous ways kept her fully occupied.

"One of Rory's fellow officers at the Customs House and his wife have kindly offered you and me accommodation at their home," Ellen told Sophie. "I arrived there yesterday and couldn't be more content. They are a delightful couple."

Before they reached the house, she and Sophie were on first-name terms and full of plans as to where they would go and what they would see when Rory was not with them. They both agreed they should visit the Royal Academy, the Tower, which Sophie and Antoine had seen only from a distance, and take a boat ride as far as Hampton Court.

"I'm having the day off tomorrow," Rory reminded them.

They laughed and promised that his company would be the highlight anytime he could be with them. The house, where Ellen was already installed, faced a leafy square. Sophie was warmly welcomed and shown to a charming room with every comfort. Then she and Rory and Ellen sat down to dine with their host and hostess. Much of the talk was of the royal wedding to take place on the morrow. Sophie heard that alterations had been made at Carlton House to create a suite for Princess Caroline, who was presently staying at St. James's Palace, where the ceremony was to be held the following evening in the Chapel Royal.

When Sophie opened her window to the sunny wedding morning she could hear the early celebrations, and when Rory called at the house to escort her and Ellen through the busy streets, she saw London in full splendor. The Prince of Wales's feathers adorned every available point. The gilded wooden initials G and C of the royal couple hung on buildings, and specially erected street archways were entwined with hearts and roses. People were in a festive mood, flaunting flowers on their coats and in their hats. Peddlers were selling souvenirs of the day and street musicians played patriotic music. Vivid banners, pennants, and flags fluttered everywhere. Garlands were looped from pole to pole all along the Mall. The King and Queen would come that way to St. James's Palace and after the marriage ceremony guests would be received at Buckingham House.

Sophie had expressed a wish to see Carlton House, which overlooked the Mall. Since she knew the Marine Pavilion so well, she was interested to see the Prince's London residence. It was every bit as grand and gracious an edifice as she had expected, with a vast colonnade and pediment like that of a Greek temple. Plenty of people had gathered in front of the gates, giving Prinny a cheer every time anyone came in or out. Then suddenly a drunkard began singing loudly the romantic ballad of the Lass of Richmond Hill. It had been written some years ago when Mrs. Fitzherbert, who then lived at Richmond Hill, was young and beautiful and the Prince was wild with love for her.

"That fellow is making his loyalties known," Rory remarked dryly.

But it was not for long. People were in no mood to let anything spoil the wedding day, and the drunkard was soon thrust and kicked on his way. Within a stone's throw of Carlton House was the house Mrs. Fitzherbert had had for her use until everything ended between her and the Prince.

"Where is she now?" Sophie asked quietly.

"Still in retreat at Marble Hill to be well away from the marriage celebrations."

"The poor woman," Sophie said sadly.

As the streets became more and more crowded, Rory hired a curricle and the three of them went for a drive out into the countryside. They were on their way back again through Twickenham when Rory indicated a large white house set in wide lawns, with willow trees trailing their branches in the clear water of the Thames.

"That is Mrs. Fitzherbert's residence."

Sophie gazed at it as they went past, her compassion going out to the woman within. Then from ahead came a horseman riding as if the devil were after him, the horse's mane flying, clouds of dust billowing up from its flashing hooves.

"It's the Prince!" Sophie exclaimed in astonishment.

He thundered past as if they were not here, his desperate eyes fixed on the house as he went past. Then he wheeled his horse about, making it rear, and galloped to and fro several times. But no beckoning hand appeared at the window, and the door did not open. When he had finally accepted the awful disappointment, he rode back the way he had come. As he swept past the curricle, Sophie saw his face was wet with tears.

There was no question of Mrs. Fitzherbert not having heard him, for this was a quiet area and he had made a great commotion. Rory and Ellen were as subdued as Sophie by what they had witnessed, and there was little conversation for the rest of the drive back.

London was alight with flares as the hour of the royal wedding drew near. There was music and singing everywhere as people danced in the streets. Sophie, with Rory and Ellen, joined their host and hostess in going to watch the guests arriving at St. James's Palace. There was a special cheer for the Prince's sisters, who had everybody's sympathy. They led a closeted existence, because the King was much too possessive to be willing to find them husbands. The pretty creatures waved to the crowd, bound for yet another wedding at which none of them was a bride.

So dense was the crowd by the time the bridegroom's coach arrived that Rory had to protect Sophie and Ellen with his arms from being pushed too close to the wheels. The little lamps were alight within the coach and Sophie could see the Prince clearly. He wore a formal white wig and was clad in gold brocade; the Garter Star, his diamond buttons, and his rings sparkled, but he was obviously drunk. She had seen him often enough to know he was deep in his cups, his face crimson, his eyelids weighed down with brandy. She could not begin to surmise how much he had imbibed in his wretchedness since that mad ride in the afternoon. Sadly she watched the coach disappear.

When the marriage ceremony was over, the Prince had almost no recollection of the service. He had a hazy image of his bride in ornate attire with flowers and pearls in her yellow hair. There was a moment at the altar when the wish to escape became so overwhelming that he had turned to flee, only to be thrust back again by one of his brothers.

He needed still more brandy to fortify him before he could face going to the marital bedchamber. As he entered the room he thought it would be easier to put a gun to his head than to perform his duty. But somehow he managed to consummate the marriage, and left the bed immediately afterward to seek his own chamber. Unsteady on his feet, the brandy finally striking home, he tripped against the fender of the fireplace and fell senseless into the ashes.

Princess Caroline rolled over onto one elbow and looked down at him in disgust. What a husband she had been landed with! Before leaving Brunswick she had heard of his philandering with Lady Jersey, so the insult of being met at Greenwich by that same woman had almost made her turn for home again. But she had believed all she'd been told of the Prince's eagerness to marry her, that he had fallen in love with her portrait, and that there was no man more charming and witty and handsome than the First Gentleman of Europe. Lies! All lies!

Furiously she punched up her pillows. Let him stay in the fireplace all night! What did she care! She hoped the glowing embers in the grate would singe his hair!

SOPHIE'S TIME IN LONDON slipped by all too quickly. Every evening Rory had an outing planned to go to one of the many theaters or to dances with a party of his friends at some exclusive assembly rooms. Once they went to the best pleasure gardens in London, which were illumined by thousands of colored lanterns. In addition to all else Sophie and Ellen had planned to do each day, they also went window-shopping. It was in St. James's Street that Sophie spotted the hanging sign picturing a mother-of-pearl box twinkling its patterned surface in the sun.

She stopped to gaze at the objects displayed in the window. There was an arrangement of exquisite Venetian glass, the goblets and claw-beakers with silver-gilt mounts and a pair of small ewers of a breath-taking blue. She could not begin to guess the age of all these beautiful objects. To one side was a magnificent silver tureen on an ornate plateau, a small card informing the beholder that it had previously belonged to Louis XVI. Yet another treasure from ravished Versailles.

Ellen had walked on to a neighboring milliner's, and now she returned to pluck Sophie by the sleeve. "There's a hat I simply must have! Do come and see."

Eventually Ellen made many purchases at various shops in St. James's Street. It was too expensive there for Sophie, but in another street she bought a new cloak the color of holly berries, knowing that at last she could designate to rough wear the one in which she had escaped from France. She wore the new cloak on the last day of her stay, which was a Sunday, when the three of them went to morning service at St. Paul's Cathedral. Sophie had never heard bells more beautiful than those that rang out over the roofs of London.

When the time came for parting, Ellen invited Sophie to visit her. "Do let Rory bring you and your nephew to stay with Mother and me as soon as possible. I've so enjoyed your company and do want to keep in touch."

"We'll write to each other and I'll remember what you've said about a visit," Sophie promised.

The stagecoach taking Ellen home left an hour before Sophie's, so she and Rory went into the White Horse Inn to wait. Throughout her stay, Rory had not lost a chance to kiss her whenever his sister had tactfully left them alone for a few minutes, but this was the first chance they had had to talk on their own.

"Now that Ellen has invited you to my home," he said, holding her hand in both his own, "you can go freely without my family jumping to any conclusions about us."

"That's true. I wouldn't want what we have between us to be exaggerated and speculated about groundlessly by others."

"That doesn't stop me from hoping for much, much more eventually."

SOPHIE ARRIVED HOME with gifts in her arms. There was a length of ruby striped silk and a lace-edged fichu for Clara. For each of the boys she had a toy rapier.

"Captain Morgan suggested I buy them," she said when she could make herself heard above the excitement. "He said that Antoine could pass on his instructions to Billy, and then you could practice together. Next time he comes to Brighton he'll give you both some more lessons."

Later, when she and Clara had exchanged their news, Sophie asked if Tom had opened his shop yet.

"No, it's still closed. Perhaps he's waiting until Prinny and his Princess come to the Marine Pavilion."

"That seems most likely," Sophie agreed.

But the shop was to be opened sooner than that. Sophie was walking along Middle Street early in May when she saw the shutters were down from the bow-fronted window. She stopped to look in as she had done in London. Here the window was full of chinoiserie. There were jars and bowls and vases, but the centerpiece was a magnificent cream horse with a green-glazed saddle cloth and an amber saddle. She was sure that if the Prince happened to see it, he would find it irresistible.

When the door of the shop opened she gave a start, but it was Richard who had seen her through the window.

"Come in, Sophie. Don't stand outside. Let me show you around."

"Is Tom not here then?"

"No, he's traveling, I'm afraid."

She entered the shop and caught her breath with pleasure. "So many lovely things!"

The premises had been transformed. The shop, as well as the large display room, had been hung with hand-blocked Chinese wallpaper.

Richard pointed out that nowhere was the same bird or flower repeated in sequence. She told him of seeing the Foxhill shop in London.

"Did you go in?" he asked immediately.

"No. There was no time then."

The gallery had been rebuilt, and Richard accompanied her up the new curving flight of stairs to view the many paintings hung for display there. A glass dome had been set in the roof to give ample light and to add elegance to the whole setting. She looked down over the balustrade to where Tom had fallen and where he had propped the ladder for her. The space was taken up now by handsome furniture, marquetry, and ormolu gleaming, its rich carving full of highlights and shadows. There was statuary too, and displays of silver and porcelain. One of the two male assistants was dealing with a customer, who was considering the purchase of a Roman bust; the other had just sold a pair of sumptuous corner cupboards.

Before Sophie and Richard descended the stairs again, he showed her how the area above the shop had been converted into a spacious apartment with two bedchambers.

"It's most convenient to be able to stay on the premises now," Richard said when they were back in the shop again.

"When will Tom be taking over here?" she asked, picking up a little silver casket from a display shelf to examine it.

"I believe his comings and goings will continue to be erratic for some time to come. Tom has promoted the undermanager from the London shop to be in general charge here. The man is moving to Brighton with his wife this very day."

"Where is this casket from?" she asked.

"Persia. It's superb craftsmanship and dates from the sixteenth century."

"It's lovely." She replaced it and although she looked at other of the small objets d'art arranged on a table her thoughts continued to dwell on Tom. "Did you know that your brother and I quarreled the last time we met?"

Richard sighed. "Yes, he told me. He should never have waylaid you at the stagecoach the way he did. I only wish I'd known in time to stop him."

"Do you think he would have listened to you?"

Richard compressed his lips wearily. "No, I suppose not. He never has."

Sophie opened a large, handsomely bound book that lay within reach. On every page there was an engraving of an Indian palace with exotic domes and lacelike ornamentation. "This is fascinating!"

"Tom has earmarked that book for the Prince of Wales. His Highness has such an interest in architecture. This is a rare book that should please him well."

As Sophie left the shop, she thought that the book on Indian architecture would please the Prince on two fronts, not only by appealing to his sense of beauty, but also by reflecting the British power that was growing in India.

WHEN HENRIETTE AND HER HUSBAND arrived in Brighton for the season, they rented the house that had been previously occupied by Mrs. Fitzherbert. Sophie was in the atelier when Henriette came sweeping in, gowned in pink muslin with ribbons aflutter, her face radiant beneath her fashionable hat.

"Dearest Sophie! La! How I've missed you. Letters are not the same as being together!" She threw her arms around Sophie, heedless of her friend's sugary apron. "Say you're glad to see me too!"

"Of course I am." Sophie's face was alight with laughter. "What a vision of fashion you've become!"

"I have, haven't I?" Henriette twirled around for inspection. "Guess who's my dressmaker? Madame Rose, who used to sew for Marie Antoinette! She's an émigrée too." Then she darted across like a little pink bird to Clara. "How are you, Mrs. Renfrew? I was so excited to see Sophie again that I forgot to greet you immediately."

"I'm well," Clara replied, looking at Henriette with a cynical glint in her eyes. "You'll be the belle of Brighton this season if I'm not mistaken."

"I hope so. I want to turn every man's head. Aren't I wicked?" Henriette giggled mischievously. "It will make such a change from my previous time in Brighton, when I trailed everywhere in hand-me-down clothes with my aunt and uncle or else sat for those dreary hours making hats. The only happy time I had was in this atelier." She flitted across to Robin. "You'd just started when I left. Are you happy here too?"

The young man flushed. "Yes, madam."

"What are you making?" She peered with interest at his work.

"It's a new line. Vases of rock sugar on pasteboard pedestals covered with gold or silver. They're for buffet tables and so forth. The idea is to put flowers in them."

"How pretty they are. I shall order some for my parties."

"We've a variety of molds. You can choose the shapes you like best."

Her butterfly attention had flickered to the young apprentice at the end of the table, who was engaged in the task of wrapping bonbons in romantic papers, a task she remembered very well. "Who are you?"

"I'm Oliver, madam."

"So! Let me watch you wrapping. Nobody can judge better than I if you're good at your task." Gaily she picked up one of the papers and glanced at it, but she did not read it aloud. Sophie noticed a subtle change in her expression before she dropped it again as if it burned her fingers.

"Am I doing well, madam?" Oliver asked impishly. This pretty young woman was creating a pleasant diversion in an otherwise monotonous routine.

Henriette answered him almost absently, patting his shoulder maternally. "Very well. I couldn't have done better myself." Then she became her bubbling self again, full of chatter as she tripped across to where some packed caskets of sweetmeats were ready for dispatch. "I want to place a regular order for some of these to be delivered to our summer residence."

Sophie came to her side. "Which would you like? I'll fetch my order book."

"I'll come with you." Henriette hooked her arm through Sophie's and hastened her outside.

"Wait! My order book is in the atelier," Sophie protested.

"Never mind that for a moment. There's something I want to ask. Did you read in the last edition of the émigré newspaper an account of a political meeting in Paris that was held in support of the Government?"

"Yes I did. Among those who spoke was Emile de Juneau. It can only mean he has gone back to France. Heaven be praised for it!" Sophie declared thankfully.

255

"Now you have nothing more to fear. Your enemy has given up his search."

There was a pause before Sophie answered. "For the time being anyway."

"Don't be so pessimistic," Henriette insisted cheerfully. "The wretched fellow couldn't search forever and it looks as if he's making a grab for the political power he missed when Orléans was guillotined. He'll be too busy to return."

"I'm going to tell Rory about it when he comes down from London again. I wish I could believe your prediction, but all my instincts tell me that sooner or later Emile de Juneau will return. Meantime I'm thankful for the respite."

"Now you can fetch your order book."

"I'll make you a gift of the sweetmeats."

"Indeed you shall not! This is a business arrangement, because I'll be needing a constant supply throughout the summer. Then in the winter I'll want deliveries to continue." Henriette rolled up her eyes thankfully. "No more traveling around to visit all the Westonbury kinfolk. Scottish castles are freezing! Sir Roland has promised we shall spend half of next winter in London while the other half will be in Gloucestershire. He can't live without his hunting and shooting. Are you going to do linenwork again at the Marine Pavilion?"

"Not on a regular basis. With the Princess of Wales coming to Brighton with the Prince this summer, two more full-time linen maids have been taken on. I shall be called in whenever I'm needed for fine stitching. With the Marine Pavilion half encased in scaffolding once again, it's not going to be a very comfortable stay for the royal lady."

"Whatever is being done now?"

"Some major alterations, including the creation of a special suite for the Princess of Wales, which, unfortunately, is not yet finished."

"The Prince will still entertain in spite of the building work, won't he?" Henriette's face was anxious. "Roland was expecting we would be invited as he has been in the past."

"Don't worry. Parts of the building are still habitable. You'll be able to dazzle everyone in your new gowns."

To Henriette's relief not only was a royal invitation soon forthcoming, but she and her husband were among the elite invited by the town's Master of Ceremonies to attend all the splendid festivities arranged for the royal couple in celebration of their marriage.

When she went to work at the Marine Pavilion, Sophie soon heard that all was not well between the Prince and Princess Caroline, who had a loud voice, a raucous laugh, and a bawdy sense of humor. There was nothing graceful about her and she walked like a plowboy. She was untidy and careless. As Sophie had heard previously, her attitude toward water, whether the sea or her bath, was much like that of a cat, and sometimes the servants held their noses behind her back. Somehow she managed to spill wine or drop food on all her clothes, but that was not surprising since, according to the footman who waited at table, she had a greedy appetite and poor manners.

In the sewing room, there was plenty of mending. The Princess was forever catching her heel in a hem, or tearing a skirt or ripping a lace cuff. To add to everything else, she seemed to have no sense of direction and frequently blundered into areas of the Marine Pavilion where builders were working. She complained bitterly about this inconvenience.

"That nasty banging and hammering gives me a headache and dust gets up my poor little nose." She sneezed frequently and noisily, which made the Prince shudder.

Yet all who worked in the Prince's employ agreed that Princess Caroline was likable in many ways, for she had no false pride and was openly friendly. She loved people and took to Brighton immediately, appreciating the town's enthusiastic reception of her and reveling in all the welcoming speeches and festivities. The crowds responded warmly to her, and children ran to hand her flowers, which she gathered happily to her ample bosom. She adored children, never thinking twice about stopping to talk to little ones or take a baby from its mother's arms to hug and kiss. She was experiencing all the early symptoms of pregnancy herself and believed she had conceived on her wedding night, since she could count on the fingers of one hand the number of times the Prince had come to her bed. In fact, since she had told him of her certainty that she was with child, he had not been near her.

For the Prince, her presence in his beloved cottage was a nightmare. Gone was the peace and the elegant pleasure amid his wonderful treasures. Unwittingly she ruined every occasion with her vulgarity. The whole of his aesthetic nature was offended by her in every respect. She thought nothing of tossing her hat onto a priceless Ming vase or leaving a trail of gloves, scarves, fans, and handkerchiefs in a kind of cheerful litter whenever she passed through the exquisite rooms. The servants could tell he was getting close to the breaking point. Princess Caroline's resentment at being compelled to have Lady Jersey as her Lady of the Bedchamber exacerbated matters between them. One of the footmen summed up the situation.

"Anyone can see with half an eye that Lady Jersey never misses a chance to add to the trouble between them. Prinny ought to kick her out."

But there was no sign of that. Sophie felt pity for the Princess, knowing what it meant to be a foreigner in a new land having to face difficulties never experienced before.

When Sophie arrived for her linenwork one day, she glimpsed the Prince throwing himself into his coach and being driven off, his personal retinue following in other equipages.

"Where is the Prince going?" Sophie asked Nick, the footman.

"Back to Carlton House for a few days. He don't know how to tolerate the Princess of Wales any longer."

Sophie wondered if he would ever return to Brighton, but he did. Lady Jersey coaxed him back again.

Twenty

AS USUAL, Tom took Sophie by surprise. She was at a horse auction being held in a meadow when suddenly he was at her side.

"What are you bidding for then?" he asked, as if they had parted only the day before on the best of terms.

She glanced at him. "A pony and trap. How are you?"

"I've never felt better. And how have you been managing since you sent my horse and gig packing?"

"I've been hiring, but it's a shabby cart and I feel it does my business no good to be seen in it."

"So which of the ponies have you chosen to bid for?"

"That one." She stood on tiptoe, for there was quite a crowd of people present, nearly all of them men. "It's being led forward now."

He looked and gave a nod. "I saw it earlier. It's not the best of the bunch, but it's strong and sturdy." He saw she was getting ready to bid at once and gave her some advice. "Don't appear conspicuously eager. The owner himself might start sending the price up against you. Come with me and we'll stroll casually to a better position. Bid from the start or else the auctioneer might not notice you if the last-minute bidding should become concentrated in another part of the crowd."

The bidding was sluggish at first. It did pick up by small amounts, but the pony was finally knocked down to Sophie. She turned to Tom with shining eyes, their differences temporarily forgotten.

"It's mine!"

He smiled. "Indeed it is."

When she had paid her money, Tom took the pony's bridle as it was handed over. Sophie produced some sugar bits, which she held out on her palm, talking to and patting her new possession as the offering was accepted.

"Now to bid for a trap." She indicated another part of the meadow. "All the vehicles are over there." She led the way, her hat ribbons rippling down her back, and Tom followed with the pony. Nobody seemed interested in the traps that day, and she acquired one in need of paint at a bargain price. Her excitement was undiminished as together they put the pony in the shafts.

"I'll call in a painter to make the trap look like new. I'm going to have lettering too." She stood back and framed a rectangle in the air with her hands as she visualized what would be painted on the side of the cart.

He eyed her sparkling face. "What shall you call your pony?"

"Bijou. It was a horse with that name that helped me escape from the château with Antoine and the Marquis."

"Then it's well named."

When she was seated in the trap and holding the reins, she looked down at Tom. "Would you like a lift somewhere?"

"No, I haven't finished looking around here."

A sudden suspicion crossed her mind, and her expression grew cool. "Are you buying horses for a band of acquaintances? I understand they're always in need of fast steeds."

He knew immediately what she meant. "No, I'm not! I need another pair of horses for a second delivery wagon at the shop. Damnation, Sophie! Must you mistrust my every action? Are we never to remain on good terms for more than a minute at a time?"

They were some way from the noisy auctions taking place, with no chance of being overheard, but she still lowered her voice in caution.

"You have the solution to that. Do you suppose I like this conflict with you?" Her eyes were bright as if not far from tears. She had enjoyed sharing her success at the auction with him and now all the pleasure had been dashed away. "There have been good moments between us. Times when we've laughed, times when we've become deeply involved in each other's lives, times when we've been friends.

Even this past hour made me happy to be with you." Sudden hope filled her. "If you really care for me, forswear all dubious dealings in the future!"

His lips tightened in a bitter smile. "How lacking in trust you are, Sophie." Then he stepped away, raised his hat, and left her sitting there.

She shook the reins and did not look back as she drove out of the meadow. There was no more anger in her. Only the heartbreaking certainty that she and Tom had created a gulf between them as wide and deep as that between the Prince and Mrs. Fitzherbert.

She had the trap painted a soft sea-blue with the name of Delcourt in delicate gilt lettering. Beneath it was painted a bonbon in rainbow colors.

In January of the new year of 1796, almost exactly nine months from her wedding night, the Princess of Wales gave birth to a daughter, who was baptized Charlotte Augusta. The Prince thought it typical of the woman that she could not even atone for her faults by producing a male heir. She would not have another chance, since all was over between them. Although he was very fond of children, he could not take to the squalling infant, seeing too much of her mother in her, although he hoped with time to feel paternal affection for his daughter.

In the same month the royal birth was celebrated, Rory's tenacious-ness paid off when, after a long and meticulous investigation, he uncovered a great ring of swindling and tax evasion that had links throughout the country. Many arrests were made and a gap closed that had cost the nation countless thousands of pounds. With the cost of the war mounting, there was not a penny to be wasted and Rory was highly commended for his work. He was offered a permanent post in London, which he declined, knowing full well that a similar high position would be offered to him again whenever he let it be known he was ready.

"I thank you, gentlemen," he said to the board, "but I have unfin-ished business with the Broomfield gang on the coast. To date they have a long list of vicious murders to atone for, quite apart from their smuggling activities. So, after careful consideration, should you offer me the now vacant Shoreham post, I would be prepared to accept, on the condition that apart from my administrative duties I could also be in personal command of any sorties where I deemed my presence necessary."

It was agreed and he was congratulated on his appointment. Before taking up his post, he went to Brighton to collect Sophie and Antoine for a visit to his home. His mother, widowed some years before, had settled in Lymington, a little town by the sea in the county of Hampshire. It was less than a day's journey from Brighton, and Sophie anticipated with pleasure seeing Ellen again.

When the house came into sight, it proved to be large and rambling, built of russet brick that flamed in the afternoon sun, with creepers hanging like curls over the porch. Ellen had been watching for them and came running out to embrace Sophie and her brother before Antoine was presented to her.

"I've heard much about you, Antoine. You are most welcome."

He bowed as he had been taught. "Your servant, madame."

When outdoor garments had been discarded in the pleasing accommodation that was provided, Sophie and Antoine went downstairs to the drawing room where Rory and Ellen were chatting to their mother. Rory sprang to his feet immediately, smiling happily at the sight of Sophie in his home.

Mrs. Morgan was seated on a striped sofa. She was in black, her gray hair softly dressed under a pretty lace cap. She was gracious and smiling, but her eyes were hard and assessing. She was distrustful of this beautiful stranger who had ensnared the affection of her beloved son.

"Sit down beside me, Miss Delcourt," she invited. "No doubt you have heard from Rory that we are a very united family. Now I should like you to tell me about yourself."

It did not take Mrs. Morgan long to decide that this young Frenchwoman would never be right for her son. Sophie Delcourt was far too independent for her liking. Mrs. Morgan had the uncomfortable feeling that Rory might have proposed already. Then as the days went by without any mention of a betrothal, she concluded that it was most likely that the Frenchwoman had not yet given him an answer. Clearly he was full of hope, and there was love in his eyes every time he looked at her. Mrs. Morgan yearned to tell him not to make a mistake, but Rory was as obdurate as his late father, ready to hang on like a bulldog to whatever he thought right. For her to offer open opposition would be pointless. All she could do was to hope he would come to his senses and find someone more suitable.

Although Mrs. Morgan wanted to be tactful, she could not stop herself from referring a little too often to Lucy, the daughter of her dearest friend. Such a dear girl! So thoughtful and attentive to older people. And talented! Nobody could paint watercolors or dance or sing or play the harpsichord like Lucy. It was no wonder everybody loved her for her gentle ways and many kindnesses.

Sophie wondered if Rory would have married this paragon of maidenly virtue had she not come into his life, but she did not ask him about it. She had suffered enough probing herself since her arrival to submit anyone else to such questioning.

Mrs. Morgan, being a skilled needlewoman herself, had shown particular interest in Sophie's linenwork at the Marine Pavilion. Since this was one topic not of a personal nature, Sophie was pleased to discuss it.

"It's all delicate work for me, now the housekeeper knows my abilities. I suppose the finer skills of a confectioner in sugar work are close to those with a needle. On my first day I had lacework, but after that there was often mundane mending such as braid loosened from a footman's livery, endless buttons to be restitched, and often gussets to be let into the back of breeches for those manservants whose waist-lines were expanding in the Prince's good service."

Mrs. Morgan clearly disapproved of such humble tasks, though she did not voice it directly. "Even though you have delicate work now, why do you continue to do it? Surely you are kept busy enough with your confectionery."

"That's true, but I don't want to surrender the privilege of an entrée to the Marine Pavilion, albeit on a lowly level, and I intend to retain it as long as possible. I like keeping my finger on the pulse of royal events. I'm a very ambitious woman, Mrs. Morgan, and I'm aiming to take my confectionery business to the very top."

Disconcerted by this determined attitude, Mrs. Morgan thought longingly of dear little Lucy, who had no such unfeminine notions in her pretty head.

The visit was not helped for either Sophie or Antoine by the rain, which rarely ceased, curtailing outings away from the house. For

Antoine there was the excitement of fencing lessons with Rory in the conservatory, and there were walks in the New Forest with Sophie and Ellen and Rory, but otherwise he was thoroughly bored. He had nobody to play with and the visit seemed to him to be mostly taken up by polite conversation among the adults in the old lady's drawing room, for Mrs. Morgan rarely wanted any of them to be spared her sharp-eyed company. Worst of all, the house was so full of valuable porcelain that Antoine was scared to move, lest he knock something over. Once he did bump into a small table, and Rory saved a piece of Sèvres from smashing to the floor. Nobody else observed the incident, and Rory had given him a conspiratorial wink.

For Sophie, who was also finding the visit difficult, a diversion was created when Rory's sister Jane and her husband, Francis, made a special drive from their home in Winchester to meet her. His other sister, Elizabeth, with her four-month-old baby in her arms, came as well from Portsmouth with her husband, Alan, who was an officer in the Royal Navy. All four were likable, friendly people. Yet in spite of this generous show of goodwill, Sophie was as relieved as Antoine when the two of them were on their way back to Brighton with Rory. The best to come out of the visit was the strengthening of her friendship with Ellen.

SOPHIE HAD THOUGHT that with Rory stationed such a short distance away at Shoreham, she would see him at least once a week, but that was not the case. His aims had expanded with his new powers. He was no longer dedicated only to the elimination of the Broomfield gang, but wanted systematically to clear the whole Sussex coast of smuggling activities. Before long, as his arrests mounted, he began to be feared by anyone remotely connected with the Gentlemen's trade. Clara, whose fishermen friends had always dabbled in smuggling, told Sophie that Rory had been nicknamed the Hawk.

"Just the risk of facing a cross-questioning by him has made them hesitate about bringing in the smallest amount of contraband."

"I'm thankful to hear it," Sophie said. "There is no harm in those men, and I wouldn't want to see any one of them go to the gallows for a keg or two. Rory has always been obsessional about capturing the Broomfield gang and he's no longer showing mercy to others."

Richard made occasional visits, calling on her whenever he was in town. He always conveyed Tom's regards and she returned hers to him. But otherwise there was no communication between them. She knew Tom did visit the shop sometimes, and once Clara had met him in Duke Street, but she herself never caught a glimpse of him.

Sophie had been looking forward to Henriette's return for the summer, but that was not to be. She had known for a while that her friend was pregnant, and it did not come as a total surprise to learn that she had been advised not to travel. When Henriette gave birth, it was to a boy, who was to be baptized Alexander. She wrote the good news to Sophie, whom she would have liked to be godmother, if Sir Roland had not had other ideas. The reason he gave was that certain members of his family would be offended if not invited to undertake the duty, but he had decided privately that it was high time his wife severed all connection with her early days in Brighton. He had no intention of ever taking her back there. His bugbear was her uncle, who was always wanting to borrow money from him with no thought of repayment, and far worse, he suspected the Baron of cheating at cards. As for the Baronne, she was as detestable as her husband in Sir Roland's opinion, and he was determined that neither should cross his threshold again. Moreover, Brighton itself was no place to visit anymore now that its royal patron had disgraced himself by separating from the Princess of Wales. Their daughter remained with the Prince at Carlton House and the Princess visited the child at erratic intervals. There were rumors that Lady Jersey was falling from the Prince's favor and he was looking again in the direction of Mrs. Fitzherbert, who had reappeared in society. She was gracious to him in company while steadfastly refusing ever to see him alone.

At the Marine Pavilion, the Prince found consolation in having freed his beloved cottage, as much as himself, from Princess Caroline's presence. He entertained as lavishly as before, but when he sat at the center of his long banqueting table, he never failed to miss his darling Maria at his right hand. No face, however lovely, could make up for hers. It was also distressing to him that as his popularity with the people continued to wane, that of Princess Caroline increased. In many quarters, the kingdom had taken her to their heart, seeing her first as the forsaken bride and then as the wronged wife and mother. It was not as though the marriage had brought him all the benefits for which he had sacrificed himself. Far from it! His income had been increased considerably, but not as much as he deserved, and Parliament had not settled his debts in their entirety, having cited the cost of the war as an excuse. He should never have listened to the persuasions and meddling of others, for he alone had ended up the loser. If only Maria would take him into her arms again, he could endure the rest.

Yet nothing the Prince had been through had made him cynical about love. He was always romantic. Whenever his steward gave permission for two of the servants to wed, he liked to know of it and was always optimistic it would prove a good match.

"There's to be a celebratory drink in the main kitchen at eleven o'clock this morning, sire," his equerry informed him as he sat at his desk. "The footman, Nick Barlow, and Betsy Dawson, the linen maid, have become betrothed."

"Good!" The Prince glanced at the clock. Perhaps he would call in on the occasion before he went out. He knew that his concern for the well-being of his servants was considered eccentric, but he felt paternal toward every one of them. He returned his attention to the book on Indian architecture that was giving him much food for thought. He already had ideas about how it could be incorporated with other styles to his seaside pavilion, making it the most beautiful palace ever seen. But he needed time to think out every detail of the vision, which had yet to loom fully in his mind. It would have to surprise and delight the eye from every aspect, magical and ethereal and yet be built to withstand the test of time.

It was good to have a purpose other than trying to win Maria back. Love letters had no effect on her determined will, even though he poured his soul into them. He'd even sent her a lock of his hair, hoping to remind her of an earlier one he had given her in a gold locket when they were still bride and groom. Surely it would make her recall the loving inscription and accept that he still felt the same. It was a wonder his hair wasn't gray with all the worry and sadness he had endured, but surprisingly it was darkening from its earlier light brown and as thick and strong as it had ever been.

He regarded himself in the mirror and smoothed a hand over his hair with satisfaction. There was no doubt he was still in his prime, his good looks unspoiled, and the weight he seemed to gain steadily only set him off as a fine figure in his Dragoon uniform or in the sumptuous coats and breeches he wore. Was Maria never going to come to her senses? At forty years old she should be glad to be still deeply loved by a younger man who set her above all other women. Over and over again he had written to her that he would always regard her as his true wife.

The striking of the clock reminded him of the betrothal. He heard the merry hubbub in the main kitchen before he reached it. As he paused in the doorway nobody noticed him at first. Their attention was focused on a beaming Nick and blushing Betsy who stood on a bench, arms around one another. The Prince's quick glance took in Martha Gunn, the dipper, who often called to see her kitchen-maid niece, and there was Tom Foxhill's young Frenchwoman, laughing and raising her glass with the rest as the steward proposed the toast.

"Our felicitations! We wish you long life and happiness in your forthcoming marriage!"

"Wait!" The Prince's voice kept all glasses in midair as he entered. "I want to drink the toast too!"

He had created a flurry of bobs and bows. Martha Gunn muttered to a maidservant standing just in front of her, "It's bad luck to interrupt a toast!"

The girl glanced back over her shoulder. "Ssh! We don't want no gloomy talk here today."

A glass of ale was poured for the Prince and he advanced with it to the happy couple on the bench. "I add my felicitations to those already offered."

He raised his glass and everybody followed suit. As soon as the toast was drunk, the glasses were returned to trays for washing up and the servants dispersed to go back to their duties. The Prince faced Sophie as she was about to follow the others.

"'Pon my word! Have you ended up as a cook at my cottage after all?"

"No, Your Highness. I've been a part-time linen maid for some time."

"Such versatility! Do you still prepare feasts for the Baron and Baronne de Bouvier as well?"

Sophie's eyes danced. "No, that was a special occasion that led to a betrothal between their niece and Sir Roland Westonbury."

"So it did! I remember now. It's an old adage that the way to a man's heart is through his stomach, and it certainly worked that evening." His eyes twinkled. "Tell me, was that your aim on the young lady's behalf?" When she had admitted it, he laughed heartily, much amused. "So I can add matchmaking to your list of talents. Our paths have crossed so often I feel sure they will again soon." He had spotted Martha Gunn about to leave and called to her. "Wait a minute, Mrs. Gunn. Why no dipping today?"

"The tide's out, sire, and there's a cold wind blowing."

"Yes, there is, and it's most unseasonable. Come to the fire and warm yourself before you go out again."

She had no choice but to move where he had indicated, close to the turning spits and the roaring flames. To her dismay he pulled a stool forward for her and another for himself. With his eyes full of almost boyish mischief, he sat down and set his hands on his knees. He still appreciated the opportunity to play a good joke, and Martha had given it to him. She did not know that in those moments when he had stood on the threshold of the kitchen, he had seen her whip a wrapped block of butter from a table into her pocket.

"I don't like to sit in your presence, sire," Martha mumbled, anxious to get away.

"I respect your old bones, madam. Pray sit."

She obeyed him, uncomfortably aware that the butter in her pocket was on the side closest to the fierce heat of the fire. He chatted to her about her work and spoke again of the chill of the waves when he had gone swimming himself earlier that day. A grease stain began to appear on her pocket and she tried to hide it with her hand. She was thankful to rise hastily to her feet when at last he stood, bade her a pleasant day, and left the kitchen. A telltale pool of melted butter dripped to the flagstones at her feet.

The Prince was still smiling at the joke he had played when the housekeeper answered his summons. "Send Mrs. Martha Gunn a new gown of good cloth, enough fabric for two petticoats, and a pound of butter."

"Yes, sire," she replied, mystified. She had not yet seen the grease stain being scrubbed out of the kitchen floor.

AT THE CLOSE OF THE SEASON, Sophie was pleased with the profits from her confectionery business, which had risen well, and she had a list of regular orders to be dispatched throughout the winter, not only to London but to other parts of England as well. Calling in at the shop one morning, she handed Richard a sum of money. "It's repayment for the winnings from a horse Tom backed for me on the Prince's advice at the Newmarket races," she explained.

"I'm not sure about accepting this on Tom's behalf," Richard said doubtfully. "You say there was nothing written and he doesn't know anything about it."

"I've always thought of it as a loan and as a gentleman's agreement on my part. Please give it to him. It means the Delcourt confectionery business will then be entirely mine."

"Very well. I'll do as you ask."

When Sophie next had supper with Richard, as she did from time to time, he said that Tom had been surprised to receive the money.

"My brother thanked you and said he accepted the monies in the manner you had once received his gift of a pistol. Tom also wishes you continued success in your business."

"I'm glad it was all done without animosity." Sophie smiled slightly. It was amazing how well she and Tom understood each other in some matters, and how hopelessly they were at odds in others.

QUITE UNEXPECTEDLY, Sophie came across a little house. She had been resigned to waiting quite a time for a place of her own. Without exception, the only Brighton properties she had seen that had low rents all the year round were ancient buildings, small and cramped, standing shoulder to shoulder along narrow ways. Then, on a crisp November Sunday, Sophie took Antoine and Billy for a walk, letting Clara have a quiet nap on her own by the fire. As a change from walking along the shore, Sophie decided to follow a route inland.

The boys ran ahead, scooping up armfuls of fallen leaves and hurling them at each other in faded coppery showers. It was along a winding lane about a mile from the sea that Sophie spotted the little house. On a piece of board by the gate were the words "To Let" daubed in dark blue paint.

She stood and looked at the property. Built of flint that winked in the pale wintery sunshine, its roof of slate, the house could have been designed from a little child's drawing. It had a square frontage with two windows up and two down, a centrally placed door, and a stout chimney. The wide gates led to a pebble-strewn path curving to the front stoop and to a track that, she guessed, led to some shelter for a horse. The garden was well tended, suggesting that the house had been only recently vacated.

She called to the boys. "Wait! Come back! I'm going to look around here."

They came running back to find her peering through a downstairs window. Then they followed her around to a vegetable patch at the back. There was a stable with a single stall.

As the boys explored, Sophie took in the environs of the house, meadows and fields and woods on all sides. It was exactly what she wanted. All that remained now was to find out the rent. As there was an arrow on the sign, pointing westward, she concluded that the property belonged to the farmer whose thatched house and barn she could see about half a mile away.

"You can stay here and play if you like, boys," she said, looking up at them in one of the trees. "I'm going to ask for a key."

It was the wife of the farmer who opened the door. She was a healthy-looking woman with a friendly smile. She had a baby in her arms and a toddler hanging on her skirts. Two more little children, alike as two peas in a pod, came running to stare at the visitor.

"Come in, miss," the woman said when she had heard the purpose of Sophie's calling. "The house was only vacated two weeks ago. The couple were townfolk who thought they'd like a change, but they only stayed eight months. These little ones you see here are four of my seven, but we'll be far enough away for you not to be disturbed by their noise. Aren't you the young lady who has the sweetmeat business at Mrs. Renfrew's place? I thought so. I've seen you driving about. I admire that smart blue trap you drive and the matching ribbons on the pony's bridle."

Sophie smiled. "I like to advertise my confectionery as much as possible."

Mrs. Ketley had sent one of the twins to bring her husband to the parlor where Sophie had been shown. Farmer Ketley had an open, honest face and was of medium height, broad, and stockily built.

"So you'd like to look over Beech House, would you, Miss Delcourt? It's a snug little nook. My grandparents lived there years ago." He was obviously pleased at the prospect of getting another tenant so quickly, making Sophie wonder if prior to the last tenancy the property had stood empty for a long time. Perhaps that was why he offered it to her at a low rent.

"Would you be living there alone?" he asked as he gave her the key.

"No, I have a young nephew with me. He's eight years old and goes to the Duke Street school."

"Then he'll probably know my lad, William, who's a couple of years older."

He offered to go with her to the house, but Sophie wanted to view it on her own. The boys were still climbing the apple trees when she unlocked the door at the front and entered. A flagged floor led to a parlor on one side and a kitchen and one smaller room on the other. Upstairs there were three bedchambers on the same scale. From the largest she could see the sea in the distance. The house had been in good hands, with signs of its having been redecorated by the previous occupants. There were striped wallpapers in pastel shades on all the walls except the kitchen, where whitewash had been applied. Sophie sighed with satisfaction.

Opening one of the upper windows, she called down. "Antoine! Come and see your new home."

Antoine looked startled and he obeyed with less speed than Billy. Both boys were puzzled until Sophie explained her intentions. She took them with her when she returned to the farmhouse to pay a month's rent in advance. Farmer Ketley and his wife hoped she would be happy in her new home and said they were pleased to have her as a neighbor.

Clara wished her well. She had known that Sophie would get her own place one day, but thought the young Frenchwoman's change of abode would have come through marriage to Captain Morgan. Now that did not appear to be in the cards. At first Antoine was uncertain about leaving Clara's cottage, although he liked the idea of having his own room. Sophie reassured him that some things would be the same as before. She would drive him with her to the atelier in the mornings and he would return with her in the evenings to Beech House, enabling him to walk to and from school with Billy as he had always done. His last misgivings faded when he was at the house one day while Sophie was cleaning it in readiness for the delivery of furniture. William Ketley came with a mongrel puppy in his arms.

"Pa says would you like it, miss. It's the runt of the litter and no good to him."

Sophie rose from her knees where she had been washing the floor. There was nothing to commend the black and white puppy in looks, but it had irresistible velvet eyes. She nodded to William with a smile.

"We'll have it. How much?"

"Nothing. Pa'll be thankful to place it. He don't like putting down animals he don't have to."

"Please thank him very much." Sophie took the wriggling puppy. "Call in at my atelier tomorrow on your way home from school. I'll have a box of candies ready for you to take home."

"Thanks, miss." The lad went darting off again.

Sophie handed the puppy to Antoine, whose face was blissful. "You must train him well," she said, "and there's one rule he must never break. He will not be allowed to cross the threshold of the atelier. I'll not have dog's hairs floating into the sweetmeats."

"He'll be good. I promise, Sophie."

"What shall you call him?"

There was no hesitation. "Barnabas. Barney for short."

Previously Sophie had not given any thought to a dog, but now she was glad to have Barney. A barking dog would be good protection since her neighbors were not within earshot. Barney was a poor little scrap at the moment, but he would have the best of care. Already he had endeared himself to her.

Twenty-one

SOPHIE BOUGHT cheaply and quickly most of the basic require-
ments for her new home. With the continual changeover of a visiting
population in Brighton, the markets always had plenty of furniture
and domestic items for sale. Once the contents of an apartment were
being auctioned, and she picked up some bargains in crockery and a
large Turkish rug that looked splendid when spread on the parlor
floor. A long-neglected table and a mahogany chest of drawers soon
regained their glow under her energetic polishing. She still had some
chairs to re-cover and more curtains to hang when Rory came to see
the house. He had brought her a silver-framed wall mirror as a
house-warming gift, and she immediately decided where it should be
hung. She almost danced from room to room radiating happiness as
she showed him over the house.

"I'm putting down roots at last. My own place, Rory! Think of it!
I haven't felt so settled since before the Revolution." She spun to a
halt in the largest of the upper rooms, which was to be her bedchamber. It was still empty, except for the restored chest of drawers and a
rag rug that Clara had given her from the cottage. "I've bought a bed
from a landlord about to refurnish an apartment, but he can't give it
up until after Christmas. As soon as it comes I shall move in."

He was leaning a hand against the wall, his head lowered as he
looked out the window, taking in the distant view of the sea beyond
the treetops. "I wanted to speak to you about Christmas," he said,

straightening up and turning to her. "Would you and Antoine come to Lymington with me? My mother hasn't been very well recently, and I want to see for myself how she is."

Sophie felt her spirits spiral down. She had been looking forward to spending Christmas with Clara and both boys, but she could see Rory was concerned and it would be unkind to disappoint him. "Yes, Rory. We'll go with you."

When she broke the news to Antoine he became frantic with distress. "I don't want to go there! It's no fun. Let me stay with Ma Renfrew and Billy. She always invites jolly people and their children to drop in and we're going carol singing on Christmas Eve and there'll be games and fun."

Sophie did not have the heart to refuse him, nor was Rory offended. "It's as well," he said understandingly. "There'll be no young company for him. Neither Elizabeth with her young child nor Jane, who is now expectant, wish to travel at this time of year. So it will be a quiet celebration with my mother and Ellen."

It was even quieter than he had expected. When they arrived on Christmas Eve, Ellen expressed her relief that they had come.

"Mother has had to take to her bed. I've sent for the doctor."

Although Rory had intended that he and Sophie should stay only three days, their visit was extended as his mother's condition deteriorated and there was nothing to be done for her. Sophie helped Ellen with the nursing. Less than an hour before Mrs. Morgan died, while Sophie was holding one of her hands and Ellen the other, she whispered a last request.

"Promise me something in case you accept my dear son."

"What is it?" Sophie asked gently.

"Don't let him take second place to your ambitions."

"I would always put the man I loved before all else."

"Thank you, my dear." Mrs. Morgan's eyelids drifted shut once more.

Rory was standing at the foot of the bed, and Sophie rose from her chair to let him take her place at his mother's side. Then she left the room to let him and his sister have what little time was left with their mother. When they emerged from the room half an hour later Ellen said their mother had not spoken again.

There was a large gathering at the funeral. When it was over and the mourners departed, Ellen, a lonely figure in black, would have liked Sophie to stay on, but that was not possible. Like all three of his sisters, Rory was deeply grieved. The journey back to Brighton was a cold one with flurries of snow, and they stopped for refreshment at an inn where a cheerful fire roared on the hearth. Sophie did not sit at once, but held her chilled hands to the flames. Rory removed her cloak and put it aside with his own. Then he stood with his arm about her waist, looking into the fire.

"I've been thinking again about my mother's last words," he said quietly. "She virtually gave us her blessing. Surely you will agree now to becoming betrothed to me?"

She was full of sympathy for him, wanting to give him comfort at this time, but unable as yet to do as he wished.

"Give me a little more time, Rory."

"Yes, of course. I know better than most how to be patient."

At the reading of his mother's will, he had made a mental note to revise his own at the first opportunity, but when he returned to his duties, the matter slipped from his mind.

As the weeks went by, Rory did not mention the betrothal again. Sophie thought sometimes that his nickname, the Hawk, also reflected a change in him. His loving attitude to her remained the same, but he was becoming totally obsessed by his aim to destroy the Broomfield gang. A chance encounter when he was undermanned had left him with three revenue men dead, five wounded, and himself with a minor injury that took a while to heal. His rage that the moment he had been waiting for had gone awry made him difficult and moody for a considerable time, causing him to speak sharply to Antoine, who was as noisy and boisterous as any eight-year-old boy. Rory was also merciless in his criticism when they fenced. Sophie explained to Antoine that Rory was under stress. Antoine shrugged and grinned. "When I can fence better than Captain Rory I'll be able to criticize him!" he replied cheekily, quite unabashed.

Rory became more and more preoccupied by work, seeing Sophie even less than before. Often when he did come to Beech House, he was exhausted and went to sleep in a chair. There were other times when he was more amorous than he had ever been in the past, but he knew the force of his own passions, and cherished her too much to risk leaving her pregnant if he should be killed before their marriage could take place. In any case, instilled in him throughout his upbringing had been the gentleman's code of honor toward decent women. For his physical needs, there was the other kind.

SOPHIE ENJOYED entertaining friends at Beech House, where she was able at last to return hospitality and give card parties and suppers. Henriette, although in London for the season, was not permitted to travel to Brighton, but she sent Sophie a pretty clock with a face of English porcelain covered with tiny flowers. It was chosen at the Foxhills' London shop and delivered personally by Richard. With it came a touching little note in Henriette's rather childish hand.

Think of me at least once a day when the clock strikes.

Its dainty chime was an appropriate reminder of its donor and of the friendship that had been forged out of a deeply troubled time.

Richard's own gift was a handsome little rosewood games table inlaid with ivory. The tabletop could be used for chess or draughts and reversed for backgammon. Sophie was delighted with it and opened a little drawer that had slots for dice, chess, and backgammon pieces.

"I've taught Antoine to play all these games," she exclaimed, "but I never thought we should have such an elegant table to play on."

"I admit to an ulterior motive," Richard confessed humorously. "I thought you might invite me for a game of chess sometime."

She invited him that same evening. After that it was quite a while before he returned to Brighton. Even then, she was unable to have supper with him as she was expecting Rory to arrive in time to dine with her. But the evening was wasted as she and Antoine waited in vain for him to appear. When they sat down to eat alone, Antoine let his feelings be known.

"I don't see why you ask Captain Morgan to dine. He's always saying he'll be here and then he doesn't come."

"When he has an alert somewhere along the coast, his duty has to come first."

Sophie had been three months at Beech House when eventually she met Richard again at the Old Ship. As usual when she was out late, Antoine slept in his old bed in Billy's room. Clara was even indulgent enough to let Barney sleep on the foot of Antoine's bed, although the dog had grown larger than would ever have been supposed likely when he was a puppy.

Richard had booked the alcove table he liked best. Polly waited on them as she had done in the past. This evening she was particularly pleased to see Sophie.

"I'm going to let Mr. Hicks know you're here, Sophie. It's been chaos in the kitchen today. The confectioner and the head chef came to blows!" She giggled delightedly. "You never saw such a scene! Anyway, the confectioner walked out and his assistants had to manage on their own. It may be a chance for some work to come your way."

She finished serving them and left with a swirl of her apron ribbons. Richard smiled across the table at Sophie. "Would you be prepared to take it on?"

"It depends on what is required. I'm always interested in extra business."

"Things are still going well?"

"Extremely so. Recently I took on some outworkers to make the boxes and frills."

"Shall you expand soon?"

"Not till I judge the time to be right. Then I hope it will be on quite a large scale, which means it's still a way off."

"I recall that on my first visit to the atelier Lady Westonbury was wrapping bonbons. I haven't seen her since the day she bought the clock. How is she?"

"I had a letter from her last week. She is well, but her little son has been ill. Her husband will be taking them to Ramsgate for the summer. It's a disappointment to her and to me that he has taken a dislike to Brighton."

"Mrs. Fitzherbert will be spending the summer there too."

"How do you know?"

"She was in the shop recently and chose a very fine writing table to be sent direct to Ramsgate at a certain date."

"I hear the Prince is still trying to restore their relationship."

"I can't see that ever coming about. How can a lady of her deep religious faith agree to mend matters when she doesn't know if she can think of herself as his true wife or not?"

"But surely her marriage was first and therefore the binding one," Sophie argued.

Richard shrugged. "Probably if all the lawyers and all the church-men in the land put their heads together they would go on arguing about it till doomsday."

"I believe the lawyers would sift away the authority of the Church in favor of the Law," Sophie conceded regretfully.

"That is what Mrs. Fitzherbert must fear herself. She'd never sacrifice her moral principles to become the Prince's mistress, no matter that once she loved him as her husband."

They turned to other topics, until Mr. Hicks came into the dining room and stopped at their table. After greeting Richard and Sophie, he put a request to her.

"Could you spare me a few minutes of your time before you leave this evening, Miss Delcourt? Normally I wouldn't ask, but I have an emergency on my hands." When she had agreed, he bowed again and left.

Richard raised his eyebrows approvingly. "More work for the maker of candies fit for a king!"

"We'll see," she replied with a smile. Then she voiced the question that was uppermost in her mind. "How is Tom these days?"

He scrutinized her questioningly. "Do you really want to know?"

"I'll never lose my concern for his well-being."

"Nor he for you."

"I suppose that sums up his attitude to all women."

Richard took a sip of wine. "Until he met you."

"And since?" she added dryly.

"They never last."

"Eventually he will forget me."

"I can't believe that."

As SHE HAD EXPECTED, Mr. Hicks offered her the position of confec-tioner. Once she would have skipped with joy at such a chance, but now she shook her head. "I have my own business to take up my time."

"I know, and I'll be able to order from you in future. The confectioner I've just lost would never have tolerated it. The assistants he left behind are thoroughly trained and they will manage well enough, but tomorrow evening the Prince is giving a ball here and I shall need a spectacular sugar centerpiece for the buffet supper table."

"You shall have it. Is it to be a galleon again?"

"Not necessarily. I leave the choice entirely to you. I would also like a selection of your finest sweetmeats."

After a short discussion about prices he escorted her to the main door and they bade each other good night. Richard had summoned her pony and trap and stood holding the bridle himself.

"Tom is here," he said as she came down the steps.

"How do you know?" she demanded quickly.

He nodded to the other side of the deserted, ill-lit street. Tom stood there in his long-skirted coat and tall hat as if he had just left a gaming table. Her guess was that it was more likely he had come from a rowboat drawn silently into the shore somewhere in the darkness. He carried nothing, but maybe his spoils had been already deposited to keep his brother in ignorance of his smuggling ways. She tensed as he began to stroll slowly across the cobbles, and she knew a terrible gladness at seeing him again. Even more alarming, her bones seemed to be melting, although she told herself it was only relief that once again he had escaped death.

He stared at her hungrily in the glow from the candle lamps above the Old Ship's entrance. "Damn you for being more beautiful than ever, Sophie. I had hoped to find you thin and wretched through missing me."

"I would never do that!" she flashed back, hurt almost to tears that after such a long time he should meet her with a savage taunt. "Quite the reverse!"

She would have stepped into the trap to leave, but Tom grabbed her arm to stay her. She feared she might faint at the electrifying contact of his hand through her thin silk sleeve.

"I've been meaning to tell you, Sophie. A week ago I was at the Château de Juneau."

"You went there! Is it still standing? It wasn't burned down, was it?" She was voicing a fear she had harbored for a long time, not knowing what might have happened after she and Antoine had left and the Comtesse de Juneau had been dragged away.

"No, it stands locked and bolted. I found a loose shutter and managed to look into one of the rooms. It had been stripped of everything."

"What a disappointment for you," she retorted. "There were no mother-of-pearl boxes for you to take away!"

He went white about the mouth. "You have lost none of your venom! I'll tell you the rest of what I discovered when you're in a more receptive mood." He flung her arm from his grasp and went striding away.

Pride prevented her from running after him, and she wished she had not given vent to hasty words. She turned to Richard. "Where is he going?"

"To the apartment. Shall I take you there?"

"No, he's tired and out of patience with me. Perhaps he will tell you whatever he has to say. Then you can pass it on to me."

But Richard was not ready to let her go yet. "What did you mean about the mother-of-pearl box?"

"It's a private matter between Tom and me," she replied evasively. "Please don't ask me anything more."

"As you wish," he replied patiently.

Sophie was almost home when she saw in the lights of her vehicle's candle lamps that the five-barred gate to the meadow that neighbored her garden was standing slightly ajar. She was annoyed. Antoine had been playing there that afternoon with Billy and some other children. Farmer Ketley permitted them to play there on the condition that Antoine obeyed the rules of the countryside and closed the gate afterward. It was not a stiff latch and easily slipped into place, and so there was no excuse for neglecting the task. Once the privilege was almost withdrawn after Antoine left the gate open and a flock of sheep came through a gap in the hedge from the next meadow and wandered far down the lane.

Drawing up, Sophie jumped out to latch the gate. She would have to reprimand Antoine severely when she fetched him from Clara's cottage in the morning. Then she led the pony the last few yards to her own gate and took him in. After she had stabled him she lit a lantern she kept hanging there to show her the way to the front door of the house. When she heard the sound of galloping hooves approaching from the direction of the town she felt no alarm. Every nerve and fiber of her body told her it was Tom in the saddle.

He reined in when he saw her standing in her own pathway, the lantern in her hand, but he did not dismount. "I had no right to deny you what you should know," he stated crisply.

She came out of her gate and stood looking up at him, the lantern light throwing its golden beam onto the planes of his face, his eyes glittering in their shadowed setting. "I was at fault too," she admitted. "Please tell me everything."

"I broke a window at the château, having forced the shutter back, and made an entry. I was bent on loot, but not for myself. I hoped to find something I might bring back for Antoine. I discovered that though several of the rooms had been ransacked, most were left virtually intact. It was as if the intruders had been checked in their scavenging. It should settle your mind to know that I left everything as it was and only brought away these two items for the boy." He took a small velvet bag from his pocket and reached down to hand it to her.

Sophie set the lantern on the garden wall and opened the bag. Two miniatures slid out on her palm. She recognized the sitters instantly in the lantern's glow. "The Comte and Comtesse de Juneau! Antoine's parents!" She was blinded by tears. "Oh, Tom! How did you know these miniatures were of them?"

"Because other portraits of those two people had been slashed. Antoine also bears a resemblance to both his parents."

She brushed the tears from her eyes. "But why were you in the vicinity of the château?"

"I had some time on my hands and thought I'd do a little investigating. Your enemy, Citizen Juneau, was there a month or two ago. And not for the first time, either. In the village I presented myself as a traveler in wares and picked up quite a lot of information. The villagers were generally wary of talking to strangers, but one man in his cups told me that Juneau was always asking about the servants who had been employed at the château during the time of the riot. Sophie, he was seeking a name!"

"Do you think he gained it?" she asked uneasily.

281

"As far as I could discover, he was no more successful this time than on his previous visits. I assume you had no direct contact with the villagers."

"None. I knew the other servants were all royalists and so I felt safe enough at the château, but I tried to remain as much out of sight of strangers as was possible. I never knew if I'd been traced from Paris." She hesitated, having something so important to ask him that when she did speak her words came in a rush. "Did you get a description of Emile de Juneau?"

"Only that he is tall and dark with aristocratic features and bears some family likeness to the late Comte de Juneau."

Sophie threw up her head fiercely. "At last I shall recognize my enemy."

"The villagers mistrust him, knowing that he was the rabble-rouser who led the attack on the château and others in the district."

"Perhaps it was also he who called a halt to the looting," Sophie suggested bitterly. "Maybe he was already seeing the château and its treasures as his own. Do you know his present where-abouts?"

"He's in Paris, trying to wheedle his way into Government, but his past association with the traitor Orléans is going against him in the present political climate. He was lucky not to have lost his head at the same time as that notorious gentleman. I don't think you need fear his return in the near future. He's short of money. No doubt his search for Antoine has cost him a considerable amount. He will need to strengthen his position at home before coming back to England. As yet he hasn't dared lay claim to the château, but undoubtedly he will when memories of his past associates have faded and, above all, if he can claim the rightful heir is dead."

"I read in an émigré newspaper last summer of his political activity. The peace of mind that news gave me was backed up by your giving me the training in shooting from Sergeant Jones."

"You did well, he told me."

"He was a good instructor. Were you in Paris too? Is that how you found out so much?"

"Yes, I was. That lovely city is finally drawing breath after all its horrors, although the prisons are still full of political prisoners and the rumors of the late King's son having escaped death in prison have now been proved false. So the new King of France is still Louis XVI's brother in exile. Fashion has revived and enthusiasm for the war prevails throughout your homeland. The name of young General Bonaparte is on everyone's lips. He's flooding France with looted treasures from Italy."

"I've been reading about him in the émigré newspaper. Tell me more about Paris."

"The bells of Notre Dame still ring out, folk still gather in the wine shops for the latest political gossip, and the trees are budding green again. I remembered your telling me where your father's shop was located and I made a point of going there. It's no longer boarded up as when you last saw it. It has become a bakery."

She nodded wordlessly in an acute wave of homesickness that took no account of the changes that had occurred. Then she moved a step nearer as she looked up at him.

"I'll not be able to tell Antoine how you obtained these miniatures," she said, sliding them back into the velvet bag. "He knows that to speak of his home as the château could be misconstrued as boasting, but the gift might make his tongue run away with him, imperiling you far more than him."

He laughed softly without humor. "Do I detect some remnants of concern for me, Sophie?"

"Why can you never be serious," she asked with a flare of exasperation. "I told you long ago I abhorred waste. Surely you have some suggestion as to what I can tell Antoine about where you obtained the miniatures."

"Tell him they are a gift from my stock. That's true enough. I'll tell him the whole story myself one day if ever circumstances permit."

"Then I thank you a thousand times on his behalf as well as for myself. It hasn't been easy keeping the memories of his parents alive, but these fine likenesses will renew them for the rest of his life."

"That's it then. Good night to you, Sophie. I'll be in Brighton for a few days. I've a couple of fine paintings and a Chinese cabinet I'm going to offer the Prince."

He wheeled his horse about and rode back through the darkness. Sophie wondered if he thought she might call in at the shop to see him, but that would be pointless. For his sake as well as her own, the less they saw of each other the better.

Sophie reprimanded Antoine severely about the gate before he went to school the next day. He never tried to avoid responsibility for his actions and she often found it hard to punish him. This time she let him off with a warning.

Throughout the rest of the day she worked on the centerpiece for Mr. Hicks. She had chosen to sculpt a vessel named *Surprise* from a painting that hung in the Old Ship. The sugaring of the threads of the rigging was particularly intricate.

When the centerpiece, tinted and gilded, was delivered to Mr. Hicks, he thought he had never seen better and it was the first time a confectioner had thought to model the *Surprise,* which had links with the Old Ship's history. His only criticism was directed toward himself for letting Sophie slip from his employment when he could have had this kind of work from her for a very modest wage. Now she charged as much as any male confectioner would have done.

That evening Sophie gave Antoine the miniatures and sat a long time talking to him about his parents. There was much about their social standing and his father's political career that she had to hold back for his own safety, but he listened attentively and spoke of the memories he had retained. She thought he might shed tears at seeing his mother's face again, but the span of time had been too long. Sophie realized she had filled the gap in his life.

"May I have these miniatures in my room?" Antoine asked when it was bedtime. Sophie gladly agreed. The boy had revealed his awareness of the importance of his parentage and of the link that could never be broken. He chose a place on the wall for the miniatures where he could see them before he went to sleep and when he opened his eyes in the morning.

When Antoine had written a letter of thanks to Tom, Sophie let him go on his own to the shop to deliver it. He was away much longer than she had expected, and she was beginning to feel concerned when he came bursting into the house, red-cheeked with excitement.

"Mr. Tom Foxhill fought a duel!"

"What?" Sophie was aghast, thinking she had not heard him properly.

"With rapiers! In his stableyard!" Breathlessly Antoine flung himself down on a sofa. It was easy to see he had run most of the way home in his eagerness to tell her about it. "Mr. Richard acted as his second. I don't know the name of the other man's second, but old Dr. Moore was on hand and very cross about the hour. He said dawn was the time for duels and they were all likely to be arrested, but they weren't because Mr. Tom told me and one of the shop assistants to shut the stable gates and then no passerby could see in from the street."

"Was Tom hurt?"

"Not much."

"How much?" Sophie shrieked.

"He was nicked on the chin, that's all."

She sank down into a winged chair. "How did the duel come about?"

"Well, I'd given my letter to Mr. Tom and he showed it to Mr. Richard and they both said I wrote well and how was I getting on at school and all that. They weren't busy, because there were no customers in the shop. Then suddenly this angry gentleman from London came stalking in and demanded satisfaction for his wife's honor. Mr. Tom said the matter should be settled there and then, which was when the shop was shut and an assistant sent for Dr. Moore. You should have seen those blades flash!" Antoine sprang to his feet and darted about the room imitating the actions of a duelist and making the hissing sounds of a blade cutting through the air.

"Stop it!" Sophie drummed her fists down on the arms of her chair. "Be still and tell me how the duel ended."

He obeyed her, somewhat chastened by her distraught expression. "Mr. Tom sliced the gentleman's sleeves and cut him about a bit. Then he knocked the rapier from his opponent's hand and set the tip of his own blade against the man's heart." Antoine rushed to Sophie and flung his arms around her. "Don't look so frightened! Mr. Tom didn't kill the man! He just flung aside his rapier and walked across the stableyard back into his shop. I saw him in the apartment before I left. He was dabbing blood from his chin and drinking champagne in a merry mood."

Sophie set Antoine aside and sprang up. Once again she drummed her fists, but this time it was against the edge of the mantel shelf.

"That Tom Foxhill!" she expostulated furiously. "Will he never stop inviting death?"

Yet she was miserably aware that there was another cause for her rage. It shamed her that she should feel a screaming jealousy of the unknown woman who had been the cause of the duel.

Twenty-two

SOPHIE HAD NOT SEEN RORY for a month when he arrived at the atelier with tickets already purchased for the theater that evening. She was pleased with the surprise, and Antoine stayed on to sleep at the cottage while she went home quickly to change into a new velvet gown whose silk ruched neckline set off the creamy smoothness of her neck and shoulders.

The play was excellent. On the way home Sophie told Rory she had decided to give up sewing at the Marine Pavilion in the coming season.

"I can no longer spare the time. The winter months have been so busy at the atelier that the summer orders will take every minute of my working days. People from London and other places have ordered far more than before, even some who have never been to Brighton. As for the sugar centerpieces, ever since I made that one for Mr. Hicks, I've been getting regular weekly orders for the supper buffets at various balls. I've also been inundated with orders for private festivities."

"That's good. What centerpieces are you working on at the present time?"

"Neptune in a chariot of cockleshells! Yesterday I finished a Grecian temple."

The night was chilly and as soon as they were in the house she knelt to put more logs on the fire. Sitting back on her heels in a tumbled circle of velvet skirt, she nodded approvingly at the flames.

"That's better!"

Rory had put aside his hat and shrugged off his greatcoat in the hall. The silver braid glinted on his jacket as he came to sit on the rug beside her. Leisurely he rested an arm on the side of a chair, unable to take his gaze from her. The firelight was dancing on her face and deepening seductively the shadow of her cleavage.

"I've been telling you all I've been doing," she said, twisting around to face him and sitting with her legs tucked up under her. "What about you? I wish you'd talk about your work too. It's more worrying not knowing anything. Sometimes I can't sleep when I start thinking about what you might be facing."

"When you're lying sleepless," he said cheerfully, "I'm probably safely asleep in my own bed. You imagine my work to be far more heroic than it is. I have such reinforcements at my command now that I would have no need to call in the military, not even on the day of reckoning with the Broomfield gang."

"Do you expect that to be soon?" Something in his tone had alerted her, even though it had not been intended. "Tell me. I insist!"

He hesitated for a few moments, but since she seemed to have guessed anyway, he gave a nod. "I'm closing in. Think what it means, Sophie. My great task will soon be done."

A sudden wave of anxiety swept over her and she flung herself across his chest as if to protect him with her own body. "Take care, Rory! The Broomfield gang will know you as the Hawk. You'll be their prime target!"

Such a spontaneous demonstration of concern touched him deeply, and he folded his arms about her. "I'm prepared for everything. Never trouble yourself on that score. All I've ever feared is losing you."

She drew back onto her heels and looked into his face. "I didn't know. You had no cause for that." She felt her whole being melt toward this good man, who was shortly to face the most appalling danger with quiet, resolute courage. Suddenly she knew how all women must feel when a lover or husband is about to leave for war. Her voice came in a whisper. "All I ever asked for was time, Rory."

His whole face became suffused with hope and happiness. He put his hand into his pocket and drew out a small crimson box, which he opened to reveal a sparkling ring—a diamond set in rubies. "I've been carrying this with me for a long time, awaiting the moment when I could be sure you would accept it. I'm not mistaken now, am I?"

"No, Rory," she said softly. "And it's a beautiful ring."

She held out her left hand and he slid the ring onto her finger. Then he caught her by the shoulders and drew her toward him, his kiss full of love. He had never wanted her more; the bouquet of her warm flesh made his senses reel. It would be easy to awaken her sensual nature to high passion in his arms, but he had the grim knowledge that within thirty-six hours he would be engaged in perhaps the fiercest battle of his career. He could not chance leaving her to bear a child out of wedlock.

Her eyes were understanding. "Soon I'll be your wife, Rory."

He had no illusions. He knew she loved him, but not yet with a depth that matched his. When she found fulfillment in their marriage bed she would cross the last short distance to him.

Then he had to leave. A band of his men were already riding to a meeting point and he had to be there before them.

Sophie went to the gate to watch him ride away. Before mounting his waiting horse he swung her joyfully up and around before setting her on her feet again with a farewell kiss. Before he was out of sight he uttered the triumphant rollicking yell of the revenue men in victory and she smiled, glad to have given him such pleasure.

Returning indoors she looked down at her ring. At last she had driven Tom from her life. Why then did she not feel released?

SOPHIE WAS UP EARLY the next morning. She wrote two letters to tell of her betrothal, one to Ellen and the other to Henriette.

That same evening she wore the velvet gown again when she went to a card party with fellow émigrés. A widow partnering Sophie was full of gossip about what had happened recently in a London theater.

"As soon as the Prince of Wales appeared in the royal box, he was booed by most of the audience. Isn't that horrifying! It reminds me of those times in Paris when our late Queen received the same reception."

Sophie knew better than the rest how it had all come about, but as she had obtained her information when calling on members of the staff in the kitchens of the Marine Pavilion she refrained from saying anything. Somehow it would be like passing on tittle-tattle about one's own family, even though much of it was generally known and none could deny the increasing popularity of Princess Caroline at the Prince's expense. At the time of separating from him, she had dismissed Lady Jersey from her service and set up her own motley and indiscreet court in the mansion she had been allotted in a village on the Thames. Among her new friends were some powerful enemies of the Prince, no doubt chosen for that very reason, and they seized every chance to defame him. Worst of all, the press took up each allegation and used it cruelly.

"Your deal, madame," Sophie said firmly, putting an end to chatter about the Prince's humiliation.

It was late when the final game was played. Everybody gathered on the steps with last-minute farewells. Eventually Sophie took the reins to drive herself home.

It was a fine night with a sliver of moon that came and went amid slowly drifting clouds. As she drove past Clara's cottage all the windows were dark. Antoine, staying overnight, would be asleep with Barney at the foot of his bed. In a few short hours the atelier would be bustling with activity. Her investment in extra equipment had paid off. There was the tall iron cupboard with its layers of drip pans, also the new apparatus for making marzipan flowers with incredible swiftness, and she even had her own still for distilling vanilla, spirits of angelica, cinnamon, and other flavorings, as well as many kinds of flower waters. Her domain was now as well equipped as her father's had been.

Out in the countryside the primroses made patches like fallen moonlight under the trees. Earlier that day Antoine had picked her a large bunch, enough to fill two bowls with delicate little blossoms. As Sophie passed a deserted barn she started with alarm as a man drew back swiftly into the dark shadows. But she had caught the glint of brass buttons and was reassured. It was only a revenue man keeping watch, as happened sometimes on nights such as this, when a smooth sea and a slight moon favored the Gentlemen. She drove the rest of the way without seeing anyone, but had to stop when she noticed that the gate to the meadow stood open even wider than it had before. She groaned aloud. "Not again! Oh, Antoine!"

He must have left it unlatched when he went to pick her flowers. Although it had looked shut when she drove past earlier, the gate must have gradually swung back on its hinges as far as it would go.

Her heels sank into the soft damp earth of the meadow as she went to pull on the gate. It failed to budge. She complained aloud again in her frustration and tugged once more with all her strength. When this attempt proved unsuccessful, she stooped down to scoop aside the grass and see if a stone was holding it. What she discovered was a stout wooden stake that had been driven deep into the earth, ensuring that the gate remained open. It would have needed a heavy mallet for the task. No child could have done it.

She felt herself go cold with fear. Hoping desperately she was mistaken, she gathered up her skirts and ran across the meadow to where another, rarely used gate was located. It had also been wedged open and the cows that normally grazed in the meadow were nowhere to be seen. She knew the next gate in line led to a cart track through the woods to a fast road beyond, but she did not need to check on that one, for she had evidence enough that it too would be wide open. Farmer Ketley had opened his gates for smugglers on horseback, and that could only mean the Broomfield gang was to operate tonight. No wonder the revenue men were about! Rory would be leading the ambush.

She rushed back to the lane and extinguished the lamps of the trap. Then she raced into the house to fetch and load her pistol, which she thrust into her sash. A few minutes later she had taken the reins again. The Broomfield gang would most surely land in the cove and she wanted to be at the confrontation. After all, she had a cause too in the death of the two revenue men she had alerted. All she could hope was that this was not one of the times Tom was sailing with the smugglers.

She left the lane to drive as fast as she could along tracks she knew well, for she had walked these ways many times. It was still quiet. The smugglers could not have landed yet. When she reached a grove she threw off her cloak, afraid its bright color might be easily spotted. Her dark blue velvet gown blended with the shadows. Leaving the pony tethered, she continued on foot through the trees until she came

291

to a stretch of rough grass and large clumps of bushy weeds that lay
between her and the tamarisk hedge that rose just above the shingle.
The sliver of moon showed her a group of a dozen or more wagons
and strings of saddled horses waiting quietly a short distance away.
Their sheer number was certain indication that an extra-large shipment of contraband was to be moved tonight. She had no idea how
many smugglers and their accomplices would be involved, but as she
crept across to the shelter of the tamarisk hedge, she remembered
from what Rory had told her that often more than sixty of the Gentlemen themselves would ride in armed escort as their wares were carried inland. She could just make out some of the accomplices waiting
amid the wagons and horses, but they maintained a strict silence.

Cautiously Sophie peered down through the feathery tamarisk
branches at the cove below. The pale beach was almost luminous and
quite deserted, but she knew that in the blackest shadow and behind
rocks Rory and his men were waiting. Sophie felt at one with his
tension and excitement, even though there had never been between
them that curious communication of the senses that seemed to exist
between Tom and her. That was as well at the present time, for it
would have worried Rory to know she was within the danger zone.
This was to be the confrontation with the Broomfield gang he had
long awaited. In the meantime there was nothing to hear except the
whisper of the sea breeze in the grass, the soft lap of the waves, and
the occasional jingle of a harness as a horse moved restlessly. Then a
light suddenly blinked twice out at sea, and Sophie's heart began to
beat so wildly that she was afraid it could be heard far and wide.

She was not at a point where she could see the answering light
from the shore, but the signal must have been given, for those waiting
with the horses clearly had no suspicion that everything was not as it
should be. Now and again she caught the gleam of weapons. She
wondered how many pairs of eyes were watching for the boats that
would be coming in from the mother ship.

Before long, black shapes began to converge onto the shore and
there was a glitter of water as oars were lifted and silently stowed.
Immediately the waiting accomplices began to stream down onto the
shingle. Still there was nothing to give them or the Gentlemen cause
for alarm. Sophie realized they were all being allowed to disembark to
ensure that none would escape. The unloading began. To her intense

relief, no solitary figure detached himself from the rest to set aside loot of his own. Wherever Tom might be, he was not here.

Then suddenly the silence was split by a great shout that could only have come from Rory. "Charge!"

Instantly there was a roar, and flambeaux blazed forth in a wide semicircle, giving illumination to the revenue men, who came rushing from all sides, shouting as they descended on the surprised smugglers. Within seconds it was like a scene from Dante's *Inferno* as cutlasses shone red and gold, flashing back the light from the flares. Pistol shots rang out and the scores of waiting horses on the grass above became frightened, pulling at their tethers and neighing and snorting. Whoever had been left in charge of them must have taken fright himself at the unexpected ambush on the beach, for Sophie could just see him mount one of the horses and gallop away.

There was no way she could tell from her viewpoint, crouched down by the hedge, how the bloody conflict was going. The sands were being churned up in the melee. The screams of the wounded and the dying mingled with the clash of blades. She was filled with horror, consumed with fear for Rory. Once in a while she could pick out a smuggler in the flickering light as he slashed ferociously with a cutlass, but it was impossible to guess which among the uniformed men might be Rory. She wished she could be at his side using a rapier with the same skill he had shown when teaching Antoine. Surely there was something she could do!

The horses! If she released them, at least she would cut off the smugglers' means of escape. Keeping close to the cover of the tamarisk hedge, Sophie reached the first string of horses. She whispered softly to them as she released their tethers. They needed no slap to set them going, but bolted away one after the other across the grass and off through the trees. Immediately a shout rang out, halting her before she could begin untying the next batch.

"Who's there? What the devil are you doing?"

So at least one guard had been left! She could see him running toward her, a bludgeon in his hand. She reacted automatically as Sergeant Jones had taught her. The guard slowed his pace as he heard the pistol cock in her hand and saw it pointed at him. He was also near enough for the two of them to recognize each other. Her neighbor lowered his bludgeon.

"Don't shoot, Miss Delcourt," he implored in dismay.

"Are you alone, Mr. Ketley?"

"Yes, the others are all down on the beach. Why are you here?"

"The manner in which you wedged the meadow gates open alerted me."

His expression was utterly wretched. "I had to do it. Nobody argues with the Broomfield gang. I didn't want my house burned down. These brutes show no mercy, you know."

"Is one of the wagons yours?"

"Yes, I was ordered to be ready to transport."

"Then get in it and drive back to your farm and close your gates, but not before you've taken the other wagon horses out of their shafts."

"I can't do that! I daren't!"

"Whatever the outcome of this battle, I can tell you the smugglers will be in no state to get their goods away. My guess is they'll either fight their way to their boats or scatter to ride or drive whatever is available. That's why I'm letting the horses go free. You're bound to be arrested if you stay, but if you follow my advice you'll be all right."

"Do you mean you'll say nothing to the authorities? You'll forget about seeing me?"

"Yes, I'm considering your family." She returned her pistol to her sash. "There are patrols about, so follow the coastline for a distance and then turn inland. You should avoid them that way."

He dipped his head and tossed his bludgeon away with relief. "I thank you and I'll not delay."

Soon he had unfastened the wagon horses and gave her a wave as he turned his own for home. By then Sophie had unfastened the last tethers. Not all the horses galloped away. Some covered only a few yards before coming to a standstill, but these she drove off, waving her arms, her shrieking lost in the tumult resounding from the beach. Soon a few sticks and pebbles thrown harmlessly left not one of the riding horses to be seen. Even the wagon horses had thudded away.

She ran back then to view the scene of battle. To her intense relief she glimpsed Rory briefly in the light of a flambeau, his face taut and grim as he wielded his blade. Not only was he unharmed, but he and his men had gained the upper hand.

Those of the smugglers still able to fight were taking rearguard action, backing their way up the shingle to where they believed the horses would be waiting. Others, separated from this last defiant and desperate group, were making individual bolts for freedom. Some were coming her way! Sophie dashed into hiding in the undergrowth and saw them burst through the tamarisk hedge. A few cursed the vanished horses, but all disappeared into the woods. When no more appeared, Sophie judged the route had been cut off by Rory's men.

Even as she rose cautiously to her feet again, wanting to return to where she could see Rory's advance, she felt a hand grab hold of her skirt. She choked back a scream, every instinct telling her even before she looked down that it was Tom. He lay on his chest looking up at her covered in blood.

"For mercy's sake, Sophie, help me! If I'm seen I'll be finished."

Her anger flashed. "What a fool you are, Tom!" Yet she almost wept at the state he was in and guessed what torture it must have been for him to crawl up from the beach. "Can you manage to walk at all?"

"If you'll give me a shoulder."

She helped him up and he reeled and staggered, his left arm hanging limp, his head bowed in pain. He dragged a foot as if his leg was injured too, making his agonizingly slow walk more of a sickening lurch. It was difficult for her to keep her balance.

"I've my pony and trap in the woods," she encouraged. "You'll not have to walk very far."

He gave a wry laugh that was no more than a gasp. "I never thought your pony and trap would be of use to me."

"Don't talk now. I'll soon get you to Dr. Moore's house."

"No, not there! To Richard. He'll know what to do."

Sophie was desperately afraid he might bleed to death. Perhaps when she had him farther away she could pad the worst of his wounds. She also feared that one of the fleeing smugglers might have made off with her pony and trap.

She strained her eyes as they reached the full cover of the trees. Then relief swept through her as the clouds parted, and the fitful moon revealed Bijou still there. The escapees must have avoided following the track.

"Only a few more steps, Tom." She dared not stop to let him rest, for she could tell he was close to collapse. They staggered together over the last few yards.

Getting him into the trap was the hardest physical task Sophie had ever had to perform. He had no strength left, and she had to haul and push him aboard. His attempt to be of some help finally defeated him, leaving him unconscious on the floor of the trap. It was actually the best place to conceal him. She remembered the revenue man she had glimpsed earlier and guessed that Rory had set a ring of his men to catch any escapees. Springing into her seat, she spread her skirts over Tom and had just spread out a plaid rug to give him further cover when there came a crashing through the undergrowth. A large man of considerable bulk, a tricorn hat pulled well down on his brow, a kerchief covering the lower half of his face, came charging toward her.

"Get out, woman! I'm taking this!" he shouted, grabbing hold of the trap.

She aimed her pistol instantly while her mind registered something familiar about him. Another local man, but this grocer or butcher or whoever he was had violent intent!

"No!" she hissed. "I've got one of your badly wounded confederates here and it's a matter of life and death! Get away from the trap!"

He hesitated briefly at the sight of the pistol, but he had no time to lose. Her movement had drawn the covering back from Tom's face, and for a second the man peered down at him.

"He's a goner! I saw him pierced in the guts." His huge hand seized Tom to drag him out. "I'll have that pistol for the revenue men and you can drive me instead!"

She fired. He fell back with an awful yell and lay groaning. Tom had been left with his head and arms dangling and she pulled him back in, terrified that the shot would bring others to the spot, perhaps even Rory. Swiftly she rearranged the rug, covering Tom completely, and cracked the whip to speed the pony away. The whole incident had probably lasted little more than a minute, but it had seemed interminable. The man's description of Tom's wound filled her with dread.

"Don't die, Tom!" she implored as the pony sped back along the track. "Please, God! Let him live!"

Not until she was in sight of the lane did Sophie feel it safe to draw up, for the escaping smugglers would avoid places where they might easily be caught. She listened, but could hear nothing except an occasional pistol shot in the distance. She pulled off two of her petticoats and made a wad of them against Tom's side, where his coat had been slashed to ribbons. She could tell his blood had soaked into her bodice where she had supported him, but fortunately her cloak had remained untouched in the trap and she draped it about her to hide the stains. She hastily re-lit the candle lamps, considering it now safer to do so, and continued on her way.

Caution kept her at a steady pace. From now on she would have to appear as if everything were normal. As she had anticipated, she had not gone far when two revenue men appeared from the cover of the trees and halted her from the middle of the lane, shining their lanterns. Both were strangers to her. One stepped forward.

"State your name, miss."

"I'm Mademoiselle Delcourt and betrothed to Captain Morgan of the Excise Service."

The man looked questioningly at the other, who nodded. "He is betrothed to a Frenchwoman."

The first man addressed her again. "Why are you abroad at this hour? It's three o'clock."

She feigned impatience. "I'm as aware as you are that Captain Morgan has special duties tonight. I've become anxious waiting alone. I'm on my way to spend the rest of the time with a friend in town. Surely one of you saw me drive home soon after midnight? I'm returning to seek company."

The second man came forward a few paces to shine his lantern into the trap. Sophie held her breath, not daring to look down in case she should arouse suspicion. But the revenue man lowered his lantern again.

"Very well, miss. I'm sorry for having delayed you, but we're having to check on everybody abroad tonight."

As soon as they were out of sight she picked up speed and bowled into town. In Middle Street the stable gates of Tom's premises stood wide and she drove straight into the cobbled yard. Richard must have been watching from a window, for the door from the display room opened almost immediately and he ran out.

"Sophie, what on earth are you doing here? Have you seen Tom?" Then he gave a despairing groan as she drew back the covering from his brother's face. "Merciful God! Is he dead?"

"No!" she cried in protest to ward off that possibility. "He must not be!"

"Take his feet and help me carry him in," Richard instructed as he began to draw Tom from the vehicle. "You can tell me what happened later."

Together they bore Tom indoors. The door to the apartment opened off the gallery and they had great difficulty carrying him up the curving flight of stairs. In the kitchen, they laid him full length on the table. Sophie threw off her cloak and took Richard's coat from him. He rolled up his sleeves and she ran to gather all the candlesticks she could find to bring extra light. As Richard cut away his brother's clothes, she fetched warm water from the range, followed his directions in finding a box of medical supplies, and fetched the spirit he wanted for disinfecting Tom's wounds.

Tom remained unconscious throughout all this. He had a deep cutlass wound in his side, but fortunately it had missed the vital organs. His arm was broken with the bone sticking out, and there was a gunshot wound in his leg. Richard worked swiftly and tirelessly; Sophie helping him in every way she could. His competence in setting Tom's arm in splints, dressing the wounds, and stitching up the slashed flesh astounded her. Throughout it all the only talk between them was connected with the task in hand. Finally they bathed him carefully and put him in a nightshirt, one sleeve cut off to accommodate his broken arm. Richard wrapped him in a blanket and once more Sophie supported his feet as they carried him to a bed.

Richard unrolled his sleeves as he stood looking down at his brother. "Tom is like a cat. He has nine lives. Unfortunately he's been using them up fast, and I'd say this was his last. He'll not get away with anything like this again."

"Do you mean you think he will live?" It was the first time Sophie had dared to ask.

"He's lost a lot of blood, but he has a good chance. As soon as he recovers consciousness he must have plenty of water to drink." Then Richard saw that Sophie had covered her face with her hands and was trembling violently. He put an arm around her and led her to a chair. "Sit down here. I'll pour you a brandy. We can both do with one. I'm sure you've many questions you want to ask, but tell me first what happened. I assume there was an ambush."

She gave a start at his words. So he had known about Tom's activities all along! No wonder he had been watching at the window for his brother's return! "Yes," she said coldly, "and there's much to talk about."

When the brandy was poured, Richard seated himself by the bedside, where he could keep a close eye on Tom while he listened intently to Sophie's full account. He asked a few questions and then invited her to ask him anything further she wanted to know. She took a deep breath.

"First of all, I must say that I never suspected you were involved in Tom's smuggling."

He raised an eyebrow. "I'm not. Tom confided in me only when he found it necessary."

"And you condoned his lawbreaking!" she exclaimed incredulously.

"I didn't say that, but Tom has always been headstrong and fearless. I was away in the army when I might have had some influence over him, and when I came home again it was too late. He has always gone his own way."

"Yet you went into business with him. You must have known that smuggled goods were passing through the shop."

"All the stock in the London and Brighton shops has always been legitimately purchased. Tom has evaded taxes by smuggling in French goods, but he has disposed of these privately. Remember, he's my brother, Sophie. Sibling loyalty is a strong bond. You couldn't expect me to denounce him."

Sophie looked wearily down at the glass of brandy she had barely touched. "Surely Tom has finally learned his lesson."

"I doubt it."

She raised her head again. "Then we must both try to persuade him never to be so foolhardy again."

Richard shook his head slightly. "Not even you, Sophie, could stop him from going back to France if his broken limbs and wounds heal well enough to permit it."

Sophie took his pronouncement to mean that however much Tom cared for her, he would always follow his own path. The thought hurt her so deeply that it would have been easy to weep. She passed a hand across her eyes as if to keep tears at bay.

"How did you acquire such medical skills, Richard? Did you once train as a surgeon?"

"No, although I believe I have a vocation in that direction. When I was a fresh-faced lieutenant during the American Revolution, I lost a good friend because I did not know how to save his life when he was wounded. After that I began to read every medical book I could get hold of, and the army surgeons were glad to have me on hand when they were rushed off their feet after a battle. When I came out of the service it had been my intention to take up medicine, but Tom was anxious for me to go into business with him."

"Didn't you tell him what you had planned?"

"No, but I've no regrets."

"You're very unselfish," she said. Then she glanced toward the window. Dawn was spreading a pinkish glow in the sky. "I must get home. Rory will still be busy, but I want to be there when he comes to tell me of his victory."

Richard stood up. "Wait! There'll be bloodstains in your trap. I'll take a bucket of water down and scrub them out."

When he returned, she had moved to the chair by the bed and sat looking down at Tom. As she rose, Richard put her cloak around her shoulders. Even as they were about to leave the room, Tom stirred and muttered. She put a hand on Richard's arm.

"Don't leave him. I'll see myself out."

"How can I thank you for all you've done?"

"No thanks are necessary between friends."

As soon as Sophie arrived home she hung away her cloak and burned all her other garments. Then she bathed herself and washed her hair. She had just finished pinning it up when her daily maidservant arrived with the woman who did the laundry and scrubbed the floors. They were full of talk as they entered the kitchen. Sophie could hear them as she came downstairs, and guessed the subject of their animated conversation. Physically and mentally tired, she hoped to get a little sleep before Rory came, and she intended to tell them to leave the parlor undisturbed as she would be resting on the sofa after a sleepless night.

A knock on the door halted her halfway across the hall. Rory's second-in-command, whom she knew well, stood on the threshold. "Good day, Mr. Pearce. Have you—" Then her voice caught in her throat for he looked so grave. She stepped aside as he entered, his hat under his arm. "What's happened? Has Rory been wounded?"

"I think you should sit down to hear the sad news I bring."

"Tell me!" She was ashen.

"The Broomfield gang was finally smashed last night in the operation planned by Captain Morgan. The fighting was over when a smuggler trying to escape brought out a concealed weapon and shot the Captain in the heart. Death was instantaneous. He knew nothing. It happened in his moment of triumph."

He was just in time to catch Sophie as she collapsed.

AT THE FUNERAL, there were full honors for Rory, fellow officers bearing the coffin and revenue men lining the route all the way to St. Nicholas's Church. Top officials had come down from London and a salute was fired at the graveside. All his family were present, including many from other parts of the country whom Sophie had not met before. All were kind and sympathetic toward her, Ellen being particularly thoughtful.

"Would you like to come back with me to Lymington for a while?" she asked when everybody else had left, Antoine had gone to bed, and they sat, black-gowned, by the fire.

"That's very considerate of you," Sophie said gratefully, "but Antoine mustn't stay away from school and I can't leave him now."

When he was told of Rory's death, the boy had flung himself into her embrace and sobbed. "First *Maman* and *Papa* and *Grand-père* and now Captain Rory!"

She had held him tight, shedding her own tears.

"Perhaps you'll come later on," Ellen suggested, interrupting the flow of Sophie's thoughts.

"I'm sorry, but I can't promise anything. There is my work. I shall need to keep busy as never before." Then it dawned on her how much her company would have meant to Ellen, whose loneliness in the Lymington house since the death of her mother would be even greater after losing a much loved brother. "May I reverse the invitation and ask you to stay on here for as long as you'd wish?"

"You've no idea how pleased I am to accept," Ellen replied without hesitating.

Sophie threw herself into work again. Ellen was a restful presence in the house and always had meals ready when she got home. She never intruded on Sophie, but was an understanding companion and soon on good terms with Antoine. It did worry Ellen that Rory had not had time to change his will and make Sophie his beneficiary. Ellen and her two sisters were to share equally in his estate. Sophie, who had not thought of the matter until Ellen had mentioned it, was quick to reassure her that it was of no consequence. "I have the lovely ring he gave me," she said, "which I shall always keep."

Sophie's grief made it difficult to think beyond a day at a time. It tortured her that she had not been present for Rory's last moments of life. Richard was the only one to whom she could speak of it.

"I should have driven Tom to Clara and let her bring him on to you. Then I could have run back to the cove."

"You would still have been unable to save his life. For your own safety, you would have been prevented from getting near Captain Morgan. He himself would have ordered it."

She covered her face with her hands. "But I would have been there!"

Richard put an arm about her. "If that happened, my brother would be dead too. The delay of waking Mrs. Renfrew from sleep and getting her on her way would have been enough to cost him his life. And how do you know she would have done it? She would have been risking arrest, and I believe she would have put the thought of her young son before Tom's well-being."

Sophie knew he was right, but still her distress stayed with her. Richard tried to tell her it was quite normal for the bereaved to feel guilt, but neither did this leaven Sophie's abject sorrow.

Tom passed the time of crisis and began to recover. Sophie never went to the shop, but Richard called regularly on her, and Ellen took pleasure in serving him tea. Sometimes he came for supper. Then one day he spoke to Sophie on her own.

"I'm taking Tom back to London tomorrow. He has a long convalescence ahead of him, and he wants to see you before he leaves."

Sophie stood very straight and still. "For all I know Tom crossed blades with Rory on the beach that night. At the very least he fought with those who killed him. I want nothing more to do with Tom ever again."

Twenty-three

SOPHIE WAS AMONG THOSE in Ship Street who hurried to buy a newspaper from a vendor shouting out the good news.

"Napoleon's fleet sunk in the Nile. Admiral Nelson's great victory!"

She scanned the first few lines that summarized the hard-fought battle and concluded with the information that Nelson was presently in Naples, where he was being entertained by the British Ambassador and his wife, Sir William and Lady Hamilton.

As Sophie folded the newspaper to read at home later, she saw that Tom was also buying one. Their eyes met and he spoke without smiling.

"Good day to you, Sophie."

"Good day, Tom."

She walked on. It was sixteen months since she had last spoken to him. When she declined to see him before he left for London, Richard had produced a letter, which she had refused to accept. After that it was almost a year before she heard he had been sighted in Brighton again. Antoine had been the first to meet him.

"Mr. Foxhill has a new scar on his cheek. I asked him if he had been in another duel. He laughed and said he had, but he had won as before."

Sophie made no comment. She had seen Tom a number of times since then, for he was almost permanently at his shop now, or so it seemed. If they passed one another on the road, he in a high-wheeled breakneck phaeton with spirited horses capable of dangerous speed, she in her sea-blue trap with her trotting pony, he would salute her with his raised whip and she would incline her head in return. If they met on foot she did the same when he raised his hat, his hard and serious stare fixed on her. Except for the scar on his cheek, there was nothing to show that he had brushed shoulders with death more times in his twenty-nine years than most men did in a lifetime.

He could not know that she felt no more anger or bitterness toward him. Forgiveness had come with the slow healing of her grief, but she could not forget. At least the score was even between Tom and herself; she had saved him as once he had saved her, and she was no longer under any obligation to him. The slate had been wiped clean.

A cheer resounded a little distance away, and Sophie saw that the Prince was approaching in an open carriage. He was always transparently pleased by any show of goodwill after all the hostility that had dogged him. There came another burst of cheering, which the Prince acknowledged with a smile.

He might have noticed Sophie if a little girl had not run too close to the carriage wheels, causing him a sharp moment of anxiety before the child's mother pulled her back again. There had been a look of his own little Charlotte about the child. The initial dislike he felt for his daughter had been replaced by paternal tolerance. It was unfortunate for them both that she was boisterous and self-willed, for he continued to connect these traits with her mother.

What a blessing it was that since Caroline's one visit, Brighton remained unspoiled by her vulgar presence. There were times when his hatred of her made him almost ill. She had steadily undermined his royal dignity, his stature in society, and his esteem. What was reported to him of her wild antics and extraordinary behavior made him wonder if she was wholly sane. There had been some madness in her ancestry. Yet the public, ignorant of the immodest and questionable side to her nature, continued to give her a rapturous reception wherever she went. Many of those in political circles used their support of her as a weapon against him.

Maybe some resented his renewed interest in politics, but there were many times when he wearied of his life of aimless pleasure and there surfaced in him again that enormous urge to be of service to his country. If only his beloved Maria would return to him, all his troubles would be eased.

He had long since rid himself of Lady Jersey, who no longer dared to show her face at Court since her malicious meddling had personally offended the Queen, but all his outpouring of remorse and renewed declarations of love in letters to Maria had failed to make her relent. In his first courtship of her it was his attempted suicide that had extracted her promise to be his. Now he would have to find some equally desperate measure to bring her back to him. He had considered and tossed aside countless schemes, but sooner or later he would discover the means he was seeking.

His carriage had brought him to the door of the Marine Pavilion. Before entering, the Prince turned to survey the garden. The roses had been superb all summer and every flower bed was colorful, with blended fragrances drifting in the air. He had had a hand in creating every aspect of the garden here as at his other residences. It pleased him that there were no high walls to shut out the sight of all these lovely plants and blossoms from the people of the town.

SOPHIE RODE HOME with Farmer Ketley, who had also given her a lift into town since Bijou was being shod at the blacksmith's forge. Through her timely advice, he had escaped any suspicion of being involved with the Broomfield gang, and in their gratitude he and his wife had told Sophie always to call on them if there was anything they could do in return.

"How's Miss Morgan?" Farmer Ketley asked conversationally as they turned into the lane. He had come to know Rory's sister through her visits to Beech House.

"Very well, thank you," Sophie replied. "I'll tell her you were inquiring after her."

After the funeral, Ellen had stayed two months until various matters had compelled her to return home. During that time she had met Richard and enjoyed sharing Sophie's outings with him, refusing to admit even to herself that she had become attracted to him and he to her.

"It's just a passing thing," she had said to Sophie, defensively. "Richard and I just like each other, that's all."

Nevertheless, a correspondence had sprung up between them, and whenever Ellen came to visit, Richard always traveled down from London to see her, even if he was not needed at the shop. Sophie hoped for a match between them. She believed Richard was an honorable man, who should not be denied happiness through the errant ways of his brother, and he and Ellen were well suited. They were both quiet, serious people with the same interest in books and music. Moreover they had had much the same experience, for Richard had told Sophie once that he had been in love with a girl he had known since they were children together, but when he returned from the American war and left the army she had married someone else.

When Farmer Ketley drew up to let Sophie alight, she saw Richard sitting with a newspaper on the garden seat under a shady tree. He glanced up and then sprang to his feet with a smile to come and open the gate for her.

"I was just thinking about you," she said with a little laugh.

"That's good to know. I'm at the shop for a few days."

Her eyes twinkled. "Would it be anything to do with Ellen arriving tomorrow?"

He grinned. "It might be."

"Has my little maidservant, Ruth, served you any refreshment?"

"She would have done, but I said I'd wait for you."

Ruth must have been watching from the window, for she appeared at that moment with a tray of lemonade, which she set on a table by the bench.

"Thank you." Sophie handed the maidservant her newspaper and her straw hat. She lifted her flattened hair with her fingers before taking a seat to pour the lemonade.

"I see you've been reading about the new naval victory." Richard took the place beside her.

"I've only had time to glance at the news, but it's most heartening. Yet I have to admit, it tears me apart to have to side against my own countrymen."

"May the day come when it will never be like that again."

"Amen to that," she said with feeling. They had not mentioned Tom since her refusal of his letter, but now she chose to speak of him. "Tom and I met today when we were both buying newspapers."

Richard eyed her speculatively before he commented. "Tom has been hoping for a meeting."

"We only exchanged greetings. Nothing has changed." She sipped her lemonade and put the glass down again.

He measured his words. "Try to show him a little mercy."

"Why?" she challenged, her eyebrows raised. "Just because he doesn't go to France as often as before?"

"That's right," he admitted.

She threw up her hands. "You amaze me, Richard! Do you take me for a fool? There is no point in Tom crossing the Channel so often now that the French Government is commandeering all the treasures it can to restore the grandeur of France."

"Believe what you must. I was simply trying to put in a good word for my brother."

She leaned toward him, her voice softening. "Don't suppose I haven't forgiven Tom, because I have, but what happened is a barrier that nothing can break down."

He shrugged and sighed. "You and Tom are equally stubborn. Let me just ask you one favor, Sophie."

"What is it?"

"Think about Tom now and again. Ask yourself why he is such a madman at times. Try to find the cause."

"I have no need to think about it. He is in love with danger. Let's not talk of him anymore." She topped up Richard's glass with lemonade as she changed the subject. "Would you be able to meet Ellen off the stagecoach tomorrow? I had business with my banker this morning and an agent showed me a couple of shops that are to be let, so tomorrow I must be all day in my atelier."

"I'll do that gladly. So you're thinking of opening a shop?"

"It's been in my mind a long time, but until recently it was financially out of the question." She glanced at her fob watch. "I'm sorry to hurry you away, my friend, but I have to change and get back to work. Come and dine tomorrow evening."

He accepted, and then, when he was on the point of leaving, he spoke of his brother once more. "Please do as I ask. Give Tom some thought."

When Sophie was at work again she considered what Richard had said and wished he had not made such a request to her. It was a burden in itself, and where was the point of it? She didn't want to think of Tom. It might reawaken all those tumultuous feelings that only brought confusion and distress. There had been no such savage heights and depths in her love for Rory, no heart-tearing quarrels or desperate confrontations. He had been a haven to her, loving and loved.

Ellen's visit passed by once more without a betrothal. "Richard was on the point of asking me," Ellen confessed when she was packed and ready to leave, "but I forestalled him by saying my life was too settled for me to consider any change."

"But why?" Sophie demanded. "Don't you care for him at all?"

"Of course I do, but I still can't forget the man I loved."

"But that is all in the past. Fate had given you the chance to regain the happiness you lost."

Ellen took her by the shoulders and regarded her seriously. "Maybe you should follow your own advice. Rory was my dear brother, but I think it's time you put your bereavement behind you. That doesn't mean there won't always be a part of your heart for Rory that nobody else can take away, but it's an old adage that life must go on, and you're too young to let love and fulfillment pass you by."

"Listen to yourself!" Sophie exclaimed.

"I was scarred by my experience and let it ruin my life, but the circumstances were entirely different. What's more, I'm ten years older than you. I know what I'm talking about." Ellen kissed Sophie on the cheek. "Farewell. I may not come again for a long while, but you're always welcome to visit me."

It was a disappointing end to Ellen's visit. Yet Sophie thought it was true that those whom one had loved, whether parent, husband, friend, lover, or child, never lost their established place in one's heart. Ellen knew, and yet could not accept for herself, that the heart also has no boundaries and no closed doors.

SOPHIE STILL HAD NOT FOUND the right premises for her shop when one of Tom's assistants came to deliver a sealed letter to her. Clara would have taken it at the door of the atelier, but the man shook his head.

"Mr. Foxhill said I was to give it to Mademoiselle Delcourt personally. As you can see, it's marked urgent, but I don't have to wait for a reply."

Somewhat dubiously Sophie broke the seal and opened the letter.

Sophie,

You told me once you had an emergency plan for escape if ever you suspected your enemy was closing in on Antoine. I know he has sent a spy to this neighborhood. You must get the boy away immediately. Collect him from school and take the closed coach that will be waiting opposite the gates. Stop for nothing and get Mrs. Renfrew to cover your tracks. If your original plan is no longer viable, take the boy to Richard, whose address at home and in St. James's Street you know. Go now!

Tom

Clara saw the color fade from Sophie's face and feared she was about to faint. But, with a curious sharpness in her eyes, Sophie thrust the letter into Clara's hands and turned to address Robin and Oliver.

"I've just received an urgent message that necessitates my going away on business. You'll have to take over all the centerpiece work, Robin. If you need an extra hand, call in that retired confectioner, Mr. Salisbury, who helped me out once before."

"Yes, miss. Will you be away long?"

"I've no idea, but I shall return as soon as possible." Then she swept outside, her apron and cap already discarded. Clara rushed after her.

"You'll need money in London!"

"How much is in the cash box?"

"Quite a lot. Yesterday was the last of the month and several customers paid their accounts. I'll put it all in a purse for you."

Sophie threw on her cloak. "Give me half and please be quick. I'm going this instant on foot to do as Tom said. I know he would never have given me such instructions without urgent reason. Look after Bijou for me. Let Ruth go half a day to Beech House for however long I'm away." Sophie clamped a despairing hand to her brow. "Barney is at home! I didn't bring him today! Antoine won't go anywhere without him!"

"You mustn't delay by going back there! I'll bring Barney to you myself if you have to stay away for any length of time. Tell Antoine that."

Sophie flung her arms around Clara and hugged her. "Thank you for taking over for me."

"Here! Take this canvas bag! I've thrown in a few things you might need. Go now and don't worry about anything here. Just get Antoine to safety."

As Sophie hurried off, Clara put Tom's letter into the flames on the hearth. It struck her what extraordinary trust Sophie must have in Tom Foxhill to follow instantly and without question the guidance he had sent.

In Duke Street the coach was waiting. Sophie spoke briefly to the driver, who had been pacing the pavement as he waited. Then she hastened into the school. Miss Stanton was teaching, but she left the classroom to show Sophie into her study. She looked uncertain when Sophie said she wanted to take Antoine out of school immediately, and it might be some time before she was able to return him.

"This is very unwise, Miss Delcourt. He's a good pupil and working well. Such disruption could be unsettling. Naturally I can't stop you, but—"

"If I tell you why it has to be done, may I have your word that the information will remain only with you?"

They had come to know each other well since Antoine had started school, and Miss Stanton gave a nod. "You have my word, Miss Delcourt. Is it anything to do with Antoine's being in reality an émigré aristocrat?"

"How did you know that?" Sophie asked, taken aback.

"Once I set the children a composition to write on their earliest memories. Antoine's effort was revealing. He wrote that when he came to England a bad man had killed his grandfather, just as other bad men had made him leave his home with you. He had written 'château' but crossed it out to write 'house' instead."

"It's true. I'm removing him from school now to get him away from a dangerous enemy. There is a fast coach waiting in the street. Every moment may count."

"Then I'll fetch him for you immediately."

Antoine was puzzled when Miss Stanton brought him to her study. "What's happening, Sophie?"

"We're going on a coach ride," Sophie said, automatically straightening his coat collar and trying to smooth his unruly hair. "I'll explain everything on the way. Say farewell to Miss Stanton. It may be a little while before you're back at school again."

His face brightened. "Are we going on a holiday?"

"Something like that."

He addressed his teacher with the perfect manners he had at his command when needed. "Au revoir, Miss Stanton." His bow was deep.

In the next minute he was bounding ahead of Sophie to snatch his tasseled hat from its peg and toss it at a crooked angle on his head.

In the coach he immediately snapped open a box lying on the seat. It contained a pistol and ammunition, and Sophie was quick to take it away from him. Next he inspected a basket of food provided for the journey, and she refused him when he wanted to eat at once. Then, while she replaced the cloth over the food, realizing it had been provided to prevent lengthy stops along the journey, Antoine opened a purse that had been lying beside the basket and, before Sophie could prevent it, sent a shower of golden guineas all over the seat and the floor.

"Settle down, now," she said firmly, making allowance for his excitement. After all the coins had been collected and returned to the purse, she put it safely away in her cloak pocket, regretting at the same time that she was traveling in her old cloak and a cotton working gown.

Antoine stopped bouncing on the upholstery when he saw the coach was turning out of Brighton onto the London road. "Aren't we going home first?" he asked anxiously.

"No, we're traveling fast, because there's someone important we're going to meet."

"What about Barney?" He was frantic. "He'll be looking for me to come home from school."

These ecstatic reunions were a daily occurrence. Sophie spoke reassuringly. "Clara and Billy will look after him until he can be fetched. I'm sorry for the haste, but we're having to leave Brighton as once we left the château. The difference is that this time there'll be nobody following us."

"But will we be going back?" he persisted.

"As soon as Tom Foxhill tells us all is well again, but I can't give you any promise when that will be."

He liked both the Foxhill brothers and saw Tom more frequently than Sophie knew, often talking horses with him in the stableyard, or being shown some new novelty in the shop, such as a little gilded bird that sang when wound with a key. Remembering the duel he had witnessed, he was sure that whatever danger had to be sorted out in Brighton, Tom would soon see to it. In the meantime, if Barney was shortly to be with him, he could put up with being away from home for a little while. He noticed a signpost go by. London was an exciting city. Yes, it would be an agreeable visit.

"Where shall we be staying?" he asked.

"I'm not sure yet. We're going first to Tilney Street. Mrs. Fitzherbert removed from Twickenham some time ago and came back to London where she has another house. You've heard me speak of her many times." Sophie paused and took both his hands into hers. "I made up my mind a long time ago that when the time was right I would reveal your true identity to her. She stayed at the Château de Juneau with your parents before you were born."

"The Château de Juneau?" he repeated slowly. "You never told me my home had such a name."

"It's your surname too. At last I'm able to tell you everything I've had to hold back for so long. To protect you from possible danger, I gave you my mother's maiden name when we came to England. I hope you will understand that this was necessary."

He nodded, still somewhat bewildered, but he smiled. "Antoine and Barney de Juneau. I think that suits us both very well."

She sighed with relief that her revelation had caused no trauma. Even when she had given Antoine the miniatures on Tom's behalf, she had spoken of the Comte and Comtesse only as his *papa* and *maman.*

"When your father died," she continued, "probably before we even left the château, and most certainly when we were still in the orangery, you became the new Comte de Juneau. It's a title to be proud of, because it's steeped in the brave history of France and in honorable traditions."

He sat still and serious. "Nothing shall stop me going home one day."

She knew he was not referring to Brighton.

During a short stay at a coaching house to change horses, Sophie took the opportunity to obtain paper and a pen from the landlord and wrote a hasty note to Mrs. Fitzherbert, asking to be received with

Antoine, son of the late Comte and Comtesse de Juneau, to discuss a matter of extreme urgency.

At Tilney Street the coachman sprang down from his seat. Sophie quickly handed him the folded note and he went to lift the brass knocker of Mrs. Fitzherbert's door. Sophie had known only a few days before when calling in the kitchen at the Marine Pavilion that the lady was in residence, but if she was at home now was another matter. While Sophie watched from her seat, Antoine gazed out at a peddler with a trayful of puppies on the other side of the street.

There was some delay while the footman who answered the door went to make inquiries within the house. Then the coachman returned to open the door of the equipage.

"Mrs. Fitzherbert will receive you, ma'am."

"Thank you. Please wait."

The hall was coral-hued with a sweeping staircase. Antoine had removed his cap, and Sophie led him with her as they entered the drawing room where Mrs. Fitzherbert, attired in a gown of bronze-colored silk, stood waiting to greet them. She came forward and spoke in French.

"Mademoiselle Delcourt, I remember you well, and here with you is Antoine, Comte de Juneau, the son of two dear friends, who were so hospitable to me in my time of trouble." Her lovely smile widened and Antoine bowed deeply to her.

"*Enchanté*, madame."

Mrs. Fitzherbert clasped her beringed hands together, obviously well pleased with him. "I could easily believe you had come straight from Versailles, Antoine."

"No, madame," he replied seriously. "I left France when I was four, just two months before my fifth birthday. Now I'm ten."

"Tall for your age too. That's splendid! Let us all sit down." She indicated a lemon-striped silk sofa for her guests and took a chair gracefully herself, speaking to Sophie. "I'm most eager to hear how you knew what a pleasure it would be for me to meet Antoine. His late mother wrote to me after his birth, but then the Revolution engulfed France and correspondence didn't get through."

Sophie hesitated. "On the basis of your friendship with the Juneau family, may I be impertinent enough to ask if Antoine might have something to eat elsewhere while we talk. As he has told you, he was only four when we fled with his grandfather to England."

Mrs. Fitzherbert guessed immediately that Sophie wanted to speak freely out of the boy's hearing. She rang the footman, who took Antoine away with the promise of tea. When she had heard everything, she shook her head seriously.

"It is a terrible thing for an innocent child to be stalked by such an evil enemy of his father. How may I help? There's something I should like to suggest, but scarcely dare to ask."

"What is that, madame?"

"Would you allow Antoine to be in my charge temporarily. I have a secret retreat in the country where I stay incognito. The couple who are my caretakers have a twelve-year-old foster son. Antoine can stay until the danger that stalks him is banished. He shall have a French tutor. Does he know how to ride? No? Then he shall be taught. He fences? Good, there can be continued instruction, as well as music and singing lessons. Then, when he is able to walk safely abroad again—and if you would permit it—I'd continue to be his benefactress. If he has grown to manhood by that time, he shall have his own establishment."

"His teacher told me he is destined to be an academic."

"Then Oxford awaits him, and the profession of his choice."

"Your kindness overwhelms me. It is exactly what his parents would have wished for him."

"I can tell by your voice that you have reservations. What are they?"

"It's only that so much has happened in his young life to bereave and distress him that I can't let him suppose I'm deserting him too." Her voice faltered. "At your retreat he would miss me as much as I should miss him. I came here today in the hope that you would give him a home and in some part fill the maternal gap in his life once I have left, but I can't let him be shut away in the country. I know him well enough to realize he would only run away."

Mrs. Fitzherbert spoke compassionately. "Do you suppose I would want Antoine to stay there if he is unhappy? There are other alternatives, but it would not be safe for him here. Unfortunately, everything I do or say is noted and gossiped about, and it would not be long before all society began speculating about him. No stone would be left unturned to discover his identity, and if it came out that he is an émigré, who is to say that Emile de Juneau might not also start making his own investigations. Perhaps he has found out already that his prey has flown from Brighton."

"I can see your point, but—"

"Say no more." Mrs. Fitzherbert interrupted with a smile. "Let the three of us travel to my retreat tomorrow. See for yourself what a pleasant place I have there, and stay for as long as you wish. If at the end of what you judge to have been a good testing time, Antoine is still not at home, then other arrangements can be tried."

Since Sophie had come with only the sparse contents of the canvas bag, she used the waiting coach to go shopping for enough garments to clothe Antoine and herself until a trunk could be collected from her home with Barney. When her purchases had been carried into the Tilney Street house, she dismissed the coachman, tipping him from her own purse.

When the three of them set out from London, Mrs. Fitzherbert told Antoine the surname she used when she traveled incognito. "Will you remember that, Antoine?"

"Yes, madame."

He had mixed feelings about this expedition. Traveling was always fun, but Sophie had explained where they were going and why, which had put a cloud over the journey. Although she had promised that he should not stay if he wasn't happy, he was still ill at ease.

It was quite a long while before the coach entered through tall gates and a moderately sized country house came into view, the sun dancing on its windows. Antoine's interest quickened when he glimpsed a group of riding ponies being exercised in a paddock. Mrs. Fitzherbert had already told him that the couple in charge were to be addressed as "Pater" and "Mater," because Jamie, their foster son, used the Latin term. Since Antoine was to be one of the family circle, that form of address would be acceptable for him too.

The couple, who had been alerted to their arrival, came out onto the porch to greet them. They were in their mid-thirties and aristocratic in appearance, speech, and manners, which made it apparent to Sophie they were not born to be employees, but there was nothing austere about them. She found their kindly welcoming of Antoine very reassuring. Within minutes he had learned that Pater liked horses as much as he and would give him the riding lessons for which he had been yearning. Tom often let him sit in the saddle and had given him basic instructions, but none of his horses was right for a boy to ride.

Antoine had expected to come face-to-face with the boy of the household immediately, but to his relief, he was first shown his own room and also the schoolroom where a tutor gave lessons daily. He had already made up his mind not to stay. It would be better to conceal himself in Mrs. Renfrew's attic and be fed by Billy through the trapdoor than to be away from everyone he knew. It might be exciting to do that, as if he were a Cavalier hiding from Cromwell's troops. Here he would be forced into the company of a boy two years older than himself, who would despise him for being younger just as the senior boys did at school. There, it had not troubled him, but here it would. Not even the riding lessons were worth that. He'd wait until he was grown enough to ride one of Tom's horses.

Then Jamie, coming from a private reunion with Mrs. Fitzherbert, appeared in search of him.

"There you are, Antoine!" he exclaimed with a grin, fair hair framing his round face, his expression eager and friendly. "Do you fence? Can you ride? It's been so dull here on my own. What of cricket and football? There's time before dinner for you to see my collection of tin soldiers, if you like."

The ice was broken.

As THE DAYS SLIPPED PAST, everything turned out to be better than Antoine had expected. There were plenty of dogs and cats at the retreat, which was in its favor. He shared lessons in the schoolroom with Jamie, who could ride as if born in a saddle and Antoine was determined to surpass him in time. He was already close to being the older boy's match in fencing and was faster in kicking a ball, although he could not compete with Jamie's musical ability. By the time Barney arrived, knocking him flat in exuberance, Antoine realized he was quite happy in this new household.

"Barney is the best dog I've ever known," Jamie told him, won over by the animal's amiable willingness to romp and run and fetch. This remark sealed Antoine's approval of his new friend. He missed

Billy, but Jamie presented a challenge in achievement such as he had never known before.

Mrs. Fitzherbert stayed only a week, but she made it a happy time for Sophie and the boys, who took all their meals with her. In the evenings she and Sophie played chess or backgammon, and although the Prince was never mentioned, Sophie soon realized that this house had been their private hideaway. Two weeks after Mrs. Fitzherbert's departure, he arrived. Where once they had enjoyed being together at this retreat, their visits now were arranged not to coincide.

Sophie happened to be coming from her room, and met the Prince in the corridor. He gave a surprised exclamation when he saw her.

"Mademoiselle! I declare! Are you following me everywhere?"

She shook her head, and since they were alone, she gave him a full explanation. The Prince's face creased with genuine concern.

"This is a grave situation, but I assure you the boy will be safe here."

As Sophie continued on her way downstairs, she realized how easily the Prince and Mrs. Fitzherbert were able to remain unrecognized here. As Mater had explained, the villagers all thought they came periodically from abroad, which could just as easily be India or any large city in the kingdom as far as these country folk were concerned. Not only would none of them ever have gone far afield, but the only royal likeness known to them was the King's face on the coinage. If by some slim chance a satirical cartoon ever reached this remote area, the caricatured figures were too grotesque ever to be linked with the quiet-living squire and his wife who came to stay at the house on the outskirts of the village.

Later that day, the Prince spoke again to Sophie when he came across her in the library.

"I want you to know, mademoiselle, that as Mrs. Fitzherbert has entrusted you with the knowledge of this retreat, I have no reservations either."

"I'm honored, sire."

After that she only saw him occasionally. Whenever he went riding, always on a black horse from the stables, he took Antoine and Jamie with him on their ponies. Antoine was learning quickly, and the Prince himself gave him both instruction and encouragement.

When the Prince left for London after a few days stay, Sophie talked to Antoine about staying on at the retreat without her. He thought about it carefully before he answered.

"Yes, I'll stay if you promise I can return home as soon as Mr. Tom says it's safe and if you'll come and see me sometimes."

She smiled. "I promise."

They managed to part with a brave show of cheerfulness that deceived neither one. As the coach bore her away, Barney, at Antoine's side, began to howl. He continued to howl all that night, and Antoine knew his dog was going to miss Sophie too.

As she journeyed home, Sophie gave thought to Jamie's position in the household she had just left. Although Pater and Mater showed him affection, so did the Prince and Mrs. Fitzherbert. The boy's fair curly hair and topaz eyes, his charm whenever he wanted his own way, and even his musical talent also set a question mark in Sophie's mind about his true parentage. But if the truth was never spoken, who would ever know except the parties concerned?

Sophie recalled again one of the cartoons she had seen in a print shop when she first arrived in Brighton. Dated 1786, which was a year after the secret marriage between the Prince and Mrs. Fitzherbert, it had shown her with a baby in a cradle. So rumors had been rife twelve years ago.

Let the guesswork continue. Sophie knew her own lips would be sealed. She turned her thoughts to other matters and the work that would be awaiting her at home.

Twenty-four

SOPHIE LOST NO TIME in going to see Tom after arriving home. He was in his office at the shop and showed no surprise as she entered. Closing his ledger, he put his quill in its stand.

"I've been expecting you," he said easily as he rose to his feet to draw a chair forward for her. "I thought enough time had gone by for you to have settled the boy. Obviously your own emergency plan went well, as you didn't take him to Richard. When exactly did you get back?"

She seated herself. "I arrived home late last night. Tom, once more I'm in your debt."

"Whatever was done I did for Antoine," he countered brusquely. "You owe me nothing."

Her eyes flashed. "Unfortunately I believe I do."

He lounged back in his chair and a slow grin spread across his mouth. "I'm pleased to see that your most recent tribulation hasn't subdued you."

"Nothing could do that!" She opened her purse to take out the one with the gold guineas that he had left for her in the coach. "I appreciate your covering every contingency, but I was able to take enough money with me." After placing his purse on the desk, she took out the box containing the pistol from the pocket of her cloak and put that beside it. "I came today to thank you for your warning and your help." Her voice was crisp, her chin high. "I took Antoine to Mrs.

Fitzherbert, who was acquainted with his parents before he was born, and he is in her care at a secret country retreat."

"Well done!"

"Do you know if my enemy is still in the area?"

"Yes." He saw her start. "Don't be alarmed. Juneau's spy is behind bars. His name is Claude Monclar. Does that name mean anything to you?"

She shook her head. "So it was not Emile himself who came."

"No. He's achieving some political success in Paris at the present time."

"How did you find out about Monclar?"

"Through a contact of mine, who had heard about the landing of a known French assassin a few miles west of here."

"So what happened then?" she asked.

"Although I had no idea if the new arrival had been sent by Juneau, I decided to follow his trail. He had come when the harvesting was in full swing and posed as an émigré seeking work. Farmer Millard took him on without question, glad of an extra hand. Monclar worked part of the time with the daughter-in-law. As they chatted she told him in all innocence, though through some clever prompting, no doubt, about the French girl who had struck up a friendship with the family after being attacked and robbed in the lane."

Sophie's mind floundered. "She gave him our names?"

"Yes, I'm afraid so. When I arrived at the Millard farm he had been gone a week. I've never ridden faster than I did getting back to Brighton, afraid of what might have happened already. I rode straight to the school, knowing Monclar would try to snatch Antoine at the first opportunity. I was in time to see the boy going into the school-house with Billy and knew that at least he was safe until playtime at noon."

"No wonder you sent me that message with such urgency."

"Getting you both away from Brighton took the pressure off the situation, giving me time to trace the assassin. I finally cornered him prowling around Beech House at night. My pistol in his back was quicker than his knife, which I took from him. The threat of a little surgery unnerved him. He wasn't to know I didn't want his purpose to become public knowledge. So when, with apparent magnanimity, I offered him the choice of being denounced as a French spy and shot, or charged as an émigré receiver of smuggled goods, which would bring transportation, naturally he chose the latter, probably hoping for escape, but he's chained hand and foot."

"How did you make it believable about the receiving?"

"I brought him back here and shoved a roll of French lace into one of his pockets, a packet of tea in another. Then I hauled him off to the nearest magistrate."

Sophie dreaded the reply Tom might have to her next question. "Did Monclar say if he had already communicated with Emile de Juneau?"

"Yes, he admitted it. That had caused him some delay while he awaited a messenger returning to France, and fortunately it gave me time to send you and the boy away. No doubt Juneau had wanted a report stage by stage in case Monclar should never return." He paused, seeing how pale and anxious she had become. "Monclar seemed sure that Juneau wouldn't send another agent now he knows where to find you."

She tensed sharply. "So he would come himself on another attempt?"

Tom nodded. "But not for a while. He has gained a foothold in the Government at last and can't take leave at the present time. I've come to believe there's more than greed behind Juneau's pursuit of Antoine. I think it's something far more deadly."

"Vengeance?" she whispered falteringly.

"Yes, he wanted to see the Comte de Juneau go to the guillotine. Having been foiled in that, he's taking other means to settle the score."

She regained her voice almost on a note of triumph. "At least Antoine's whereabouts can't be traced. That is all that matters. Has Monclar been tried yet?"

"Yes, at Lewes with seven other men charged with the same offense. The trial lasted no more than ten minutes, because every one of them had been caught red-handed. They were sentenced jointly to be transported to the colony of Australia." Tom opened a drawer and took out a printed list of names, which he handed to her. "Among those being shipped out next week are some accomplices of the smugglers caught at the ambush of the Broomfield gang. Their departure was delayed through wounds they had suffered at the time. The prison authorities see no point in sending out men likely to die on the voyage."

Sophie glanced down the list, wondering if she would recognize any of the names. The man she shot had not seemed entirely a stranger. It was odd to think now that he had almost vanished from her memory.

Suddenly her hand shook, making the paper rustle. One name had leapt out at her, jerking her back to that horrific moment in the grove when her pistol had exploded. John Barnes! Now she knew him. It had been the same Barnes who had attacked her and her charges when she first arrived in England.

"There's a name on the list that you know?" Tom queried with interest.

She nodded. "The man who tried to drag you out of the trap was the same Barnes responsible for the death of the Marquis!"

"Are you sure?"

"Yes!" She returned the list to Tom, letting him see the name for himself. He thumped a fist on the desk. "This means Barnes must have a new trial for murder."

"No," she cried. "The result would be a hangman's noose for him, and there's been enough death. I want the present sentence to stand. The life he'll endure in exile will be punishment enough. But I want to see him before he's shipped out."

"That would be very unpleasant for you."

"I have to do it on the Marquis's behalf. It's what he would have wanted."

He saw her mind was made up. "Very well. Richard will arrange it for you. He is well acquainted with the governor of Lewes prison."

She rose to leave. "I'll write to Richard today. Who would have thought that when Barnes crossed my path again I shouldn't have known him instantly."

The corners of Tom's mouth curled wryly. "You did have other matters on your mind."

If there had not been barriers between them she might have smiled. Tom saw her to the door of the shop and almost brushed against her as he leaned forward to turn the handle. They bade each other good day and Sophie left, walking briskly. She was aware of wanting to put a distance between herself and the man whose physical presence seemed to charge the very atmosphere for her, even though their minds were at war. There had never been that dangerous excitement with Rory, and now she was glad of it. She wanted nothing to steal into her memories of Rory.

Inevitably, since Sophie had emerged from mourning, she had met other men eager to further an acquaintanceship with her. But none of those men would have been like Rory, Tom, or Richard, who accepted and respected her independence.

RICHARD REPLIED PROMPTLY to Sophie's letter. Not only did he make the necessary arrangements for her with the authorities at Lewes prison, but he came to Brighton specially to escort her there and remain with her when she met Barnes.

The prison was a large gray edifice with great studded doors. As Sophie and Richard were led by a guard across the prison courtyard, there came an awful medley of shouts and jeers and howls from the high barred windows where prisoners fought each other to get a glimpse of a woman.

The governor's office with its glowing fire and paneled walls was a noticeable contrast to the bleak, chill corridors along which they had passed.

"Your request was most unusual, Miss Delcourt," the governor said from behind his desk when she and Richard were seated. "However, Mr. Foxhill presented a strong case on your behalf, and as nobody else has asked to see Barnes I decided in your favor."

"What of his wife?"

The governor shook his head. "It is common for prisoners to be abandoned by their next of kin once they have been convicted."

The room adjoining the governor's office was where inmates were brought to wait until he was ready to see them. Sophie and Richard were shown in there even as Barnes, in the custody of a guard, was admitted through another door. In spite of herself, Sophie drew her breath in pity. He was a broken hulk, his head bowed, his wrists and ankles in chains. She took an involuntary step forward and was restrained by Richard's grip on her arm. Then she recalled again the brutal killing of the Marquis.

"John Barnes," she said firmly. "Do you know me?"

He raised his head and blinked, as if unaccustomed to the light pouring in through the large windows. Then his gaze cleared and hardened as he snarled at her.

"You're the bitch who shot me! I can't use my left arm because of you!"

"You forced my hand. But I want you to think back beyond that meeting to another at the harbor at Shoreham. You were the Reverend Barnes, then. Do you recall offering help to a young Frenchwoman with a boy and an elderly aristocrat in her charge?"

She had never seen a man's face turn gray before. His lower lip quivered and his mouth fell open.

"Have you come to lay a fresh charge against me?" he asked in fear. Then to her dismay, he dropped to his knees in abject appeal. "No, miss! Don't do that, I beg you! It was an accident, nothing else. The old man was still alive when I left him!"

The guard became suspicious. "What's all this, sir?" he demanded inquiringly of Richard.

Sophie answered instead, irritated that the guard should suppose a woman could not speak for herself. "This is a matter between the prisoner and me. Whatever the outcome, the decision will be mine alone." Then she spoke to Barnes again. "How long ago did you become involved with the smugglers?"

"Since the flow of émigrés dried up. Pickings became poor. I had to make a living somehow." Something of the old cunning crept back into his eyes as he shuffled a little nearer to her on his knees. "Be merciful, miss. You had your revenge when you took that dying government man instead of me on the night of the ambush, shooting me for good measure."

He went babbling on with his plea, but she was no longer listening. She turned wide, dilated eyes questioningly on Richard, who met her penetrating stare but said nothing. She turned back to the kneeling man. "What did you mean by that? A government man?"

He showed his yellow teeth in a grimace. "Took the wrong fellow, did you? I saw him myself fighting alongside the captain of the revenue men. I suppose when it came to the crunch, it was natural he should side with the law. Which of the gang had you meant to save?"

She ignored his question and, shaking off Richard's hand, went to look directly into Barnes's ugly face, heedless of his foul breath.

"Who was it I had in the trap then?" Her fists were raised as if she might strike him. "That man who you thought would die?"

He shifted back on his knees, ankle chains rattling. She looked so fierce with her blazing eyes that he was afraid. "I never knew his name, but it wasn't for trinkets he went to France. One of the gang told me he once fought a man to the death because he'd dared to steal a packet of documents from him out of curiosity."

"So he was a spy." Sophie straightened up and drew back a step, outwardly composed again. "Some of the Broomfield gang were French," she said, remembering Pierre Froment. "Didn't they care that he was smuggling out their nation's secrets?"

"Why should they? He paid well for sailing with them whenever it suited him." Barnes saw she was turning away and thought she had decided to send him to the gallows. "I'm not a killer! I never was! I didn't mean to let the old fellow die!"

Sophie paused and looked back at him. "I believe you. I hope you learn to build an honest life for yourself in the colony when your seven years punishment is through."

When she and Richard had left the prison, Sophie asked the burning question he had been expecting.

"Why didn't you tell me?"

"Tom told me of his missions on my oath of secrecy, such as he had made in the presence of the Minister of War himself."

"I can see now why you told me to try to decide why Tom appeared to act like a madman in his wild deeds, but stupidly I refused to listen."

"I'm certain you would have understood eventually." Richard was watching her sympathetically, for she was consumed by remorse.

"But how many more long years might have been lost in the meantime! Why could I not have seen that when Tom lay desperately wounded he feared being killed by a revenging smuggler, and not being arrested by the revenue men?" Another question sprang to her lips. "Do you know how many sorties Tom has made to France?"

Richard shook his head. "He only told me when he wanted me to stand by in case of emergency. His smuggling was a front to conceal his true missions. It gave him the freedom to come and go as he pleased. By associating with men on the wrong side of the law, his sea trips could be made easily and secretly."

"But why did he choose to sail with the terrible Broomfield gang?"

"Being well armed, they always gave him the best cover. If they had ever suspected him of being a government man, they would have turned on him like dogs and slit his throat."

"Wasn't the gang suspicious after the fight over the documents that Barnes told us about?"

"Tom managed to convince them that by chance he had come across papers with which to blackmail an émigré. I believe it was touch and go for him at the time."

Sophie shuddered. "Yet still he risked his life over and over again, not only in France but at their hands as well." She turned her head to look unseeingly out at the passing countryside, not knowing how to bear the thought of how often Tom had brushed shoulders with death. "How long has he been doing this?"

"When France declared war on England he volunteered the same day and was recruited at once. Gradually he built up contacts on the other side of the Channel by posing as a French wine merchant or a seaman or even a peasant mad for the blood of the aristocrats. Over the past year in Paris he played the role of a politician and bluffed his way into various departments to gain special information. He was daring enough to strike up acquaintanceships, so that on subsequent visits he was remembered and given immediate access to the files he wanted."

Sophie had turned back to Richard in amazement. "Tom must have nerves of steel!"

"He has had many narrow escapes."

"Why doesn't he go back to France anymore? Surely you can tell me that now?"

Richard shook his head. "That is something you must ask him yourself."

She raised her clasped hands agitatedly and let them fall again. "When I think of all the harsh things I've said to him! The accusations I've made! He must have hated me at times!"

"I can deny that on his behalf straightaway."

"But how can I face him? However can I make amends?"

"Let him come and see you at home."

"No." Beech House was full of memories of Rory, and she did not want those blotted out by Tom's vital presence. "Neither do I wish to go to his shop. We've exchanged too many harsh words there."

"Would you like me to arrange a meeting point on neutral territory?" He thought she was about to agree when she snapped her fingers in sudden enlightenment, her smile wide.

"I have it! Just the place!"

When he heard where it was to be, he smiled too. "I can't think of anywhere better."

When they arrived at Beech House, Sophie rushed indoors and Richard followed. She went straight to the kitchen where old papers were kept in a basket for lighting the fire. Ruth, preparing vegetables for dinner, stared as Sophie knelt to scrabble through the pile, sorting out old letters and other papers that had been crumpled into balls.

"What have you lost, ma'am?"

"It's all right, Ruth!" Sophie had found what she had been looking for. "It's something I threw away the other day, thinking it was of no interest, but I've changed my mind."

Excitedly she sprang up and rushed back to the parlor where Richard was waiting. Spreading out the crumpled paper on the table and smoothing the creases, she invited him to read the agent's description of a shop to let.

"As you see," she said, leaning over his shoulder, "it has everything I want. It's in a good area and the shop is the right size, with plenty of room for me to have a larger atelier than my present one. That will be when I can afford to take on extra workers."

Richard grinned at her. "The only thing not previously in its favor was that it's located alongside Tom's property and you would have been neighbors. Now there's nothing to stop you taking the place."

"Tell Tom to meet the new proprietor there tomorrow!" Then suddenly she looked alarmed. "As long as the shop hasn't gone to somebody else already."

· Richard glanced at his fob watch. "It's not too late to go to the agent now."

Half an hour later Sophie and Richard were being shown round the premises by the agent. It was on the same scale and layout as Tom's property, except that instead of a gallery it had an upper floor made into living quarters. Moreover, as it had been occupied until recently by a draper, it had been well maintained. When Sophie returned home she had the key, and three months rent had been paid.

SOPHIE WAS NERVOUS as she paced the empty shop. She had no idea how many times she had glanced at the little watch suspended on a silk ribbon from her waist. Every minute seemed to be taking an hour. In her mind she had gone over and over all the cold and hostile things she had said to Tom. How could she have been so blind! So stupid!

The shop door opened and she turned, as startled as if she had not been expecting him. Tom was silhouetted against the winter sunshine. The door clanged as he closed it behind him.

"That must be fixed," he commented. "A little oil should do it."

"Tom," she began uncertainly. He looked so serious and uncompromising, although she had asked his brother to tell him all that had taken place at the prison. "I've been sadly in error."

"No apologies, Sophie. You were not to know. I'm here, somewhat unnecessarily, to get you to promise that you will keep all you learned to yourself."

"You had no need to ask."

"That's it, then." He glanced about the shop. "You have good premises here and should do well. Delcourt confectionery is finally coming into its own. It's what you've always wanted. I'll be in to purchase from time to time."

She could see he was on the point of leaving again. "Don't go yet. Let me show you round."

"I know this property. I bought it at the same time as the place next door with a view to expansion when the draper moved out, but after all I have enough space. So I'm your landlord, Sophie. I would have offered this shop to you personally when it became vacant if I'd thought you'd tolerate being my neighbor, but I didn't want another rebuff." He turned to go.

She raised her hands in appeal. "I'm asking you to stay a little while. There's so much I want to say. Please, please give me the chance!"

He raised his eyebrows. "I can't think of anything that needs to be said. You know the truth and I assume you've absolved me of all the sins I've committed either in reality or in your imagination. So we have a clean slate. That's good enough. Good day, Sophie." Once again he turned away.

Her temper flared and she drummed her fists on the counter. "Don't you dare leave this shop until you've heard me out, Tom Foxhill! And I will be told why you don't go to France any longer!"

He retraced his steps and set his hands on the opposite side of the counter as he leaned toward her. There was mirth in his eyes at last. "That's better. I didn't like to see you acting the abject little mouse."

She flung up her hand and struck him across the cheek, causing his head to jerk to one side. The sound of the slap resounded in the shop. Horrified at what she had done, Sophie turned and ran from him through the storeroom and up the stairs to the empty living quarters, slamming the door after her. Flinging an arm against the wall, she buried her head against it and sobbed convulsively. She had ruined everything! Thrown away her last chance to make amends!

She did not hear the door open. When Tom spoke she did not know how long he had been present.

"Sophie, my darling Sophie, there's no need for tears."

Slowly she raised her head and looked over her shoulder at him, blinking through the sparkle of her wet lashes. "I thought you had gone."

Framed by the doorway, he gave a slight shake of his head. "I've waited so long for you that nothing could drive me away. Not that you haven't done your utmost to make it happen."

She lowered her arm to her side and turned to lean back against the wall, her tears still flowing, although silently now. She spoke gently. "That dates from the moment I opened my eyes and first saw you."

Stepping forward, he drew a handkerchief from his pocket and carefully dried her eyes and her cheeks. "You were always running to me whether you knew it or not. The magnetism between us has been impossible to deny."

She was rendered speechless by the way he was looking at her. There was such a blend of adoration and passion in his narrowed eyes that she feared her legs would give way and she'd slither down to the floor. If he as much as touched her hand, she might cry out with joy.

"France," she prompted huskily. "You haven't told me yet what I want to know."

"I was withdrawn from active service during my convalescence to reorganize our spy network. When I'm not here, I'm in London. I recruit and instruct when the need arises and have trebled the number of our spies. Does that answer your query in full?"

"Not quite. I find it hard to believe you would willingly exchange an active role for sitting behind a desk."

He smiled, nodding approvingly. "You're beginning to know me at last, Sophie. It's true that if it were possible I would have demanded to return, but unfortunately on my last mission things didn't go according to plan and my cover was blown."

"What happened? Please tell me."

"That night of the ambush of the Broomfield gang I was already injured when I boarded the smugglers' boat. It was not serious, but I had cut myself when leaping through a window."

"Why did you do that?" she gasped.

"I know Richard has told you how I secured an entrée into certain Republican ministerial departments. On this particular day I was alone in an office, copying out information about the movements of French ships, when the door was thrown open. On the threshold stood the politician whose name I had used, a lazy fellow who consistently neglected his duties. He had a pistol in his hand and looked extremely nervous, even though he had armed soldiers at his back. I stood up with my hands spread to show I held no weapon, seeming to surrender. Then I grabbed the paper I had been copying and leapt by way of a strategically placed chair through a window."

"You could have killed yourself!"

He grinned, shaking his head. "The first rule for a spy is never to be caught. So in any potentially tight situation, I always made sure of an escape route in case of emergency. In this case, there was an extension to the building jutting out just below. I ran along it with a few potshots whizzing past me and jumped down again into a courtyard. There I reentered the building, a hand clapped to my sleeve to prevent leaving a trail of blood, and strolled out to freedom through the main entrance."

"What did you do then?"

"I had a horse waiting and as I rode out through the gates of Paris, I knew it would be a long time before I could return. I was not mistaken. An extraordinarily good likeness of me is pasted up in Paris and elsewhere in France, with the promise of a large reward for my capture."

"You're lucky to be alive," she breathed.

"I was never closer to death than when you took me away in your trap."

She looked down. "You fought at Rory's side."

"Yes, until it became necessary for us to fight back to back because we had been cut off from the rest of his men."

"Is that where you sustained your terrible wounds?"

He hesitated before answering, seeing where she was leading. "It was, but fortunately Morgan's men broke through at that point, because I had already lost my rapier, and I couldn't have used it any longer anyway. I had to try to avoid being trampled underfoot and drag myself away in the hope that I'd survive."

She raised her eyes to his again. "Then Rory would have been killed in the midst of the battle if you hadn't been with him."

Tom crossed to the window, although there was nothing to see but the rooftops of Brighton. "I only did what he would have done for me. That's how it is in such conflicts."

"You gave Rory his moment of triumph. He died knowing his ambition had been fulfilled and the Broomfield gang was no more."

"If I was instrumental in that, then I feel honored. Morgan was a brave man and the loss of his life a tragedy." He spun about and returned to the door. "You must have a lot to do. I'll not delay you any longer. Will you have dinner with me this evening?"

"Gladly."

She went to the head of the stairs to watch him descend. "There's one more thing I'd like to ask you before you go."

He smiled up at her from the bottom of the flight. "What's that?"

"May we begin knowing each other all over again?"

No man could have rushed faster back up the stairs than he, and she flung herself against him. They met in a kiss such as she had never experienced before. He devoured her mouth and she was as frantic as he, all her long dormant passion flaring forth. Her fingers gripped his hair as if to prevent his ever ending the kiss, and yet his arms were crushing her body to his as if they were already one.

They swayed with the force of their kissing, all bonds released, all restraint gone. When they drew breath, it was to smile in mutual jubilation that after such a long time and so many hazards they had finally come together.

"Where shall we live, Sophie?" He held her radiant face between his palms.

She answered at once. "Above the shop. It's what I'd planned to do. We could cut a door through to your apartment."

"There already is one. Come, I'll show you." He took her by the hand.

In one of the rooms, there was a tall cupboard, which she had supposed was a fixture. Tom put his shoulder to it and thrust it a yard to one side to reveal a door. Taking a bunch of keys from his pocket, he turned the lock and flung the door wide. Beyond was the gallery. But Sophie was looking back into her room, having suddenly noticed another piece of furniture that had not been there the evening before. It had been placed in front of the window, a lady's secretaire of great beauty with Boulle marquetry of engraved tortoiseshell, the moldings chased with acanthus foliage. It was almost jewellike in the soft light. She ran a hand gently over the surface, at a loss for words.

"Does it please you?" he asked from where he stood.

She nodded and spoke in a whisper. "It's from France."

"More than that." He came across to stand behind her and lift her soft shining hair to kiss the nape of her neck. "It was the personal property of Marie Antoinette."

"Oh, Tom!" She spun round and flung her arms about his neck, the sparkle of tears in her eyes from happiness this time, and kissed his lips lovingly. "I'll treasure it always and so will our children and their children forevermore!"

She laid her head on his shoulder and he stroked her hair. The secretaire had come into his possession lawfully not long after he met her, and he had saved it for her ever since. After the agent had brought him the name of his new tenant, he had removed the piece from storage and brought it here.

"You're talking of descendants," he teased gently, kissing the top of her head, "and we're not even married yet. What about tomorrow? My uncle happens to be the Bishop of Chichester. He could arrange everything."

"Yes," she agreed contentedly. "That would suit me very well."

They did not dine together that evening after all. Tom had to send a letter to his uncle and Richard had taken it while Sophie had much to organize, for Tom had insisted they should have at least two weeks away together before returning home. Sophie also had letters to write, telling the news to Antoine, Ellen, and Henriette.

In the morning, Clara, Billy, and the atelier staff were waiting by the roadside as Tom and Sophie rode by on their way out of town. Sophie waved until she could see the little group no more.

Richard was waiting at the Bishop's palace in the heart of Chichester when Tom and Sophie arrived. But there was to be a disappointing delay. The Bishop, white-haired and distinguished, who was addressed by Richard and Tom as "Uncle" and by Sophie as "Your Grace," said they must wait three days for him to make the necessary arrangements.

"However," he added, holding up his hand to forestall any argument from Tom, "it would be a pleasure to have Miss Delcourt—Sophie—to stay here in the palace as the guest of your aunt and myself. Richard will have the room he has always had, but you, Tom, must forgo yours this time and take a bed at the Dolphin Tavern across the street from the Cathedral."

Tom did not have to ask why he was being excluded from the palace for the first time. Neither his uncle nor his aunt would consider it seemly for a groom to sleep under the same roof as the young woman he had yet to wed. Tom consoled himself with the thought that he would have Sophie's company by day, but his aunt took her over completely after hearing that she had had no time to order a wedding gown.

"I'm only doing what your mother would have done if she had lived until your wedding day." The Bishop's wife, resolute and firm-chinned, had long experience in handling the ladies of the diocese and many others who came into her sphere. Within an hour, a team of seamstresses was at work on a gown to Sophie's specifications.

From there she was whisked to the milliner, the glove-maker, the hosier, and the silversmith for a pair of shoe buckles, then on to the cobbler. In addition to all this activity, Sophie found herself sitting in at sewing circles for the needy, visiting the local orphanage, and taking food to the poor. The Bishop's wife was not one to waste any extra pair of hands that came her way. Soon the wedding gown and the accessories were safely delivered, the Bishop, at his wife's instigation, footing the bills as a way of welcoming Sophie into the family. She was quite overwhelmed. The only time she saw Tom was at supper, and then, by tradition, not on the wedding eve, which he and Richard spent in the taproom of the Dolphin Tavern.

Both Sophie and Tom had wanted a private marriage ceremony with only his aunt and Richard as witnesses, but word had spread and a large number of people, including those whom Sophie had met during her three days sojourn, took places in the pews of the great cathedral at midday to see the Bishop's nephew wed. The bride, with her inherent Parisian instinct for fashion, had the latest bonnetlike curve to the brim of her hat, with bunched ribbons trimming the side of the crown. Her gown, of champagne-colored silk gauze in the new simple lines, was gathered at the neck and under her breasts, giving a high-waisted and slender silhouette. The hem was appliquéd with the lily of France.

The wedding feast was a family meal with Richard proposing a toast. He embraced Sophie as she and Tom were on the point of leaving.

"This is the day I've wanted to see for a long time," he said. "It may not be long before I'm also a married man."

"Oh, Richard! Are you winning Ellen round at last?"

He was smiling. "The signs are good."

"I'm so glad."

She thought this was the final touch to the perfection of the day, but there was far more to come. The Bishop had offered them his country home for two weeks, but neither of them wanted further family links during the time that was to be entirely theirs. They stayed the night in a quiet country inn where they were the only guests.

In the firelight of their room after supper, Tom slid off his coat and let it drop on a chair. The only candle stood on a table with a tilted mirror before which Sophie had begun to take the pins from her hair.

"Let me do that," he said. As her hair tumbled, he caught it with his hands and put it to his lips. She stood motionless, feeling naked already, for no man had ever seen her hair loosened before. But when he took hold of her waist and gently swiveled her round to face him, she pleased him by untying the bow of his high white stock, freeing his collar. He tossed it away and drew her by the hand to the warmth of the fire.

There he began to remove her garments, slowly and sensuously. The very touch of his fingers against her skin sent waves of pleasure trembling through her. Her gown descended in a rustle of silk to her feet and she stepped out of it. He embraced and kissed her then, a tender violence in his mouth, until once more he resumed his pleasurable task with the same fond care as before. Such restraint and patience was not what she had expected of this fiery, passionate man, but it was soothing to her, and perhaps somehow he knew that.

"I've loved you for so long, my darling," he said softly, stroking his palms over her bare shoulders and down her arms to lower her untied chemise to her waist. Instinctively she covered her breasts with her arms, which made him smile lovingly. He took her face between hands and looked into her eyes.

"I first saw your lovely figure by lantern light when you were lying in the dust of the lane with your bodice torn away. You've no cause to hide your beauty from me now."

As she let her arms drift down to her sides, he lowered his head, caressing her, and his exploratory lips traveled her curves and sank erotically upon her taut nipples. Her eyes closed and as her head fell back, his hand moved to support her arched spine. He released the petticoat tapes at her waist and her last garments descended into soft folds about her feet. By now she was aflame, and as he dropped to one knee in his continued kissing and caressing she dug her fingers into the fine linen of his shirt, aware only of the wild tumult of her body. When she cried aloud against the exquisite torment, he swept her up in his arms and carried her to the bed.

His clothes flew in all directions and then suddenly they were together again, arms about one another, mouth on mouth, her pale silky limbs entwined with his hard muscle. Frantically eager for him, she did not notice the pain of his entry, for it was a wild and adoring coming together. Although he prolonged the intense, almost unbearable pleasure for them both, the final moment of ecstasy might have tossed them apart in its crescendo if he had not been so deeply embedded in the beloved and passionate woman who was the other half of himself.

It was a night beyond her wildest imaginings, full of blissful and ecstatic revelations. Then at dawn, when she stirred drowsily from a brief sleep in Tom's encompassing arms, she smiled with pure happiness as she received him yet again.

They spent the two weeks at that inn, content with the simple accommodation and fare. By day they roamed the countryside, their cheeks stung by the sharp air, or hired horses and rode for miles. By night and in the early morning they made love, and sometimes, during the daylight hours, on a bed of dry leaves in a quiet wood, or with their laughter carried by the wind on an isolated stretch of the frosty hillside.

Not until the day of their departure did Sophie remember that their troubles were not wholly behind them. A shadow still lurked in the shape of Emile de Juneau.

Twenty-five

AS SOON AS POSSIBLE after their returning to Brighton, Sophie went to visit Antoine. She traveled to London with Tom, who had government officials to see, and arranged to meet him there upon her return. One of Mrs. Fitzherbert's carriages took her from Tilney Street for the rest of the journey.

"I don't know which of you is the most pleased to see me!" Sophie laughed merrily as Antoine almost choked her with his hug and Barney barked and leapt about.

During her stay Sophie could not go anywhere in the park without the dog keeping close to her, and more than once she almost stumbled over him. Being such a large dog, he was not allowed in the house as the other pets were, and whenever Sophie and Antoine went indoors he would sit on the steps and howl until one of the servants put him on a leash and dragged him away.

"Barney pined after you left him here," Antoine said, sitting with Sophie on the window seat of the schoolroom after showing her his work. "He's chained up most of the day, because I can't always be with him. I think he gets homesick."

Sophie took the boy's hand into hers. "And what of you, Antoine? Do you still get homesick?"

"Sometimes, but I like it here and we have a good time. It's just that I miss everyone in Brighton. Why didn't Mr. Tom come with you? After all, you're married to him now. I wanted to hear about his horses. I'd like to see Ma Renfrew and Billy too."

Sophie explained that as this place was a private retreat its whereabouts could not be revealed to others. Seeing the boy looked cast down, she tried to cheer him. "Come. Let's take Barney for a walk."

From a window on an upper floor Maria Fitzherbert saw Sophie and the boy setting out with the dog along a boxhedge-lined path. She was coming to know Sophie very well, for on this visit they had spent the evenings together. Now she herself had to return to London, but before that she had an important letter to write, for over the past months a great crisis had arisen between the Prince and herself.

Having failed in every other way to win her back, George, in his desperation, had given her an ultimatum. If she did not agree to return to him as his wife, he would declare his love for her to all the world, letting it be known publicly at last that their marriage had taken place exactly as everyone always supposed. Not only would such an announcement endanger her uncle and brother, who had broken the law by acting as witnesses to the marriage, but the scandal would be devastating. Most surely George would have to surrender his right to the throne, and the social ostracism would make him an outcast until the end of his days. His life as well as hers would be in ruins. What was more, the King was in uncertain health and the shock of this outrage might kill him.

The correspondence on this impasse was going to and fro between the Prince and herself like a ball on a tennis court. An envoy was forever at her door. Her head ached constantly as she tried to think how a solution might be found, for the Prince was not bluffing. She knew what he was like when he dug in his heels.

So she had come to accept that there was only one person to whom she could appeal for personal guidance, and whether he advised for better or worse she would abide by it. Leaving the window, she went across to a secretaire where she sat down and drew a sheet of paper toward her. Taking up her quill pen, she began to write the letter she would send to Rome.

When the time came for Sophie to leave, Mrs. Fitzherbert had been gone two days. As she and Antoine walked down the steps, Barney bounded ahead and sprang into the waiting coach. Normally the mildest of dogs, he growled ferociously and showed his teeth when the coachman attempted to drag him out. Antoine's coaxing was equally in vain, for Barney only settled his head on his paws. Sophie's sharp command finally made him stir. The manner in which he slunk forward to obey showed that he knew he was in disgrace. Then, before he jumped out, Antoine pushed him back again. The boy's face crumpled as he fought against tears.

"Barney has to go with you. He's missing his freedom and is miserable here. I think he's been cuffed and kicked by the servants for his barking and howling when he's chained up. Please take him."

"If it's what you wish." She was full of pity for the boy's distress. "But I don't like leaving you without him."

"The head gardener's terrier is soon to have puppies. I'm sure Mater will let me have one of them. It won't be like Barney, but I won't let the puppy know that."

Sophie hugged the boy to her. "I often think how proud your *papa* and *maman* would have been of you, Antoine."

Back in Brighton, Sophie had much to do. She took no furniture from Beech House, except the games table that Richard had given her and the clock that was Henriette's gift. She and Tom had decided that since her apartment was the larger, his should be left as a guest suite for Richard or anyone else who came to stay. In the meantime they continued to live in it while the new one was being decorated. Silk panels were installed, floors polished, the windows adorned with soft swags and drapes.

Since the choice of everything was Sophie's, she had a splendid time selecting whatever she wanted from his stock. She shared something of the Prince's fascination with chinoiserie, and while she and Tom were in London she had become enchanted with a gilded bed in his St. James's Street shop. Its canopy was of cream silk, gold-fringed in the shape of a mandarin's parasol, and edged with tiny bells. It was removed to the Brighton bedchamber that she had decided should be hers and Tom's. A Chinese wallpaper with a silvered background made the room a bower of exotic flowers and butterflies. The chairs were gilded bamboo with cushioned seats, and the toilet table that held Sophie's perfumes and cosmetics was lacquered a pale green, as were the cupboards and the tall chests.

The first night she and Tom slept in the lovely room the tiny bells edging the canopy created such a tinkling cacophony that at first laughter mingled with their lovemaking. Next day, he removed all the tiny clappers, saying with amusement that he did not want the whole world to know every time he took his wife to bed. Sophie put them away in a tiny drawer in the mother-of-pearl jewel box Tom had given her. They would always remind her of a memorable night of lovemaking out of which their child was conceived.

Pregnancy did not diminish Sophie's energy in any way, and no matter what else she had to do during the day, she never failed to take Barney for a walk along the sands. He bounded about, barking at sea gulls, making friends with whomever he met, and clearly enjoying the freedom that had been denied him at the retreat. There was no doubt in her mind that the decision to bring him home had been the right one.

It was a proud moment for Sophie when the sign writer finished painting the name of Delcourt above the shop. Her hanging sign was in the shape of a bonbon in a rainbow-hued wrapper. Alterations and redecoration of the business area had been taking place at the same time as the work in the apartment above. The shop walls were papered in pale pink stripes, the paintwork white, and there was a spacious counter where she could display her sweetmeats in crystal bowls. The shelves behind would hold glass jars, giving a jewellike look to the varied contents. Some time ago an émigré had come to her with a sample of the work he had once done for an exclusive confectioner in Rheims. It was an exquisite little casket set with tiny polished pebbles from the beach, for he had no money to buy the semiprecious stones that had been provided by his employer in the old days. Sophie had taken him on immediately as an outworker, and since gems were also beyond her means at that time, she had supplied him with an excellent line of false pearls and colored glass stones that had been equally effective. But on opening day there would be semiprecious stones glowing from the casket placed on a length of draped silk in the bow-shaped window. It would be filled with fake bonbons, all made of wood, that would appear to tumble out of it in romantic wrappers.

After a final look at the sign, Sophie reentered the shop and went through to a hallway with a private entrance from the street. Beyond was the great room that corresponded with Tom's showroom next door and that was to be her atelier. Her heels tapped as she strolled across the newly tiled floor and let her gaze wander over the white walls and the new windows. The stoves and boilers were already in place, and the latest form of ventilation had been installed. There would never be the intense heat that she and her workers had had to endure at Clara's, where yesterday she had supervised the packing up of all her utensils ready for the removal wagons today.

She had never expected to be able to transfer her workers so soon, but Tom had insisted that all the alterations be done while the builders and decorators were on the premises. Her protest that she could not afford this as yet had been waived aside.

"Remember that technically you're still my tenant," he had teased, "and I can do whatever I like to my property. If I choose to change it about to make an atelier it would only be sensible for you to make use of it. As for the business itself, that remains yours entirely and I'll never interfere."

It would have been expected, she thought as she continued her wandering around her new domain, that because he was so understanding over important issues, theirs would be a peaceful match. But they had each discovered that it was as easy for an argument to flare up between them these days as it had been in the past. Both of them had strong views on almost everything, but that was what they wanted of each other. Sophie had come to realize that the placid partnership she had once thought ideal would never have suited her.

There came the clatter of heavy hooves at the front of the shop. Sophie ran through to open the door. All her confectionery equipment had arrived. Clara, Robin, and Oliver had ridden with the drivers and were ready to start work as soon as everything was in order.

The opening was planned for Midsummer Day. It could have been a little earlier, but Sophie had made special arrangements for Antoine's eleventh birthday. Since she knew from the émigré newspaper that Emile de Juneau was still occupied in Paris, she thought it safe for Pater to bring him to London, where they could meet for an outing together. The surprise for the boy when he arrived was that Tom, Clara, and Billy were there too. As they were all staying overnight, there was a visit to a comic play at the theater, and the next day they attended a fair where Antoine and Billy rode so high on the swings that Clara shrieked in alarm. When Antoine left for the country again his pockets were full of souvenirs and the coach seat piled high with gifts.

"It's been the best birthday I've ever had!" he called out the window as he was borne away.

Sophie, well into the third month of her pregnancy, was thankful that the child within her would one day ease the heartache she felt every time she had to part from the boy who had become as her own son.

The Delcourt confectionery shop had a grand opening. Sophie had hired a band to play in the street. Her three shop assistants were attired in pink with white aprons. As it was the height of the season, crowds were soon attracted by the music. Fashionable people began streaming into the shop. Sophie served behind the counter that day, and she and her assistants were all rushed off their feet. Deliveries were made in the sea-blue trap driven by a smart youth, newly hired, who had been fitted out in a livery to match.

In her large new atelier Sophie was able to take on extra hands. She herself continued to carry out most of the centerpiece work, for which there was much demand. A piece was almost finished one afternoon when one of her shop assistants came rushing into the atelier.

"The Prince's carriage has just drawn up outside. Beau Brummell is with him!"

Sophie rushed to the alcove where there was a sink with a pump and quickly washed the sugar from her hands. Beau Brummell was a young man possessed of a huge fortune, who had become one of the Prince's circle, no doubt through the penchant they shared for sumptuous living and wild extravagance. Brummell's immaculate appearance and high sense of style had made him an undisputed leader of fashion, his dictates followed by society on everything from correct etiquette to the manner in which women should drape a stole to be most elegant. Such was his power that Sophie knew he could make or break her business by whatever opinion he might air about it. Hastily she glanced in the mirror, smoothed back a tendril of hair, flung off her apron, and swept forth to meet her two distinguished customers.

The Prince paused on the pavement before entering the shop as he burst out laughing at an amusing remark Brummell had made.

It suited the Prince well that such a man was not in Caroline's court, or else he himself would be the butt of that caustic wit. Always generous to his friends, he had made Brummell an officer in a fine regiment, but the fellow turned out to be hopeless at soldiering and interested only in the handsome uniform. However, it was done, and the commission couldn't be withdrawn. At least Brummell was an indefatigable and willing source of advice on everything from the cut of a coat to the very latest way to tie the bow of a neckcloth, which seemed to change from week to week.

As the Prince turned for the shop's entrance, he saw his own compressed reflection caught several times over in the small panes of the bow-shaped window. He had had his hair clipped shorter in the latest style, which he thought suited him even better than Brummell, and the high points of his collar, rising to the jawline above his neckcloth, were flattering, the whole arrangement hiding the swollen glands that had troubled him for as long as he could remember.

The door had been opened from within before one of his own carriage footmen could reach it. A neat little creature in a pink gown bobbed to him, then he saw there were two more behind the counter. Brummell raised a triangular quizzing glass by its slim gold handle and regarded them appreciatively.

"Strap me! These young women are as pretty as the candy and equally delectable."

Then the young Frenchwoman herself appeared and curtsied. The Prince smiled at her. "My felicitations on your marriage, Mrs. Foxhill."

"Thank you, Your Highness. May I welcome you and Mr. Brummell to my shop?"

"Indeed you may. I learned of your marriage when your husband took me to an auction last week, but I had to find out about the shop from others. Come! Let me taste some Delcourt confectionery. I want to discover if you're as accomplished at candy-making as you are at cookery."

Sophie's three assistants each offered a different selection of the very best of the chocolates and other sweetmeats. The Prince expressed his approval of each variety. Brummell ate one slowly, his expression showing neither pleasure nor distaste. Her heart sank when he shook his head with a frown on being offered another. On impulse she took up a bowl of nougat, a candy of French origin made of honey, eggs, nuts, and fruit. To her disappointment, he ate a piece without comment.

"My steward shall come to see you," the Prince said when he had enjoyed several of the richest sweetmeats and looked as if he would have liked more. "You are an asset to Brighton. Good day, Mrs. Foxhill."

He left and Brummell followed him out. Sophie leaned back against the counter in disappointment. She dared not begin to contemplate the damage Brummell might do to her reputation. Then, while the door was still open, he suddenly took a step back to the threshold.

"Perhaps you would like to know, Mrs. Foxhill, that I shall commend your confectionery to all."

Sophie rushed to tell Tom what had happened. He was as pleased as she, but not impressed. "Your success was assured, anyway, my love. Even if Brummell hadn't liked what he sampled, I know of nothing that could keep you from reaching the top."

She flung her arms about his neck and kissed him soundly. "No wonder I love you, Tom! You have such faith in me!" Then abruptly she stepped back with a puzzled expression and pressed both hands to her stomach.

"What's the matter?" he asked with concern.

Slowly her expression became radiant. "The baby has quickened!"

As THE MONTHS ADVANCED Sophie began to consider hiring a nurse-maid in time for her son's arrival, for she was as sure as Tom that their firstborn would be a boy. She saw several applicants, but finally chose a smiling, neat-looking woman named Emma, who had been well trained in a baronet's nursery but now wanted a position in Brighton.

Sophie gave birth to a daughter even as the nineteenth century was born. As she lay exhausted with the infant in her arms, Tom seated by the bedside, she could hear the cheering and shouting outside as well as noisy trumpets. They had both been so sure she was going to bear a son that they had given no serious thought to what they might name a girl.

"So what are we to call this little girl, who has so surprised us?" Tom asked. "Would you like the name of Fleur?"

She smiled. "Ah yes! The fleur-de-lis of France!"

At Fleur's christening in St. Nicholas's Church, Henriette was one godmother. Although recently widowed and genuinely distressed by Sir Roland's death in a hunting accident, she was also feeling liberated and had decided to cast aside mourning completely on this occasion. Ellen was the second godmother and Richard the godfather, but in spite of his earlier optimism nothing had been settled between them. Henriette had brought her four-year-old son, Alexander, with her. He was a thin, pale-faced little boy and quick to give way to tears, but like his late father in features.

"He needs the sea air," Henriette said. "The climate in Gloucestershire has never suited him and the doctor advised a long spell at the coast. So I'm taking a house here and we're staying on."

It was good news for Sophie, for she and Henriette had taken up their friendship as if they had never been apart. What she did find worrying was that Napoleon Bonaparte had become First Consul of France and wrought far-reaching changes in the Government. Emile de Juneau was among those who had been tossed out. If there was ever to be a time when he would take up his mission of vengeance, this would be it. There would be no more visits to Antoine for a while, for Sophie could not risk being followed.

Antoine had been home a few times, Tom having judged it to be safe again, swimming in the sea and playing cricket or football with old school friends. He always hugged Sophie hard when he left her, but there were never any tears. He had adjusted to life at the country retreat and saw it as another home. The Prince had given him his own pony, and his ambition was to follow the hunt with his royal benefactor, wearing one of the pink coats that Beau Brummell had declared de rigueur for a huntsman.

Tom was fully on the alert at all times. He made his visits to London as short as possible. At his instruction, Sophie kept the pistol he had given her always in her pocket or purse. Then one day in London he learned that Emile de Juneau had laid claim to the family château and its lands in view of the late Comte's heir being presumed dead.

It was shattering news for Sophie. "Oh, no! I promised Antoine's mother that I would take him home again one day!" She clenched her fists and pressed them together, her head bowed.

Tom put his arms about her consolingly. "Don't distress yourself. Nobody could have done more for Antoine than you, my darling. Try to look on the bright side. Now that Juneau has what he's always wanted, he might let his old hatred slip by. This new development might have lifted any threat to the boy's life."

She looked into his face with worried eyes. "But does the lust for vengeance ever cease in such a man?"

"Let's hope he gets fat and lazy on his ill-gotten gains and will let the old grudges fade away. Remember also that Antoine is rising thirteen. He has been taught to shoot and to fence. Before long he'll be able to defend himself against any enemy."

Except, Sophie thought with a terror she could not voice, the coward's attack of a dagger in the back.

To set Sophie's mind at rest, Tom made contact again with a retired French smuggler, one who had never been connected with the Broomfield gang. A widower and living in an uncomfortable garret, the man was willing to settle, at Tom's expense, in the village adjoining the Juneau château posing as someone weary of city life. He was to keep check on Emile de Juneau's movements and report any suspicious absences.

"Now," Tom said to Sophie, "it shouldn't be too long before we hear how well Juneau has taken to the life of a country gentleman."

In contrast to the bad news from France, there was good news at home. Mrs. Fitzherbert and the Prince became reconciled. The Pope had confirmed the canonical validity of their marriage, and with her sensitive conscience clear Maria was able to become once again a loving wife. Sophie and Tom received an invitation to a reception in London, which they both knew was to be one of celebration, although that was not to be announced in the resumption of the masquerade that had prevailed before. By the same courier came a letter in Mrs. Fitzherbert's own hand, offering Sophie the most important commission she had ever received, to make the sugar centerpiece for the reception.

Since it would be impossible to transport such a sizable and delicate confection all the way to London without damage, Sophie immediately planned to go ahead of Tom, stay with Richard, and spend four days in Mrs. Fitzherbert's kitchen. She had chosen as her motif a dramatically large cornucopia from which appeared to tumble in great profusion a cascade of every kind of spring flower, symbolizing the rebirth of happiness for the Prince and Mrs. Fitzherbert. Other small flowers would be placed individually about the table as if scattered by the breeze.

When the evening arrived, Sophie dressed her hair in the shorter style that had come into vogue. There were curls over her forehead and the rest of her hair was drawn back smoothly into a knot high on the back of her head, leaving her slender neck entirely exposed. A band of pearls completed the simple coiffure, and pearl earrings danced in her lobes. She spun around in her décolleté gown of coral silk for Tom to admire, while streamers of gold ribbon tied under her breasts fluttered out across the straight skirt.

When they arrived at Tilney Street, the windows of the house were open wide to the warm June air. Tom and Sophie were welcomed by both the Prince and the lady he had recaptured at last. The magnificent diamonds Mrs. Fitzherbert was wearing, enhancing her oyster silk gown, were his gift to mark this turning point in their lives.

"You look lovely, Sophie," she commented admiringly. "That color suits you so well."

It was also the opinion of many other people present when they caught sight of Sophie as she surveyed the glittering scene. The reception was of such scale and splendor that it was a proclamation in itself of marriage vows privately renewed. Although female eyes raked every detail of Sophie's appearance, it was Tom who drew the women's attention. Among the tallest men in the sumptuous room, he looked particularly handsome with his skin tanned by the sea air. The cut of his crimson coat set off his broad shoulders, and it was noted that his knee breeches, still worn by all men on grand occasions, were attractively taut over his hard muscled thighs. Had he wished it in that scented, music-enhanced atmosphere, he could have made a score or more assignations during the evening.

When it was time to leave, Mrs. Fitzherbert spoke to Sophie of meeting again in Brighton. Their friendship had become so firmly established, in spite of the difference in age, that she wanted it to continue.

They saw one another often that summer. Barney always gave the distinguished visitor a friendly but restrained welcome, having become far better trained under Sophie's sole control. Mrs. Fitzherbert loved Fleur on sight. Large-eyed, with hair as curly as her father's and as dark as her mother's, the baby clutched at the amber necklace that dangled enticingly from Maria's ample bosom. Sophie would have loosened the strong little fingers, but Mrs. Fitzherbert removed her necklace to let the baby make a plaything of it.

The Prince had once more given his beloved Maria a fine large house of her own on the Steine, everything falling into place as before, and Sophie became a frequent visitor. But the exchange of calls was not the only social connection being formed. The Prince and Mrs. Fitzherbert had been less than two weeks in Brighton when Sophie and Tom received an invitation to dine at the Marine Pavilion.

Sophie found herself seated between two royal dukes, both of whom were the Prince's brothers and, like him, renowned for having an eye for a pretty woman. The footmen were astonished to see her there, although their rigid training prevented them showing any change of expression. Only Nick gave her a mischievous wink when he held out a dish for her to select from, and she gave him a smiling glance.

For the first time Sophie ate from a gold plate, but then everything on the table was gold, except the exquisitely engraved wineglasses. She had always admired the twenty-four salts, which she had seen being polished more than once. They were well suited to a seaside residence, being in the form of nautilus shells supported on waves by a swimming triton. Although Sophie had seen all the other pieces before, and knew that the Prince had several gold services for two hundred settings or more, she was still charmed by it. What gave her most pleasure, however, was the sight of the Prince himself seated at the center of the table in his high-backed red chair with Mrs. Fitzherbert once again at his right hand.

Two hours later the company moved from the table to follow the Prince and Mrs. Fitzherbert down a long wide corridor for a concert that was to take place in one of the salons. As Tom and Sophie strolled side by side he asked her with twinkling eyes if she was enjoying herself.

"It's a dream," she confided humorously. "At any moment now I'm going to wake up!"

But it was far from a dream. Through her friendship with Mrs. Fitzherbert, there were many more such invitations.

Twenty-six

IN THE TWO YEARS that followed the Prince's first visit to Sophie's shop, her business expanded with a swiftness beyond her wildest dreams. Delcourt confectionery and her sugar centerpieces went regularly to the Marine Pavilion, and not only was she sending her sweetmeats to Carlton House as well, but the Prince's brothers were also kept supplied. The Duke of York had a particular weakness for her orange-flavored candies. She had taken on more hands and had three large sea-blue wagons to take her deliveries far afield. At last she was able to have semiprecious stones set in caskets for special presentations, and her ribbons, lace, and other trimmings were of the finest quality. Tom had imported crates of Chinese lacquered boxes for her, and these became equally popular as containers.

There were times when Sophie almost caught her breath as she considered the wave of good fortune that had swept her along. So many good things had happened. Fleur was as bonnie as any child could be, and Henriette's Alexander had put on weight and become a lively boy. His future domicile had been undecided for a while when Richard and Henriette married a year after Ellen had made it clear that she intended to remain a spinster.

"My love for Henriette hasn't come on the rebound," Richard said to Tom and Sophie. "I've never forgotten meeting her in the atelier, but she was betrothed then, and I had to put her lovely face out of my mind. When I met her again it was as if the years between had never been."

Since Henriette did not want to expose Alexander to the winter fogs of London, she and Richard compromised by settling in a village that was within easy reach of the city. She also retained the Brighton house she had bought, and the three of them were frequent visitors.

To add to everything else that had given Sophie such happiness, Emile de Juneau had never gone farther from home than Paris, and that very infrequently. She began to hope that he was letting bygones fade away at last. Not that she didn't intend to fight him legally for possession of the château on Antoine's behalf if ever she had the chance.

When the ringing of the church bells was heard early one morning, Sophie and everyone else in the atelier paused at the task in hand, thinking instantly that it must be another naval victory. Before anyone could speak Tom came hurrying in waving a newspaper.

"Great news! Peace has been agreed between France and Britannia. A treaty has been signed at Amiens!"

There was a moment of stunned silence, and then Sophie burst into tears of relief and joy. The others reacted similarly or began shouting and cheering. Tom, his arm about Sophie, made an announcement on her behalf.

"Take the rest of the day as a holiday!"

He led Sophie away. "It's incredible," she said, still dazed. Although great changes had come about in France under Napoleon, he was such a military man that peace had always seemed far away.

"It is indeed," Tom agreed, keeping his doubts to himself. His private belief was that Napoleon was gaining a respite to rearm for the invasion of England. "Would you like me to take you to Paris?"

She threw her arms about his neck. "Yes, Tom! Fleur and Emma can stay with Henriette."

But it was not to be. By the time Sophie had made the arrangements, there were already reports of returning émigrés having been arrested in France on dubious charges.

"That warrant for your arrest will still be in someone's file, Sophie," Tom said gravely. "If the charge should be something that applies today and somebody recognized and betrayed you, there's no telling what might happen."

Although bitterly disappointed, Sophie had to abide by this wise advice. Yet it was hard for her that countless numbers of her rich English customers were streaming across the Channel to France. An outbreak of fever in the village near the Château de Juneau did not reach either the French or English newspapers, but among the villagers who died was the man Tom had hired to watch Emile de Juneau. And Tom continued to think that no news from that source meant all was still well.

As Sophie had presumed, Antoine expected to go home immediately. When her letter of explanation failed to satisfy him, she went to see him in person. The Prince and Mrs. Fitzherbert, who visited again these days, had been there only a few days before. Antoine and Sophie hugged each other as they always did after he had formally bowed over her hand. Then he took her to his study. It was a place where he could do his schoolwork and withdraw from other company when he wished.

"Going home at the first opportunity was what you always promised me," he stated as soon as they were seated. At fifteen he was a tall, strong, and good-looking boy, who still retained some likeness to each of his parents. "There's peace now, Sophie! You'd be safe if we avoided Paris, which is easily done. I've studied enough maps over the years to know that is possible. We'll go straight to the château. All I have to do is tell that relative of mine to get out. He wouldn't dare
· raise a hand against me when everything is changing."

"It's not as easy as that. A claim must be made through the French courts with proof of your identity."

"Well, that wouldn't present any difficulty." He sprang to his feet and moved energetically about the room.

Sophie shook her head regretfully. "It's not the right time. Tom says things are too unsettled as yet, and claims aren't receiving sympathetic consideration."

Antoine was seized by a fresh idea. "Tom and I could go on our own to the château. At least I'd see my birthplace and make myself known to the villagers, because I'm sure they're working on the land and tending the vineyards again as they did in my father's day." His words came in a rush of eagerness and he gestured wildly in his enthusiasm for all he had planned. "I'll tell them they'll always get a steady living wage with bonuses, and good relationships shall never be abandoned again."

Sophie hated to dampen the very longing for home that she herself had always kept alive in him. "I know it's hard, my dear, but you and I must be patient for a while longer. Believe me, I'm still as determined to fulfill my promise to your mother as ever I was, but it can't be yet."

He clenched his fists in frustration and went to the window, standing with his back to her as if he did not want her to see his distress and disappointment. She wished Antoine still had Jamie's company, but the older boy had left the retreat to start out in the world under the Prince's patronage. There was another child in the house now, a toddler named Mary Anne, said to be Mrs. Fitzherbert's niece. She was taken into Pater and Mater's foster care as a baby some little time after the Prince and Mrs. Fitzherbert had reconciled, but she was far too young to play any part in Antoine's life.

Sophie waited until she saw his shoulders straighten, signaling his apparent resolve to accept the present situation for the time being. Then she went across to him and put her hand on his arm.

"The time will go quickly. Think of all you have to do here. Next year you'll be going up to Oxford. It's what you've wanted and worked for."

Antoine looked at her with a half smile. "Yes, I've thought of that and of how much I should miss, but I have a duty toward the home of my ancestors."

"Yes, you have, and the day will come when you'll fulfill it," Sophie said with wholehearted conviction.

He nodded and turned away from the window with her. "Could I go back to Brighton with you for a week or two?" Catching her quick glance, he smiled, shaking his head. "It's not to pressure Tom as I did you. I won't mention the matter, I promise. But I've had a long spate of working hard and I've passed all my examination papers."

As soon as Antoine was back in Brighton he slipped once more into the daily routine. He went riding with Tom, saw his friends, and walked the sands with Sophie and Barney. The only difference she could detect was that he'd become quick to eye a pretty girl. When he was invited to a party one evening at a neighbor's house, Sophie told him not to be late and went to sleep without any qualms. Barney would bark when he returned, and she would know he was safely home. Yet she and Tom woke in the morning without having been disturbed, and she imagined Antoine had been quick to quiet the dog.

He was not up for breakfast when Sophie went into the atelier, but she decided to let him sleep on. He had been so active the past two or three days, coming and going restlessly. It was when she went to spend a little time with Fleur at midday that she learned Antoine was still abed.

"Have you heard him about?" she asked Ruth, the maidservant who had come with her from Beech House.

"No, ma'am. There hasn't been a sound."

Suddenly Sophie was afraid. She dashed to Antoine's room and flung open the door. His bed had not been slept in, and a note lay on the pillow.

Dear Sophie,

Please forgive me, but I have to go to France. I intend to rouse the support of my village tenants. Then I can make my claim in Paris with their signatures to show that it is I, the rightful owner, whom they want to see again at the château. Do not worry about me. I shall write soon.

Antoine

Tom was not in the shop, but she found him in the stableyard where a valuable cupboard was being lifted onto a wagon. The sight of her frantic face made him fear some harm had befallen their daughter, but she gasped out at once. "Antoine is gone!"

He seized her by the elbow and steered her to a chair in his office. Sophie thrust the note into his hand. His brows contracted as he read it.

"My God! If Antoine goes to the château alone he'll never come out alive. He's been safe for so long, he must have forgotten your warnings or thought them exaggerated. I must go after him!"

The two things she dreaded most had come about. Antoine was in terrible danger and now the man she loved was to share it. Tom saw how stricken she looked and he raised her up to hold her close.

"I'll bring the boy back. My guess is that he's taken a fishing boat." He kissed her swiftly. "I'm going to make a few inquiries. You go ask Clara if he said anything of his plans in her hearing. Then go to the bakery where Billy works and speak to him. I'll meet you back here. Have some provisions ready for my journey."

Sophie returned before him. Clara knew nothing, and all she had gained was that Antoine had bought two loaves the previous evening at the bakery, and Billy had been with him one day when he had purchased a traveling bag in the market. Tom had more to report. Antoine had taken one of the smaller sailing boats for hire, saying he wanted it for the rest of the vacation, which obviously had been to cover his retaining possession of it. The neighbor said the boy had left the party at nine o'clock.

"But we hadn't gone to bed then!" Sophie exclaimed.

"Antoine didn't come home. He collected his baggage and the food wherever he had concealed them and went straight to the boat." Tom sighed. "I never thought I should regret teaching him to sail."

Sophie remembered how Antoine had straightened his shoulders in the study at the retreat. It had not been in resignation as she had supposed, but in determination to get to France at all costs. "He planned this expedition the moment he knew he wouldn't get our cooperation."

Tom put his fingertips under Sophie's chin and tilted her distraught face to his. "The boy has spirit and courage," he said with a serious smile, "and I commend him for it. I have a feeling that you and I might have done exactly the same if we'd been in his shoes at his age."

She spoke ruefully. "You may be right. At least I would have known that it was not signatures I could expect from the villagers, but their mark of a cross."

Tom kissed Fleur, and then he and Sophie went downstairs together, their arms linked, her cheek resting against his sleeve. At the door they kissed lingeringly, as if this might be the last kiss they would ever share. It was the hardest parting that either had ever known. Then he broke away and flung himself into the saddle of his waiting horse and galloped away to take the evening packet from Newhaven to Dieppe. There was no need for subterfuge any longer with travel between England and France open again at last.

When Tom disembarked at Dieppe the following morning he went first to hire a fast horse. He thought it most likely that Antoine had done the same wherever he had come ashore. Although Tom did check at the occasional hostelry along the route he was taking, he found nobody who could remember seeing Antoine. There was always the danger that the boy had fallen foul of tricksters or robbers along the way.

Tom snatched as little sleep as possible and changed horses several times before he finally rode into the village of the Château de Juneau two days after stepping onto French soil. He went first to the cottage rented by his spy, keeping a sharp eye for any glimpse of the boy. To his surprise the cottage was empty and deserted. A neighbor informed him that its occupant had died of a fever some time ago.

Instantly Tom was filled with foreboding, and he galloped back along the village street, scattering a flock of geese being driven to market. When he reached the gates of the château itself, he brought his steaming horse to a standstill. The gatekeeper spoke to him through the ornate ironwork.

"What's your business, monsieur?"

"I'm here to see Monsieur Emile de Juneau. Make haste and open these gates. I've no time to spare."

"The master isn't here. He left the château three days ago."

"Where was he going? It's a matter of life and death that I know!" Tom tossed the gatekeeper a gold coin and it was deftly caught.

"He usually only goes to Paris," the gatekeeper replied significantly.

"What do you mean? Don't you think that was his destination this time?"

"All I can tell you is that he didn't go by coach with all his usual baggage, but on horseback with saddlebags. So his destination can't have been either far distant or important."

Tom thought it meant exactly the reverse. "Has a boy been here asking for him? A tall, well-built lad with brown hair."

"Yes, there was one of that description not long after the master left."

Tom wheeled his horse about and rode back into the village. He did not find Antoine at the first inn, but discovered him in the second. The boy was on his feet addressing three old men, who sat at a table listening to him. A serving wench was also in his audience, although her interest was clearly more in his good looks than in what he was saying.

"It means so much to me that you good men remember my father." Antoine was in full spate. "Not only shall I emulate him in all his wise and just ways, but I will—"

Tom's voice cut across his words. "Your pardon, Monsieur le Comte. A private word with you, if you please."

Antoine turned to him in a blaze of fury and disbelief. "What are you doing here?"

Tom had no intention of humiliating him before the old men or the girl. "I've an urgent matter to bring to your notice. I'll wait for you outside."

Tom left the taproom and went to the stables, where he hired a fresh horse for himself and one for Antoine. When the boy emerged into the courtyard he was crimson with temper and glowered at the sight of the second horse.

"I'm not leaving here! Damnation! I'm not a child anymore and you shall not treat me so, Tom Foxhill! Emile de Juneau is away, but by the time he returns I'll have the support of every villager."

Tom swung himself into the saddle, his face grim. "I happen to believe that Emile de Juneau is on his way to England. I'm not wasting another second here. Sophie is alone and unprotected. I pray to God I may not be too late."

He wheeled his horse about and rode out of the courtyard. Antoine stood for a moment in shock. Then he threw himself onto the waiting horse and galloped to catch up, which was exactly what Tom had expected.

NEVER HAD SOPHIE KNOWN DAYS to be as long as those she spent waiting for news that did not come. Normally she could have done with forty-eight hours in every day to suit her busy life, but now it seemed that long from one dawn to the next. She slept badly, often springing from her bed when it sounded as if carriage wheels were drawing up outside, but every time she was doomed to disappointment.

Barney sensed the change in her. When they went for walks along the shore he behaved more soberly, ambling along at her side. They had more walks than ever before, because she either flung herself into work as if every order for a centerpiece had to be finished in half the normal time, or else she left the creative tasks entirely to Robin, absenting herself once more for the sea breezes. Whenever possible she took Fleur down onto the beach, making sand castles for her while Barney lay watching or sleeping. The child also paddled happily in the warm rock pools, getting her petticoats soaked until Sophie took her home for a meal or a bath.

After Fleur's bedtime, Sophie invariably felt unable to endure the quietness of the apartment. Clara would have kept her company as would Mrs. Fitzherbert, as well as other friends who invited her out, but she declined every invitation. She was consumed by the conviction that she must keep her vigil alone if she wished to see Tom and Antoine safely back. More and more she went for evening strolls with Barney by the sea. As there were plenty of summer visitors about on the promenade and attending parties with bonfires on the beach when the tide was out, she walked on until she reached the quieter stretches of the shore. It never occurred to her that someone might be taking note of her lonely wanderings.

The first stars were out on a light summer night when she reached the rocks from behind which she had once glimpsed Tom in his smuggler's guise. She had turned to retrace her steps when she saw Barney running from her to wag his tail at a man also strolling toward her along the sands. She guessed the dog was hoping for a stick to be thrown, since she had become halfhearted about it.

"To heel, Barney!" she called, for the man had made a threatening gesture. The dog cowered back and then to her dismay bolted toward home.

The stranger spoke in French. "Your dog is not very obedient."

She supposed he knew her by sight through her business as so many did. "Barney suffered some mistreatment once for his tendency to howl when troubled. He has been nervous ever since if anyone raises a hand to him."

She had drawn level with the man and hoped he would not turn about to fall into step at her side. It would not be the first time when a stroller had wanted to engage her in conversation. But this man did something far more sinister. Tall and thickset, he stepped forward to deliberately block her path.

"I've been waiting a long time for this meeting, Sophie Delcourt."

Then she knew him. Terror struck at her heart. It was Emile de Juneau!

She could see his face now, thin and aristocratically boned, dark eyes deep-set, a thin merciless mouth, and yet curiously like Antoine's father.

She made no pretense. "What do you want, Emile de Juneau?" she demanded, determined not to show fear while bitterly regretting her failure to have come armed on her walk. With all her anxiety centered on Tom and Antoine in France, she had given no thought to the possibility that her enemy might be in England.

"Tell me where I can find the boy you whisked away from my potential guardianship over ten years ago," he demanded, "and have kept from me ever since!"

"From your murderous clutches, don't you mean?"

His voice became persuasive. "Be sensible. The boy is nothing to you. You've been burdened with the responsibility long enough. I'm releasing you from it."

"You're mistaken," she gave back fiercely. "I love Antoine as my own son."

He snorted contemptuously. "Don't try to fool me. The Comte must have paid you well to get his brat away. Is it on those ill-gotten gains that you've risen so high in the world? However, if it's money you want, I'm prepared to compensate you."

"I want nothing from you but your departure from Antoine's life and mine," she exclaimed angrily. "You've haunted us far too long! Not that you have heard the last of us, because when the chance comes, I'll fight you in the courts for the Château de Juneau to be returned to its rightful owner." Her voice became mocking. "If you had only been patient, you could have had Antoine in the palm of your hand. Now it's too late. You've lost that chance forever!"

She hurled herself into a run, swerving away from him. But he had been prepared and she covered no more than a few yards before he grabbed her with a force that knocked her off her feet. He yanked her up immediately and shook her in his rage, crushing her arms against her sides, until her teeth chattered. Her attempts to kick him in the groin were in vain. She did not scream since nobody would hear her and she feared he might become even more violent if she did.

"Where is Antoine?" he demanded again, grinding out the words. "I've known for some time where you were living! In the taproom of a local inn someone told me that Antoine is with you again, but I've not seen him. Where is he?"

Sophie was thankful he had been misinformed. "He's where you'd never think to find him. And you'll never get that information from me."

Neither of them had noticed Barney come running back until with a rushing leap he buried his teeth in Emile's ankle, growling ferociously. Sophie seized the opportunity to break away and run off again, almost weeping with thankfulness that Barney had come back to find her. Then she stopped as there came a terrible yelp of pain from the dog and she saw Emile tossing away a thick chunk of driftwood. Barney lay sprawled on his side, his awful whimpering causing her to cry out in distress. Then her enemy was charging toward her again and as she reared away he had her in his grip.

"What have you done to my dog?" she shrieked, clawing at his face before he dragged her hands away.

"Nothing compared to what I'm about to do to you!" He hauled her, kicking and screaming, into the sea. The water pulled at her skirts and she lost a shoe. When he was boot-high in the incoming waves he thrust her backward under the surface. Then he pulled her up again, her hair streaming away from her face, and put his relentless question to her.

"Where is the boy?"

"I'll never tell you." The salty water closed over her face again.

Again and again he ducked her, never holding her under long enough to drown, but inevitably she swallowed water and came up spluttering each time. The possibility that someone might see them struggling made him brutal in his urgency. From the start he had intended to drown her when she had given him the information he needed, and the thought that she was going to thwart him with her stubbornness evaporated the last of his sanity. He heaved her up, limp and dripping, coughing and gasping from the water in her lungs, and brought his face close to hers.

"This is your last chance!" he shouted. By now she could only whisper, but her words were the same as those she had uttered between each ducking.

"Never . . . tell . . . you."

He hurled her down again, determined to finish her life. Just then his shoulders were seized from behind by powerful hands that whirled him about and the crash of a fist to his jaw sent him falling backward into the water with an enormous splash. Tom snatched up Sophie and swung her forward to be caught by Antoine, who had come plunging after him. Then Emile was on his feet again. He had never learned the English art of self-defense, but he had a dagger under his coat and he swung up his arm to deal his assailant a death strike. Tom flung all his strength at the Frenchman's wrist and twisted his arm back until the dagger fell harmlessly into the sea. After that the fight was Tom's. One more punch to the ribs, another to the point of the jaw, and Emile was senseless. Tom hurled him onto the sand at the edge of the sea before running to Sophie, who lay slumped in a heap with Antoine rubbing her wrists.

"That's no good," Tom shouted. "Get down on your hands and knees!"

It was the old seagoing method of throwing a half-drowned seaman over a barrel to pump the water out of him. Antoine's back gave the support as Tom threw Sophie face downward across him and began to pump and pummel her ribs until the water gushed out of her mouth and she coughed and retched before making a little murmuring cry.

"Is she all right?" Antoine asked anxiously.

"Yes, she is." Tom lifted Sophie from the boy's back into a sitting position. "Give me your coat to wrap around her—mine's wet."

When this was done he left her with Antoine and ran to Barney. The dog's injury was a broken leg with considerable bleeding, but it was nothing that would not heal, and the bone could be set. In spite of the pain, Barney managed to thump his tail weakly as Tom spoke soothingly to him and patted his head.

Antoine, watching from where he sat beside Sophie, regretted wildly his going to France when it had brought harm to both Sophie and his dog. He would never remember how many horses he and Tom had changed in their desperate race to get back across the Channel and then to Brighton. Now he saw Tom was returning to take Sophie from him.

"I'm so sorry for everything," he said in a choked voice. "I never thought anything like this would happen."

"We were in time, thank God! But when Emma told us at the house that Sophie was walking alone on the beach I dreaded what we might find." Tom adjusted the coat around Sophie's shoulders. "Now fetch the dog. He'll be heavy, but you're strong enough to manage."

Antoine gathered Barney across his forearms as carefully as he could. Then he glanced in the half-light at Emile, who still lay where Tom had tossed him.

"What are we going to do about him, Tom?"

Tom was lifting Sophie up in his arms, his back to the sea. "I'll send a keeper of the peace to arrest him for attempted murder. His future is settled. He'll never threaten you again."

"But look at him!"

Tom turned with Sophie in his arms, and saw that the incoming tide had overtaken the Frenchman. Emile de Juneau lay drowned in a few inches of water.

Epilogue

IT WAS PRIOR TO THE BIRTH of the twins that Tom had bought the country mansion on the outskirts of Brighton. Sophie, returning home from her office at the atelier one warm May day in 1823, knew from the quiet that fifteen-year-old Edward and Henri were still at a cricket match. Fleur, who had grown into a beauty with laughing eyes, was married to Henriette's son, Alexander, and living in Gloucestershire. It was a match that had pleased everybody, although Sophie missed Fleur's carefree presence as did Tom, for although he was proud of his sons it was his daughter who was the apple of his eye.

After removing her hat and gloves, Sophie wandered through to the glass doors that stood open to the verandah. There she sat down in a cane chair and gazed out almost unseeingly across the butterfly-hazy flower garden. The mingled perfumes of the blooms seemed to intensify in the late afternoon hour. She had much to think about. Earlier that day she had received a confectionery commission sent at the special request of her royal patron of long-standing, first when he was Prince of Wales, then as Regent for the last madness-racked years of his father's life, and more recently as King George IV.

It was to be a special sugar centerpiece for a banquet to celebrate the final completion of the rebuilding of the Pavilion, which had been under way against the backdrop of dramatic events that had followed the painfully short peace of Amiens. There had been the dreadful

362

threat of invasion by Napoleon until the great sea battle of Trafalgar under Admiral Nelson had destroyed the French fleet. Then, at last, the glorious victory by Wellington at Waterloo. The Royal Pavilion, so renamed over two years ago when George IV ascended the Throne, was an inspiration in itself.

It had been transformed into a vision from the Arabian Nights. Its roofline alone was pure fantasy with a vast central dome set off by smaller domes, soaring minarets, Chinese-inspired tentlike roofs, and castellated turrets, all as delicate and beautiful as if they had been fashioned in sugar. Windows and glass doors were framed by Indian arches, with graceful tracery, loggias, colonnades, and recessed verandahs all adding dignity and charm. The overall effect was magical and ethereal, as if the whole of that huge pearl-hued palace might detach itself from its foundations at any moment and float away across the sky.

Not everybody liked the architecture. One wit, eyeing the domes, declared that it looked as if St. Paul's had come down to Brighton and pupped. Others criticized the exorbitant cost of the transformation, but money had never deterred its royal owner from having whatever he wanted.

Sophie was not the least surprised that her royal patron should continue to be the focus of criticism as he had been in the past. There had been a wave of sympathy a few years ago when his daughter, Charlotte, died in childbirth after her marriage to Prince Leopold of Coburg. The King, then Regent, had been distraught, but public compassion soon waned, even though his servants knew he had continued to grieve for his child ever since. Many people were outraged by his refusal to allow Princess Caroline to be present at his coronation. She had hammered in vain on the doors of Westminster Abbey for admittance. And his profligate ways continued to be a bone of contention with people genuinely concerned for the good name of the Monarchy.

Although the King's faults could not be denied, Sophie would not allow anyone to criticize him in her presence. She was quick to remind his detractors that it was his mind and aesthetic taste that lay behind many of the artistic improvements to Windsor and other places of national heritage. Even London itself had been transformed through his great plan, executed by the architect John Nash, with leafy Regent's Park, the graceful sweep of Regent's Street, and the destruction of ugly areas to make way for fine terraces and broad thoroughfares. With his love of gardens, the King had brought new beauty not only to those of the Royal Pavilion, but to many others as well. As for the priceless art treasures he was still collecting, surely no monarch would ever bequeath more to a nation?

When Tom came home he found Sophie still sitting in the late afternoon sun. He dropped to the seat next to her, stretching out his long legs and taking one of her hands.

"Come back to me," he teased, for her greeting had been abstracted.

Sophie answered dreamily. "What a lot has happened since I first applied for work at the Royal Pavilion."

"I agree. Not least your achievement in reopening a Delcourt confectionery shop in Paris with exalted patronage and all the success you so richly deserve."

She smiled. That had been the same year she kept her vow to the long-dead Comtesse and accompanied Antoine back to the Château de Juneau. It was the autumn of 1815, just over twenty-two years since the day she had run with him from the Revolutionaries. He was well fitted for the responsibilities that awaited him, having been trained in the husbandry of the land on a royal estate through the goodwill of the King when he was still Prince of Wales. Antoine's claim to the château had gone through almost without question. Properties had been returned whenever possible to their rightful owners after Louis XVIII of the House of Bourbon, uncle of the uncrowned boy king who had died in a Revolutionaries' prison, returned to France after the defeat of Napoleon.

Antoine was not alone at the château. He had taken with him his lovely young wife, Louise, and their baby son. She was as French as he, for although she was born in England, both her parents had been émigrés. When the time came for Sophie to return to England with her promise fulfilled, Antoine had embraced her fondly. He would have thanked her once again, but she put her fingertips gently against his lips.

"Caring for you, my foster son, enriched my life."

"Come with Tom to see us often. I hope the family will do the same. Louise and I want always to keep in close touch."

"As we all do, my dear," Sophie said emotionally. "Mrs. Fitzherbert will visit you when she is in Paris. She appreciates your friendship over the years."

"I've never forgotten how she gave me shelter in my hour of need."

He also kept in contact with Jamie, who was presently with the East India Company and leading the life of a gentleman. As for Mary-Anne, the little girl fostered by Pater and Mater, she now lived as a beloved daughter in Mrs. Fitzherbert's care and was not unlike her in looks.

On the verandah, Tom broke into Sophie's reverie. "Have you made up your mind yet about the design for the banquet's centerpiece?"

"Yes!" Sophie spun back to the present, eyes sparkling, and sprang to her feet. "I didn't have to think twice about it. It will be the Royal Pavilion itself in the best sugar!"

WHEN THE DAY of the celebratory banquet arrived, Sophie went to the Royal Pavilion, dressed for the evening hours even though she would be in the kitchens. She had chosen a gown of lapis-blue with silver embroidery under the still-high waistline fashion decreed. Having been a guest of the King in his days as Prince, etiquette demanded that she arrive at the main entrance, which was all but unrecognizable with its new domed porte cochere shaped like an Indian temple.

From the green-walled entrance hall, Sophie blinked with surprise as she saw the startling sunset-pink and Chinese blue of the reception corridor, exotic now with chinoiserie, tasseled lanterns, and nodding mandarins on gilded pedestals. Double doors stood open along the corridor to equally beautiful rooms, each with its own special color, as if a treasure chest had been plundered for the varied hues of precious jewels.

Although her enchanted gaze went everywhere, the corridor was not the way for her. Instead she hurried along the servants' tile-walled passage, which ran parallel to the corridor, and came to the new kitchens. There her sugar centerpiece had arrived by a tradesmen's door and was being carried through to the cool storeroom away from the steaming copper pans and savory aromas. Servants whom she knew were amused by the delight she showed in finding that the great new kitchen had its own unusual décor. The pillars that supported the high ceiling had been painted to resemble the trunks of plantain trees, while at the top three-dimensional leaves spread out to create the illusion that the frenzied activities of the chefs and all their assistants were taking place in some lush jungle. The King, in a jovial mood, had dined there on his own one evening, surrounded by his kitchen servants, and Sophie thought it was not surprising when this area had become grander than some people's drawing rooms.

Sophie saw that the menu for the banquet was chalked on a board. She ran a professional eye down the list of ninety-seven different dishes, which at the end included the fruit and sweetmeats that would be served in gold and crystal bowls with her sugar pièce de résistance. Turning away, she noticed that the footmen, whose livery had been changed from the red and green of earlier days to the scarlet and blue of the Sovereign's service, were busy taking the last items through to the banqueting table before the guests began to arrive. Sophie followed, but on the threshold of the Banqueting Room she halted in astonishment at the splendor of the vista before her.

"Magnificent!" she exclaimed, clasping her hands in wonder.

In spite of all she had already seen of the Royal Pavilion, Sophie had not been prepared for the flamboyant, dazzling, and beautiful exoticism of the Banqueting Room that hit the eye as if the sun, the moon, and all the stars had suddenly burst forth. It was like stepping into a magical Chinese fairy tale with paneled Oriental scenes on silvered grounds, cornices of golden bells, gilded moldings, and a ceiling curved like that of a mandarin's tent. Crowning everything and drawing the eye upward was a vast chandelier cascading crystal brilliants above the banqueting table. Opaque lotus flowers cradled candle flames, the whole was suspended through a mirrored star by silver chains clasped in the claws of a winged dragon that flew beneath a vast spread of gigantic plantain leaves against a painted blue circle of summer sky.

"You've stars in your eyes, Sophie," Nick quipped as he paused to grin at her on his way past.

She laughed and spread her hands wide. "There can be no other room in all the world like this one, and none that is more *fun!* I could almost believe the King had his tongue in his cheek when he decided on all that is here. It's his golden *coup de theatre!*"

When Sophie returned to the kitchen she thought how sad it was that Mrs. Fitzherbert would not be there to share this night, but after several happy years together following their reunion, the Prince had once again been lured away by the charms of other women. The end had come one evening during a grand banquet at Carlton House to celebrate the Prince becoming Regent when, instead of Mrs. Fitzherbert being seated at his right hand, she had been placed at the far end of the table. He could not meet her eyes, and she withdrew with dignity, knowing that the final break had come. Thus, she had never seen the present glorious interiors of the Royal Pavilion.

The atmosphere in the kitchen suddenly became electrified. Footmen dashed to take their places. Music could be heard in an adjoining room and the banquet was about to begin. Sophie was quick to get out of everyone's way, for kitchen servants were hurrying with covered dishes into the deckers' room, which lay between the kitchens and the Banqueting Room. It was from the table there that the footmen would pick up the many dishes for each remove. She found a seat by the wall where she could watch everything and nobody would be in danger of tripping over her feet. Once a chef handed her a slice of turkey on a fork, and when the first remove was brought out she received a plate of venison. She was also given a glass of wine when one too many had been poured out in the Banqueting Room.

The banquet had been in progress for almost three hours when the King's valet strolled into the kitchens. When he sighted Sophie, he came across to greet her.

"It's a long time since we last met, Sophie." Then, as he failed to hear her smiling reply in the clatter of copper pans, he made a grimace. "There's too much noise here to talk. Let's find somewhere quieter."

They found a bench in a passage and exchanged news of their respective families. Then, as if his thoughts had been running along the same lines as hers, he spoke of Mrs. Fitzherbert.

"A splendid lady," he said with a sigh. "During those last years together before His Majesty became King, she gave him so much guidance and wise counsel, as well as seeing that he drank less and ate more sensibly. She cared for him when he was unwell and once nursed him back from death when the doctors feared nothing could save him. Do you know what her life is like now?"

"Yes," she replied. "Having visited her only recently, I can tell you that she fills her days with good company, is still as hospitable as she has always been, and concerns herself with the happiness and well-being of the young people she has long had under her wing." Sophie shook her head slightly. "I still find it hard to believe that such love as she and the King shared should have died out completely, even though I know that when she is staying at her Brighton house and he is at the Royal Pavilion that they are like strangers to each other and their paths never cross."

The valet looked uncertain, as if hesitating to say what was in his mind. Then he made his decision. "If I should tell you something nobody else knows—I haven't even told my wife—would you keep it entirely to yourself?"

"You have my word. I've kept many secrets in my life."

Although the valet glanced cautiously to the left and right to make sure there was no chance of being overheard, he still lowered his voice as he spoke confidentially.

"As you may remember, the King never throws anything away, whether it's a coat or an old letter. It's a habit with him. His cabinets and desk drawers are littered with love notes and keepsakes and locks of hair sent by various ladies throughout the years, but none of them mean anything to him. They're simply forgotten items like so much else. Yet around his neck by night and day he wears a locket containing a miniature of Mrs. Fitzherbert that was painted when he was first in love with her. I happen to know that he has stipulated that when his life nears its end nobody is to remove it. It's to be buried with him."

Sophie was deeply moved. "So the memory of her still means all to him. I thank you sincerely for telling me."

Before the valet could answer, there came a shout from the kitchen doorway. "It's time for the centerpiece!"

Sophie hastened back to the kitchen to supervise the two footmen designated to lift up the gilded base of the sugar concoction between them. Before they had taken a step, Nick came looking for her.

"His Majesty wishes you to help bear in the centerpiece too!"

She was astounded. After her royal patron had parted forever from Mrs. Fitzherbert, she and Tom had never been acknowledged socially again, although their business associations had continued harmoniously.

"I'm ready," she said, placing her fingertips in token support at the middle of the base and going with the footmen through the wide door into the Banqueting Room. The brilliant scene was further enhanced by the glittering jewels and rich clothes of the guests. Yet her sugar creation sparkled in its own right, for she had gilded and silvered all its intricate ornamentation. Spontaneous applause broke out as it was seen in all its splendor.

When Sophie rose from her curtsy she was taken by the King's almost boyish pleasure at the sight of his Pavilion in sugar. Always emotional, he wiped a tear from his eye. Although his self-indulgent living had taken a heavy toll on his once handsome looks, he still retained the regal air of his youth, and his old charm was undiminished. To her astonishment, he rose to his feet and raised his glass to her.

"Mrs. Foxhill, you've presented me with a jewel within a jewel. I only wish your masterpiece could be preserved forever."

Everybody rose to their feet to join in the toast. Sophie was overwhelmed and curtsied deeply again. Outside, fireworks suddenly burst forth like a cannonade in the sky, adding a spectacular touch to her triumph.

Tom was waiting in the entrance hall when she left. Her radiant face told him immediately that all had gone well. He grinned at her approvingly.

"I can see that felicitations are in order!"

She whirled her arm through his and drew herself on tiptoe to kiss his lips. "Oh, yes, Tom! Let's walk by the sea. I'll tell you everything on the way. I'm too excited to go home yet!"

By the time they reached the sands Sophie had finished her description of all she had seen and the triumph she had enjoyed. Fireworks were still filling the skies with cascades of colored stars and the sounds of celebration drifted around them. After they had walked quite a way, Sophie drew Tom to a standstill, her hand tucked in his elbow.

In silence she looked across the sea as once she had stood on the French coast and gazed toward England, wondering what the future held. She had not known then that she was to avenge her father by making Delcourt confectionery renowned above all others once again, even to gaining the patronage of the kings of both England and

France. Neither had she realized that her hope of finding love would be fulfilled by a man who had already been on his way to meet her by chance.

Suddenly Sophie turned to Tom and his arms immediately closed around her. This time it was he who kissed her for all that had been between them and for everything that was yet to come.